Dear Dad + Bar...,
Thanks so much for your
hospitality this past
weekend

INTER STATES
EMERGENT DISORDER

and
for your patience! I
thought I had sent you
this! Tell me what
you think.

RALPH MEIMA

Love,
Trip
4/3/2017

FOUNDERS HOUSE
PUBLISHING

Inter States: Emergent Disorder
Copyright © 2016 Ralph Meima
Published by Founders House Publishing, LLC
Cover Art by Matt Forsyth
Cover and interior design © 2016 Founders House Publishing, LLC
Paperback Edition: June 2016
ISBN-13: 978-0692734902
ISBN-10: 0692734902

For more information please visit www.foundershousepublishing.com

Published in the United States Of America

For Kristina, Joseph, Alexander, and Gemma

ACKNOWLEDGEMENTS

In addition to the acknowledgements below, which apply to the entire Inter States series, I wish to add my salutations to Thomas Piketty and Yanis Varoufakis, who I have read more recently, and to direct profound appreciation to Vermont Senator Bernie Sanders, who—based on what he has said during his presidential campaign—seems to grasp what needs to be done to avoid a scenario as arresting as the one depicted here.

Many deserve my sincere thanks for advice and encouragement on the decade-long path that the Inter States project has so far trodden. Rob Williams, source of the series' title and flag/shield logo, has cheered for IS since early-on, and provided valuable opportunities for promotion. My community of readers around the world has been supportive and informative, notably François Bartsch, Eve Ermer, Bob Fairchild, Magnus Nilsson, George Oprisko, Bill Perry, Beth Porch, Michel Salim, Sandy Schaudies, Mark Starik, Alex Wilson, Flemming Ørneholm, and scores more. My father Ralph and mother Barbara have been steady muses and advocates. Great gratitude goes to my publisher, Shaun Kilgore, for providing fabulous structural feedback. And big thanks also go to Matt Forsyth for his inspired cover art. You all believed in me, and this.

Finally, I salute those whose own explorations of the present and the future have been especially thought-provoking in my own project (not that I agree with them, necessarily): Ed Abbey, Gregory Bateson, Edward Bellamy, T.C. Boyle, Frank Bryan, Lester Brown, Ernest Callenbach, Fritjof Capra, Herman Daly, C. Lee Dravis, Sibel Edmonds, John Ehrenfeld, Dave Foreman, George Friedman, Joel Garreau, Ross Gelbspan, John Michael Greer, Paul Hawken, Chris Hedges, Richard Heinberg, Samuel P. Huntington, Aldous Huxley, David Holmgren, David Cay Johnston, David Jonstad, Naomi Klein, David Korten, Paul Krugman, James Howard Kunstler, Sinclair Lewis, Amory Lovins, Douglas MacKinnon, Lynn Margulis, Chris Martenson, Bill McKibben, Walter M.

Miller Jr., Thomas Naylor, Gerard K. O'Neill, Naomi Oreskes, David Orr, George Orwell, Ayn Rand, Jeremy Rifkin, Karl-Henrik Robert, Ken Stanley Robinson, Mark Satin, George R. Stewart, John Todd, Naomi Wolf, and Yevgeny Zamyatin. There is a lot to make sense of, but—fortunately—also a vibrant, creative web of sensemakers.

AUTHOR'S NOTE

I did not originally set out to write a novel. In the years around 2003-2004, as I awoke to the rising chaos and corruption in American politics during the first George W. Bush administration, and pondered our growing understanding of climate change and resource depletion, I began to wonder with growing alarm about the long-term effects of bad governance, corruption, willful ignorance of science in public policy and education, and the economic stripping of the middle class. Having spent a sizeable portion of my life living outside the United States, where I witnessed cases of profound political-institutional change, I knew that things would not necessarily always stay the same in the USA—that there would have to be consequences of some kind.

At that time, I was teaching a graduate course in strategic management at the School for International Training in Brattleboro, Vermont that included a unit on forecasting and scenario planning, so I invited students to write scenarios that addressed some of the latest trends, and tried my hand as well. The results of my work were less than satisfying. This short-format futurism felt linear, uncreative, obvious, and self-important. Plus, I had once organized a "future seminar" in the early '90s in Sweden for LM Ericsson that attempted to predict the cell phone business 15 years into the future (2005), and we (laughably) completely failed to anticipate the Internet and WWW. I was therefore well aware of how inaccurate most attempts at scenario-craft tend to be.

Nevertheless, frustrated by what I felt was a lack of thorough explorations of the future consequences of current trends, I decided to embark on the deep dive of an extended work of fiction set in the future, because I concluded that its real learning/thinking value rests not on how accurate a particular prediction is, but rather on whether the people in the narrative act in an interesting and plausible manner as the future throws new circumstances at them. If we don't want certain circumstances to appear in our own future, it's useful to contemplate how to avoid them, but things are never going to turn out exactly as one expects, so the most important thing is to train one's capacity to act flexibly and resourcefully as the future unfolds. Characters in a narrative can model this.

A final note: I have been experiencing a disturbing phenomenon first-hand as I write. I call it "severity inflation" or "plausibility creep." Again and again, a fictional future situation or event (political, economic, climatological, etc.) that felt implausibly extreme to include upon first imagining—alarmist, corny, melodramatic—has, as time passed and current events piled up, started to feel increasingly tame and predictable. I don't know whether this reveals more about me or about the future. But the early chapters of *Inter States* were written well before Hurricane Katrina, Tropical Storms Irene and Sandy, Abu Ghraib, the financial crash of 2008, the Arab Spring, Occupy Wall Street, the European debt crisis, the rapid spread of the acceptance of same-sex marriage, rapid advances in space technology, and much more of both a positive and negative nature. Most of these have entailed the arrival and acceptance of a strange, unfamiliar future circumstance sooner than imagined. And I have had to go back many times to earlier chapters to "turn up the heat" because—you know what?—the future seems to be consistently arriving ahead of schedule!

INTER STATES
EMERGENT DISORDER

1—AFTER THE STORM ON MOUNT ST. ALBAN

Sunday, October 28th, 2040

"Why don't you come upstairs, with us?" Mrs. Singh spoke with a note of urgency and concern. "It very dangerous down here." She stood silhouetted in the light of the stairwell's narrow window, glancing back and forth between Honorée and the boys.

Honorée leaned wearily by the side of the shattered living room window, watching the hurricane-bedraggled side street and the short section of Wisconsin Avenue that was visible. Her pistol lay on the chair beside her. Hot, muggy air filled the apartment. Aware of Mrs. Singh's presence, she remained at the window, unable to complete her processing of the scene. There were broken windows and pieces of debris scattered around. Yet it was an oddly festive scene, with garlands and wreaths of still-bright-green leaves plastered against walls, stuck in shutters, and caught in electric wires, where the force of the wind had torn branches from trees and impaled them on small projections. The trees, however, were stripped. In her exhaustion and shock, Honorée was having a hard time reconciling her impressions.

"Come on, Miss! You really shouldn't stay here, with those boys." Mrs. Singh was not going to give up.

Honorée reluctantly tore her bleary gaze away and met Mrs. Singh's attention. "Somebody's coming down to get us," she answered finally.

"Nobody's coming anywhere today. Except looters. You come up with us."

Asa let out an angry scream and Lee started crying. The boys were playing on the floor by the entrance to the kitchen. Honorée had rolled back the wet carpet so they could play on dry floor. The boys' fight penetrated her numbness for a moment. She glanced with a shuddering breath from the boys to the window to Mrs. Singh. The fight died back

1

down quickly, before she needed to intervene. Mrs. Singh stood looking at her expectantly.

Honorée sighed. "Oh, thanks for coming downstairs to check on us, but a friend called on the satnet about two hours ago. He's coming down with a wagon." The cellular networks were all down, so only the satnet was available. But Honorée was almost out of credits in her telecom account and with the price of the satnet, she had to be careful of every minute she used.

"Sweetie, there are trees and wires and poles and all sorts of other things across every street. It's martial law and they might not even let him through. Where does he live?"

"He's staying at my grandma's house in Chevy Chase."

"Chevy Chase, DC?" Mrs. Singh asked.

"No, a few blocks over the line, in Maryland."

"Oh, no...," replied Mrs. Singh. "No, no. The border is closed. Absolutely closed."

Claudia abruptly came out of the bedroom, where she had been lying down. Mrs. Singh started. "Oh! I didn't know..."

Claudia smiled coolly at her, and apologized with a faint "Sorry". She stood surveying the situation. Honorée slung a non-committal glance at her mother. They had been getting on each others' nerves.

Mrs. Singh recovered her composure and returned to the topic. "Sweetie, they're not even going to let him cross the state border. You come up with your boys and talk with Omar. He's listening to the radio and keeping track. He said, 'Go down and get the neighbors because it's going to be a bad night.'"

"I guess I can text Marcus..." Honorée reached for her phone. Mrs. Singh nodded approvingly and opened the door wider. But after several unsuccessful attempts, Honorée gave up trying. She frowned. "No, it's not going through. Even on satnet. That's odd." She stuffed the phone and pistol in her bag, swung it over her shoulder, and scooped up Asa. She grabbed a backpack with her free hand. Mrs. Singh took Lee's hand, and they started up the stairs toward the fifth floor.

"I suppose we're leaving?" asked Claudia accusingly, still motionless.

"Yes, come on, Mother. Mrs. Singh says it isn't safe down here, and I guess she's right."

Claudia waved her hand, and drifted after them. Not even the impact of the hurricane penetrated her compulsion to feel like excess baggage.

"You know, the water's off, too," said Mrs. Singh, ascending the stairs ahead of Honorée. "But we filled up everything with water before it happened, so I think we'll be OK until they get it turned on again." As they neared their door, they heard a murmur of voices. "My son's over too, with his wife and kids. They live in Adams Morgan, but they walked up late last night after the wind stopped. No buses, no Metro. Leland heard gunshots and said it was time to get somewhere safer."

"Good, more kids will keep my bored boys occupied," puffed Honorée gratefully.

They went in. It was a busy scene, in sharp contrast to the lassitude in the streets. Several older children, playing a card game on the floor, moved out of their way. Omar rose to meet them, a courtly older man with the dastaar and long beard of a Sikh. Honorée did not know them well, but he had a market cart and somehow knew Grandma. They exchanged greetings, and then he led her to the panoramic living room window. Honorée gasped. The view took in the avenue, a triangular park, various alleys, and Washington's skyline. The rain had stopped early in the morning, and it was beginning to clear. Weak, hazy sunlight dappled the city, and long, swooping banks of ragged cloud marked the flung-off wake of the hurricane. Signs of destruction were everywhere.

Honorée had known it would be bad. The night was long and terrifying. The wind howled and howled, and the darkness outside was filled with cracks and crashes as things broke up under its strength. Sometimes, the old brick apartment building itself seemed to shudder. A while after the electricity went off and the cellnet went down, the picture window exploded inward in thousands of shards, hit by a branch carried by the wind. Honorée had tried to call Jenny and Grandma, but had not yet been able to get through for over twenty-four hours. Not accustomed to being without at least email and the phone, her sense of isolation grew. But she was not even remotely prepared for what Omar Singh brought her to see.

The streets were impassible for any vehicle—even bicycles—and looked like they would be for days. Practically every tree they could see had been toppled. Roofs and other pieces of buildings lay piled and draped and up-ended everywhere. The streets were a tangle of wire as well.

3

Streetlamps were pitched at odd angles. Sidewalks were buried in detritus. The few vehicles parked outside had been blown over. Looking down the block, she registered an impossible scene: one side of a venerable old apartment building had collapsed, spilling an apron of masonry out into the street. An enormous tree, snapped off near its base, had impaled the opened building several floors up. She studied it for a moment. You could see right into the apartments. The building looked like a doll house.

Scanning the streets, she saw a few people. Some were just sitting or standing. Some picked their way gingerly over and under the debris. No vehicles moved. There was an illusion of Sunday-morning calm hanging over the savaged neighborhood.

"See out there?" asked Omar Singh, pointing toward the horizon.

"Yes." She peered out at the view that their vantage point on Mount St. Alban afforded, looking southeast and east. "Smoke!"

"Yes, see the smoke?" In numerous places in the far distance, black smoke drifted diagonally through the muggy air.

"Uh huh." She looked at him, wondering why things were burning after more than a foot of rain.

"The city's falling into anarchy," said Omar. "I've been following the news all day. The Army and police are just sealing zones off, letting the rest go to hell. Everyone's stuck. They can't get around. Outside, people are looting, rioting. All those poor, frustrated people. I've always wondered why it never really happened before. People have lost so much." Claudia joined them by the window. He went on. "But all the suburban migrants and the veterans down on the Anacostia Flats, and the natives up in Tuxedo and District Heights, they're just burning everything, and taking the civil defense stores."

"They won't let them get here, I hope!" Claudia spoke up loudly, in alarm.

"Nothing is sure right now, Mrs. Loporto," said Omar Singh politely. He and Mrs. Singh recognized Claudia but didn't exactly know who she was, and wondered where the black-haired young woman was. But they hadn't pried. They were as a rule very discreet.

"Um, no, my last name's Kendeil. I'm Claudia, Honorée's mother." She instinctively held out her hand, hesitant. "Sorry I didn't introduce myself. I'm forgetting my manners." Omar took it and shook it warmly.

"Anyway, nothing's sure," he repeated. "It's not going to be safe around here, either. Just imagine how desperate people are. We'll have to guard our door." He pointed at a rifle lying up on top of a tall bookshelf, out of the childrens' reach.

"We have to get out of here," sobbed Honorée suddenly, to the others' embarrassed surprise. "We have to get to Grandma's."

"Does she live in a safe area?" asked Omar Singh. "Is she in a stockade?"

"No, no stockade. So, maybe it isn't," said Claudia slowly, putting her arm cautiously around her daughter's shoulders. "I mean, probably not— it's a big old wood Victorian with lots of windows—but I think the police and militia in Chevy Chase will be better-organized. They do have neighborhood checkpoints..."

"I hope so," said Omar. "Because that's where the rich people are, so looters and vigilantes might try to get in there."

Honorée rubbed her eyes, driving away her tears. "How long is it going to take before things get back to normal?" Then she reflected that things were already far from normal for her before the storm hit. And it then hit her that she had not given Sanna or the van a moment's thought for hours. Those were minor problems now. Imagine that!

They were all silent for a moment as they watched a man run across the Avenue a block down toward Georgetown, ducking under and leaping over tree limbs. What was he running to, or from?

"Oh, I think it will take a long while," replied Omar Singh slowly. "Clearing the streets will take time. Getting the power and the water back on. Getting food in. We don't know what has happened to the markets, the bridges, the river." He narrowed his eyes and stroked his gray beard. "You know, I think it will take many weeks and months."

"I've got a bad feeling about Mike and Grandma," said Claudia. "And Jenny."

"Oh, *don't* say that!" said Honorée. "I'm sure we'll be back in touch with them today."

"You've been trying since last night, even on satnet," she shot back.

"So? So what? What are you saying? Why be so negative, *Mother*, when you don't even *know*!?" Honorée's voice rose in anger. "You don't know any more than I do! You're talking about your own kids and mother!"

5

Omar Singh watched the exchange, stepping back a little. He decided to change the subject. "Ah, we have enough room here, but shouldn't we go down and bring up any food or water you might have? Supplies, such as ammunition?"

The women fell into silence, nodding in agreement with Singh. By unspoken pattern, Honorée turned to follow him downstairs while Claudia went to see what the boys were doing.

* * *

It was late morning. They had brought up everything edible and potable from the first floor, along with Honorée's bicycle and trailer and assorted valuables. With its main window gaping open, and its glass kitchen door, the once cozy, sunny apartment now felt terribly vulnerable. If for no other reason than the message it would send, they fastened a table-top to cover the door's pane, and nailed up a heavy old carpet and several boards over the open picture window, using a hammer and a jar of rusty used nails that Mrs. Singh fetched. The darkened apartment became close and dank with humidity. They quickly withdrew.

Honorée's cell phone, clipped to her collar, quietly emitted its satnet tone. She answered it instantly. It was Jenny, voice only.

"Mother, it's Jenny!" Honorée cried over her shoulder toward Claudia's receding back. Then she lifted the phone to her ear. "Jenny, baby, where are you?!"

Claudia dashed over to where Honorée stood, leaning to catch what Honorée was hearing. Honorée flicked on the speaker, spoke briefly with her sister, and then passed the phone to her mother.

Jenny was weeping. She was just outside Fredericksburg, in a newly organized Red Cross refugee staging center near the interstate. The building where she lived had been blown apart. She had her horse—she had ridden out to the highway—but her roommate Portia was dead, crushed by a section of the roof when what must have been a tornado hit them. Julius had escorted her to Falmouth, but then gone back into the devastated city to retrieve his logging team and Portia's body. Jenny had begged him not to, in the darkness and chaos. He was not even armed. But he had gone, and she was left alone at the center, with nowhere in town to live and no idea what to do next.

"Jenny," said Claudia. "Can you stay there tonight?"

"I don't know. I don't know. Maybe."

"Oh my God...," muttered Claudia, looking ashen.

"What?!" interjected Honorée. "What's she saying?" Her mother was visibly confused. She let the hand holding the cell phone drop.

"Here, let me," said Honorée. She grabbed the cell phone back. "Jenn, honey. What? What did you say?"

"I don't know if I can stay here," sobbed Jenny.

"Ask them." Claudia and Honorée waited in silence for a minute or two, faces stricken, listening to the babble of voices and radio tones in the background. Jenny's voice returned.

"Yes, they're talking about putting us in a church basement."

"Good," said Honorée. "You stay put and when we can reach Grandma and Mike, we'll get them to come get you."

"Where are they, Hon?" Jenny's weeping had calmed.

"They were in Petersburg, last we heard. It's going to take a couple of days, Jenn. You sit tight there. Stay close to that Red Cross center."

"Oh, I'm not going to leave it at all," Jenny muttered, sniffling. "That would be crazy."

"You sit tight, Jenn. 'K?" Honorée tried to sound encouraging. "We'll see you soon."

Jenny sobbed.

"I love you, sissy."

Suddenly, the incoming-call melody sounded on the line. It was a VNET call. Honorée hastily said good-bye to her sister and terminated the call, answering the new call in voice-only mode: "Hello?"

Claudia watched abrupt surprise pinch her daughter's face. Her hand over the phone, Honorée whispered, "It's Sanna."

2—BREADLOAF AFTERMATH

Sunday morning, October 28th

"It looks like Philadelphia's about as far as I'll be able to get by train," said Wilder. "After that, maybe I can get a ride with the military down I-95."

"Didn't Philadelphia get it pretty bad, too?" asked the state senator in the other back seat.

"Apparently not nearly as bad as the stretch from Norfolk to Baltimore, and then up through New Jersey," Wilder replied. "The railroad's still open to Philly, if you come in from the west. Not from New York, though. At least, not yet."

"When does the congressional session end, officially?" asked Roy Kapp.

"The regular session can run right up to the election. We're technically in session now, although nothing has happened since last week. I have no idea what Laugherty and the leadership are planning. I need to track them down. Not much info yet. Washington is a complete mess."

Kapp leaned forward, resting his arms against the back of the front passenger seat occupied by Wilder. "You sure you want to go back down there? They might not let you go home."

"Right," laughed Wilder speculatively. "A hostage."

"Or you could be our ambassador!" suggested Kapp conspiratorially. "Bart's not going back, and I don't think Howard would want it."

Wilder looked back over his shoulder and eyed Kapp. "I'm prepared to accept what the people vote for. But there's nothing funny about this."

Kapp looked back at him coolly. "Don't take my humor for more than it is. Or less."

"What is it?" demanded Wilder.

"I joke around," said Roy quietly. "That's my personality. But this whole crisis is no joke."

"As long as you understand that," shot Wilder, suddenly furious with this state representative who had abruptly come to symbolize for him the whole separatist movement.

"You saying I don't?" asked Roy with a more surly tone.

"Gentlemen!" the state senator interjected. "Remember your oath! We're all members of the Breadloaf Council now."

Both men fell silent. The soldier at the wheel discretely glanced at them. The state senator shifted forward and grasped a handle over the door with her right hand, turning around. She continued, "We're going to be tested in all kinds of ways. This is a whole new situation. I have very mixed feelings about secession as well, but we have to let democracy work and we have to be ready as public servants to serve the public the best we can, no matter what direction events take."

Wilder tried to take a more conciliatory approach. "You have to realize I spend most of my time in DC. I am struggling to relate several incompatible realities. First, yes, the past decade has been very, very hard on people and communities, and many states have been proactive. So people may think we'd be better off on our own. Maybe we would be. There's plenty of federal legislation on the way, like Forsa, which scares the heck out of me. People here wouldn't stand for it, so OK. There'd be more nullification campaigns." He sighed. His listeners waited.

"Second, I think we have a major crisis unfolding now—a double or triple crisis—the likes of which we've never seen before…"

"I think you're right on that second point, Jake," said the senator. "The levels of cooperation and secrecy we'll have to assume are unprecedented…"

Wilder continued. "…So, second, we have to put wishful thinking and ideology aside and just deal with things as they come at us." His eye's met Kapp's again. "And, third—and here's what bothers me the most and what I want to really impress on you state politicians, just take it from me, no disrespects, and I'm just telling you my perceptions, not dreaming this up—but the mood in Congress and DC in general, and at the leadership level around the country, is now way more aggressive and paranoid and intolerant than anything I've ever seen, and it's only going to get worse with this hurricane. You know the bills before Congress. You see

9

Laugherty's attacks." He gestured out the windows at the green landscape unfolding before them as they drove south. "Vermont may vote to secede, but a lot of very powerful people are not going to want it to happen, because of what it symbolizes, because it means a final abandonment of faith, a final vote of no confidence. It could set off a chain reaction that neither Laugherty, nor the Energy Trust, nor the oligarchs, nor the right-wing rank and file want." Wilder paused and looked searchingly at both. "It could also give Laugherty just what he wants, an excuse to move quickly and decisively 'in a time of crisis' to prevent this, and prevent or take over a lot of other things as well. Nothing would surprise me. Our voters may feel very justified in this, self-righteous, but we have to be prepared for a very nasty reaction. I worry people aren't even close to ready for this, psychologically."

"I think you're right," said Kapp. "I appreciate your sharing this." He chewed the corner of his mouth, no trace of humor or irony in his expression now.

"But Jake," said the senator. "Laugherty can say what he wants, and he might even get elected in two weeks, but he wouldn't be inaugurated until January. Are you talking about something even sooner?"

"Emily," said Wilder, "anything can happen. Look at the pressure Morales is already under. If you add to it a catastrophic hurricane, damaged election, huge humanitarian issues, migration, a state looking like it's starting the breakup of the Union, foreign pressures to get involved—even if ostensibly for humanitarian reasons—and a Congressional vote for OSCIA, all at the same time, then what the President-elect wants, who also happens to be the Speaker of the House, by the way—number three in the leadership succession order - is going to weigh pretty heavily. I'd put nothing past the Supreme Court, for instance. Or suddenly we start hearing very little from President Morales and the Surgeon-General comes out and says she has suffered a nervous breakdown and is resting... You never know."

Their driver started decelerating as the I-89/I-91 checkpoint appeared in the distance. The three politicians felt for their old-fashioned ID cards, and a collective sense of gloom grew over them as they prepared to identify themselves to the federal troops who worked alongside the Vermont Guard on the nationally controlled interstate highway. Despite the afterglow of camaraderie and shared focus from the Breadloaf Wilderness, the prevailing reality weighed heavily on their hearts. Who was on their side, and whose interests ran against it?

A large illuminated sign flashed the warning, "US Agents Ahead. Prepare to Stop and Present Identification. Remain in Vehicle. Weapons Active." Traffic slowed to a standstill. The animal-drawn queue in the right lane was long. In the east, toward New Hampshire and Hanover, Wilder saw no smoke this time, but the heavy military presence—especially the convoy of Army transports parked on the shoulder and the flatbed trucks bearing helicopters—suggested more than routine logistics.

A soldier motioned the driver forward, and signaled for him to stop. He was dressed in combat gear, with the young, bored face of a Vermont Guard infantryman doing something any civilian or state trooper could do. He leveled his retinal scanner at each of them. The driver handed him the bunch of IDs. No RFID check, noted Mike. That was unusual on a federal interstate.

"So where are you folks going this morning?" asked the soldier. "Business or pleasure?" From the roadside, a gunner in a small machine-gun nest trained his weapon at their car. Wilder studied him out of the corner of his eye. The gunner also wore the uniform and insignia of the Green Mountain Boys. Then, the soldier at their window realized who they were, and his demeanor abruptly became crisper and more respectful. "Congressmen, Senator, Representative Kapp. Honor to assist you this morning." He handed back their IDs and saluted. "Safe travels."

The gate opened, and they moved ahead, their car picking up speed as it rolled south, once again in view of the Connecticut River and the New Hampshire hills beyond.

3—BATTLEFIELD VIGNETTE

Sunday afternoon/evening, October 28th

There was a lot of smoke in the air. The big fire they had built puffed out waves of acrid smoke from the mix of green and cured wood they found nearby. In the humid, nearly windless air, the smoke hung around a while before moving on.

Mike did not mind the smoke. It held off the clouds of flies that had found their sodden camp out in the battlefield.

"Oh, my goodness gracious," sighed Grandma wearily, settling back on the wagon's bench-seat to rest, up above the mire. She looked down at Mike. "Honey, would you mind making me a cup of tea?"

"We've already made a great big pot of mint and chamomile, Mrs. Trudeau," called Lena Burhans, politely avoiding the practice of the others to call her "Florence." She motioned to Mike. "If you bring me a cup I'll fill it up for your grandmother."

Grandma smiled and nodded with unconcealed appreciation. She had just returned from two demanding hours of horsework with Bill and Sherbet, directing her team to drag broken trees from the blocked road they would use to escape the storm's tangle. Mike, Fernando, Nate, Ethan, Jim, and Carl did the heavy work, chaining the trunks and branches to the team, pulling smaller debris out of the way, and chopping loose the snags with their axes. But Grandma knew her horses, and how to lessen their anxiety. They were wagon horses, not a logging team, and the unfamiliar, dark, crackling objects dragging behind their rear hooves made them jumpy.

"Here you go, Grandma." Mike stepped up onto the lowest rung of the wagon's ladder and handed her the battered metal cup of tea. "That was hard work." He eyed the storm's trail of caked mud and new nicks and dings along the wagon's flank.

12

"Hm, yes," she replied, breathing the tea's vapor deeply as she prepared to drink. "Nice to hand it over to those local people." From where she sat, the next crew of stranded horses and humans went to work on the next several dozen yards of cluttered roadway. They watched the others move into position. There were four men in black trousers with suspenders, loose black shirts, wide-brimmed straw hats—Hutterites, it appeared—and two muscular horses that resembled small, bay Percherons. The men were laughing and talking as they backed up the team to a huge, ancient oak sprawled halfway across the road. The sound of wrought iron on gravel rang out as they set pry bars under the trunk. The driver yeahed and chanted to the horses, who chawed and stepped with accustomed, almost bored expressions.

"You must be pretty tired," said Mike. He climbed up and sat down next to her. They reclined quietly, surveying the small island of order their campground made in the middle of the endless snag. Fernando was over currying their horses while Celia and Carl worked on the four North Swedes. Nate was across the fire from them, splitting wood and singing some rhythmic song, the sort of song that was perfect for repetitive work outdoors. His axe rose with each line and flashed down between them. They were burning large quantities of wood, almost as if the big fire could symbolically expunge the storm's trail of disorder and disease and death that surely lay out beyond what they could so far see.

"Hmm, yes, I really am," answered Grandma. "Exhausted." She yawned. "Another night in the wagon, eh?" They were sleeping in the bed of the wagon, with the ground so sodden and muddy still. "I don't mind working, but oh, you *do* start to tire out at my age..." She laughed wearily.

Mike was feeling exhausted himself. They sat in silence, bathed in the soft rays of the late-afternoon October sunshine, and he felt his eyelids drooping as he succumbed to drowsiness. His consciousness withdrew from the entrancing melody of nearby civility: the crackling fire, chopping axes, jangling harness, whinnying horses, and low murmur of conversation. He leaned back, his head settling into a folded horse blanket atop the seat. A last thought hung like a gentle goad, the reminder that he had promised to fetch and filter water, of which they would all be needing more by dinner.

With an abrupt jerk, Mike ejected from his brief sleep, the lurid image of a hypnagogic dream fresh in his mind's eye. It was a scene from his recurrent dream. The girl was in it, the slave girl or dancer, or whatever she was. She spoke his Olian name sharply—Daat—and it was still echoing in his ears as he jolted awake.

"Falling asleep?" chuckled Grandma.

"Mmmm," he mumbled, rubbing his face with both hands. "Tired, too." But he hung onto the image in the brief dream. Dreams like this were a common companion of RDD. They could last for years, the doctor at the base had emphasized. There was no certain cure; some said meditation and exercise helped. RDD had some things in common with post-traumatic stress disorder, and this was one of them. It was irritating, Mike found. But along with the irritant of recurrent dreams and the nagging compulsion he could not easily shake was the annoyance of not being able to go back to Vtopia anytime he wanted. It was bad for you, sure, sure, but he had grown up with VR, and almost everyone he knew spent time there. And it could be stunningly beautiful, a world of bright colors, intense sensations, and incredible adventures—far more alluring than the dreary world RL had become, with its mud, flies, dusty animals, tension, and poverty. Mike's rational mind knew his forced absence from Vtopia—what had it been, a couple of days? - was a good thing for his health and his wallet, and the longer, the better. But his sensual mind hungered for its dramatic landscapes, grand cities, and the rush of interplanetary and intergalactic warps to visit the endless variety of planets it offered. Indeed, he realized he had been half-consciously clinging to Lara's parting invitation to know her as Myste Rains, her persona in some yet-to-be-entered corner of the V-world. And as clearly as he knew what risks this posed for his spirit and sanity, he also knew that, as soon as circumstances permitted, satnet charges be damned, he would find an opportunity to look up Myste Rains.

"Mike, do you want me to tell them you're going to take a nap?" Grandma looked at her drowsy grandson with concern. "I'll bet you're exhausted, too."

Mike looked up at her and stretched, pulling physically away from his VNET reverie, yet still partly trapped in its competing sense of real-ness—what the onliners called The Frame.

"Oh, I'm OK."

"You gave me a start when you jumped like that. And you said something!" She looked at him a bit suspiciously.

"I did?" He wondered if he had tried to talk to the slave girl.

"Yes. It sounded like you said 'get' or 'got', and then something else…"

He pretended to be mystified. "Don't know." But Mike was not interested in telling Grandma what was on his mind. He was not sure she knew much about Vtopia, beyond her produce market business. She had surely heard about his problems, and he was certain he did not want her disapproval, moralizing, or sympathy at that moment. "Oh, well. Guess I was falling into a dream." He grabbed the side of the bench and hauled himself up.

Grandma's phone started playing its little chirping cricket ring tone. They both frowned at it. The cellnet was down, so this had to be coming in by satnet—a potentially expensive prospect for the called party as well. Grandma hesitated, and then grabbed it, glancing at its display to make sure it was worth answering.

"Hello?"

With Mike looking on, there followed a brief, rushed, emotional conversation with both Hon and Jenny. Everyone nearby in the campsite paused to eavesdrop. Grandma kept saying "oh, honey" and "yes, yes, yes" and "good heavens". Then, she hung up.

"We have to get to Fredericksburg as soon as we can." Grandma heaved a shaky sigh, and sat up unsteadily on the bench. "Jenny's there, in a refugee camp. Stuck. One of her friends died. No house left."

"Fredericksburg!" exclaimed Lena in dismay from over by the fire. "Oh, *that* doesn't sound good." There was a hunger for information in her expression—for news of her own home and environs.

Grandma looked down at her, distracted. "No, very bad there…"

At that, the energy in the campsite changed perceptibly. It was not as if they could suddenly accelerate the process of clearing the trees and snags off the road. There were no shortcuts. It would take the time, the work, and the horses it took. But the challenge wasn't simply to get home any longer. For Mike and Grandma, it now included rescue. And for the Burhans, home was starting to become a major source of worry and bigger questions were looming.

Conversation around the dinner fire that evening was all about the state of affairs in Fredericksburg and how to get there promptly. With the cellnet down, there could be no casual use of the phones or VNET for surveillance, but through quick checks Nate was able to determine that the

15

damage to the city was extensive, and the numbers of people driven from their homes very large. At the height of the rain, the rampaging Rappahannock River had overflowed its banks and gouged out large parts of the waterfront, flooding much of downtown. On higher ground, the Burhans' house and workshop appeared to have fared better, although they could get little clear information. There was speculation that washed out roads and bridges would make it inaccessible, except for on foot.

As talk turned to the improving possibility of being able to leave the following day, Grandma drew Mike aside.

"The call earlier was very hurried, but Hon told me she's heard from Sanna."

"Oh?" replied Mike curiously. "Sanna?"

"She's left the country. A week ago or more, by ship."

Mike shook his head. "Poor Hon."

Grandma looked at him with mild incredulity. "Is that all you have to say? 'Poor Hon'?"

Mike felt his face warm in the darkness. "Sorry," he muttered without fully grasping why.

"Sanna sold the van! Mike! She took their biggest asset—which I helped them buy, and for which they still owe me a *lot* of money—and sold it so she could run off. She also drained their savings, and ran up a huge satnet bill."

"Oh." These were sobering facts. "Where is she?"

"Europe. Sweden." Grandma stood up stiffly with a huff of disgust.

"Shit." Mike watched the crackling campfire. "So, what do we do?" It was certainly tragic, but it all felt so distant in their current predicament, and he had never met the woman. Focusing on this dimension of Honorée's life was difficult for him at that moment.

"Hm. Good question." She sighed, and turned toward the wagon, thinking. "It's like one rescue after the next. We can talk about it as we drive. First we get Jenny and the horse. Then we get home. Hon's safe with neighbors for now. I can't imagine what's left of the stall at White Flint, or the Market Garden." Grandma stood slightly stooped, as if each of the challenges was a further weight upon her thin shoulders. "Mike, don't take my tone of voice as some sort of denial, or as confidence…I am so terribly worried about what's ahead."

He nodded in the descending darkness, vaguely realizing how differently he and she were apprehending the situation. She was a matriarch, with a child, grandchildren, and great-grandchildren—six in all—plus various employees to look after. He was a young guy, used to only worrying about himself, and—worse—used to the structured environment of the Army where he did not have to make very many choices most of the time. They were swept up in an enormous disaster, compounded by many pre-existing problems. Grandma was concerned about where they would live, what they would eat, how they would make a living, and whether they would be safe from lawlessness and the inevitable epidemics that would come. Mike was not thinking ahead at all, he realized, or, if he was, he was only thinking about himself and where they would be the next evening, and whether there would be cheap VNET. An inkling of the very mass of Grandma's concerns overwhelmed him for a moment.

"Grandma, you can count on me," he said tentatively. She smiled, silhouetted in the firelight. "Just tell me what you need me to do. We're going to get through this."

She chuckled and patted his shoulder. "There's the spirit, grandson. Let's get some sleep."

He sat thinking as she walked slowly away toward the wagon and their tent up in its bed, where Fernando stood with a lantern, rigging mosquito netting. His mind spun reluctantly through thoughts of wagons, horses, bandits, disease, and recovering from the storm. "Grandma?" he called toward her receding figure. She stopped and walked a few steps back toward him. "Grandma, when we're all together again, do we have what we need to get by in Chevy Chase for a while, until things improve?"

"Maybe," she replied. "Probably." He noticed several of the Burhans family pausing to overhear their conversation. They were probably wondering the same thing.

"All winter?" Mike found himself pondering about the food, fuel, and supplies a large non-farm household would need to get to the next growing season. This was always the damn problem with hurricanes, he said to himself. They time their arrival perfectly to destroy harvests, and at a time when the next growing season will not start for half a year.

"Honey, let's talk about this tomorrow," Grandma said. She stood musing, swaying slightly. "Mike?"

17

"Yes, Grandma?"

"You know," she said, "I think I might give the Daniels a call, to see how they are. If they are anywhere near Fredericksburg with that truck, maybe they can step in and get Jenny until we get there in a few days. If they made it home to Blacksburg, then they probably came through all this in pretty good shape... If they can get across the rivers..."

Mike listened, her pause inviting a reply.

"Blacksburg got a lot of rain," interjected Nate, "but it did OK. I read they're using it as a base for refugee relief."

"Grandma, Blacksburg's a long way from Fredericksburg," responded Mike. "Even further than here, I think." He tried to envision Virginia's geography.

"Yuh, sure is," confirmed Ethan, who was passing as they spoke.

"Well, I was just thinking that, if they had the truck, and were..." She trailed off.

Mike heard a low chuckle from where Celia, Nate, Carl and Jim were hanging out, opposite him across the fire circle. Possibly amused by Grandma's outdated optimism about distances, thought Mike.

"I think I'll call them anyway," said Grandma. "You never know." And she walked off toward the wagon with a mixture of defiance, hope, and fatigue.

Mike considered her reaction. They often said that the old generation had a travel compulsion. When they wanted to escape or regroup, younger folks dove into the VNET. The older generation always wanted to hop into some expensive, fast vehicle and physically travel somewhere. That's where their heads were at. Only the few with cars to drive or money for trains or airplane tickets could actually indulge that impulse, of course

Mike's thoughts turned back to the earlier question of how they would live, once back in Chevy Chase, with things so damaged and conditions so risky. He suddenly recalled that they still had the pomador. That could surely buy all they needed for a while, assuming they found a safe and efficient way of cashing in the gold. They would be OK, all holed up in Grandma's rambling old house with the winter ahead. There, the family would get things back on track, and rebuild.

He stood up, dusting off his trousers. Yes, it was time to sleep.

18

4—WHERE'S DARYL?

Sunday night, October 28th

"Daddy," said Lara softly. "Daddy, wake up." She touched his exposed arm gently.

Ari Daniels opened his eyes, and lay motionless for a moment, trying to recall why he was on the sofa in the living room, and why his daughter was there and not in Salem.

"Daddy, sorry to wake you up but I just got through to Hon and Claudia."

"Mmm," replied Ari from his exhausted grogginess, slowly reconnecting disjointed mental dots. "What time is it?"

"Only about ten-thirty," she said. "You've been asleep for maybe an hour."

He raised his head and looked around. "Where's your mother?" he asked with foggy concern.

"In bed. We stayed up and cleaned up the kitchen and checked the latest VNET reports, and then she went to bed."

"Good." Ari sat up. "I shouldn't be sleeping here any longer anyway. Oy, my back is stiff." He stretched in several directions, and then swung his bare legs off the sofa and onto the wooden floor. It had been a demanding past twenty-four hours. The winds had been relatively moderate in Blacksburg, slowed by their long, bumpy scrape over the foothills of the Appalachians, but the volume of rain that had fallen had broken all previous records. The Daniels' house was high and dry, far from the creeks and ravines where the destruction was worst. But the already-intermittent electric power had failed, the roof had leaked, and their yard and street were full of broken tree limbs and other debris.

"Here, have some tea." Lara handed her father a warm mug she had just made on the kerosene stove.

19

He smiled. "I miss having you around all the time, Lari. Now, this is service!"

Her tired, worried face broke momentarily into a sweet smile, but then the tension and urgency returned. She sat down in the armchair across from him.

"Daddy, it's funny that we ran into Florence and Mike only the week before last. I probably wouldn't have thought of them so quickly. But as this hurricane started building up, I wondered how they were doing, with that wagon. They couldn't have already made it home. I started calling them yesterday. I didn't know if the VNET is down or just completely overwhelmed. So I tried to call Honorée, and got through, partly by satnet. I just got off the phone with her. And what's funny is that, when I was talking to Hon, Florence left a satnet message for me, which I haven't replied to yet."

"Where are they?" asked Ari, sipping his tea. "They OK?"

"Yes, Hon's OK. She's with the boys and her mother in their building, upstairs at a neighbor's. They had a terrible time there. You know the eye went right through Washington."

"Um-hum," he affirmed.

"So," she continued, "they don't know anything about where Florence and Mike are, or how they are. No contact since Friday afternoon. They were hunkering down—um, well, not in a hunker—some tunnel—in Petersburg. No news since then. Hon's been trying both their numbers constantly."

"My God," said Ari slowly, shaking his head, the lines around his mouth drawn. "Are Honorée and her family safe now?"

"She sounded calm, but it didn't sound good. The city's apparently a complete tangle of trees and everything else, and it's getting dangerous to go out. You know that other stuff we saw earlier—everybody shooting at everybody—well, in parts of the city but not around where they live, apparently."

"Where do they live?" Ari knew Washington, D.C. fairly well.

"Near the Cathedral, off Wisconsin Avenue."

"That's high ground, all right," he noted. "We stopped by there once."

Lara nodded in delayed recollection. "Yes, that's right. Wasn't it when she married that awful guy? They were already living there together."

20

"Yes, yes." He saw it again in his memory. "No kids yet. Must be seven, eight years ago. During the last Arabian War, and the pre-Morales crackdown. We had to get special passes. Remember?"

"Yes." But Lara had no interest in reminiscing. She went on with the original topic. "So, Hon wants to get out to her grandma's house in Chevy Chase. Thinks she'll be safer there. Her neighbor and her mom are totally against it, so they're staying put for the time being. They're not sure they could even make it across town, in terms of debris and roadblocks."

"Are they getting relief? Water? Food?"

Lara shook her head. "Hon said there's been nothing at all, not yet." Then she remembered her other main piece of news. "Oh, Daddy, you know her little sister Jenny, in Fredericksburg?" He nodded. "She's apparently in a total predicament—lost her house, barely saved her horse— and she's in a refugee camp along I-95 trying to get up to Chevy Chase."

"Fredericksburg was terribly damaged," Ari reflected. Earlier, they had seen drone footage of Fredericksburg, where all the bridges over the Rappahannock River had been washed away, excluding the I-95 bridge, and deep fingers of mud extended through the devastated downtown area. "How's she going to get up to Chevy Chase by herself? And with a horse? And can they get across all the rivers?"

"Hon didn't know," she answered. "It's apparently packed on the interstates and they're not letting people leave where they're from, just return home." She took a drink from her own tea. "It's about fifty or sixty miles, but who knows, maybe she doesn't have all her tack, and I wouldn't want to put a horse through that after everything that's happened. Plus, no lone woman in her right mind would take the back roads up through those counties."

Her father chuckled ironically. "Florence and that Spaniard did, and probably ten times the distance. Of course, that was before the storm..." His expression changed to puzzlement. "Odd about this selective travel ban. I wonder how they are enforcing that. What about family groups where some of them are traveling 'away' while the rest are heading home. Are they kicking people off wagons and out of carts, saying families have to split up?"

Lara shrugged.

They were both silent for a moment. Outside in the warm, humid darkness—all the blacker because of the total electric power outage - the summer sounds of nocturnal creatures clicked and rattled, unfazed by the storm's recent visit: katydids, crickets, geckos, tree frogs.

"Oh, it sure is hot," sighed Ari, wiping perspiration from his face. "Almost November…"

"All this humidity…" agreed Lara.

Through the open windows came the distant sound of a diesel engine, growing in volume as it crept closer. They glanced at each other. As it approached up the long, steep hill toward their house, they heard the crack of crushed branches, occasional shouts, and the rise and fall of a revving engine.

"Home Guard, I'll bet," said Lara.

"Who else has diesel trucks?" asked Ari rhetorically, his civil engineering authority aroused. "Army? They're staying down by 81 or working around federal facilities somewhere. VDOT has plenty to do elsewhere, not up here where the only problem's some downed trees and no power."

"Mmm," mused Lara. She was instinctively wary of the Home Guard, especially around Blacksburg. As a whole, they seemed more dangerously right-wing than their counterparts in Roanoke. She thought of the unpleasant atmosphere some years before, not long after high-school, when she and her parents had accompanied Daryl to the Blacksburg Fourth of July parade. A small riot had broken out at the Rec Center afterwards, with a lot of racist name-calling aimed at a small group of diverse Tech students. That was when she first found out about the Home Guard. They were supposed to be keeping order, as a National Guard auxiliary, but then they started telling some people they weren't welcome, and got into a confrontation with the police. The scene was ugly, although no one was seriously hurt. On their way home, she was shocked at how angry and frightened her father was. "Nazis," was all he seethed through gritted teeth. "Homeland Front!?"

Her attention returned to the present. "Where do you think Daryl is now, Dad?" Thoughts of the Guard had reminded her of her brother, who lived with her parents. "Should we call him?"

"Oh," murmured Ari from his mug, "I'm sure he's still with the Home Guard on the VDOT detail and we'll hear from him soon. Although he said he might sleep with the crew tonight at the barracks, and stop in tomorrow." He was not concerned. Daryl did this sort of work periodically—disaster or no disaster - and it was local and routine, and did not involve handling weapons. He drove a truck and handled field administration, as far as Ari knew.

"I wouldn't want to be out there now," sighed Lara. "Dangling electric wires, looters, loose animals, who knows?"

"Yes, well," said her father. "There are risks, but compared to what people a little east of here are dealing with, we're OK." He raised his eyebrows. "Which reminds me, we're probably going to start seeing a lot of refugees coming out of the Tidewater. They don't have much left to live on..."

The truck outside was very loud now, and then they realized that it was stopping at the foot of their driveway, and that men were outside on foot. Lights played across their windows, and footsteps started crunching up the gravel path toward the front door. There was a loud knock.

"Open up! Guard orders!"

Lara and Ari looked at each other, startled. Lara jumped up.

"No, no, I'll get it." Ari heaved himself upright and started walking toward the front door, carrying the tilley lamp Lara had placed on the coffee table when she brought his tea. The knocking was repeated. He opened the door.

There were five or six Guardsmen outside, with flashlights aimed into his face and past him into the house. Ari noticed several weapons out. He also saw a few neighbors peeking out their doors nearby. He was not unduly frightened—this had become increasingly common around town as the Guard was called upon to help keep law and order—but he had irrationally expected to see Daryl among them, so he peered around at their faces, trying to recognize someone in vain.

The abrupt treatment seemed to fall back into more courteous behavior for a moment. The captain in charge spoke. "We're looking for Daryl Daniels. He is your son, is that correct?"

Ari stared at him in confusion. "Ah, yes, of course, but ... isn't... isn't he with you?!" He wondered if they were from his unit.

"No, sir. He abandoned his Home Guard platoon this evening. He is away without permission. If he is here, you are required to cooperate and disclose this information."

Lara had come up behind Ari in the narrow hallway. She felt the men's eyes on her.

"My brother is out working with you guys!" She showed her irritation at their heavy-handed intrusion into her parents' home. Off to her left, she could hear her awakened mother calling out with a trembling voice. "Just phone him." Lara turned to her father. "Can you believe this?"

"That's negative, miss. If y'all don't mind, we are coming in to take a look." The captain's body language indicated a readiness to push past them into the house. His companions tensed up, weapons cradled, barrels down. But they waited.

"On whose orders?" Ari's mystification was giving way to anger. "Did the police send you here with a warrant?!"

"Sir, this jurisdiction has been under martial law since Friday night. That's all the warrant I need. I take my orders from Major Willow, 116th Infantry Brigade." He held up a tiny T-pad. "Orders."

Then it suddenly dawned on Ari and Lara simultaneously that this was not the Home Guard—not the irregular militia; these were regular Virginia Army National Guard troops. Lara recognized the horseman silhouette in the captain's sleeve insignia—the Stonewall Brigade—and the spear-and-chain VANG insignia on his other sleeve.

"What in God's name....?" Ari made no move to permit them to enter, struggling to regain his composure. He swallowed with difficulty. "Well, this is crazy. Daryl has been out with his Home Guard unit for days, working like a dog, you know, cleanup, rescues. This is a mistake." Lara put her hands on her hips, shaking her head. The soldiers, responding to some unvoiced cue, relaxed slightly.

"Are you absolutely certain he's not here, sir?" The captain looked around, clearly without relish for a forced entry when these people appeared honest.

"We are absolutely sure," said Lara, "but is he in trouble?" She could not believe this.

"Miss, we have orders to bring him in for questioning. Quickly. That is all I can tell you." He appeared to not know the reason himself.

Ari's intellectual acumen was returning as he started to grasp the situation. "Well, there is sure to be some mix-up, and we'll know sooner or later, but with everything such a mess, why would they waste your unit's valuable time to go looking for one local Home Guardsman? This is very strange, and I'm sorry your time is being wasted like this." Ari tried to smile.

The captain retreated from Ari's invitation to answer the question, staying neutral and tense. "We're going to take a look around outside your house and garage, Mr. Daniels." He spoke quick words to his men and gestured left and right. The men quickly spread out, shining their blinding LED rifle lights through windows, among the boxwoods, around corners, and deep into the back yard, around the Daniels' stable where Missy, Lara's Morgan, was tied up.

Ari Daniels shrugged wearily. "What on earth…"

"We will be going," the captain said after several minutes. "We apologize for any inconvenience." And then they vanished in a swirl of lights and rumbling engines into the sticky night, leaving the tree-shaded residential street dark and quiet again.

5—DARYL'S DARK LESSON

Earlier on Sunday, October 28th

It was earlier on Sunday morning. Daryl was beginning to wonder whether they were on a new militia patrol, or still doing volunteer service for State Highways. They were using a State Highways truck, but everyone in the crew was Home Guard, and most were from Bravo Company. And as the morning wore on, Pierce spoke and acted more and more like the Guard Master Sergeant he was, and less and less like a civilian VDOT volunteer detail crew boss. It was subtle. Nobody was saluting, but Dee and Wilson were calling him 'Sarge,' and so was Tade Porter, who had joined them that morning. There was a harder authority in Pierce's eyes and tone. Maybe, reflected Daryl, it was just the tension brought on by the emergency situation.

The calls they were responding to varied. In the big diesel, they could drive into standing water and pull folks out of drowned homes and waterlogged trees where they had taken refuge. Today, forty-eight hours after the peak of the storm, there was less call for that, owing partly to the topography of Blacksburg: most water had drained precipitously away down the many creeks feeding into the enraged Roanoke River, so there was little standing water. There were washouts everywhere, however, and undercut buildings on the verge of collapse. The Blue Ridge Mountains had received much less wind than the Tidewater, but their elevation had caused Rhiannon to dump epic quantities of rain. VDOT was reporting that in one area of Albemarle County, nearly four feet of rain had fallen in a day. In Blacksburg, it was well over two. Bridges were gone, roads swept into creeks, houses swallowed up into ravines, and the wash-out debris and enormous snags of branches and building materials made travel very difficult. So, road clearing and keeping people away from unstable banks and structures was a large part of their work that day. The only merciful

26

element in all this, reflected Daryl, was that the harvests were mostly in. Otherwise, they would be out harvesting rot-threatened, flattened crops as well.

"State troopers finally up here, huh," drawled Dee, slowing down for a police checkpoint ahead. Pierce was in the front passenger seat. He opened the window and leaned out, his right elbow resting on the door. A trooper was approaching him, holding up his hand rather unnecessarily to motion a stop. There were several cruisers parked alongside the road, radios softly crackling.

"Mornin'," said Pierce in a friendly, no-nonsense fashion.

"Mornin'," answered the trooper.

"Nice to see y'all here. Things are goin' from bad to worse in a couple areas."

The trooper squinted at the rest of them in the rear seats, and returned his attention to Pierce. "Things're goin' from worse to worser in a lot of places. Your crew doin' all right?"

Pierce looked over his shoulder at the crew, and then back at the trooper. "Nope, they're a sorry bunch, and getting sorrier." He laughed his abrupt, whisky laugh. Dee and Tade Porter grinned and looked appeasingly at Pierce. The trooper smiled cautiously, and asked where they had been and what they had seen so far that day. Pierce responded, and the two men talked. Another truck drove by, heading the other direction, and the radios crackled louder. Daryl strained to hear what Pierce and the trooper were saying. Something about looters and snipers. Pierce looked grave. Another trooper came over and joined the conversation. Wilson opened his window, which had been closed because of the mud and spray, to listen. Daryl wished he was not seated in the left side of the truck.

When they had finished talking, the troopers stood back and waved them through the roadblock. Dee drove further down the long grade toward Harding Road, the diesel engine silent as the regenerative brakes took over. Pierce swung around to address them all.

"There's more trouble goin' on, I heard. Troopers said some looters been shot over other side of the campus. Stealing livestock. Poultry and calves." His icy blue eyes narrowed, and he shook his head imperceptibly. "He asked us to refrain from shooting 'em if we run across it, but we need to report it immediately and we can detain 'em if we get a chance." Pierce rattled a low laugh. "I'm going to personally 'detain' any fuckin' looter I see with enough metal to slow 'em down good and final!" The crew was quiet. They knew that they were technically *not* on Guard duty, and there were only a couple of weapons between them. Pierce was visibly armed with his service piece on his belt, but getting into an exchange with a concealed sniper was nothing anyone wanted, and the word making the rounds was that snipers and the serious looters often came in a package.

At their next call, they hauled away used sandbags for an hour, and then joined a large crane crew in the late morning to pull wreckage out from under a bridge that had barely survived, but was still passable. It got warmer and warmer. The men sweated in their T-shirts, and drank volumes of water. There were more rumors of looting, and gloomy conversations about the wider effects of the storm, the costs of rebuilding, and the food situation with winter coming.

"That's why we're moving out to Wisconsin," remarked Tade Porter. "Before Christmas. My uncle's got a dairy farm. Nobody goes hungry there, boy. And no malaria!"

They were back in the truck again. It was late afternoon. They were coasting down a long incline. Daryl spotted what seemed to be an intersection a short distance ahead. Their latest call involved helping a newly-homeless family get some trees and swamped vehicles out of their driveway and street so they could move their own wagons out. There was no end to such calls. Even with the main roads open, the parking lots, drives, cul-de-sacs, and small streets were in many places impassable, and people needed to go out for food, water, and other supplies.

Bang, bang, bang! Dee braked the truck hard, throwing Daryl against his seatbelt. Everyone in the back seat bounced around like loose groceries. Pierce was already hanging out the window, taking aim with his handgun again. Bang! Bang! A fourth and a fifth shot. His targets, a small cluster of black kids, jumped unscathed down a steep hill into the ravine by the right side of the road, dropping bags and boxes as they ran. In a second, they had scattered and vanished behind the buildings separating the road from the ravine—at considerable risk, thought Daryl; he could see how the creek's bank was seriously scalloped out below one building, all the vegetation scraped away to reveal earth with bands of gray marl and red clay.

"Holy fuck!" Pierce was breathing hard, excited. He sat back down in the seat. Dee stared at Pierce, his eyes popping out, a question mark on his face. "You see them go? Grabbing everything they could get their hands on." He gestured toward the houses that they had apparently run from. A driverless horse and cart still stood in front of one of them. "Still all down there just th'other side of those buildings, hidin'." Daryl expected Pierce to jump out of the truck any second and run down to catch them. But he stayed in his seat for several heartbeats, breathing with agitation and looking everywhere ahead of the truck. "Dee, pull up there," Pierce snapped. He jerked his index finger toward a place opposite the horse cart. Then he swung his head over his shoulder and barked, "Prepare to dismount!" Daryl felt his hackles rise at its military ring. This was wrong. Wilson came back at Pierce, incautious in his confusion. "Sarge, you sure they was looters?"

Pierce whipped around and glared at Wilson. "Sure I'm sure. As shootin'. You payin' attention?"

Wilson persisted. "They looked like young kids loading up the family cart." He chuckled inappropriately. "I'd like to be loading up and getting' out of here myself right now, too."

"No question. Pay attention. My ass." Pierce was annoyed, energized. He fired off the commands. "You heard the troopers. Dee, call it in. I'm goin' to look. Daniels, come with me. Dee, Wilson, Porter, secure our position." Daryl got warily out of the truck. No one appeared to be around. Dee looked confused. Pierce was in command, but under whose authority? And they did not have enough weapons to secure anything, much less their truck in a 360 perimeter, right out in the open. Pierce threw on a chitrex vest he had up front with him. Daryl had no armor. It was not part of their gear. The situation felt weird, out of control. Pierce was on his feet now, gun at the ready, stalking tensely toward the cart.

The horse, startled, stood nervously in the filtered, humid sunlight, its eyes wide and ears flapping. The scene was quiet, except for the chatter of a flock of grackles in some trees above the ravine and the distant braying of a donkey. No one appeared from the dozen or so multi-family houses and garden lots grouped around the crossroads. They seemed deserted. Daryl stood close to the truck, his back to it. In a stiff crouch, Pierce paused and glanced back at Daryl. "Get the fuck moving!" he hissed. Daryl began to follow, torn between the fear of being shot at by some invisible, imagined sniper and the ordinary calm of the country road. He didn't know whether he wanted to run back to the truck or walk normally over to Pierce and tell him there was no need for this. But he did neither. Pierce was firmly in command.

In the right corners of his eyes, Daryl registered motion. He looked to the side, in search of its source. But Pierce was already moving fast, unlocking his pistol as he ran, screaming up at a figure coming down the front steps of the cabin closest to the cart: "Down! Down! On the ground. Get down, face down, get fucking down on your face. Arms out! Get the fuck down." The figure of a woman dropped an armload of something and fell down onto the brick walk leading up to the steps. Daryl ran. Pierce was already there, about ten feet from the woman on the ground, his gun aimed rigidly down at her. She lay across the edge of the walk, her waist on a border of ivy and her torso on a battered strip of lawn.

"What's going on? What's going on?" she kept screaming. Daryl saw she was in her forties or fifties, dark-skinned. She had dropped a thick pile of blankets and bed linens, which now lay on the slimy brick walk soaking up the damp. His impulse was to go help her up, but then he looked at Pierce again and held back. Pierce's face was a mask of wild anger. The gun was still aimed.

"Daryl, check her!" Pierce motioned with his head toward the woman. Daryl hesitated for an instant. "Check the woman!" he ordered again, still shouting but sounding more controlled. Trancewise, Daryl ran over to her and started frisking her sides and back, feeling for metal. He had never done this in his life but he had seen it so many times, in person and on the screen that it came like instinct. The woman was breathing in big, moaning sobs, afraid to move. "Thorough!" drilled Pierce. "No surprises!" Daryl felt nothing. It seemed so unnecessary. "OK," called Pierce in disgust, clearly dissatisfied with Daryl's half-hearted attempt at a pat-down. "Get back." He walked closer to the woman. "Roll over! Slow!" The woman turned her head stiffly to the side, looking at his feet but not up at his face. "That's it. Roll over and look at me!" The woman rolled over onto her back, her full dress all twisted around her knees and calves. There was a jumbled mix of terror and indignation on her face. Pierce trained the gun on her head. "The state cops are shooting looters to kill," he finally said, aggressive but quieter, the trace of a grin on his face. "You're fuckin' lucky it's just me you got this time."

"Oh, no, no," the woman was panting over and over.

"What you got to say for yourself?" demanded Pierce.

30

"Not a looter, not a looter," she repeated, taking a deep breath, which she let out with a shudder. A small cloud of gnats was starting to form around her, down near the saturated soil.

"Oh yes you fucking are," said Pierce. "I saw those boys, running with all they could get."

"No, no, not my kids!" The woman became agitated again, starting to cry.

"The state police'll be here any minute to take over," said Pierce. "You better pray they're feeling lenient." The woman moved as if she were getting ready to get up. "Back down!" yelled Pierce. "Stay right there!" Daryl became aware of a police siren in the distance.

"I'm not a looter!" the woman gasped. "This's my sister's house!"

A frown lashed Pierce's lips. His gun dipped a few inches, but then he steadied it on the prone woman again.

"This is my sister's house!" the woman said again with bolder emphasis. "Those was my kids going over the road. We're moving, not looting!" The siren got louder. "We're getting away from this mess!"

Pierce laughed, and glanced at Daryl as if they were both witnessing something very funny. Behind Pierce, two state police cruisers came over the brow of the hill. "Getting away? Well, that sounds like a very good idea. The fewer fuckin' coons around here, looters or not, the better!" Pierce chuckled at his own clever joke, and stared hard at Daryl for a tense instant, his eyes bright, a smile strung on his leathery face. Daryl looked away, his mouth dry and sticky. He could not meet Pierce's eyes. Pierce lowered his gun and holstered it, turning to face the police. Their cars crunched to a quick stop behind the cart. Several troopers in helmets and chitrex suits jumped out, machine rifles at the ready. The horse let out a loud whinny and stomped its feet.

"She's all yours, boys," smiled Pierce. "Very suspicious." And he turned again toward Daryl with a curious look before preparing to give his report to the state police.

6—A TEST OF LOYALTY

Early morning, October 29th

Jessica Daniels was not ordinarily a light sleeper, but after the commotion of the National Guard's visit, she had lain awake in bed for hours, long after Ari had fallen into soft snoring beside her, and after Lara had returned to her bed in the guest room. Jessica lay there, worrying, thinking about all the subjects her mind frequently returned to: their financial struggles, her children's challenges, her own precarious health, the disrepair of their house, the general insecurity of the times. The hurricane was a blow. There had not been electricity for several days, coming after a summer of many blackouts. Who knew what longer-term effects the storm would inflict on them? She hoped the power would come back on soon. The air was so close. She longed to switch on the ceiling fans. That would provide some relief.

It had been years and years since they could afford air conditioning. That was humiliating enough. But there were other humiliations, so many of them—the sorts of things that a girl growing up in Northern Virginia in the Eighties and Nineties was never prepared for. Such as having to walk everywhere, take the vegetable gardening seriously, repair old clothes endlessly, and keep patching what had once been high-end household appliances. Ari had fixed the microwave numerous times. He was getting good at that. But since the washing machine had broken down again two years before, they had not been able to fix it, and washing everything by hand was a daily burden that always seemed to fall to her. As long as Lara was with them, she could count on her help with that chore.

She wondered how long Lara would be there. Lara's visits meant laughter, a sense of safety, help with the work, and the social thrill of having company. Once upon a time, Jessica had led a fairly active social life. Their part of town was home to a lot of college families, and she had been busy as a volunteer in schools and local non-profits, especially when the kids were young. She had also been a regular and relatively good tennis player. When they moved to Blacksburg in 2010, even in the middle of the Great Recession, it had seemed like a dream come true, with the cooler summers, scenic mountains, a friendly community, and good work for Ari. Lara and Daryl had both been born there. Once upon a time, they had had no qualms about retiring there. Many of their friends planned to as well. A lot of retired faculty tended to stay nearby. Who wanted to move to Florida anymore? And moving back to Arlington was not even thinkable. Her own family was no longer around there. Her parents had passed away, and her two brothers both lived up near Boston now. Besides, she reflected, the whole D.C. area was so overcrowded, so expensive, and so, well, messy. You never knew what might happen next there.

So they lived on in Blacksburg, in their red ranch, with views of the Blue Ridge. They had a network of old friends and acquaintances. Lara and Daryl were never far. Jessica tried to feel comfortable with their choice. But, as much as she tried, deep dissatisfaction and vague dread gnawed at her. They no longer had a car, and it was almost a half-hour's walk down to the markets and the Mercantile. She was unwilling to ride a bicycle or horse now, with her incessant vertigo. Ari could bike around—she was grateful for that—and through Lara they had acquired a middle-aged cob that was now stabled in their back yard, in the pole barn that Ari and Daryl had built with wood from an abandoned home. Ari ran most of their errands, and with the cart that had come with the cob, he took Jessica anywhere she wanted to go. There just weren't that many places she wanted to go anymore. You could only go so far in a cart. The malls had closed, and so had most of the downtown stores. So she pretty much stayed put in their dilapidated neighborhood, worked in the garden, washed and dried the clothes, visited on the porch with a few of the more friendly neighbors, watched the abandoned homes slowly get stripped of useful materials, and chatted in the VNET with Lara and a few of her old girlfriends who were similarly entrenched in places like Chapel Hill, Charlottesville, and Williamsburg—friends she had not actually seen for a long time and might never again, as far as she could tell.

Jessica's thoughts swirled slowly as her interrupted sleep returned. She slumbered; she did not know for how long. Suddenly she was awake again. There was light coming from the living room. Someone was moving around out there. She got up stiffly and pulled on her bathrobe, wondering if Lara had been unable to sleep. Opening the door slowly, she peered out into the soft tilley light, which was turned down very low. It was Daryl, in his Home Guard uniform. He was making himself a sandwich and tea.

"Mom!" He looked up at her anxiously. She squinted at him, taken aback. Daryl was sweaty, disheveled, and grimy. He was also as pale as a ghost. Her surprised eyes took in the additional fact that he had pulled down all the blinds.

"Honey," Jessica whispered sleepily. "What are you doing up so late?" Then, the memory of the National Guard visit returned to her. "And what is going on?"

"Oh, mom," Daryl began. He looked like he was going to cry. "Mom, I have to get out of here."

"Why? Why do you have to get away?"

And then he told her.

After the strange shooting incident, Daryl had felt a growing fear of Pierce as he contemplated his anger, violence, and dominating attitude. What would he do next? He was a bully—a skilled, decisive, ruthless bully. Daryl just wanted to get away from him. He contemplated resigning from the Home Guard—sometime after the storm aftermath had quieted down. He thought about what that would do to his income. He would lose the milscrip they distributed, which he could use at the Mercantile. He would get grief for it. The other guys would look at him as a traitor. Not everyone was a Home Guardist—not the farmers, the skilled tradesmen, the professionals, the real military, the police and emergency services... But if you were none of those things and not even Home Guard, you were pretty low in the food chain. People would wonder whether he had been expelled. Whether he no longer qualified.

Daryl went through the rest of the day like that, working, feeling a bit shocked, pondering his limited choices. He was on a fifteen-hour rotation. When their State Highways truck pulled back into the parking lot beside the Armory, he had two more hours to kill before he could leave. Being Bravo's quartermaster, there was always paperwork to deal with. As most of the men dispersed toward the locker room, he headed toward the office. As he neared the door, Pierce called him. His ears involuntarily pricked up, and he pivoted reluctantly back toward the source of Pierce's voice. Pierce was walking quickly up the sloping corridor from the garage.

"Hey Daniels, I need you for a minute." He gestured for Daryl to continue into the office. Once they were both in, Pierce closed the door behind him. Daryl, heart pounding, turned and waited, switching on another light as he spun on his heel.

"Yessir," he replied.

"Daniels, you keep all that situation with those looters confidential, understand?"

"Yessir," nodded Daryl. He felt a blend of shame, disbelief, and disapproval about the incident, but if Pierce wanted it kept secret, who was he to argue?

"Real confidential. I may file a report, but I think the police know everything they need to know, understand?"

Daryl met his eye for a moment, nodded, and looked away. Then it dawned on him that, if Pierce had used his service weapon, he was supposed to file a report anyway. He must have fired at least five rounds, he mused. He wondered if that report would be filed.

"Good soldier," said Pierce, radiating a pleasant satisfaction that was utterly devoid of respect. "In these times, there's a lot of crazy shit going on, and we have to be able to trust each other. To keep the peace, keep our city safe." He kept smiling.

Pierce walked closer to Daryl. Daryl felt his tension rise. He was afraid to look at Pierce. His neck hairs rose. He could smell Pierce's sweat.

"We uphold the trust, we live. Betray that trust, and we're dead." Pierce's smile was a net of sinew. "Dead men. Know what I'm sayin'?"

Daryl swallowed dust and ash. "Yessir." His reply came out as a raspy click. Pierce laughed. He patted Daryl on the shoulder, provoking a reflexive jump, at which he laughed even more.

"Good man. You understand me."

Daryl let out a suppressed breath, hoping this was now over. But he was wrong.

"OK. Soldier, follow me." Pierce turned and started walking back toward the garage. Relieved to be moving, the excruciating moment over, Daryl followed unwillingly, wondering what was next. Pierce was already way ahead, opening the door into the truck bay. He hurried to follow. In the bay, the lights were on now, as the autumnal dusk fell out on the street. A couple of guys worked noisily on a truck at the opposite end, but the rest of the bay was quiet. Pierce was over on the other side, by the light vehicles. There was a battered L-8 parked by the wall, one Daryl did not recognize. Its bed had a dark green canvas tarp over its cargo that Pierce was busily pulling back.

"Give me a hand and you can get back to the office." Pierce pulled away the buckles and dropped the tailgate. Extending from under the tarp were three green wooden crates about three meters long. Pierce dragged them out onto the tailgate, pulling on their handles. Daryl came up warily beside him.

"Know what this is?" Pierce shoved one crate diagonally across the bed, and started opening the top.

"Nossir," replied Daryl.

"This is for when the EU tries to come in here with their Trojan horse relief supplies," smiled Pierce, grunting to lift the top, which was partially weighted by the canvas. "Or if some disloyal National Guard brigade or faggots from up north try to take away our liberties."

This made no sense to Daryl at all, and for a second he stared at Pierce, unsure of how to respond. But Pierce got the top open, and gestured at the contents with his head, his thick arms holding the top up so Daryl could see. There was a large-caliber machine gun of some kind.

"XM505's. Twelve-millimeter autocannons. Coil guns. Cryo. Six hundred RPM. Two-click range. Mach 7 rounds." Pierce looked at the weapon in awe. "Two-man crew. Totally electric."

Daryl studied the gun. He had only heard about these, but never seen one. They were very new. What did the Home Guard need these for, in Blacksburg? To stop a smuggler running a road block? This could slice a helicopter in half two thousand meters away. And he was the quartermaster, anyway. He knew about any new weapons orders. There was no order for these.

"Uh," started Daryl. He was not sure what to say. The situation was all wrong. His shaky, panicky feeling returned.

"Here, help me get these off the Later." Pierce used the nickname for the L-8 light truck. He dragged the crate towards its tipping point on the tailgate. "Here!"

Daryl stepped over quickly, grabbing the handle at the far end as Pierce pulled. With a heave and a stagger, they put the crate down on the cement floor.

"Go get that hand pallet over there," ordered Pierce, pointing next to the forklifts by the wall. "It should take all three."

As Daryl turned to obey, he noticed a label stapled onto the side of the first crate. "Deliver to U.S. Army Garrison, Fort Detrick, Maryland, MCHD, Bldg 810." There was a date: August 2040. He quickly turned away and walked toward the hand pallet, his knees wobbly. At this point, he was not going to say anything to Pierce. Not after everything today. But he knew that something illegal was going on, and that these guns had been diverted. Why, he had no idea. It had to involve more than Pierce. Pierce was a local bully, but what larger network was involved? The National Guard? The Army? The Front? The Brotherhood. Who could tell? And who was the enemy? It was crazy, unhinged. He just wanted to get back to the office, so he quickened his step.

"OK, let's get 'em loaded," said Pierce, when Daryl had the hand pallet lined up. They stood at either end, and settled a crate down onto the forks. "Since you're our quartermaster, you can fix up a manifest. You don't need my signature." Pierce winked. "Put 'em in under 'special equipment.' File the paperwork."

Daryl nodded, but stayed silent, moving to lift the second crate.

"This is also obviously confidential, Dickie." Pierce grunted at the weight. "Just between you and me. And the Later." He grinned conspiratorially. "Trust. You break it, you buy it." He chuckled at his joke. Then he looked hard at Daryl, no trace of humor lingering on his face. "Boy, you sure are learning a lot about my business today." Daryl reflected in that instant that he had asked for none of it, but to make a comment about that would not be remotely appropriate. Pierce continued, "Should I be concerned?"

"Nossir," said Daryl emphatically, shaking his head and wondering if he would ever feel any self-respect again.

"Cuz if I start to feel the slightest concern, if my precious trust in you starts to waver..."—he drew out the word "waver" into a long drawl, and paused—"snap!" He snapped his fingers. "We can't be loving our homeland and taking on so many sacred duties to protect and defend it when that trust ain't there. It would sow dissention in our ranks. We'd fail in our duties."

Daryl nodded, sticky-gummed. He just wanted to run.

Pierce was all smiles again. "Good. I knew I could count on you all the way." He motioned to Daryl where he wanted the hand pallet pulled. "Oh, and your shift is extended to oh-one-hundred. Sorry. I gotta be somewhere else—duty calls—and Wright has been reassigned for the rest of the week. Grecco will relieve you at oh-one-hundred.

Shortly thereafter, Pierce left on some unknown mission, the clock passed eight o'clock, and in a state of panic, confused and revolted, knowing he was in a very serious new kind of danger, Daryl abandoned his post. Staying off the main roads, and bushwhacking through woods and fields to get home, Daryl fled. When Pierce unexpectedly returned around ten o'clock, he found the office empty. No one had seen Daryl for hours. He now knew he could not count on Daryl. He was not up to the game. Pierce immediately called the police and the National Guard. Daryl was AWOL during a state of martial law. Had he committed any additional crimes, the police and VANG wanted to know. "His patriotism has always been a little weak," Pierce told them. "I have reason to believe he has been smuggling weapons for partisans." "Partisans" was their term for the small, armed bands of radical environmentalists, socialists, and secessionists that had occasionally been caught in Virginia over the past decade. They were seen by the Homelanders as evidence of Europe's and China's fifth column, and as a supposed but never proven Democratic Party militant wing. (Some Homelanders were also in the habit of calling SIF personnel partisans as well—at least, as long as a Democrat was sitting in the White House.)

"Thank you, Sergeant Pierce," the Virginia Army National Guard captain said. "We'll bring him in."

7—LAUGHERTY'S RUSE

Early morning, Monday, October 29th

Prokop Vulk closed the glass door, and the busy open-plan hive of Op Center Level Three—bustling even in the hours before dawn - became a silent tableau behind the sealed panes.

"That's better, Prokop," said Laugherty. "Now we can hear ourselves think."

"Do you want me to repeat what I just said?" asked Vulk.

"No, hold it. I heard you. Let me just think about it for a moment."

Martin Laugherty leaned back, removed his glasses, and rubbed his eyes between his right thumb and index finger. He had been going for almost forty-eight hours on about four hours of sleep since the evacuation. Having Suzanna along had not helped. Secure in the depths of Mount Weather—"the humbum to beat all humbums," the marines called it—he had a private suite, where she lay fast asleep now, and some of the comforts of home, but events were spiraling ever faster, and he needed to stay on top of them, which meant maximizing wakefulness. Vulk replaced his glasses and sat up again to face his chief of staff.

"OK. Now let's work this one through. You're saying that Morales might *accept* the airlift, without consulting Congress, and even though she has been saying she wouldn't?"

"Uh-huh." Prokop Vulk's beetle brow was furrowed, but his face remained otherwise expressionless.

"How do you know? She hasn't contacted me. I thought this was going to be open-book, like she said."

"My sources in the SIF," said Vulk quietly.

"They're not exactly celebrating this, eh?"

"No…," mused Laugherty ironically. "I imagine the Oath Keepers just *love* it."

Vulk nodded in amused agreement.

"She can do this, of course. She's still the POTUS, for a while, at least...Of course, it would absolutely kill any remaining chances for Hedges, but..." Laugherty chuckled in wonder. "But maybe Lucia Morales really might put people's lives before politics!"

Vulk cracked the remotest shadow of a smile.

"'Course, if she does, we need to be all over it, and head off what the Front might do with it." Laugherty was thinking out loud, working to stay clear and focused. "How many planes and personnel they talking about again? What are we looking at?"

"Ten thousand personnel," answered Vulk. "Almost five thousand flights. To start with."

"Where are they right now?"

"Several big airports—Frankfurt, Madrid, Paris, a few in the UK."

"When will they be airborne?"

"Davis said they'd be ready to start launching by Wednesday evening, their time," replied Vulk. "So that's, you know, around noon, afternoon, here. Wednesday. Maybe later, depending on Morales."

"Even if they could land, and that's not altogether clear—Dulles and BWI for instance are pretty fucked up, from what I hear—this is going to be a PR disaster for us, or worse." Laugherty got up from his chair and started pacing along the glass wall, his lanky frame slightly stooped from fatigue. "If Morales is successful, she's going to look well-connected, to a lot of voters. European goodwill is going to shine through, and the loan deal is not going to look so terrible any more to a lot of people. Fewer refugees. Some happy governors and DRR managers...Might even tip the election, even with voting numbers down in the disaster areas. Our clients, especially the Trust, are going to go ape-shit."

Vulk pursed his lips at the word 'clients'. This was not how he saw them. 'Overlords,' perhaps, or 'masters.' But not clients. Laugherty went on. "So is the HF. Their supporters are going to think D-Day has finally come, and hit the streets," said Vulk. "The more HF-leaning militias will be up in arms, too."

"...Which means very bad news for us unless we can look just as hard-line against the airlift as the Front itself, and actually stop or delay it. If we don't, the Front will try to just push us aside, and paint us as just as soft on the foreign powers as the Morales administration...as hypocrites. Which we're not. But if we don't swing this story our way, one week before the election, we're looking at major political risk. Our voters may fall for the Front rhetoric. The GOP can't look like a fifth wheel. Above all, we don't want the EU to have a human face. Absolutely not! Or the Chinese and the others." He laughed ironically. "Where's the frickin' Tea Party when you need them? They were nothing compared to the Front!"

"'Cuz if it does," responded Vulk, ignoring his reference, "it means, to the swing voters, that Lucia Morales was right all along."

"...and even if the hurricane depresses the progressive-Democrat turnout in the Mid-Atlantic, where they're so strong, there could be enough of a positive reaction in the Midwest that the Dems do well there, too. And of course the Northeast is theirs to win, or lose."

Vulk nodded. "So, hmm, let me think..." He played with numbers on his T-pad. "So, it wouldn't take much for the pissed-off Front voters to take another 3%, and the left to gain about the same, and—poof—our margin's totally gone. We get, let's see, another four years of the Morales-Hedges bunch, a president who'll veto OSCIA and Forsa, the Trust on our ass even worse, a stronger Front in Congress, foreign troops on US soil, happy talk about the EU, and...have I forgotten anything?" He paused, six fingers in the air for emphasis, a hint of insubordination in his eyes. "Oh yeah, and you probably won't be Speaker after that."

Laugherty glowered at Vulk in silence for a moment, and then relaxed. "Well, it ain't gonna happen."

"No?" Vulk waited. Laugherty was renowned for his die-hard optimism in most circumstances, and for his calm under fire. He could quietly work out the most dreadful details of his opponents' demise, closeted away with Vulk, his PR team, and the rest of his core staff, and then appear shortly afterward kissing babies and marching in parades like the breeziest, happiest favorite uncle anyone could imagine. His smiling, hearty face was his brand, and never once in his long political career had he lost his sunny public demeanor under pressure.

Vulk knew the odds had suddenly shifted against them with this hurricane's destruction. The federal and state governments would have trouble mustering relief fast enough to forestall serious disorder and out-migration from the affected areas. How could the Laugherty team prevent foreign assistance on the scale needed, when Morales was still firmly in the White House, without looking like the bad guy? There were still a lot of

Republicans who didn't like the Front, and who would not be especially hysterical about a foreign relief mission as long as it was limited in scope and duration. How could they appease the HF swing voters, appease the Democrats who were uncomfortable with the Morales policies, and keep the Republican base happy? Vulk was very curious to hear how Laugherty would tackle this. He waited, intrigued and doubtful.

Laugherty was standing up, rubbing his jaw, looking out into the Op Center. His cell phone warbled on his ear, but he ignored it. Their DOD liaison, June Ellis, came to the door, but he waved her away with a beaming smile and a "one-minute" gesture. After a dramatic pause, he turned back to Vulk.

"Prokop, it ain't gonna happen."

"OK?" grunted Vulk in expectation.

"It ain't gonna... Look." Laugherty made a fist and raised one thumb. "On one hand, we need an injunction. We need the law to slow things down. We only need to delay things a week. Let people speak first. The states will have to come up with the first round of relief." He grinned, and did the same with his other hand. "Then, we need an incident, something that scares the dickens out of any voter who doesn't trust foreigners enough already."

Vulk's mind was still on the first item. "An injunction..." He raised his chin and closed his eyes. "Is there any precedent for deployment of foreign soldiers on US soil? Since 1812?"

Laugherty nodded. "I think that some country—maybe Mexico— offered to send a convoy of relief supplies after Hurricane Katrina, and were told they had to leave their weapons at home. "

"Anything else?" Vulk asked.

"I don't know...1812?" Laugherty became emphatic. "Look, I'm not a historian but I can tell you that it *must* be unconstitutional for the President of the United States to authorize the deployment of foreign soldiers within our domestic borders without the consent of Congress. She's, um, she's the Commander-in-Chief, but only of US forces... And think of the Presidential Oath. No way. It's for Congress to approve, and if Morales makes a move without us, the Court needs to put a hold on it."

"Mm," said Vulk. "The Senate has the power to approve treaties with foreign governments...Constitution..." He frowned. "Do we even know where the Chief Justice is?"

"We can find him." Laugherty stood up straight, allowing June Ellis to catch his eye. He nodded at her through the glass. "OK, let's get going. I want to talk to Rubino, Landers, and the media team at 6 AM."

Ed Rubino was his counsel. Jeff Landers was the Clerk of the United States Supreme Court.

"We're gonna have to file some sort of proposed writ today."

"Yessir," said Vulk fighting a yawn.

"And we'll need a special session of Congress. Somewhere besides DC. ASAP. Before the election. Like, Thursday or Friday. Philly? We gotta get ahead of Morales on this thing. How do we set that up?"

Vulk reached into his coat pocket and pulled out the tattered copy of the U.S. Constitution that he had carried since he was a law student. "Hm." He flipped through the pages. "I think you've got lots of recourse…Like, Article I, Sections…hmm… Sections 1 and 8. Gotta watch Article II; the President can adjourn a session of Congress if the two houses are in dispute about meeting. But you and the House have plenty of powers, and no one can stop a meeting."

"Good. Get the staff going on this. And yeah, I want Philly. Independence Hall. Enough seats? Check that! … Um, close enough to the destruction for the melodrama, but far enough away that the infrastructure's working. Get me scheduled to be there by Wednesday. We're done, for now." June Ellis hurried through the door. Laugherty turned to greet her, but was still talking with Vulk, his head over his right shoulder. "This gives me about 2 hours to get some sleep. And, oh," Laugherty added, "we'll need to speak to Carl Holt about the incident."

Prokop Vulk knitted his forehead. "Carl Holt?"

"We don't want to hand him the big win he's looking for, of course," chuckled Laugherty. "But he's got some skin in this game already, and more muscle on the ground than we do."

Carl Holt was the national chairman of the Party for the Defense of the Homeland. What very few people knew was that he was also the commandant of Sword and Shield, an elite militia associated with the Front.

"See you later." And then Laugherty was gone, his hand on June Ellis' slender shoulder, beaming benignly at her.

8—A CHOICE OF FATES

Early morning, Monday, October 29th

By this time, Lara had awakened and joined them at the kitchen table. Ari snored quietly in the bedroom, exhausted, the door ajar across the wide central living area of the ranch. With dawn less than two hours off, the louder insects had quieted, and the silence of the muggy night breathed through the house, a gentle myrtle-scented breeze pushing the lowered shades in and out with a slow rhythm. But they were on edge, nervously alert to the approach of any vehicle or footstep.

"And there was the Murphy boy, Alex Murphy," muttered Jessica. She had never spoken of such things before. Ari would bring them up, even with closer friends and a few neighbors—he had strong opinions about politics and society—but Jessica's own drive was for family, relationships, the seasons of life and home—and her mind consistently shied away from what people did to one another in the service of ideology, political interests, and pure power. It simply would not happen if people tried to be nice, and left each other alone. It was so unnecessary.

"I thought he was a criminal..." said Daryl, his voice trailing off. Pale, haggard, his eyes dark, he looked as if he still was not sure where the truth had lain in that case earlier in the year.

"Daryl! Whether he was or wasn't doesn't matter!" Lara was urgent, fuming. "He never had a trial. He was just shot along the road and dumped in a ditch. And *so what* about the rumors? He was a leader in the Brotherhood and the Guard, all proud in the Fourth of July parade with his uniform and speeches, loved by all the girls, Mister Patriot, and then there's gossip about foreigners and partisans, and bang, dead." She looked up at the ceiling in exasperation, and pressed her palms against her cheeks, shivering with a suppressed yawn.

44

"I heard it might have been because of not paying his rent," said Jessica.

"Oh good grief, mother!" exclaimed Lara. "His landlord was Justin Smith, Katey's uncle. He's tough but he never would have done that."

"You never know what else he was involved in..." murmured Daryl.

"What, are you still thinking maybe he deserved it?" Lara almost shrieked, and then restrained her voice to a low hiss, aware of the open windows. "After what you told us—you're not making this up, are you?—and then you run away from your post; do you really think he was dealt with fairly, and that you're going to be met with understanding and love and compassion? Bobby Pierce showed you really, *really* powerful, illegal weapons, after he's been pushing you around and bullying everyone. Jenny Ferris has told me about him—what her dad says. He was testing you, maybe he had doubts about you, you have a dad who's a liberal professor and who has spoken out against the Front. And now you've failed his test *right* away." Her words were interrupted by a faint sob. "Daryl, you went into all this Front and Brotherhood stuff a few years ago head-first, and we never supported it at all, and now we are in danger, too. It's not just you now!"

"OK, I'll go kill myself!" Daryl erupted from his tired stupor with wide eyes and a manic clarity in his tone. "I'll go friggin' hang myself from a stop sign, so all your problems will go away! Is that OK? Huh? Will you feel better?!" He was shouting now. Lara's and Jessica's faces blanched with fright—at what he might do, and at being overheard by nosy neighbors.

"Shoosh, shoosh!" Jessica waved at him to sit down, panic rising in her voice. He sat back down, his mania abruptly draining away. They could hear Ari groggily calling out from the bedroom.

"You've woken dad," said Lara with alarmed resignation. "Should I just go call the police and tell them you're here? If the neighbors aren't already on the phone?" Lara knew her brother well, knew his aimless tempers, his clichéd statements, his social clumsiness. She knew his bark was a lot worse than his bite. "Maybe they can save you from yourself." Her last statement stung, was intended to sting. She did not believe his threat for a second. She had seen it all before. She needed him to stop the dramatics. There was only one course of action. He had to get out of

45

Blacksburg, with a plausible reason they had to spread around quickly, and with no evidence of his parents' involvement.

Daryl was sitting slumped in his chair, looking deflated and defeated. So deep was his estimation of the Home Guard's and Brotherhood's power, and so profound was his lack of confidence in his own abilities and means, that—in his moment of crisis—his inclination was toward nothing short of apathy. He looked like he was now resigned to simply waiting for them to come get him.

"What is everybody doing up?" asked Ari blearily, tying the cloth belt around his bathrobe as he joined them.

"Daryl's fallen out with the Guard," said Lara. "They are after him."

"Hm," said Ari. "So that's what all that stuff was about, earlier." He did not appear flustered. The others stared at him. "What?" He looked around expectantly, very much awake now. "Didn't you think this was going to happen sooner or later?"

"Huh?" Daryl sat up slightly, a note of curiosity rising above his misery.

"Of course, you idiot." No one could ever recall Ari ever having addressed his children as idiots before. "I have been studying this for years now. I've been hoping you would find some other, safer way out of the Brotherhood, once you really found out what it was. They're Nazis! Fascists! Reformers, tag-along intellectuals, moderates like you who are impressed with their so-called decisiveness and their hard line against all these supposed enemies and conspiracies... The real tough guys eventually sniff you out and either enslave you or kill you. Or scare you far away, if you can run fast enough. The sadists. The psychopaths who movements like this empower and activate. They're taking over here in Blacksburg. You're on their black list now, no pun intended. You have to get away. We have to get away."

They all looked at Ari, taking in what he had just said.

"Or we can stay here and hope it's all a bad dream, hope that the fine normal moderate nice people—like Daryl here—can keep the Home Guard and the Brotherhood legal and kind and gentle. Convince Bobby Pierce to just stop worrying about partisans and relax and live and let live..."

"What, leave?" Jessica looked shocked. This eventuality had never occurred to her, despite Ari's occasional talk.

Lara looked intrigued. She had grown increasingly uncomfortable with the atmosphere in Blacksburg, although the Roanoke area was little different. "Where?" she asked. "And are you sure you should do it now? I mean, shouldn't you just stay here to make things look normal? What if they come after you, um, I mean, us?"

Ari laughed with no mirth. "What, do you think they are that stupid? As if we don't communicate? Daryl is living here, with us. So, he just up and runs away, and here we are, just us chickens, no idea where he went? They wouldn't believe that for a second. They would give us a hard time... no idea what they might try. They are always looking for enemies, for evidence they can use to convince people that they are right. To scare their base into supporting them even more." He looked through the kitchen doorway across the room at their wall of family photos, steadying himself on the doorframe. "Good God. The whole thing would be almost laughable if it weren't so tragic. Tell me exactly what happened."

They told him, quickly, furtively, the passing time suddenly on their minds. Ari listened silently. When Daryl finished with the final details, Ari sighed. They all watched him.

"This is just what I expected." He stretched his stiff neck, and groaned. "Do you know what happened almost exactly one-hundred-and-two years ago, this time of year, in Europe?"

They looked at him expectantly. "Nazis?" asked Lara.

"Mm hm," Ari nodded. *Kristallnacht.* There's no time now to describe it, but it was all a setup, all a trap. Coordinated. You can read about it anywhere. But I had relatives who were arrested, their shops set on fire."

Daryl groaned shakily, confused. "Dad, oh God, look, Bobby Pierce is a nasty bully, but really... Most aren't like him. This isn't Nazi Germany..."

Lara looked at Daryl in disbelief. "Are you still trying to *defend* them?"

"No, it's Virginia in 2040—different problems, different times," said Ari with agitation. "But do you really think this is about nothing worse that some mean-tempered good ol' boys who don't like university people, Jews, foreigners, diverses? Where did those coil guns come from? Of course there are conspiracies, networks, people with influence, people who will take power when it's available to them. And, damn it, there is a national Homeland Front party with a whole narrative about partisans, foreign plots, sabotage…They are public with this. No real secrets. People are going to vote for them. They mean what they say. This is all breaking loose like a dam collapsing…"

Not far off, in the pre-dawn silence, a bird sang out a song for the new day. They started, and glanced at one-another with worried expressions.

"We have to move very quickly now," said Ari, more wearily.

"I have to get away," said Daryl with resignation.

"We have to get away," Ari corrected him.

Jessica looked back and forth at the two men, her husband and son, still uncomprehending. Lara, seeing this, took a deep, wide-eyed breath and looked away, seeming to search for something in the distance.

"Well, honey, look …" Jessica started to say.

Ari stood up abruptly. "Darling, no, look at this." He walked over to the broad bookshelf in the living room, and searched nervously for a few seconds, pulling off a couple of books and putting them on a coffee table to one side. "Here." He brought an old, gray, cloth-bound book back to the kitchen table. Lara squinted to read the title, which appeared to be in German.

"*Also sprach Zarathustra,*" pronounced Ari slowly. "*Thus spake Zarathustra.*" They looked at him in dull surprise. "By Nietzsche. Friedrich Nietzsche. 'God is dead,' he declared." Ari laughed ironically. "But that isn't why I wanted to show you this."

He blew dust off the text block, and tried the pages carefully, to see if they would separate. Deftly, he opened the book in the middle, revealing an old, yellowed envelope. "This belonged to my great uncle Jakob. He was a lot older than my grandfather. They went to England before World War Two broke out, because he was a successful geographer, and was able to get a job in England making maps for the military. I guess they were planning ahead. I've never shown you this… It didn't seem relevant, until now."

He opened the envelope, and removed a small, folded letter on onionskin paper.

"He wrote this to my grandfather after the war ended, when he was a refugee and had decided to travel to America, not join Jakob and his family in England."

Moving the letter closer to the center of the table so that all could see, Ari slowly read the English translation of the letter, penned in blue ink below the spidery black-ink German hand:

You can go anywhere—America, Israel, Australia,
But we saw our own flesh and blood stand obediently like pets,
Quietly, deferring properly to authority,
And get herded off to their terrible deaths.
Remember that this can happen anywhere.
How tragic it all was, brother.
You were so lucky to live, that I give thanks in prayer daily.
So you must promise me that, if you and yours face the same threat ever again,
Because it can happen anywhere, and sometimes does,
You must never become the obedient cart-horse.
You must put caution ahead of comfort.
You must study the signs and be honest with yourself.
You must never be persuaded by the sad pleas of those who have not.
Houses, belongings, pretty gardens, local friends, your own history,
These can be re-created.
These mean nothing when they have been stripped away,
And your life sold to butchers and lunatics for a purseful of happy wishes.
When the time comes, you must move in an eye-blink, toward safety,
And never look back.
Nietzsche examined "eternal recurrence" in this book.
You must love your fate, but first you must grasp your fate.
And you must know that you can choose the path ahead of your fate, or the path behind it.
Choose the path ahead always, Benyamin.
Peace.
Jakob

Daryl, who had been listening with a frozen raptness, let out a long, shuddering sigh.

"Well, that's pretty much that," said Lara, standing up. "We need to go." She barely even looked around at the house she had grown up in—the dark mahogany furniture, the white curtains, the open brick fireplace. "I'll get my things and make some food and hot drinks for the trip."

"Where are we going?" Jessica remained frozen at the kitchen table, looking around in sheer panic.

"Well, first, Salem," said Ari, glancing at Lara. "It's about a day's ride. Lara, who actually lives there, is our pretext. If we go east first, and get on the other side of I-81, we can take the small back roads, and I imagine that, since it's closer to the storm's path, things will be less organized—easier to slip through. Daryl, you'll have to…"

But his words were cut off by a sudden woeful wail from Jessica, dissolving into tears at the table. Lara rushed over to comfort her. Daryl seemed to snap out of his apathy, sitting up straight and looking at his mother.

"No, no, I can't leave all this!" she sobbed. "This is all we have."

"Mother, no, Daddy and Daryl and you and I are all we have," said Lara. "I agree with Daddy that we have to go, now. Daryl found out what we didn't want to know and could have gone on for a long time deliberately not knowing, and maybe nothing bad will ever happen— maybe Bobby Pierce and a few other men are bullies but decent people will prevail. But we don't know that anymore and we can't stay to find out."

She looked up at Ari, who stood nervously watching, poised between coming to join them and rushing off to gather the things they would need for the trip to Salem.

"But what about our friends?" protested Jessica, casting about for some logical refuge. "They won't know where we've gone. Or the neighbors."

Ari took her hand. "Look, we can just email or call them, silly. As far as everyone is concerned, we're just going to see Lara in Salem, to help with the storm cleanup, or something. Aside from the National Guard and Home Guard, who are looking for Daryl, no one knows anything. And besides, people are too busy just dealing with the situation. We just leave, lock up, leave the house looking normal—it'll take weeks before anyone even wonders."

"Normal?" Jessica was calming down, wiping away her tears. "But we have so much packing to do first!"

Ari chuckled with empathetic disagreement at his wife of more than thirty years. "Honey, no, we have to travel very light. If this is all a mistake, and we'll eventually know, we can come back or ship things to where we are. If not, we'll just be slowed down by a lot of things and that will put us in danger. Please, trust me. Uncle Jakob's letter was based on hard experience. It was written for us, precisely us, now, here. Please." He squeezed her hand. "Just the basic things you'll need. We have to take the cart. Pack as if we were going camping. And fast fast fast!"

The Daniels family had always been avid campers in the Blue Ridge Mountains that surrounded Blacksburg, and the closets of the house contained a jumble of camping equipment dating back decades to when it was high-tech and well-made. Lara and Daryl knew the drill well. As a family that also was often late to things, and pathologically did things at the last minute, they were also used to quickly packing for camping trips under time pressure.

"If we dress and pack for camping, it will fit our story better about storm cleanup, I think," said Ari. He glanced at his watch. "Hey, everyone. It's almost five-thirty. We should plan to be out by seven, when it's still sort of dark. You have ninety minutes." He peered around for Lara. "Lari, honey. Can you harness the cob and cart by yourself?"

"No, Daddy. I'll need Daryl to help me."

For about forty-five minutes, organized chaos reigned in the Daniels household. Jessica, after several more brief teary-eyed episodes, threw water on her face and started to quickly pull together simple, rough, warm clothes and the camping cook-ware. Ari pulled out a small footlocker from under their bed, and set it on the kitchen table. "My ready-box," he called to Daryl, who was throwing his uniforms and a few personal belongings into a duffel bag. Daryl glanced over and nodded. Ari's ready-box had been a work many years in the making. Always organized and keen to be ready for emergencies, Ari had assembled a compact collection of light tools, hand weapons, flashlights, first-aid items, camping and fishing gear, maps, books, and emergency supplies. Into the nearly-full trunk, he added money, their jewelry, and their long-expired passports. Looking stressed, he glanced around, wondering what he might be forgetting. Satisfied that the ready-box contained most of what it should, he left it open on the table, and went over to find Daryl.

"Son," he called. Daryl turned around, his hands full of thick socks. "You are going to have to go on foot until well away from Blacksburg."

Daryl nodded. "I sort of figured that."

The two men stood in silent consensus for a moment. Daryl seemed more composed, Ari noted.

"Yeah," continued Daryl. "They'd nail us at the first checkpoint."

"They may nail us anyway, but I think we have a perfectly good story—enough to get well beyond where your issue is on anyone's agenda." Daryl's flight might be Bobby Pierce's concern in the town, but the surrounding counties in all directions were in so much turmoil from the storm, dealing with refugees, missing persons, looters, and other crises, that it seemed likely that the case of Daryl would be of little consequence only a few towns over.

"You should probably head north first, follow the trail on the crest of Paris Mountain," said Ari. Daryl nodded. He knew those trails and the hill terrain heading northeast from Blacksburg. And despite his lumbering walk and somewhat unfit appearance, Daryl was in fact an accustomed runner and well acquainted with long-distance hikes.

"Yep," said Daryl. "Cross that valley further up, then get up on Fort Lewis Mountain, and go over Little Brushy Mountain right down the town roads into Salem."

"It might take you longer than a day," said Ari. The distance was almost fifty kilometers. Daryl tilted his head, thinking.

"You are probably right." He gestured at a daypack on the bed. "I'll expect to spend a night out." He grunted. "Just hope I don't run into anyone nasty up there."

"Nastier than down here?" Ari made a wry face.

Daryl stood there, looking both at his father and the small pile of items beside his daypack. He did not answer.

"You must be exhausted," said Ari in realization. "You haven't slept at all."

"No," replied Daryl, chuckling slightly as he recalled this fact himself. "And I can't sleep here."

"Is there anywhere you can take a nap before you head out?" pondered Ari.

Daryl shook his head slightly. "No place I would dare, now."

Ari shook his head in sympathy. "What about ... What about holing up somewhere off the trail, a hidden bivouac somewhere?"

Daryl nodded, displaying a mixture of weariness and excitement at leaving his terrifying predicament behind. "Yes, it's going to have to be something like that."

A boom echoed in the distance, perhaps a vehicle backfiring, or some other explosion. They all hesitated for a heartbeat, reminded of the need to hurry. Lara came in the front door at that instant, causing Ari to start.

"Daryl, I need your help now with the cart. Missy's saddled up and tied out front."

"OK," replied Daryl. "My stuff is all ready." He walked out with his big sister, his bag slung over his shoulder.

"Half an hour, everyone," called Ari, his composure recovered.

Jessica stood, her eyes darting anxiously over the many neat piles of clothing, towels, utensils, and other objects arrayed across their bed. "Only half an hour." Then her eye spotted the irregular pen marks climbing the left frame of the closet door, marking her children's advancing heights at different times in their childhoods, and a lump caught in her throat.

9—DEPARTURE FROM PETERSBURG

Monday, October 29th

"We didn't bring the right tools for this stuff," said Ethan Burhans with some disgust, over the jangling of the chains in the team's harness. "Should'a had some chainsaws and more than one axe." They had been clearing the sunken road leading away from their campsite for more than two hours, and had only come about thirty meters. The Hutterites sat back in their campsite, resting for their next stint. The others who had taken refuge in the tunnel had left long before, threading their way through the wreckage on foot with their horses in tow. In the distance, as the morning waned, there were sounds of chainsaws in a few directions, and the beeping back-up signals of heavy equipment. But here in the middle of the battlefield park, Mike and the Burhans worked alone to continue the slow journey away from their tangled prison.

"From up on the earthwork, it looked like it opened up some," said Mike, peering over the plastic- and weed-festooned trunks and branches, "out maybe a hundred, two hundred yards ahead."

"Hope you're right." Burhans started the delicate task of backing his team up for hitching to the next snarl of limbs. "Watch out!" The horses high-stepped and nodded, pulling unevenly at cross-purposes for a moment.

Mike stepped back to give the horses space, and contemplated how he would maneuver around them to secure the cable they would shortly pull on. When they had settled down a little, and were standing in position, Nate reacted on cue from his father and stepped nimbly up on the nearest flank line, and in an instant was astride one horse aft of the yoke, facing backwards, pulling in and coiling the cable for another toss to Mike. They had to keep doing this because it was too risky to retrieve the cable from directly behind or under the horses. The horses were remarkably calm in these unusual circumstances, reflected Mike.

"Are these horses trained for this kind of pulling?" he asked Ethan.

"Oh sure, that's how we started training them, when they were younger. Plows and skids, that's a good way to get 'em used to harness before you train them for carriages. Less to break."

Nate sat as high as he could and threw the coiled cable back over the tree branches. One horse started as the falling cable flicked its rear-end. "Shhhh, shhh," Ethan intoned. Mike grabbed the hook and fastened it around the trunk and back onto its cable, being careful not to put his hand or arm in harm's way should the horses suddenly decide to pull. They had nearly had a serious mishap this way when they started clearing the road earlier.

There was a brief moment of calm. Mike gave the father and son the thumbs-up, and Nate jumped down off the horse's back. Ethan looked across the team at Mike, and then glanced briefly back in the direction of the campsite, where the tops of the coach and wagon were visible over a low shoulder of the berm.

"Your grandma OK?"

"Not sure. There's been a lot to take in yesterday and today," answered Mike. "She's been pretty quiet. She's worried about my family because we haven't heard much yet."

Burhans nodded. "I'm lucky, with all my nearest folks right here with me. The rest of my relatives pretty much live outside the storm's track."

"Anyway, thanks for asking," said Mike.

"No problem," said Ethan Burhans. "Ready?" Mike and Nate nodded, and fell back. He looked at the harness, to make sure the lines were straight and that the forward path was clear. The horses stood like statues for an instant. Burhans grinned. "Yahhh!" he shouted, slapping the long rein. The North Swedish pair surged forward against the loaded yoke, muscles and veins popping out across their low, stocky bodies. The tree held for a moment, and then burst free of its entanglements and swung easily across the center of the road and out of the way, arcs of twigs, leaves, and bark scraping behind it.

"Nice job, girls!" shouted Burhans. "That's thirty feet of progress in one pull!"

The sweaty work of clearing the road went on like this for several more hours, with the Hutterites and Burhans-Trudeau-Kendeil teams spelling one another. The air was full of the pungent aroma of broken greenwood and leaves, from the black locusts, oaks, sweet gums, tulip poplars and other species snagged across the road. As the sun got hotter and the flies thicker, they took only a few short breaks, and replaced the North Swedes with Bill and Belle. Grandma came down to drive them again, since they really only knew her. Mike saw her perk up when called upon to help. He was impressed with her skill, as he had only seen her drive the wagon until yesterday. But Grandma clearly knew pulling and plowing as well. Ethan Burhans and Grandma traded comments about harnesses and yokes as they continued down the gradually curving road. Around noon, they saw that several men with a tractor were clearing the road ahead, coming fairly rapidly in their direction. Behind the tractor crew waited a bus and an open truck. Before long, the two crews met. The others were locals who were working for the city of Petersburg, friendly middle-aged men and a couple of boys. They were making their way toward a passenger train that was stranded at the other end of the battlefield, its tracks undermined and washed out. Behind them, a path was now clear all the way to Interstate 95. Mike was impressed at the work already done. "Forget 295," they advised. It was washed out in several places as it skirted Petersburg. But word had it that I-95 was clear all the way to Richmond.

"I think we should get going today," said Burhans. "Pack up fast and try to get onto 95 by darkness."

This would not entail too much of a challenge, thought Mike. They had a campsite, but the carriage and wagon had been righted and had suffered only slight damage, and the horses would make it the mile or so to the Federal Interstate Zone. Security would be better there, and fresh water available. There might be some relief supplies. Maybe they could find the telecom they needed for getting in touch with family. In contrast, staying on the battlefield until Tuesday morning would mean dwindling feed, a shortage of water, the incessant flies, and who knew what sort of human-generated insecurity?

"Sure," said Mike. "I agree."

"You know what I mean?" continued Ethan Burhans. "Nothing to gain by staying here a second longer than necessary, and plenty to potentially lose."

"Yup," said Mike. He appreciated Burhans' way of thinking. "I guess you wouldn't mind getting home as soon as possible either."

Ethan Burhans glanced at Nate and Celia, already halfway back to the campsite. "To whatever's left, anyway," he muttered darkly. "But home's home."

* * *

They were loaded and harnessed up by two p.m. That meant about three and a half more hours of October daylight, and only a short distance to travel. Grandma and Mike drove first. The road across the battlefield was now open, but there were still lots of small debris to drive over, and sometimes trees that had been pulled aside scraped against the wheels and sides as they pushed through. The landscape they passed bore little resemblance to what they had traversed only two days before. As they came to the edge of the battlefield reserve, and entered the built-up area, they saw that downed trees were only a small part of the destruction. Not a single building appeared to have escaped significant damage. Roofs were splintered, walls were blown down, and even brick structures had crumbled under the terrific power of the wind.

"There must have been tornadoes," mumbled Grandma, looking with shock at the passing scene. "More than just ordinary wind."

"You're probably right," mused Mike, who was driving. "Always more of them in close to the eye wall, I think." But his eyes and mind were more on the people and livestock they passed. There were lots of people out - sitting in their gardens, rigging up makeshift shelters, chopping at the windfalls. There were dogs and horses and chickens wandering around among flattened fences. A green new-model cell-electric sat in a driveway with an enormous oak tree resting on its collapsed roof. Next door to it, a trap sat half-submerged in the roof of a small house. He saw a lone woman collecting ears of corn from a small field of stalks that had been blown level with the ground. A huddle of men were butchering and roasting a cow that had probably been killed in its pasture during the storm. There was some smoke in the air, but relatively little.

The strongest impression, thought Mike, was the quiet. People moved slowly. Animals were silent. No birds were singing. The sun was sinking toward the horizon in a hazy blue sky of occasional small white clouds. Petersburg was slowly reawakening from its daze, a day after Hurricane Rhiannon left it behind. It was a damaged city, but populated with people with a purpose. Food would be scarce all winter, but not firewood, with all the downed trees and branches. They have challenges ahead, thought Mike. With or without outside aid, this would be a real test of the community and civic organization. He wondered how much the Triple-C affiliation would matter. There would likely be shipments of relief supplies from out West already on their way, from Fort Collins and the other Triple-C bastions. Not all cities and towns would fare as well. But a disaster like this would generate some converts...

* * *

"That must be the Fed checkpoint up ahead," yelled Ethan up from behind them. They had been crawling along in the line of dense traffic for more than an hour, dawdling behind an upright full of people and luggage, who Grandma speculated might be some of the derailed train's passengers. As they waited, they saw a good many vehicles turning around and driving back down towards and past them, away from the interstate highway entrance.

"Wonder why they're being made to do that?" asked Mike out loud.

"Mmm. Some kind of security, maybe," mused Grandma. He glanced at her. Her expression was somber. They had just been talking about the pomador again. Despite her elaborate plan, Grandma was starting to feel pessimistic about their chances. And their spirits had been further dampened by the fact that they still had no access to the cellnet.

"There goes Ethan," she added. They watched Ethan Burhans jog up between the stopped vehicles, heading toward the checkpoint. "He'll find out."

In minutes, he was back again.

"We're OK," he yelled up. "The Feds are only letting travelers onto the Interstate who are heading home. They're keeping the locals out. I guess they don't want refugees yet, just folks who need to get back home."

"That's positive," said Mike. "I was worried they wouldn't let anybody in." He knew the military.

As they drew closer, they saw how elaborate the Federal Zone checkpoint was. An elevated stretch of Interstate 95 passed over Petersburg's streets, and ramps on either side spiraled between the Interstate and ground level. The checkpoint area was surrounded by fences with razor wire, crash barriers, and floodlight towers. A tall watch tower rose up through the highway's median. Some sort of office or barracks stood beside the checkpoint. A small park had been created just outside the first gate, on Petersburg land. Set among boxwoods and clumps of rusty marigolds, a small marble statue of Saint Peter stood, this time in the robes of an elder saint. He raised his hand in a gentle welcome to travelers. His head was nearly bald, ringed by a tuft of hair. A low sign at his feet read, "St. Peter. Fisher, Follower, Rock, Martyr. Welcome to his City." Mike watched it pensively as they swung off the main road and into the final approach to the highway gate. He silently thanked whatever forces had watched over their safety since they entered the city two days before. And hoped they would stay with his little band a while longer.

* * *

Mike knew what to expect—he had just spent five years inside its all-embracing institutionality—but the re-entry was no less wrenching for it. Amidst blinding lights shining down on them from towers on all sides, and followed watchfully by numerous robocams and human guards in machine gun nests, they were swiftly directed into an inspection lane and approached by a soldier in a chitrex exoskeleton. As they came to a jostling stop, Mike deftly released the pomador for its quiet descent into the shadowy gap between the horses. He prayed it would all go according to plan. Things moved fast. The soldier motioned them down from the cab. They both climbed out the right-hand door, since the damaged left door was tied shut. Other soldiers appeared from the next lane, sweeping the sides and bottom of the wagon with their searchlights and scanners. Mike and Grandma stepped into the shakedown frame beside the lane, and grasped the handles above their heads. From the corner of his eye, Mike saw the Burhans' coach driving into a lane several positions to their right. Grandma was quiet, subdued, tiny beside him. A large display above their lane listed Mike's name, with a photo beside it. The system had already picked up Mike's RFID implant. Below his name blinked a second line with nothing but the text "1x INDIV NO SIG."

"Another retinal," the soldier muttered with mild exasperation, and—walking around to face Grandma—held a laser scanner up toward her eyes to capture the pattern of her retinas. Grandma blinked into the splash of lights. Her name and photo appeared above them, next to his. Like everyone, she was in the government databases, but like many of her generation she had resisted receiving an RFID implant, since it was not yet mandatory for civilians back then.

With the scans and other inspections complete, the pace of the process changed. The crew moved rapidly to another lane, and the first soldier drew himself up and faced them, motioning for them to let go of the shakedown frame. They did, relieved they had made it this far. No one had noticed the pomador, apparently.

The exoskeletal soldier saluted curtly, and looked into their faces. "Captain Kendeil, Mrs. Trudeau, where are you traveling to?" she asked, because it turned out she was a woman.

"Home to Chevy Chase, Maryland, soldier," said Grandma drily.

"Plan to stop off anywhere along the way?"

"No, ma'am," replied Grandma. "Except maybe in Fredericksburg, to pick up family."

"Carrying enough food?" asked the soldier. "Because the Federal government is not providing relief supplies within the Interstate Zone, and if you get off further up 95, there's no guarantee you'll be let back on."

"Why's that?" asked Mike.

"Orders," said the soldier. "There's a lot of relief and refugees on the move, and the situation keeps changing. Have to keep the checkpoints flowing, too, and some are very damaged."

"If we can't get off," said Grandma, "then where can we camp?"

"We've opened up temporary areas within the Zone."

Grandma glanced at Mike. "We'll be safer, anyway," she muttered.

The soldier stepped back. "Any further questions?" She was already eyeing the next vehicle behind them in the lane.

No, indicated both Mike and Grandma.

"Proceed," said the soldier. On the display above, Mike noticed the text "Passed" appear, followed by "Toll $600 debited."

They were back in the wagon's cab in an instant, calling the team to move and deftly reeling the secret pomador back up, out of harm's way. "Whew," whispered Grandma under her breath. Mike flashed a guarded grin at her, his hands on the reins.

As they moved out of the inspection area and onto the ramp that spiraled up to the Interstate, they began to notice details of the destruction they had missed when they first entered. Light poles leaned at odd angles, and all sorts of debris were caught in the railing and crash barriers along the road. Military personnel were everywhere. As they came up onto the level of the elevated roadway, a dramatic scene met their eyes. Where it passed over central Petersburg and the Appomattox River, the Interstate was eight lanes wide, casting a broad shadow over the ground below. In the median, on black pylons, was the Federal coal slurry pipeline that connected Norfolk with the Washington, D.C. area. The pipeline lent an industrial feel to the Interstate, with its pumping stations and maintenance sheds. Mike knew that it ran down the center of the Interstate for security reasons. Anywhere else, it would be vulnerable to sabotage and theft.

What was remarkable, however, was not the Interstate's eight lanes, or the pipeline. Mike and Grandma had seen them before. It was the traffic that was unusual. The right two lanes were absolutely packed with overloaded animal-drawn and slower motorized vehicles, bumper-to-bumper, crawling along. Many of the vehicles looked damaged. The faster lanes were nearly as full of military and emergency vehicles, streaming steadily northward with lights flashing and an occasional horn or siren. Every few minutes, a helicopter chopped by overhead, following the line of the Interstate. Alongside the highway, military personnel were everywhere, carrying out repairs or supervising the traffic.

As they crested the rise above the Appomattox River, the landscape spread out around them as it flattened into tidewater. In the distance, in the crimson rays of the evening sun, they could see some of the higher buildings in Richmond. The artful contrast of the scene caught their rapt attention for a heartbeat. The interstate highway was all color and busy movement, modern and crisp: red tail lights, the shiny tinsel of the razor wire, the blacktop, blazing floodlights, signs and displays in blue and green and yellow. But all around, down below, it was like an Impressionist painting of some ancient land, already asleep as night approached. No hurricane damage was visible from their height. Fading green and brown vegetation fused with slumbering gray buildings, yellow harvested fields of husks and stubble, soft lanterns and candlelight, and the pools of deepening darkness scattered among them. There were no headlights, no bright public lighting. Nothing moved, save lazily drifting feathers of smoke here and there. Centuries seemed to separate them from the hazy, golden vision below.

Sighing almost in unison, Mike and Grandma focused on closer matters, happy to be on the road, secure, and finished with Rhiannon, at least for now. They found themselves behind another wagon: a long, open wooden wagon full of bundles of luggage and about a dozen people. Most appeared to be dozing or sleeping under the warm evening sky. Two young girls sat propped beside an older woman, facing back towards Mike and Grandma, wide awake but not talking. Mike regarded them as they rumbled along, barely ten feet ahead of Bill's and Belle's muzzles. They met his eyes with no expression, communicating exhaustion and apathy with the language of their slumped postures. They were like refugees being evacuated from a war zone. A war they had lost.

"At least we're moving north again," said Grandma. She sighed again. "Let's hope we don't have any more hurricanes." Mike wondered what would have happened if he had given in to her two days before, and agreed to leave Petersburg. He knew the answer. So did she. This was probably why she did not bring it up.

10—A FEDERAL IMPASSE

Evening, Monday, October 29th

"Governor Remington," said her assistant from the next room. "The conference call is starting now."

"Thanks, Tina," said the Governor. "I'm all set." She looked up at the large flatscreen on the wall of her Montpelier office, and then back at the dozen-odd staff she had asked to join her. It was already dark outside, and the streetlamps of State Street glowed softly through the large windows behind them, beyond the dark edge of the State House next door.

With musical tones, the flatscreen began to fill with faces as the northeastern governors came online. They nodded tense greetings to each other, awaiting the appearance of President Morales' round, intelligent, always-serious face. The mood was somber. Several of the governors were in facilities where they had taken temporary refuge from the storm and its aftermath.

Then the President was suddenly with them, her image in the center of the screen. "Good evening, friends," came her characteristically nasal, flat voice. "Thank you all for joining me." The nine governors—five men and four women—returned her greeting. Most of them were fellow Democrats (Jeanne Remington was one of two exceptions) and they knew President Morales well.

Without pleasantries, the President moved straight into the subject of their conference. One day after Hurricane Rhiannon had left the mainland and dissipated over the Atlantic, recovery and assessment of the vast damage were only starting. Tens of thousands were believed dead. More than three million were homeless, and tens of millions more were without essential services and utilities. The center of the storm had moved out to sea over New Jersey's coastline, sparing New York City and Philadelphia. Washington was a mess, as were Wilmington and Baltimore. Areas of

63

Virginia, Maryland, Delaware, and New Jersey had received almost a meter of rain. Several coastal towns, including Cape May, New Jersey, and Lewes, Delaware, were no more.

The President was still at Mount Weather. Few government facilities in the capital region had escaped damage. She would shortly be leaving for a provisional office in Colorado, until normal White House functions could be restored. Before she left, she would be touring the damaged region by helicopter.

The danger of disease was acute. Food and water reserves were barely adequate. The ability of Federal and state governments to respond adequately was in question. Although the President was directing her staff to take all necessary measures, by the time help and supplies could be moved to where they were needed—a period that could take weeks, rather than days—it would be too late for many victims of the storm. Large numbers of refugees could therefore be expected to take matters into their own hands, and either attempt to leave, or resort to desperate measures to secure resources and safety where they were.

"We are expecting large numbers of people to try to move north, as soon as the roads begin to open up. Some westward and north-west, but most northward. I have instructed the Interstate Highways Command to only allow people to return to their homes at present, if they have been traveling. As you have heard, the Interstates in the affected areas have been filling up rapidly all day long."

The governors nodded and murmured in confirmation. She went on.

"As you and your emergency people know, this is a scenario that DRR has worked with for a good while. We hoped it would never happen. A scenario exercise four years ago called it 'Megalopolis Lost'." The basic assumption was that, as a result of the Long Emergency of the past decades, many people in the urban strip from Richmond to Boston would no longer have compelling reasons to remain living there. Making a living would be getting harder and harder. Only social ties, hurdle costs, and inertia would be keeping families and individuals from leaving the region. A major disaster, such as a hurricane or—God forbid—a repeat of Sanderborough, was hypothesized as the catalyst. In 'Megalopolis Lost,' it was indeed a hurricane. With homes and food supplies destroyed, winter coming, livelihoods at risk, civil order fragile, and infectious diseases threatening to break out, as many as fifteen million people over a period of two to four months were predicted to migrate northwards across Ohio, Pennsylvania, New Jersey, New York, and points beyond."

President Morales paused, looked at them for several seconds, and pursed her lips nervously.

"Now this scenario may be coming true. We have to take urgent steps, in a coordinated fashion. The Interstate Highways Command is only authorized to control the Federal highways. Although security is a concern, and many roads are washed out, refugees and other migrants will be taking to the smaller roads instead. Controlling or stopping this flow will be up to your National Guard units and state police. A number of you have already declared martial law..."

As she spoke, her listeners confirmed her statements and briefly added facts and impressions of their own. Some had seen the situation first-hand. Others were relying on the reports and footage starting to emerge from the Mid-Atlantic states. The conversation quickly centered on the matter of refugees.

"This process is going to have to be facilitated," said the President. "We cannot force people to stay put. We don't have the means, and they have rights. Every individual is going to be thinking about their family's and their own safety and welfare, and getting away to relatives somewhere, or just away to a safe, secure place outside the storm's track, where they can rest up and regroup." She shrugged and raised her hands, palms upward. "Wanting to do this is perfectly natural. Perfectly human. And, frankly, they won't have much to go back to for some time, with so much infrastructure and housing destroyed. We're probably talking about such large numbers that no place along the most likely highway exit routes—95, 66, 270, 81, the Jersey Turnpike—will be anywhere close to being able to house, feed, and provide medical and sanitary services to all of them. It could quickly become a humanitarian catastrophe. The worst of it would occur—is already occurring—in the areas closest to the storm's track where the refugees are concentrated and the local capacity partly damaged in many cases, although not necessarily enough to drive the locals away."

The President drew herself up, and spread her hands in an appeal that, to Jeanne Remington, looked stiff and unconfident. "I am counting on you and your state governments to provide all assistance possible to manage and accommodate this historic, tragic relocation of our people."

For a heartbeat, there was a tense silence. Then Jerry Hannity, the first-term Massachusetts governor, spoke up abruptly.

"If I just heard you correctly, Madame President, you're saying that you're going to make it your policy to regard these folks as long-term migrants, not as refugees who'll eventually return."

President Morales sat without moving for a moment, as if holding her breath. Then she sighed imperceptibly. "That is correct, Governor, although I'm not sure I'd use the word 'policy'."

There were several low whistles and mutters. Jeanne Remington glanced at her staff with a raised eyebrow, and they returned the look. New York governor Max Videtos joined the exchange: "That is a rather radical position, Madame President." Morales was silent, waiting for more. Their poor relationship was well-known. Videtos had criticized the Morales administration many times for its inability to gain the advantage against the Republican Right and the strengthening Homelanders. One of the most powerful progressive-left politicians in the country, he was a strong advocate of Hedges, the former senator from his own home state of New York. He looked around at the other governors, and continued. "I mean, have you discussed this with Robbins [governor of Virginia], or, for example, Myra Eich [Maryland's governor]? What do they have to say about what's essentially the depopulation of their states and a total change in their demographics? Is this now official White House policy? 'Cause that's what it sounds like."

Morales was shaking her head. "You misunderstand me, Max. And not for the first time." She paused, and many of her listeners wondered whether this was an attempt at humor or a glimmer of her frustration. "Official White House policy is life, liberty, and the pursuit of happiness. People can go where they like, aside from short-term martial law limits on movement. Period."

"I'd rather not get into the matter of civil liberties right now, Madame President," said Videtos with barely concealed sarcasm. "But what do the affected governors say, and is this 'Megalopolis Lost' scenario something we're supposed to be sharing with the public and using to guide our response? Because I don't want my name on it, or that of my administration!"

"The former question, No. It was just a planning exercise. The latter question—guiding our response—yes. It's a tragic situation but when you look back at lessons learned from the Dustbowl in the 1930s, the 2005 hurricanes, Sanderborough, permanent coastal flooding, when the conditions are right—in the worst way—the refugees never return. In those cases, the numbers were low enough that the nation absorbed them. Right now, we are talking about so many people moving in one predominant direction, over just a few months, combined with severe resource shortages and winter coming..." She sighed. "I'm taking a realistic position, and hoping for the best, including your generous support."

"And the Mid-Atlantic governors?" prompted Janet Jones, of Rhode Island, softly.

"Yes," said Morales, shifting tone. "I've spoken with Robbins. He's been going all-out for more than forty-eight hours, and out-migration is the least of his present concerns. We're still trying to raise the others. I'm especially worried about Myra Eich. She stayed in Annapolis, and as you know they had an enormous storm surge and some of the highest winds. So far, no contact."

Hannity spoke up again as Videtos sat back to listen. "Madame President, when you say we need to 'facilitate' and 'accommodate,' I presume you're organizing the resouraces we'll need to do it?"

"This is a question we're looking into." President Morales put on a bland smile, but her lips twitched.

"Looking into, Madame President?" Governor Hannity wrinkled his brows. "Ah, before the Commonwealth of Massachusetts commits to 'accommodating,' say, a million refugees as permanent or very long-term residents, just like that, we're going to need some firm commitments of very substantial resources from the Federal Government. We all feel awful about what they've been through, and Massachusetts is a very generous state, but this is such a huge number and we're not exactly flush with funds and capacity these days..."

The President interrupted him with an uncharacteristic sharpness in her tone. "Excuse me, Governor. I understand your perspective completely. But this is a time of national crisis and we all have to shoulder the burden." She glared at Hannity.

It was Hannity's turn again. "Yes, and this is indeed a *national* crisis, not one for Massachusetts or New England alone, and we would expect the Energy Trust and the Pentagon to be in a much better position than the average state government to be able to step in with the resources that can make the real difference here." He glanced around at the other governors, who were following this exchange with varying expressions of surprise or agitation. "I mean, in the present situation, I'm not even able to keep the roads paved or the public health clinics open as it is. A million *new* people? Who've lost *everything?*"

President Morales responded with resignation. "I am not making any additional commitments at this time. But I am counting on you to make this work. We will do what we can. The Interstate Highways Command is fully deployed. So is the SIF, and the DRR, of course. We're at the limits of what's possible, for the time being."

As the governors and their staff members digested this information, President Morales excused herself from the screen for a minute. The low murmuring of conversations drifted from the wallscreen into Governor Remington's office as participants waited.

"Echoes of the Breadloaf Council, wouldn't you say, Jeanne?" Anna Cleary smiled a worried smile. Those present who had attended the remarkable meeting only two days before shared quiet glances.

"And my boots aren't even dry yet," answered the Governor. "Good timing, eh?"

The Lieutenant Governor nodded. "Very timely."

Jeanne Remington muted the wallscreen's speaker and microphone with her bat. "Now, watch carefully what happens when the President gets back. I spoke with Hannity and Videtos and Janet J. this morning. Couldn't get through to Bourne or Longfellow in time. Or Pirelli. I think Hannity prepped Pirelli."

Anne Cleary looked steadily at her. "And?"

Governor Remington went on. "And, well, they've been having pretty much the same conversation, albeit indoors, so we have a consensus. I think we're at the point in the conversation where we have to bring it up. Videtos agreed to take the lead. Lucia won't take kindly to it. But then we can good-cop it, those of us on much better terms with her." She raised her eyebrows and took a deep breath. "I do not envy her. Poor woman. And we're her friends, comparatively speaking." Although Morales was in theory a member of the opposing party, Remington sounded genuinely sympathetic. Then, there was a flash of movement, and President Morales reappeared in the center of the wallscreen. The Governor turned the sound on again.

"Thanks for your patience," smiled the President, her body language signaling that she wanted to move on and bring the meeting to a close. "There was a quick bit of business I needed to attend to. Now, I believe we are all in agreement about the short-term priorities. Is there anything else, before I sign off? Do you have any additional items? Can we set the time for our next conference, considering the rapid evolution of the unfolding crisis?"

She paused briefly, and into the pregnant silence added, "I believe we'll need to confer at least every other day for a week or two. Maybe every day."

"Madame President," began Max Videtos delicately. "We have had some preliminary discussions about the resources needed for refugee reception and temporary resettlement, and we have developed a proposal..."

"Who is 'we', Governor Videtos?" asked the President briskly.

"Ah, the New England governors and myself," replied Videtos. The President nodded, narrowing her eyes very slightly. He continued. "In view of the tremendous severity of what has happened, and the urgent need to be prepared for both the short and long terms, we have put together a proposal that solves a key problem."

"Yes?" asked Morales. Jeanne Remington's office was wrapped in a tense silence, duplicated in all the other participating governors' offices.

"Our position is this: If the Federal Government is not prepared to give our states the resources we need—which it has, somewhere - to adequately provide for the safety and welfare of these large numbers of US citizens moving up from the Mid-Atlantic area, while still meeting the needs of our own populations in these difficult times, then we will have to go elsewhere." He paused, glancing at the motionless, now stony face of President Morales on the wallscreen. "As it happens, we have been in touch with Brussels and Beijing today about a significant assistance package that the EU and the CU can start delivering within two days, above and beyond what they have offered to the directly affected areas in the storm's track." He took a shaky breath. "I believe they have also been in touch with the White House..."

"You're all in agreement about the, um, viability and political acceptability of this offer?" asked President Morales tersely, in the form of a statement. A trace of disbelief haunted her eyes.

"Yes, Madame President, as an option, although it isn't perfect," said Jeanne Remington, softly breaking in. "We have also talked about creating a coordinated regional holding and resettlement plan, so refugees end up where there is the best possible capacity to receive and support them, and where disruption of the local population is minimized. That's a big issue. With foreign help. They are our fellow Americans in a time of extreme need, and we owe them the greatest possible effort we can muster. Of course, we also owe our own states' citizens our top priority."

Lucia Morales chewed the inside of her lip, and looked around at the governors. She sighed. They waited.

"You know I am under tremendous pressure not to authorize this," the President finally said. "Not just political and opinion pressure. Legal pressure. And none of you have the authority anyway, if you'll recall Article I, Section 10 of the Constitution. Think of all the conflict around the loan package. This takes it up a few more notches, with foreign personnel involved, as well. No no no no no...." She was shaking her head, her eyes lowered in thought.

"Madame President," said Governor Hannity with gentle urgency. "You can authorize it. It's just assistance. It's not anywhere in the remote vicinity of the loan package. Unless you know how to get the resources domestically, of course..." The storm had affected only a small fraction of the land-mass of the United States. Most states were unaffected. Yet domestic offers of aid, beyond relatively small volunteer commitments, were meager. It was in the Federal military and the Energy Trust where the most substantial resources lay.

President Morales looked trapped. "In the present situation, doing this would create more problems than it would solve. It's something I'd only want to take on with the full, multi-partisan support of the Congress." Her listeners knew this was absurd. Republican and Homelander opposition to any sort of foreign aid was compact and resolute. Yet they would never support a massive diversion of military and Energy Trust resources to this long-term regional problem either, especially a region nearly completely hostile to their positions, with few Republican or Homelander voters, only several indigenous oligarchs, and less than ten percent of the US population. There would never be support from that quarter. And to undertake this a week before the election would kill any remaining chances for Hedges, on whom this association would rub off.

Videtos came in with a bitter edge to his voice. He dropped all formality in speaking to his President. "Well, unless you want us to strip the bark from the trees and start digging up tulip bulbs to feed all these folks, you need to tell us where the resources are going to come from. This is not some little emergency we're talking about."

Frustration and anger began to rise in Lucia Morales' voice as well. "I said, I am not making any additional resource commitments at this time. Congress should be back in their chambers pretty soon, before the election at least, *somewhere*, anyway—Philadelphia, I've just been hearing - if they can't get the Capitol open by Thursday. Get your delegations to sponsor a bill. I can't appropriate funds like that."

"What about talking to the Energy Trust's board?" asked Hannity. "They're awash in cash, for God's sake. They have more money than Treasury and the Fed. Because they're a regulated monopoly, that's the American people's money!" He shook his head in disbelief.

"You know the Trust wasn't chartered for things like this," said Morales. "There's one way to do this right, and it leads through Congress."

Max Videtos held up his hand, and spoke gravely. "Madame President, we know what the possible national election impacts will be from a decision like this, but we are all willing to go on record with primary responsibility for pushing this through. It's people's safety and wellbeing we're most concerned about. This is no Trojan horse, or whatever. Waiting for a congressional appropriation could take weeks... People would die unnecessarily. Anyway, we are elected by our states' electorates, not right-leaning voters down south or out west, and *they* are telling us this is necessary."

This was the limit of what President Morales could tolerate. Her voice was frosty and strident. "Hear me very clearly, Mr. Videtos. Elections are of no concern to me if people are in immediate jeopardy—it's outrageous of you to suggest otherwise—and to suggest that I'm not concerned about people's safety and welfare is ... It's completely wrong and extremely insulting." She looked her watch.

There was a murmur of voices as several governors demurred. But Videtos stuck to his point. "Madame President, we're not insinuating anything. We're just trying to be realistic and suggest some way of sharing the ownership of this, and finding the resources we don't have. We realize it won't be popular in some quarters, but people's lives, their whole

71

worlds, are at risk and we can't just watch and let it all happen." Several others voiced their support for Videtos' standpoint.

"Absolutely not," said the President. "There ought to be the necessary resources for the very short term, and then this should go to Congress as soon as possible. I'll sign it as soon as it lands on my desk. You may not enter into compacts or agreements with other states or foreign powers, period. Read your Constitution, Governor!"

"Jesus Christ," said Videtos, raising his voice. "You're passing the buck that's supposed to stop on that desk of yours. You know that an adequate allocation for what will rapidly become OUR refugee crisis is never going to come from this Congress. This is about imminent danger *as will not admit of delay*! Read *your* Constitution, Madame President. Look at how much priority this Congress has given our heating crisis. Look at their designs on our forests." His face was dark with anger, his jaw tensed. "Look at the way this supposed nation of ours is dealing with the loan offer, not to mention relations with Canada. God *damn* it, you *know*, Madame President, that this Congress will budget nowhere near what we need in the Northeast. I can almost see the self-satisfied expressions on the oligarchs' and Homelanders' faces when they vote this down the first time. Please, *please* do not pass this buck. History will not judge you kindly." Then, with a look of surprise at his own vehemence, he looked down, shook his head, and muttered "I'm sorry."

Lucia Morales had turned white, aghast, and sat motionless in her seat before the camera. She reached absently for something before her, invisible to the teleconference participants, and then sat up straight, regaining her poise. "That's outrageous, Mr. Videtos. You're speaking to your President and acting outside your state's powers. You are kindly requested to keep your angry theories to yourself and work through your congressional delegation, like everyone else. I don't share your pessimism, which I think leads down a very dangerous path." She faked a courteous smile, and looked around. "Now, let's talk on Thursday, and let the ops folks get on with their business." Her face said, this is the end of our meeting.

"Madame President," said Governor Remington, speaking up for the first time. "Before you go, we need to mention a further piece of our proposal." The President looked at her with unguarded suspicion, her mouth pursing and unpursing nervously. The Montpelier office was sprung with dreadful anticipation.

The Vermont Governor went on. "If the Federal Government is unprepared to provide us with what we need for some very substantial challenges ahead, we are in agreement that unusual steps will need to be taken. It's obviously unconstitutional for any of us to unilaterally enter into a humanitarian aid compact with the EU and China, much as we'd like to. But think for a minute about the terrible bind it puts us into. To take my example, I am sworn under oath to uphold and defend the Constitution of Vermont, and to see to the welfare of its people. That's my sacred duty. If the Federal Government severely restricts my ability to act in Vermont's interests, but provides no compensatory assistance even when it can, then what am I supposed to do? Or my fellow governors here? And I should remind you that my state, despite my own personal opposition, is holding a secession referendum in a week, so it's clear that relations between *my* constituents and *your* government are already very, very frayed. So we have to watch this situation very closely, and act carefully." Her voice softened and dropped in volume slightly. "I was elected as a Republican, and I certainly don't want these matters to unduly disturb the election. But this is no time for being partisan, and we're not. So, because you are who you are, here is the rest of the proposal—it's NOT an ultimatum or threat, we all should stress—that I respectfully and reluctantly submit on behalf of the governors of New England and New York, and I read: Pending resolution of the resource assistance question by the Federal government, we reserve the option to close our borders to northbound refugee streams should the volumes threaten to overwhelm our capacity to meet both the immediate needs of the refugees and the longer-term needs of our own citizens." Governor Remington stopped reading, her look frozen downward toward her hands. The others quietly nodded their assent.

Lucia Morales looked both shaken and furious. Her position had become untenable, pinched between natural allies like these governors whom she was under enormous pressure not to support, and others who attacked her openly. "There's something in the Constitution called the Commerce Clause. What you propose is not yours to propose. And there's nothing in the Constitution allowing a faction of governors to blackmail the President, extorting Federal funds that just aren't there. We have a system. Use it! How dare you threaten me in this way? It doesn't even deserve an answer. As far as I'm concerned, we're done talking. We will speak Thursday about circumstances on the ground. In the meantime, try to come up with some solutions a little more connected to reality." With that, Lucia Morales abruptly ended the conference call.

Videtos was the first to speak. "The sad thing is that she basically sympathizes with our position, and would do the same in our shoes. She just can't say it."

"It's more than sad," said Janet Jones tensely. "It's an enormous, enormous tragedy."

And, with that, one of the most momentous meetings in US history between state governors and the President of the United States came to a hushed conclusion.

In later years, Bill Zeller would quip that, as far as Lucia Morales' career was concerned, this was the moment when the lame ducks all came limping home to roost.

11—CONVERGING JOURNEYS

Tuesday, October 30th

The traffic was dense, bumper-to-bumper, but it flowed steadily northward. The federal authorities needed to keep it moving. The vehicles that inevitably broke down—an overheated engine, a bad tire, an ill or injured horse—were quickly removed from the highway surface and either directed into turn-offs, or expelled from the federal highway zone.

With the Burhans' coach right behind them, there was foot traffic back and forth, to pass the time. Celia and Nate were up in the wagon's cab with Mike and Grandma as mid-morning approached. Fernando was back in the stage coach, playing cards with Carl and Jim.

"Ladysmith," remarked Celia, observing the large exit sign they were approaching.

"We're only a day's ride from Fredericksburg," said Nate.

"It's a funny name, isn't it." Celia ran her hands through her thick, blonde hair and eyed Mike shyly.

"No," shrugged her brother. "No, it isn't."

Celia sat up and poked him. "Yes, it is. It's funny. It's, like, named for someone who makes ladies, like a blacksmith." Her eyes danced.

Nate unwittingly rose to her bait. "Don't be stupid, Celie. It was obviously named after a Lady Smith, you know, in olden times."

"No." She shook her head. "That's not possible."

"What do you mean, 'That's not possible'?" sputtered Nate, becoming annoyed. Then he caught himself and smiled. "OK, OK. Very funny." Celia giggled. He laughed. "God, I am losing my sense of humor." Under the circumstances, despite the bright sunshine and cool, fresh breeze, this was understandable.

"You never had a sense of humor to start with," pushed Celia.

"No, guess not," said Nate. He turned to Mike, grinned, and rolled his eyes.

Mike grinned back. She was a pretty girl. Her coltish teenage humor put her almost beyond comprehension for a man like Mike, past his mid-twenties, hard lessons of life and Army service accreting behind him. What a difference those years had made. Beyond joking around, or practical conversations about for instance horses, there was nothing to talk about with her. Still, her physical presence was undeniable. She made him uneasy. He wondered what the future held for her.

The local cellnet had been down since the previous day, but with a scattering of little beeps and chirps in and around their wagon, it announced its return. There was a cheer from an upright clopping along in the lane to their left.

"Thank goodness for that," said Grandma. "Now we can find out where everyone is." She pulled out her T-pad's handsfree, and started a round of calls. Her first was to Honorée.

"Still in her apartment," she said to Mike, as she hung up. "They haven't let civilian traffic across the Maryland-DC line yet. Marcus offered to drive down with our Lancaster van to pick them all up and bring them out to my house, but he wasn't able to get across Western Avenue."

"Just like here: you can travel home, but you can't travel anywhere else," said Mike.

"I'm quite worried about them down there in the District. Their building isn't secure, and who knows what's going on? Have they got enough to eat? They'll be safer for now at my house."

"I hope they let them move soon," agreed Mike.

The next call was to Jenny. Grandma spoke to her for a long time, sighing and uttering short sympathies and encouragements. Mike, who was driving, strained to listen over the nearby sound of a long convoy of military trucks headed south and the frequent helicopters that followed the line of the interstate.

"We have to get to Fredericksburg by tomorrow," said Grandma, as she hung up. "Jenny is at her wits' end. She doesn't sound very good."

"Mm," Mike empathized.

"She has been through some real tragedy, with no preparation. She's never been in a situation like this." Grandma motioned to Mike that she was ready to drive for a while. "Her housemate died..." She paused, her

76

faced creased with worry. "Jenny isn't injured, and she rescued her horse, but she's lost everything and she'll have to move back up with us, until…"

Grandma fell silent as she slid into the center of the bench and Mike climbed over her to take the left passenger seat she had been occupying. Nate, to her right, offered his hand to steady her, but she managed without his help.

"We'll be quite a full house again, anyway," continued Grandma, brightening, as she adjusted the reins and clicked to her horses. Mike sensed their relief as their owner took over again. "Like never before. Claudia, Hon, her boys, Jenny…" She turned her head toward Mike. "And you." He smiled, raising his eyebrows. "That's six of you," Grandma continued, "along with Marcus and his wife and two kids, in the carriage house apartment. Six new mouths to feed, but also four who can work, well, three, anyway. Though of course Claudia's at my place almost all the time anyway, and she can watch kids…" She fell into thought as she scanned the road, horses, and nearby vehicles. "Hm. Well, there's lots to do, and there will be fewer rents to pay."

Mike was reassured anew as Grandma's practical, practiced manner reasserted itself.

Light conversation continued among the four of them as they drove. Noon approached. They discussed exactly how to find Jenny, since Nate and Celia knew the area just west of Fredericksburg, where Route 3 crossed the Interstate, and where Jenny awaited them in a camp set up on the vast graveled field where a shopping mall once stood. Nate speculated about the condition of their own home, and about what lay ahead.

"I sure hope the barn's OK." He stared off across the flat fields to their east - acres of muddy stubble, several collapsed farm sheds, and the remains of a windmill. "We stocked the loft completely before we left, for the horses, and mom and Celie spent the whole summer putting up the preserves down in the cellar."

Celia picked at her fingernails with a pensive look. She spoke up.

"I don't want to go back."

Nate stared at her. "What?! Why not?"

An angry frown flashed across her face. "I sort of wish I was also going up to Washington." She glanced at him with an open face. "We, not just me," she stressed. "You, too."

"Are you crazy?" Nate looked at her with surprise and disdain. "We have a nice life in Fredericksburg, a nice place. Washington is where people go who've lost everything—no land, no tools, no way to survive."

Grandma chuckled good-naturedly. "Oh, it's not that bad."

Celia looked at her with hope. "See, Nate."

"I know folks who've been there. Crowded, expensive, and dangerous." Nate was shaking his head. "And not Christian, which mom wouldn't like."

"Parts of DC are fine," replied Grandma. "You're talking to someone who lives there! Why, I was there just a few weeks ago, and will be again in a couple days." She sighed, pursing her lips. "Well, at least, it used to be OK. We have to see how things are now."

"Anyway, *Na*than," rejoined Celia with a taunting stress on her brother's full name, "Fredericksburg isn't the same now, either."

"But suppose it's still OK," said Mike. "Why don't you want to live there?" Jenny, he reflected, appeared to like the agrarian, small-town social life, with its big, landed plantation families, the weddings and balls, the horse shows, the country fairs.

"'Cuz there is nothing to do except get married to some poor farmer and start having babies." Celia snorted. "That's all. Period. Everybody is either a housemother, all jealous about what they have, or a housegirl, and then even the poor farmers aren't interested."

"My sister Jenny seemed to like it," mused Mike. "She lived near the College and worked for a family, and if it hadn't been for this storm, she'd still be there."

Celia pouted and looked away.

"What's wrong with being an honest housemother?" asked Nate. "That's what mom is, and she can hold her head up in any market or fair, and in church." He made a disgusted face, and—addressing Grandma, muttered, "Isn't that frustrating?"

Grandma smiled diplomatically.

"It's boring and tiresome." Celia's voice took on a jeering tone. "All anybody cares about is what the Winthrops and the Montagues and the Ginsburg-Smiths are doing—their parties, their racehorses, their fancy homes, with all their nannies and field crews and housekeepers. I'm not going to go work for them. I can ride and work tack better than any of their fancy daughters." Celia looked ahead down the long, crowded curve of the

78

interstate highway. "And I don't want to be just another sad housemother living in their shadow, worrying about whether I can knit fast enough late every night in time for winter, and about lice and bedbugs and fleas all the time, and washing, washing and washing..."

"Better not let mom or dad hear that," muttered Nate. Celia frowned glumly.

Mike watched Celia, fascinated by the new insight she had imparted. This was a girl on the other side of an invisible barrier from Jenny, who had somehow managed, as a nanny, to get into the landed families' social scene, and who liked her life in Fredericksburg—her old life, in any case. Maybe it was because she was from the city—different speech, different ways—or perhaps because she came with her own horse and the right connections, including Ginny Rawls, whose family, Mike recalled, owned a big livery stable up somewhere closer to DC. Maybe Celia, a local girl, whose Virginia drawl was perhaps less genteel, and whose father built carriages, faced hurdles Jenny did not.

"Gee-yip!" called Grandma to the horses as the traffic ahead started to move slightly faster. There was a jingling of harnesses and the hum of electric motors all around...

* * *

A soft tap sounded at the door. Lara rose and walked quickly over to answer it. "That will be Daryl."

Her parents' eyes followed her. Daryl had called a few times, reporting his progress, but the exhaustion of the previous days had slowed him to a cautious stroll through the autumn woods, holing up several times when he heard others nearby. He did not really know whom to avoid, but his nervousness was so acute that he simply avoided all contact.

"Hey." Daryl walked in. They all greeted him with smiles of relief, offers of a drink and lunch, and all the warmth a family's refuge could offer.

"You should all be resenting me right now," he said, when he had taken a long drink of water and wolfed down a cheese sandwich. "That's all I could think about. What I did chased you out of your home, our home." His eyes were dark, gloomy.

Jessica started to protest, looking upset as the topic veered back toward their sudden, wrenching departure. But Ari stood up, his palms pressing out toward his seated family. "No. Not anymore. This conversation is over. Daryl was the canary in the coalmine. What? Were we just supposed to sit quietly and mind our own pathetic business while this happened to other people's sons, until it all finally caught up with us, personally? No. Daryl, you fell in with the wrong men, but they would have gotten you somehow. This is what these things are about, these movements. You were in the middle of the Guard. You called them out. At least you know who your antagonists are. Some people never find out, until it's too late!"

"Shhh!" cautioned Lara, with a frown of warning. "These apartments have thin walls!"

Ari sat back down, and lowered his voice. "OK. Finished. OK?" He waved his hand.

As Daryl ate, their conversation moved into the subject of what their next plans should be. Lara had a job at Samaritan, and her horse work. She had taken a week off to help her parents, and had three days left. Samaritan owed her many weeks of time off. She had hoped to get back to work at the stable sooner. Would her parents stay put, or find a way to move north, to their relatives in Boston? If they stayed, was Salem safe, or was Bobby Pierce so vindictive and well-connected that he could pose a threat there? Could they sell their house? Could they send back for important belongings, like heirlooms and books? Their friends could certainly provide limited help with that. And, if and when they continued on to Boston, how would Ari and Jessica travel? Would they decide to pay for train tickets? Would the tracks be repaired by then, to get beyond the storm's path of destruction?

And, most important of all these questions, if Ari and Jessica moved north—as refugees, they realized with consternation—would Lara move with them? Daryl would, presumably. How could he stay in Virginia? He had been economically dependent on his parents anyway. Now, he was neither economically independent nor ideologically welcome.

"Oh," sighed Lara, "I have so much around here—my work, my friends, my whole life history!" She looked around the apartment, and stared for a moment out the window across the rolling landscape. They all fell silent. "Everything is changing so fast now, isn't it?"

Her father nodded.

"Well, anyway," Lara smiled at her parents, "wherever you go, I go, 'K?" Ari nodded again, gravely. Daryl stared absently at the empty plate on the table before him, picking at a row of burrs that had attached themselves to his sleeves during his hike. "We have to stick together," said Lara firmly.

At that, Jessica started weeping again, and was quickly hugged into vaguely reassured silence by both Lara and Ari.

* * *

"Yes, of course I will contact her. If I get to Washington. And that's a big if." Wilder smiled in mild frustration at Maryann. "There's no session there, for now." A few hours earlier, his state director, Mary Worthington, had contacted him with the news. The House of Representatives had been called into extended session at Independence Hall in Philadelphia, right up to election day. The extension was to start at nine o'clock on Thursday morning.

Christine took her mother's hand. "You're so worried, but try to be hopeful."

"I'm so worried about her, yes. About all of them. The information has been so random and I have barely been able to speak with Flossie. They are still scattered all over." Maryann's normally relaxed face was pinched with tension. "The last time we spoke, yesterday evening, Flossie and Mike were on an interstate somewhere, with days still to go."

A bell signalled the approach of the southbound train that Wilder awaited. They all glanced at the display hanging above the platform.

"Three minutes," muttered Wilder. He turned to Maryann, and, affecting an air of optimism, said, "I'll see what I can do. Who knows? I may get to Washington—in fact, I hope I can—and if I do I'll get right in touch with them all."

Maryann smiled in cautious gratitude. "Oh, that would be so dear. My big sister is a wonderful person, and, well, they have all had their troubles, haven't they. Even before now, of course. Such an uncertain life down there." She sighed and put her arms around her daughter and Wilder. "Think how lucky we are. No hurricanes, not really. No big, crowded cities." They murmured in agreement. Up the track, the 1:30 train to New

81

York appeared around a distant bend in the river, flashing in the sunlight as it wound its way under a canopy of trees.

Wilder pointed up at the high ridge across the river, on the New Hampshire side. A scattering of reds and yellows pointillated the soaring forest, sharp against the brilliant blue sky. "Look. You can tell that fall is finally on its way."

* * *

"It's weird. I never paid them all that much attention before," said Lara to her mother. They had just come back from a trip up Main Street to buy food and other necessities. It was early afternoon.

"I think it's just awful." Jessica put her cloth bag down on the table in the kitchen-dining area of the small apartment, and stood holding a palm against one cheek, an uncertain look on her face.

"Wasn't everything expensive?!" started Lara.

Ari looked up at them from the chair where he was reading. "Who?"

Lara smiled at Ari, trying to sound unconcerned. "Oh, we were just talking about all the Homeland Front campaign tables..."

"What about them?" asked Ari. He put his book down on the coffee table beside the chair. Lara noted how tired he looked.

"The young men in uniforms," said Jessica. "Beside all of the tables." She untied the kerchief from around her head—it was windy out—and patted her wavy hair back into place.

"You know, dad," added Lara. "The Front guards. Paramilitaries. I'm not exactly sure what they are. They're always young and aggressive looking." She clutched her elbows absently. "I'd never really paid that much attention to them, but now you're here and everything has happened, it's like they are everywhere."

"Were they doing anything? Marching or something?" Ari frowned with concern.

"Oh, just standing by the tables with the campaign workers, signing people up to vote and handing out leaflets, that's all," said Lara. "Not really doing anything else."

"Are they armed?" asked Ari.

Lara and her mother glanced at each other with question marks on their faces. Lara made a puzzled expression.

82

"Huh. I don't remember!" She looked back at Ari in mild apology. "Do you, mother?"

"No. Oops. I just noticed their baggy fatigue pants, sort of green-gray, and their tunics. And their gray berets." Jessica sat down at the kitchen table. "And how very young and serious they looked. I suppose there weren't quite as many of them around in Blacksburg."

"Women!" exclaimed Ari, with a hint of a smile at their selective recall. "I would be worried about whether they were armed. Down in town at the markets they were certainly appearing as the election campaign got rolling. Usually unarmed. But they made me nervous. Same sort who started those parade riots. I was glad that Daryl never got into that." He motioned imperceptibly toward the bedroom, where Daryl lay sleeping. "Probably report to the local Bobby Pierces." He pronounced the name with disdain.

There was a pregnant lull in the conversation. Ari looked at his watch, and then out the window at the breezy, unsettled weather. The drying leaves of a row of oak trees near the apartment house shivered madly in the wind. In the distance, down toward the college, he could make out busy activity where a tarp-city of storm refugees was accumulating.

Lara reached for the cloth bags thoughtfully, about to start emptying them.

"We can't stay," said Jessica abruptly.

"What?" said Lara. She stared at her mother. She had heard, but struggled to switch her focus. Ari said nothing, watching both of them. He had catalyzed their journey. Would they stop it here, or move farther along the road they had taken?

"We can't stay here." Jessica stared glumly at the groceries. She turned to Ari. "It's just all wrong. This isn't our home. Poor Lari has no room for us, really, in this little place. Ginny would feel invaded." Lara's apartment mate, Ginny, was away through the following week. "We're too close to Blacksburg for comfort and there are all those same sorts of horrible people out there. They might find out about Daryl and then they'll feel entitled to harass him, or even worse. What are we supposed to do? Sit here all day, inside, reading? We have to have a life, and not invade Lari's space like this. There's no garden here. How will we eat? We've only been here a day, but I just know we have to keep going...And it all seems so unreal!" She pressed her palm against her face again, and stood in mute uncertainty, worry creasing her thin face. "To Boston, I suppose," she finished her thought.

Lara waited, searching her mother's face, evaluating. The wind shook the windows of the small apartment complex—a row of town homes dating back to the 1980s, their cookie-cutter look long since augmented by odd pieces of do-it-yourself clapboard and trim. It was a cool, northerly wind, coming in long waves and brief gusts, under a bright sky of evenly spaced, scudding clouds, intimating a possibility of colder weather ahead.

"You know," said Ari, directing his words at his wife. "Besides Blacksburg, the Boston area is the only place we have family—your brothers and my cousins." Ari himself was the only surviving sibling of his family. "And there's no sense moving anywhere else. Who would help us? Why should we? But we don't have to make the full commitment right away."

The two women looked at him with curiosity.

"I was wondering whether that cell-electric truck is still available."

"I don't know," said Lara. "Daryl probably knows." Daryl was still asleep in Lara's bedroom. "Why?"

Ari stretched his stiff arms and legs, and stood up from the ragged reading chair. He walked over to the living room's picture window. "Well, we can't just sit here. I agree with you, honey." He gestured at the apartment around him. "It doesn't feel sensible. We started a momentous journey, but we're only over in the next county, so far. What threatened us there is pretty much the same here. No, we need to go to Boston, come what may. But we also need to reach out to people who can help us, who care about us, and who we can learn new perspectives from. And who we can help, too. We have to start a new life."

"God, dad," said Lara with a mixture of bewilderment and admiration, getting Ari off track. "You are being very rational about this. I mean, you just pulled us away from where you've lived all my life, as refugees, basically, but there wasn't any immediate thing forcing you to..."

"But what about Daryl's situation?!" interjected Jessica with reproach.

"I mean, no one had even arrested or attacked him..." Lara was not sure what she meant to say.

"You wanted to wait until *that* happened!?" Jessica looked very disturbed. "The National Guard came to our house at night to get him! You were there! He just barely got away. They came for him."

Lara turned to her mother. "Mother, please calm down. That's not what I meant at all. I just meant that most people would have stayed put until those sorts of things happened, until he was in jail, and it became all about getting a lawyer, going to court, all that. OK, maybe until it was too late..."

"And do you think he would have gotten a fair trial?" Ari raised his eyebrows and waited. "If he lived that long?"

"Oh, maybe, I don't *know...*" replied Lara in exasperation. "A lot of people still believe in democracy and fairness, and..." She paused, grasping for some logic to hold onto.

"Lara, first of all, what was his crime?" Ari then answered his own question. "There was no crime! All trumped up. Pierce's next level of domination, when workplace bullying doesn't work. Daryl didn't just shut up and stay in his job. He ran away. People like Pierce don't just shrug and say, oh, well, I can't bully him anymore. And if people like Pierce are already operating that way, well, we know he isn't the only one. Pierce isn't alone."

He turned and gestured toward Daryl.

"If Daryl had just sat there in our home waiting for them to come for him, all of us praying for democracy and justice, then he might well have wound up in a terrible situation, and our family would have been dragged through troubles we certainly didn't need or deserve, by hateful, scornful bullies turned on by the false license to take power that shouldn't be theirs to take. Making all sorts of claims about partisans and foreign sympathizers and whatever. And the good people we know uncertain, doing nothing..." His eyes searched the busy landscape beyond Lara's window. Outside a house nearby, a large, battered ox wagon loaded with what looked like storm refugees and their baggage had just pulled up.

He continued. "Look, yes, Blacksburg was our home for exactly thirty years, um, back in June. We loved the life there for most of those years. We'll miss it, miss friends. But that's a price I'm willing to pay! And, as far as democracy and justice go, do you know that all those fascist and communist take-overs in past history were the result of small minorities of nasty, violent people—small groups—Russia, Germany, Italy, Spain, Bosnia, Cambodia, Korea, Afghanistan. Things came back to law and justice in some cases, but not until a lot of people died and outside help became strong enough to make a difference. It's sometimes hard to remember now, but the US was once very involved in restoring law and democracy in all those places, in the days when our soldiers and diplomats reached every corner of the world. People like us were relieved when they arrived—refugees, people in concentration camps, people in hiding, people living under oppression."

He smiled at his wife and daughter, and continued.

"Well, it's happening here, now, even though I think things will turn out well in the end—yes, democracy and justice will win out." He laughed ironically. "Americans are very good at restoring democracy. Nation building, they called it! It's one of our traditions. We'll have a great deal of use for those skills, pretty soon. But Blacksburg is a just a microcosm of most of the country. Everyone is just trying to put food on the table, and ignoring the signs of fascism." He shrugged. "It may never get beyond this point. American democracy survived the Civil War, the Reconstruction era, which were much worse than this, I think. But I think we need to go somewhere else for a while. It's the best option, so…"

Lara interrupted him. "Dad, I think I understand this all better now. But I have been amazed at how calmly you have taken it. On the drive here, you acted like it was just a nice fall outing."

Ari laughed. "Well, wasn't that part of the disguise?"

Lara smiled. "OK, yes, it was. But you're so calm about this, as if you had seen it coming."

"Lari, sweetheart, of course I have. In general ways. And I talked about it, even when you were a little girl. I've always been bringing up these questions. Didn't you think I was serious? Look, we have to focus now on our next move, so I won't babble on much more right now about this."

He shot a smile at Jessica, who knew well his talkative streak.

"But remember what I have seen in my lifetime. I was already an adult when the second George Bush became president. In those days, at first, no one even talked about climate change or peak oil. Then, in the years I was in graduate school, before we moved here, ah, there—Blacksburg—deep changes kept coming, one after the other. When the second Bush took over, in 2001, America was by far the strongest nation in the world—economically, militarily, culturally. Our influence was everywhere. We were very rich compared to just about everywhere else. But the signs of change, which I guess I became aware of in my twenties, were everywhere, and the nation kept making poor decisions and living in the past as our economy eroded, our rival nations became stronger, and the climate and resource situation kept getting worse." He paused to see if they were listening. Jessica had tuned him out, and was pulling clothes out of her bag, looking for something. Lara sat in profile, her eyes toward the window. Ari laughed. "Oops. Here I go into a full-blown lecture. Want me to keep going?"

"Yes, please do," said Lara. "I'm listening. It's just hard to look at you as I hear this." Ari saw the track of a tear on her cheekbone. He continued, in a more subdued tone.

"Well, it wasn't the left or the right's fault—they all kept getting it wrong. Bigger government versus smaller government, higher versus lower taxes—they weren't the answer. As a civ-e, I was always involved in band-aid projects: energy, dams and levees, irrigation schemes, mass transit, geoengineering. Projects to deal with the consequences of humanity's bad habits. But over the years, I learned about the deeper issues, helped by everyone from dear old Nietzsche and Jefferson and Rawls, to Sen and Krugman and Galbraith and other dead thinkers—all those books back on our shelves in Hokiesburg—and by the guys at the Progressive Club, and also by Jack Trudeau, in fact. He was a very important teacher—an older brother. All those long days chatting on the beach, and evenings on the decks." He sighed a smile of remembrance. "Do you know what he did?"

Lara looked him, alarmed. "No. What?! What did he do?"

"Oh, no, not like that." Ari laughed softly at her rapt, serious attention. "I mean, do you know much about his work?"

"I have no idea," she said. "A professor or something?"

"Well, later in life he was at universities and think tanks, yes," replied Ari. "The Kennedy School. Brookings. American Progress. He did have a doctorate. But most of his career was with the CIA. He was in a unit called economic and social architecture. They tried to understand and change the societies and political systems of nations that posed a threat to the US and its allies. He was a really big-picture thinker, a systems and social science genius. But what really put him on the map, and was a key part of my education, was his book, *Graveyard of Paradigms*. You know about that?" His question was more of a confirming statement.

"Um, yes, well, no," she admitted. "I guess I recall seeing the book on our shelf."

"You should read it. He published it at least fifteen years ago, after he retired and went independent. It didn't really say anything new, but it put the whole picture together, so that a person concerned and confused about America's endless wars and economic decline and political disarray could get a sense of why, and about what should have been done..."

"I should read it," mused Lara.

Ari looked at his watch, suddenly aware again of the time's passing, and of the need to focus on the day. "Hm. We should get Daryl up and talk about that cell-electruck... But let me say a couple more things about *Graveyard of Paradigms*. He brought a lot of factors together—the corruption of democracy by money, the media monopolies, concentration of wealth and the loss of the middle class, erosion of civil liberties, the military-industrial economy, all the wars, deepening drug and VNET addiction, growing anger and frustration—along with fossil fuel depletion and climate change—and you could clearly see where America was headed. All the authoritarian moves that the Federal Government made, like the Energy Trust and the Interstate Highways Command, price controls, establishing the SIF ... which majorities of voters supported, they all backfired, and led to even less democracy and even more conflict and oligarchy, without getting us any closer to the solution—prosperity and justice and stability..."

Lara listened raptly.

"Then, pulling back from wars around the world and closing down all the bases looked like it might be part of the solution," Ari continued, losing himself again in the complexities of the national predicament. "The Coalition for Renewal. But they couldn't unseat the oligarchs and the Trust this time, and the nation is angry, poor, and unstable, and you now have all these paranoid people wanting to go to war with Canada to get its oil, and shut out the Chinese... and people fearing that the EU might invade, and these *pathetic* Homelanders wanting to go to war against imagined domestic enemies and people who are different right here at home..."

He stood up, signalling the end of his lecture. "So, you could say I have been studying this for most of my adult life. Things were already bad, leading up to this election. It was possible to imagine all sorts of terrible scenarios from my armchair, as the economic crisis slowly worsened, even years ago. Even when the Green Teens filled us with hope. History is full of examples: Weimar, the Russian Revolution, the collapse of the Soviet Union... But you know what?"

"What?" replied Lara, following him with her eyes.

"This hurricane is the spark that will set the whole damn pile on fire."

"Hm," replied Lara.

"Just a storm. Been lots before. But my gut tells me that this is the precipitating event, even if most people don't see it. Bobby Pierce's bullying is a reminder that the pile is there, but it's been around for a while and we've all been OK until now." They both glanced at the closed bedroom door, where the sound of a flushing toilet indicated that Daryl was up. "That's my hunch. Things will take off in a new and dangerous direction." He stretched his stiff back and arms. "OK. If I'm wrong, we go to Boston, visit, maybe get stuck there for a little while, and then come home if that feels like the right thing to do. But I'd rather be wrong than sorry, honey." Ari nodded to himself, and frowned. "Better to be wrong..."

Lara reached over and touched his arm. "Daddy, thanks for going over all that. What we're doing makes a little more sense to me now. Thank you for thinking about these things for such a long time. I never paid as much attention as I should have."

"Wait, I'm not finished," said Ari, searching for the right language.

Lara waited.

"I believe this storm will be the precipitating event that doesn't just lead to more chaos and poverty and senseless, meaningless decline, but rather toward a new republic."

"Republic?" asked Lara, puzzled.

"Yes, republic. Supreme power held by the people, not by the rich and the oligarchs, or locally by strong men like Bobby Pierce. See, we're not a republic any longer." He spoke more loudly, for emphasis. "The United States of America is not a republic, no matter what the kids say in school when they chant the Pledge of Allegiance."

Jessica stopped her puttering and joined Lara in watching Ari as he struggled momentarily with his words.

"The nation is no longer a republic, even if there are lots of towns and villages that are self-governing, and many states. Thank God for local democracy. But there's lots of local theocracy, too, that isn't democratic, and true democracy at the national level is gone..."

There was a silence as Ari trailed off. The trio looked at one another. Ari regained his composure and shrugged. "I'm done."

At that very moment, Daryl groggily emerged from the bedroom, his hair and clothes stale and rumpled. He did not say a word, but went over to the kitchen counter and poured himself a glass of water from the tap above the sink. He smelled the water, evaluating, and gave it a taste. "Seems pretty good," he mumbled. He turned to his sister. "Is this OK to drink?"

"Yes," replied Lara absently, still digesting Ari's lecture. "You've drunk it here before!"

"Oh, yeah," mumbled Daryl.

"Hey," said Ari, his attention refocusing. "Daryl, do you think we could use that cell-electruck for a few more days?"

"Um," Daryl took a sip. "Sure, well, maybe. Dale Shifflett might be using it for storm cleanup, but he's right over here in Roanoke. I can ask him. He still owes me two weeks."

"Can you trust him?" asked Ari. "I mean, is he good for his word?"

Daryl smiled. "Dale? Yeah, he is. He is one of the good guys." He sighed. "I wish I still worked for him. His whole family. Good people. Why? Do you want to go home and move stuff out?"

"No," said Ari. "I had something else in mind."

They all looked at Ari, their curiosity piqued. The babble of a large flock of migrating Canada geese sounded faintly through the closed windows.

"But shouldn't we move our valuables, at least?" asked Jessica. "We can't just move off to Boston and leave everything just sitting there!"

Ari smiled. He raised a finger. "Honey, we're on a family trip, right? If anyone should ask. No, I think we should get ahead of things and go help Florence and Mike pick up Jenny and get safely home to Washington. They are in trouble, and we can help them with that truck."

Lara and Daryl brightened. Jessica contrasted with a worried look.

"We can make a difference. We have our own troubles, but we aren't storm refugees, and they are very old, good friends."

"When?" asked Lara.

"How soon can we get the truck?" replied Ari with another question, turning toward Daryl.

"I'll call Dale," answered Daryl, "um, after I get the cobwebs out of my head." He appealed to Lara, "Is there any hot water or tea?"

* * *

"Isn't that wonderful?!" laughed Grandma. "Tomorrow, too!"

Mike smiled with her. It was the most happy and animated he had seen her since their meeting on Head Island two long weeks before.

"You'll see that pretty Lara again, too."

Mike groaned, embarrassed. "Grandma." He pictured Lara descending from the cell-electric truck—her lithe torso, her wiry arms—and then his vision got all mushed together with his cylphing fantasy earlier and he pushed the appealing images away from his thoughts.

"She's a smart girl, and between nursing and horses, she's practical." Grandma pursed her lips and nodded.

Mike sighed. "Grandma, OK, she's nice, but lay off, OK?" Grandma glanced sideways at him, a touch offended. "Look, I don't know what I am going to do," he continued, "especially now, and she can get anyone out there in Virginia, if she wants - guys with land, lots of land. Horses. Crops." He sighed again. "Men with means."

"Hey!" said Grandma, softly but firmly. "You have means, and experience, and you'll have a milscrip income for years to come as well, which most men your age don't." She leaned sideways toward him on the wagon's bench, and squeezed his arm. "Don't sell yourself short."

Mike sighed again, swearing silently under his breath. "Grandma, thanks for thinking of me, but I'll be OK." He met her sidelong stare. "Mom's gonna be on my case about marriage as soon as we get back to Chevy Chase." He glumly imagined Claudia's relentless passive-aggressive chiding. "Please, don't go there when Lara's around, for however long she is." He scoffed, "Anyway, we aren't some Elevener family, trying to marry off the boys and girls before they're sixteen."

"No," replied Grandma. "But it's not like when I was your age, when people built their careers or drifted around until they were in their thirties before starting a family. Now, all the nice girls go fast, and if a man doesn't get right to work on building a family and farm or trade, he loses out." She straightened up. "That's what everyone I know is saying."

"Oh-Kay!" retorted Mike emphatically. "I'm just going to enjoy the music now, all right?" In the next lane to the left, alongside and just ahead of Grandma's wagon, was a huge flat-bed wagon with what looked like an extended refugee family aboard, and some men and a woman were competently playing a mixture of folk music and bluegrass. One player's high, slightly off-key voice rose and fell as he sang the lyrics, and the woman fiddled expertly with an expression of blank distraction. At least two dozen ragged men, women, and children lay about on the flat-bed among bundles and boxes, accompanied by several large, black dogs.

"OK." Grandma pulled a wry frown. "Nothing more, except this. I want our family to survive, and you are now the key. Maybe Hon will pull out of her nose-dive after that awful woman Sanna." She made no attempt to hide her disgust. "Hon is certainly very capable, but she has the boys to think of all the time, and they are still very small. Jenny is coming home with us. She's a good girl, and could make something of herself. But I don't know how much longer I'll be around, and you'll have to look after your mother."

Mike reflected on Grandma's role and self-image as the head of their small family.

She continued, as the wagon crept slowly forward along the densely crowded interstate highway: "We own my house, but there's not much ground there for growing anything, and it's expensive to keep up. And I don't own the Market Garden. I just run it. That's good—well, that *was* good - for salary, produce, and manpower when we need it." She nodded toward Fernando, who was ahead of the wagon, walking with Nate and Celia in the dense, slow traffic. "Hon's market stall was showing promise, although Sanna's stealing the van was a very, very big setback. And we need more household income anyway—real income—so with your milscrip, and with a girl like Lara, and ..." She glanced toward the concealed bag that contained the pomador, tight up against the cross-bar of the harness pole. "... we can think about investing ..." She froze, her eyes searching for the familiar bulge of the small, brown felt and leather bag, seeing a loose flap of leather, but no bulge.

Mike sensed the sudden change in her tone and body language. His eyes followed her stare.

"Mike!" said Grandma in an urgent whisper. "Where is the gold!?"

They both leaned forward, frantically inspecting the shadows between the strolling horses' flanks. The leather bag was empty. Mike crouched over the front of the cab, with one hand on the harness pole and the other on the footboard's edge for safety. Leaning as far out as he could, he grabbed the leather pomador cover and pulled it back toward their seats, while Grandma paid out the nylon line that suspended it.

"Empty!" he exclaimed.

"Oh my God!" shrieked Grandma. "Oh my God!" Fernando and Celia jerked their heads back toward her in surprise. "Oh no!" Grandma looked around in agitation, panicked, her hands against the sides of her head. Mike jumped off the wagon, which was moving slightly faster than a normal walk, and looked under the team's hooves and among the wagon's wheels. There was nothing but smooth, worn pavement. He jogged toward the rear of the wagon, mindful of the other vehicles rolling beside and behind it. His mind worked feverishly. Where could the pomador have fallen off? How far and long had it been? Was this an accident, or a theft? Was there any hope of recovering it? He saw nothing. Running back to Grandma, he saw that Fernando had mounted the cab in concern, with Celia right behind. Grandma was looking around in consternation, ignoring them, shaking, repeating "Oh my God" over and over, starting to sob.

"What?!" shouted Fernando. "What it is?" But she kept on sobbing inconsolably. Mike did not know what to do. Should he comfort her? Had it been misplaced? Should he grab his gun and run after some unknown thief? His adrenaline soared, but he had no answers, no direction. Reflexively, he took his pistol from under the seat, stuffed it into his jacket pocket, and jogged back along the file of vehicles behind them in the lane, his eyes darting under wagons and back up at their drivers and passengers. His odd behavior was met with suspicious stares. Anyone could have stolen the pomador, or scooped it up if they saw it lying on the pavement, a fallen apple of gold. He slowed down, coming to a stop about twenty vehicles back, beside a rough oxcart. His pounding heart started to calm down. The traffic was stopped now. He glanced up at the driver of the cart, a heavy-set, older black woman. Several teenagers lounged in the back of the cart. The woman eyed him out of the corner of her eye, its white contrasting sharply with her ebony face. Mike looked away, realizing the futility of what he was doing. As his eyes swung, he saw a nest of security cameras on the nearest light pole, and remembered that anything he did would be observed by the IHC. Odd or disruptive behavior could get him thrown off the Interstate. They needed to get to Fredericksburg by the following day. He straightened up and started walking back to the wagon, hoping he had not attracted attention, and glancinh furtively left and right under the wagons.

The traffic was at a standstill the whole way back to the wagon, even in the high-speed lane reserved for motor traffic. This had been happening periodically since they entered I-95. But just as he caught up with the rear of the wagon, the traffic ahead leapt to life, and the wagon was surging forward as Mike jumped onto the lowest ladder rung and climbed up into the cab. Fernando, at the reins, shot a look of surprise and confusion at Mike as Mike sat down beside Grandma.

"Grandma," said Mike, realizing how unnecessary this sounded, "it's gone." Grandma sat twisted sideways, her head against the bench. Her eyes were red from crying, her cheeks wet, but her sobbing had quieted. Mike saw a disturbing emptiness in her expression, a vacant resignation. This was about more than a valuable object. This was about decades of hope and planning and perspective, with Jack and later with their expanding family.

"Mike," said Grandma, finally. She wiped her eyes and cheeks dry with the balls of her palms, and heaved a shaky sigh. "It's gone. The past can't save us now."

12—A MEDITATION

Early Wednesday morning, October 31st

The air moved easily in and out of her sanctuary on the side-porch, one story up, but the vines and potted plants she kept there hid Lara from the view of neighbors and passers-by. It was here she meditated—mostly in the early mornings before work—and it was here today that she took pause after the past several tumultuous days, and before starting on today's new journey of assistance and displacement.

Placing the woven hemp mat on the brick floor, she glanced with accustomed approval at her trim legs, but quickly pushed such thoughts out of her mind. She did not want distractions now. As she deftly sat into a cross-legged position, an image of Mike Kendeil admiring her legs invaded her mind. With mild irritation, she nixed that thought as well, reflecting that Mike was not even close to the kind of man she was attracted to: too shallow, unquestioning, non-contemplative, and disconnected from the world of animals and the Earth she delighted in. She imagined him happily driving around in military vehicles, shooting weapons, and enjoying who-knew-what techno-fantasy in Vtopia. And then she grimaced at the recollection she had told him her V-name when they met on Head Island. What was she thinking? Was it the spell of childhood familiarity? And then, with an annoyed shake of her head, she perceived this new unwanted train of thought, and determined to quiet her chattering mind.

Pulling a light blanket around her shoulders and across her lap to lessen the morning chill, she breathed slowly in and out, rhythmically, first letting the sensations of the world around her settle into her consciousness. The sun was not yet up, but a ripple of scarlet and gray clouds adorned the eastern sky. The air was cool and almost still, smelling of autumn, cookfires, manure, boxwood, and the naked green wood of the downed

95

trees nearby. She heard cattle in the distance, calling to be milked. Scattered roosters boasted. A jay jeered nearby, and she heard the noisy flapping of a male mourning dove. The animal voices were briefly interrupted by the ripping chops and clinks of someone cutting breakfast splints a few houses away.

As Lara breathed, the outer world receded, and her breath became the focus of her detaching mind. Yet she could not settle into her habitual pattern of distanced tranquility. Her brother's face, darkened by a morose expression, kept looming in her thoughts, and, even as she tried to brush it away, she kept falling into troubling resentments and recriminations. Why had Daryl been involved in the Home Guard in the first place? Why couldn't he leave it alone? Now he had brought down the attentions of bullies and bigots on her whole family, and they had run away!

"Oh!" exclaimed Lara out loud, in frustration with her wandering mind. The meditation was not going well. She opened her eyes, stretched her back, shook her hands, and tried to fold back into the calm, non-reactive cradle of her breathing. For some moments, her mind quieted and began to rock gently, emptily. In. Out. In. Out.

But into the rhythm came a nagging irritation with her father, Ari. She saw him back at their home two days before, lecturing them about Nietzsche and Uncle Jakob and the Nazis, using that whole narrative to mobilize them in their fatigue and fear over Daryl's misfortune, but it was *his* narrative, Ari's narrative! Sure, his family in Europe had been Jewish, and maybe he'd been raised in a nominally Jewish home, up in Connecticut, but Mom wasn't even Jewish, and Daryl and Lara hadn't been raised with any particular religion at all, and she started feeling like the whole flight to Roanoke had been a charade, an unwitting accommodation of Ari's indulgence in his own sentimental, irrelevant preoccupations with persecution and diaspora. That was *his* history. In Blacksburg, the Daniels were just another white university family. It wasn't like they were some Fiddler-on-the-Roof family getting expelled from a *shtetl* by Russian peasant mobs. And Lara herself was blonde and green-eyed—no-one could accuse her of being anything but an ordinary white American.

Here, another nagging thought crept in. Unlike Lara, who took after her Irish-English mother, Daryl did have the dark-haired, Semitic features of his father's family, and, in his teens, his friends at scout camp had given

96

him the nickname "Shalom" after a month without haircuts caused his side locks to grow long and rabbinical. Yet he could be Latino, Greek, or Italian, or any number of ethnicities, like so many others. And anyway, how pathetic Bobby Pierce and his buddies were, seizing on little superficial differences to randomly set people up as the enemy, just so they could pin their anger and resentment on some scapegoat. Why couldn't they grasp that their problems were system-wide, that they were all in this situation together?

Her meditation forgotten, Lara sat, head down, wrapped up in her thoughts. She recalled a comment by Pierce that Daryl had mentioned once—not in irritation, but in wry amusement at the time—when he was appointed unit quartermaster: that the cash and books would be safe in the hands of a Jewish banker. How silly it had sounded at the time. Maybe Pierce knew about Daryl's teenage nickname. It had not felt in the least bit menacing, then. Because it really meant nothing.

But, as Lara let out a deep sigh and prepared to abandon her early morning ritual and go in and get some tea and breakfast, she acknowledged to herself that their supposed Jewishness would probably become a pretext sooner or later, and maybe sooner had come. Daryl hadn't actually done anything to deserve the bullying, as far as she knew. And, was this just Pierce's idea, or was something bigger going on? The local Brotherhood rallies had sometimes included claims that Jews were behind the partisans and environmentalists. That horrible Homelander leader, Carl Holt, was an outspoken anti-Semite. So were some of the CCC leaders. Lara had seen them recently on 3V. Holt kept referring sarcastically to the "Emmanuel Goldsteins" who supposedly were working behind the scenes to facilitate the arrival of Chinese and EU relief forces who would turn out to be peacekeepers that enforced order as the US government was dismantled. It all seemed so ridiculous to her that she'd given it no further thought. The Chinese Union and the EU had their own problems at home to deal with. Politics was all about hype and false claims, anyway.

Goldsteins. Lara paused in her movement to stand up. She remembered the Goldbaum family, who once lived a few blocks away from them in Blacksburg. Rachel Goldbaum had run high school cross-country with her at Blacksburg High. She'd known her vaguely before then, too. She recalled Rachel's bat mitzvah, years before. Ari had looked favorably on that. For Lara, it had been a new cultural experience. She'd never had one

97

herself, of course. Why was she thinking about Rachel, she wondered, still slightly groggy? And then she recalled that, right after they both graduated, Rachel's family had moved away, to Canada. That was in '30. Rachel was really upset about it. She and her siblings wanted to stay. But her mom and dad said that the climate in Virginia was no longer 'positive'. Lara had been incredulous, and saddened. Hmm. She had forgotten about that. She wondered how many others who were not old-line native Virginians had quietly made the same decision. Years ago, all the Indian families had left. She clearly recalled that. So the Daniels family was maybe not so alone in taking this route. Just a bit late.

A train whistled, powering up the valley from Roanoke. Lara heard Salem awakening around her. Salem. City of Peace.

And then, like a struck match, a painful anger flared in her. Why was she dwelling on this? Because Daryl had a bully for a unit commander? That had nothing to do with her. And she didn't even live in Blacksburg anymore. No, it was about the purest form of evil there was—the evil in people when they turn others into inhuman objects and categories. There was a lot she didn't know about Daryl's situation, but the Virginia Army National Guard didn't come to arrest people in the middle of the night, during a state of emergency, unless they were terrorists or traitors, and Lara simply *knew* that Daryl was neither. He was being targeted, and probably because Bobby Pierce and his friends needed a target. The election was less than a week away. Homelander strength was on the rise in Virginia, but the vote wasn't in the bag. Maybe that was it—a convenient ploy. Maybe it didn't even really have anything to do with Jews. But Lara realized that Ari had made the choice to not take any chances, and there was a long, personal family history to guide choices in such situations. Maybe the world was just that crazy now. Her father was a smart and a good man. And this was her own heritage, too, as much as she might impulsively try to separate herself from it. It was hers. And her fury became red-hot as she reflected that it was also anyone's to abuse and manipulate any way they liked. That wasn't supposed to happen in a civilized democracy, where laws protected people's rights. But was it worth taking chances? No, and that made their predicament outrageous.

There was a scuffing sound behind her. Lara turned around and looked up.

"Good morning, princess," smiled Ari sleepily, standing in the doorway to the porch. A ray of weak sunshine caught the top corner of the door frame.

"Hi, daddy," answered Lara, her fury subsiding.

"What?" He regarded her tense expression with mild alarm.

"Oh, nothing. Some memories..." She shook her head and stood up.

Ari nodded knowingly. "Ready for another long day?"

"Very ready," sighed Lara. "You don't know how ready."

"Good." Ari's T-pad pinged on the kitchen table. He retrieved it, frowning as he scanned. He looked at Lara abruptly, and then held up his T-pad, so she could view the screen. "Did you see this?"

"No." She shook her head, peering at it as she stood up. "What?"

"Look. Bad news."

She took a closer look. It was the main page of the New River Valley Nexus, wishing readers a "Happy Halloween." She read the next headline: "Suspected Blacksburg Partisan Wanted for Weapons Thefts; Fear Spreads of Terrorism Ahead of Election."

A photo of Daryl stared back from the screen.

Lara stared at the photo, and then back up at her father.

"Oh, god."

"We need to leave right away," said Ari, his face a mixture of disgust and surprise. "And your mother's coming with us." He set the T-pad back down on the kitchen table and rubbed his temples with his thumbs. "We will take only back roads."

13—PHILADELPHIA

Wednesday, October 31st

"Why don't they have TVs in hotel rooms anymore?" Lola Osmanian, Jake Wilder's press secretary, threw up her hands in mock disbelief.

"It wouldn't work anyway, under these circumstances," replied Selena, always the authoritative young aide, but with a tendency to take things literally.

"It might. You know, some private network." Lola shot a glance at Selena. "Here, honey. Run down to the concierge and ask them if there are any antique stores nearby."

Selena hesitated, brow furrowed, and looked toward Steve Johnson, Wilder's chief of staff, for guidance. Lola burst out laughing—a nervous, grating, yet not unkind laugh.

"OK, look, I'm kidding, honey. Sorry. No, you're totally right, but, oh God, your expression." Lola slowed her chuckling, and looked around at her colleagues, gathered in the cramped, rumpled hotel room. "Look, you gotta laugh sometimes," she appealed. "Look at us! Frowns all around, and we have to stay sharp and on top of this stuff for, um, at least four days until we go back to Vermont, *if* we can get back there...."

"We'll get back, Lola, if we have to walk," muttered Johnson. "We'll make sure of that. Let's focus on the positive, OK?"

Lola shot him a defiant grin, but nodded her consent. "Right, of course." She smiled all around, in cooperative yet sly defeat. "Meanwhile, we need more information; the cellnet's still off; and we don't have the budget for the satnet, period, unless it's an emergency." She went to the window and looked out across Philadelphia's Center City. Their hotel, the Benjamin Franklin, was located about midway between City Hall and Independence Hall, and if she leaned out the window and looked to her left, up Chestnut Street to the west, she could have looked more clearly in

100

the direction from which all the commotion was coming. She did not. Even though the security cordon around the hotels where congressmen were lodged extended well away from their building, she did not want to take any unnecessary risks.

"A couple of us should take a walk up there, to see for ourselves." Doug Dupre had been restless all morning. He and Selena had been in Philadelphia for several days already, and in walking all over Center City as they planned for the arrival of Jake Wilder and the rest of his staff, had become more comfortable in the crowded, turbulent downtown. With the staff now holed up in the Franklin, the VNET inaccessible, and events outside spiraling in novel directions, they were starved for information. "Steve, do you mind?"

Steve Johnson hesitated. "I guess it's OK, if you stay close to the police and keep your IDs visible around your necks. If things get chaotic, no one's going to be thinking about ret scans or chips."

Doug looked around. "Anyone else coming?"

Selena stood up. "I am." Doug grinned.

Lola chuckled to herself. She was enjoying watching the electricity emerge between the two newest additions to Wilder's team. "Not me, guys, as much as I'd like to."

"OK, see you soon." Doug let Selena pass through the hotel room's door, and pulled it closed behind him.

Seconds later, a chorus of pings and chirps announced the return of the cellnet. The staff greeted this cheerfully.

"Now I can find out when the train gets in," stated Steve with satisfaction, turning his attention to the tiny cognitrol bud perched behind his ear. He paused, gaze distant, his lips working faintly. "OK, let's see... Four-thirty-five. That gives us about an hour and a half to prep a briefing." He mentally dictated a text message to the two just-departed aides, telling them when they needed to get back, and prepared to send Jake Wilder a status report.

The others took out T-pads and other devices, relieved at being able to get back to work. From the distance, through the open window of the suite, across several blocks of rooftop gardens and smoky, traffic-filled streets, came the din of a roaring crowd, punctuated by beating drums and the clatter of what sounded like firecrackers.

101

* * *

The train from New York finally reached 30th Street Station in the haze of the late October afternoon. Nearly twenty hours had passed since Jake Wilder and Howard Rosen left Hartford. Dispensing with DC-style Congressional protocol, two SIF troopers met them as they got off the train to escort them to their ride. Pulling their luggage, they emerged from the platform into the great hall and were met by a scene reminiscent of some wartime European train station a century before.

Behind the monumental statue of the Angel of the Resurrection, lifting a fallen solider from the flames of war, sections of the glass windows had been blown out. The ornate marble floor was still crunchy with mud and other storm debris.

"There must be five thousand people here," muttered Senator Rosen. Lines and clusters of people filled every part of the hall, waiting for trains or tromping down the ramps to the platforms to board. The majority were heavily laden with backpacks and wheeled luggage, carrying babies, leading young kids by the hand, steadying the elderly. As they moved down to the trains, surge upon surge of new travelers were let in through the doors to replace them. Red Cross tables and booths dotted the vast concourse.

"This is probably the first functioning station they could get to," replied Wilder.

One of the SIF troopers gestured toward an elevator beyond a checkpoint. "This way, Congressmen." In moments, they were descending into a secure garage where a vehicle waited.

"We'll have to take a detour around Center City to get you safely to your hotel," announced the senior SIF guy.

"What's going on?" asked Senator Rosen.

"There's a big protest outside City Hall," said the SIF soldier. "Been going on since yesterday."

"Who's protesting what?" asked Wilder, as the elevator doors opened.

"The last couple of days, refugees from New Jersey and Delaware been showing up in Philly, camping on the outskirts. They need water, food, medicine, care…"

"Aren't they getting it?" Rosen knew the answer.

"No sir, I don't think they are yet, not enough," answered the other one, waving at a nearby car—a green SIF van—which flashed its lights back at him.

"How many people are we talking about?" asked Wilder.

The senior orderly shook his head. "Hundreds of thousands... I don't know."

Wilder whistled. "My god."

"The PA Army Guard stopped most of them from crossing the river," the orderly rejoined. "So most are kettled up around Camden and Cherry Hill."

"I'd think most would be too exhausted to protest by now," said Rosen ironically.

"I don't imagine New Jersey's very operational yet..." mused Wilder.

The four contemplated this development as they boarded the van and spiralled up the ramp, lights flashing, bound for the reserved government lanes that would expedite their progress down Market Street, to the edge of Center City.

* * *

The hotel room was in an uproar as Jake Wilder and Howard Rosen made their way in, their baggage in tow. Right behind were Selena and Doug, who had met them as they were escorted into the teeming lobby. Senator Rosen's own staffers were on their way down from an upper floor.

"I can't believe it!" burst Moriah Oglethorpe, Jake Wilder's legislative director. "We heard from the Governor's office Monday night that this was completely off the table."

"What? What?!" asked Wilder with a bemused smile as he set down his briefcase.

"The President just announced she is approving the EU-Chinese relief mission," said Steve Johnson, drawing Wilder aside. "Minutes ago. They can be here tomorrow. Enormous. What do you recommend?"

Wilder laughed in mild exasperation, taking in the crowded room in one glance. "Let me think about it a minute! Any coffee or tea here?" Doug went off to fetch one of each. "Good," noted Wilder. He turned back toward Steve and Moriah. "So, let's get everyone settled, brief me, and we'll take a look at what this means." He turned to Senator Rosen. "You're welcome to join us. It's a bit cramped but maybe we'll be more efficient if both staffs are here."

Howard Rosen frowned and nodded. "Yeah, sure." He beckoned toward his chief, who had just entered the room.

Moriah Oglethorpe stood pensively amidst the organized chaos, one hand holding her T-pad, the other akimbo, resting on her hip. A historian by training, she flipped mentally through the decades and centuries of US history, searching for anything similar to this news. All she could come up with were events around the American Revolution and early 1800s, and those weren't relief missions, they were military expeditions to satisfy imperial goals by interfering with a young, weak America. This was about saving lives, restoring stability ... on the surface. For whatever complex reasons that continued to frustrate and infuriate her, the Federal Government was not able to come up with all the relief supplies immediately needed, and neither were the directly affected states. Promises of aid from the other states were only starting to fall into place. So the president was accepting offers of foreign aid, delivered by foreign troops.

Moriah caught her breath. Morales was yielding to need and to the northeastern states' challenge. What a terrible bind to be in. But Laugherty and every politician to the right of center would be all over this like a swarm of hornets. A showdown was unavoidable, and right before the election! And lurking in the back of Moriah's thoughts, which she would shortly seek to explain as the staff briefing started, was the uneasy awareness that, bundled together with the goodwill and stability interests of the Chinese and Europeans, was the crossing of an unfamiliar line in global power relations. The Republicans and the Front sensed this. If it was unavoidable, why did the Democrats have to take the fall for it? The injustice of it stung. Or, maybe this was intended to be nothing more than a throwaway symbolic gesture by Morales. Perhaps she thought it would never be allowed to happen, and felt she had nothing to lose by looking responsible, and possibly something to gain. She would never be blamed as the "president who lost America."

Moriah turned toward Steve Johnson as he called the briefing to order.

"OK, we're all here. Senator, Congressman," Johnson nodded at each. "We all know one another." He peered at the combined staffs packed into the suite, seated on beds and dressers, cross-legged on the floor, leaning against walls. "Yes, um, I think we do... So, a special session has been called by the Speaker, to start at noon tomorrow, November First." He looked around. "This is the first time that the US House of Representatives has assembled outside of Washington since around 1800." He glanced at Senator Rosen. "We're still waiting to hear what the Senate is planning to do." Howard Rosen remained impassive. Johnson drew himself up and took a quick breath. "These next couple of days will be historic, in ways we may not like." He turned to Moriah Oglethorpe, and extended his hand. "So, to give us some basic updates and a historical perspective as well, I invite Moriah to take over the next fifteen or so minutes of this meeting." He chuckled ironically as he stepped back to give her space. "And by the way, happy Halloween." This was met by chuckles and groans of realization. It was, indeed, Halloween.

Moriah Oglethorpe smiled wryly as she threaded her way through people and furniture to the edge of the room, the window behind her framing her slender figure.

"So, let's run through what we now know, starting with Laugherty's call for this session in the early hours of Monday morning, running right up to this afternoon..."

They were silent as Oglethorpe spoke, her voice clear and precise above the city sounds behind her.

14—CENTER CITY CONFIDENTIAL

Wednesday, October 31st (afternoon)

Suzanna drew her neon-blue happi coat around her bare shoulders and went over to the open window. She pulled the curtains apart and leaned on the window sill, still breathing from exertion. The sun was setting, filling the hotel room with red light. Prokop Vulk watched how it dusted her hair rusty. He looked at her clean, young jawline. At the muscle definition in her thigh. At the way her happi coat broke in the small of her back and swelled below it.

She glanced back at him.

"You're sweet," she said.

"What did you say your name was?" he countered.

They both laughed.

Vulk took a deep, relaxed breath and switched on the wallscreen. There was more chatter about President Morales' announcement and the anticipated opening of the session later that evening, interspersed with drone footage of the refugee camps across the river. Vulk watched for a moment, trying to detect anything he had not already seen or heard.

"You have two hours," Suzanna noted.

"I should connect with Martin at least an hour before it starts," he said. "Sharon's on situation point, and I wanna hear that."

"I'm coming to stand in the gallery."

"Sure," he said. "You have the clearance. Why not?" No one's escort comes to Congressional sessions is why not, Vulk thought to himself. But Suzanna kept demonstrating she was different.

"I wouldn't miss it," she asserted. "This is historic. Anyway," she added a bit self-consciously, following his eyes down to her naked legs, "I want to come support you, 'cuz you're going places with Mister Laugherty, and I want you to take me with you."

"Mm," he chuckled.

"How come you're not already married?" she asked suddenly, studying him.

"How come?!" Vulk laughed in surprise. "Why?"

"I can be curious." She pressed her lips into a faint pout.

"Never had time, or the right girl," he said, realizing that sounded lame, but also that he had no better answer.

She considered that for a moment, unconvinced. "Well, I'm sure you had lots of chances. Anyway, now you don't need to."

"Anyway, anyway," he mimicked humorously. "And why is that?"

"You got me."

"Where do you get your freakin' self-confidence?!" he burst out. "I pay you! I'm *renting* you."

"A rich man rents the woman he's with," she smiled. "Doesn't matter whether she's a wife, mistress or whore." She drew out the last word with an extra diphthong and rested the tip of her tongue in th corner of her mouth, grinning.

Vulk laughed. "I'm not rich! I'm a paid staffer. You've got that wrong..."

"Oh, no," she interrupted. "You are rich. You have no idea."

"Rich is assets," snorted Vulk. "Rich is wealth: investments, houses, factories, land... I get paid a good salary but, no, not rich." He wrinkled his mouth. "I know who the real rich are. I'm not rich." He grinned. "I'm rented, too."

"Ooh," she laughed archly. "Do you, um, you know...? With the Speaker?"

"Shit." Vulk flung a pillow at her. "Not funny."

She giggled, and then grew more serious. "But, so, do you own your condo?" she asked.

"Yeah."

"Any big debts?"

"No."

"Have you got cash if you need it?" She shivered slightly as the outdoor air cooled, and flopped down in the chair beside the bed, pulling a discarded shawl over her. "Like in an emergency?"

Vulk nodded.

Suzanna erupted in a derisive laugh. "Oh, sweet Jesus and Mary! You are rich, rich, rich, and you're afraid to admit it!" She crossed her legs at the knees. "You got a car, a condo, cash, lots of shoes. You can fly in planes. Where I come from nobody has any of those things. They're lucky to own any land, and it's only as good as the food and cash crop it produces. One bad season and you're dead. Off to tenant farming or housegirl work."

"Or SIF, in your case, right?" He was surprised at his lapse into personal curiosity, but decided not to regret it.

"Mm hm," she confirmed.

"So, how'd you manage that?"

She turned her head with barely concealed pride. "I got a scholarship to Allegany Military when I was fifteen."

"Where's that?"

"Cumberland."

"How come?"

"I passed the test." She looked at him with a frown. "Not many do."

"I mean," he raised his eyebrows, "how did you make it through that kind of school and into the SIF? That's pretty tough." Vulk had a cousin who was serving in the SIF, and he was a hard-ass. "What was your edge?"

"I was smart, and I was good in track and MMA," she said.

"So why did you leave?" He knew she had been out for over a year.

"Six years was enough!" She laughed, eyes bright. "But it gave me a taste of a life I never, ever tasted before. The way you people live. Oh, my God. I mean, you see it in the V, you can imagine it, but it's like, who ever goes there in RL?"

"'Us people!'" Vulk chuckled. "Well, you don't know too much about me, either, and believe me, I didn't used to be 'Us people' either."

She looked at him for a moment, calculating. "Yeah, so anyway, I thought, what's the fastest way in for somebody who's not Miss Debbie Debutante or already educated—you know, not a scientist or engineer kinda thing—and…" She struck a theatrical pose. "Ta da! Here I am."

He looked. She was clever, ambitious, and disarmingly transparent. She appeared to know what she wanted, and seemed utterly unconflicted about her ends or means. Vulk did not want to know about her means prior to the agency's referral to him only a few short weeks before. Best left unknown. But, yes, here she was. Perfectly proportioned, slim, blemishless, and displayed before him like a self-ironic tableau of feminine guile. Ta da.

Vulk felt the bedsheets amid him start to ratchet upwards.

"Mm, you have to hurry," said Suzanna softly, "but I'm not going to let *that* go to waste." And in a flash she whisked the sheets aside, settled, and with a series of flicks of her hips was giggling and gasping, pulling him along with her. The suddenness and sassy elegance of it accelerated them both to a shuddering climax. She lay down beside him, panting lightly in his ear. "Whew," she breathed.

Vulk stretched, feeling pleased with himself and more convinced about this escort than he ever had been before.

Suzanna went into the bathroom. Vulk pulled the window closed against the cooler air.

15—REUNION IN FREDERICKSBURG

Wednesday, Oct 31st (afternoon and evening)

"There they are. There they are!" Lara and Daryl spotted Grandma's wagon at the same moment, pulled off to the side of the road just beyond the interstate highway overpass over Route 3. It stood on a narrow strip of rank grass between the shoulder and a large parking lot reclaimed by vaults of sumac and chest-high weeds. Above the wagon towered an ancient sign, intended to be visible from the interstate. The words "Gateway Village" and "Plank Road Discount" were still faintly legible among festoons of sheet metal dislodged by the hurricane winds.

In the wide back seat of the truck's cab, Ari roused Jessica with an excited whisper. Daryl cautiously steered from the motorized lane across gaps in the two slower lanes, aiming for the spot right behind the wagon. With the horse trailer behind the truck, he drove a long and cumbersome vehicle, but the carts and cars paused to let them pass.

"Those must be the Burhans, and Fernando," observed Lara as she watched several others emerge from the roadside shadows beyond the wagon, where the horses were out of harness and grazing. In seconds, they were there, parking, the electronics in the cab powering down. Mike was at the passenger door, grinning wearily, pulling the handle so the door swung open. Lara hopped down in one tumble into Mike's appreciative, hasty hug. She pulled back to look at him, holding the shirtsleeves around his biceps, studying his face in concerned surprise.

"Wow, what a difference!"

He smiled awkwardly back at her clean, neat demeanor, just as he had last seen her, in contrast to his sunburned face, sprouting beard, and the shaggy remains of his military crew cut. "Yeah, well, we've been living rough."

"Oh, y'all poor things," exclaimed Lara, coming loose as Ari, Daryl, and Jessica piled out of the cell-electric beside her and the others came up behind Mike. Grandma emerged from the wagon and came straight over to Ari and Jessica, wan, uncharacteristically stiff, but smiling sweetly. They embraced with laughs of relief and delight, and greetings and introductions all around followed.

"We're not all here," said Grandma. "Jenny's bringing her horse and things over from the refugee camp. Jim went with her." She gestured north across the road, toward the expanse of tents, blue tarps, wagons, emergency vehicles, and milling people. "Ethan's sons Nate and Carl have ridden across town to check on the condition of their house."

"We've brought you all sorts of fresh food, and fresh coffee from Roanoke," said Ari. "You must be overdue for a decent meal. Is this a good place to stay parked for now, by the side of the road here, until we figure out what to do next?"

"Sure," said Ethan. "We're not in anyone's way. It's not dangerous. They're up there." He gestured up at the federal checkpoint only a short distance away, by the on-ramp of the cloverleaf.

Jessica was already bringing out her kerosene stove and a large kettle. "I'll help you, mom," offered Lara, coming to her assistance. Mike came up to the two of them. "It's just great to see you. How long did it take you to get here?"

Lara looked at her mother. As she started to answer, a helicopter flew over, low, following I-95 northward. The conversation hung for a moment as the pulsing din crested and subsided, punctuated by a faint puff of rotor wash.

"About eight, nine hours." She glanced at her mother. "We left around seven this morning."

Mike shook his head, visibly impressed. "We sure could have used a motor vehicle these last few days. What's it here, from Roanoke? Like, a couple hundred miles?"

The women frowned. "No idea," said Lara. "We only went between twenty and thirty most of the way. We stayed on the smaller roads, like 29 and 20."

Mike looked surprised. "You did? How come? Weren't they in pretty bad shape?"

"No, well, there were some washouts, but they had traffic running, and the crews have gotten the trees off the roads the past few days, I suppose."

"You got across the rivers?" Mike looked skeptical.

Lara laughed. "We had to go through a couple, but you can do that with this truck." She glanced at the big tires. "Although I wouldn't have wanted to be a horse in that trailer, fording the river back just outside Charlottesville." She turned her head toward her mother. "Mom, did you see how the empty trailer was actually floating?"

Jessica smiled, a touch excited. "Yes, the Rivanna River." She looked at Mike with wide eyes. "Very muddy, all full of sticks and broken wood that the truck just rolled right over."

"Wouldn't the interstates have been a little quicker? Eighty-one, and maybe..." He struggled to recall Virginia's exact geography.

Lara glanced in hesitation at her mother, noted Daryl's location over beside the wagon, and turned back to face Mike. "Daryl had some trouble in Blacksburg..." She lowered her voice. "He didn't do anything, but some Front people framed him, so now he's on lists... We didn't want to risk dealing with the federal checkpoints. On the smaller roads, it's just a few state police and sheriff's departments, and they're just trying to prevent looting and fights, and keep the traffic moving."

Mike took off his cap, and wiped the dust from his face. He spoke so softly that Jessica cupped her ear and Lara leaned closer to hear him. "I thought he was in tight with the Front."

"He was." Lara recalled their conversation only two weeks before. "We thought so. But I guess they were looking for someone to bully, to set up as an enemy. Scare the others into submission."

"Is he going back?" asked Mike quietly.

"Nope. And neither are we," replied Lara, to Mike's astonishment.

* * *

"I've lost something very dear," said Grandma to Ari, when the two had sat down together on the wagon's tailgate. She sat hunched over, small beside him, smelling the steam rising off her tea.

"Hm, so have I," said Ari with a sigh. "You first."

"Remember that golden apple I told you about, years ago?"

Oh, yes?" answered Ari, cocking his head. "I thought you had sold it, or put it in a museum."

"Well, no. We did try to make it seem like that, but, no, we kept it."

"Must be worth a king's ransom today," said Ari. "What's gold, $65,000?"

"We lost it." Grandma spoke very softly, clutching her arms, the tea on the tailgate now. "We lost it on the road."

"Oh," breathed Ari. He let that sink in. "I'm sorry. What, just misplaced it?"

"We had this crazy rig between the horses, so the scans wouldn't catch it, and that worked fine, but it apparently came loose." She took a deep breath and trembled as she exhaled. "And that was that. Never found it."

Ari stayed silent, looking at her, studying her averted face. A cool breeze blew over them, rustling the tarp on the wagon, the dry grasses on the embankment, the horses' manes and tales. Grandma picked up her metal mug and warmed her fingers around it. She pursed her lips.

"So, what did you lose?"

"Our home."

It was Grandma's turn to be silent, but she put her hand on Ari's arm and squeezed it.

"Maybe we'll be able to go back to it someday, but not right now."

"Ari," said Grandma. "I'm so very sorry, and I'll want to hear all about why, but don't you just get the feeling most of the time these days that, no matter what you do, everything you care about just keeps getting taken away from you?"

They sat quietly, taking note that Jenny and Jim had appeared across the six-lane road, leading her horse between them, and were preparing to cross over to them and bring their hushed conversation to an end.

"Things, I can part with," said Ari finally. "That's life. It's the people that I don't want to lose, Florence."

Grandma brightened at both Ari's words and the approaching figure of her youngest granddaughter. She studied Jenny approvingly: skinny, as tall as Mike, taller than Honorée, taller than Jim beside her. Jenny looked left and right urgently, her horse's lead in one hand, a large duffel slung over her other shoulder. Seeing her opening, as vehicles slowed for them, she stepped quickly out into the road. Grandma watched her booted stride, her long, light-brown hair streaming around her face, her heavy man's work jacket, the home-sewn cowboy hat tossed back on her head. There was still something of the adolescent about her. It looked like Fredericksburg had been good to her, at least until now.

Ari followed Grandma's eyes, and chuckled when he found their target.

"You know, you're right," said Grandma. She downed her tea, and prepared to stand. "You're very right. It's the people... So, it sounds like we're going to be traveling together for a while, then." She smiled at him ruefully and nodded.

"Where you go, we go," laughed Ari softly.

The calm was swept away as Jenny, dropping her pack and handing her horse's lead rope to Jim, burst into a wrenching mix of laughter and tears, and ran the final few paces to give Lara a hug.

"Oh, it's so great to see y'all," she sobbed, overcome by the emotion of a second reunion in barely an hour's time. She turned and hugged Daryl, Jessica, and Ari in turn.

* * *

"We're going to have a meeting in a moment, over by the wagon," said Celia politely. Lara, Jessica, and Jenny looked up, interrupted, perhaps a bit too abruptly. "If you don't mind," she added, blushing.

"About what?" asked Jessica blankly. Celia hesitated, surprised.

"Um, Mike and your husband, and my dad ..."

"Sure, we'll be right over," laughed Lara, glancing at Jenny. "We'll be right there."

Celia walked away quickly toward the next cluster.

"Mother, you didn't need to scare her. She was just sent over to tell us." She looked at the sky and then at her watch. "It's almost five, and we don't want to stay here any longer than we need to."

"What are we waiting for, anyway?" asked Jessica vaguely.

Lara chewed her lip for a moment. "We were waiting for her brothers to get back from checking out their house." She looked at her mother with concern.

"Are they back?" Jessica appeared slightly disoriented.

"Yes, they got back a few minutes ago. They're over there." Lara pointed, and took her mother's hand. "Are you feeling all right?"

Jessica rubbed her face and forehead, and sighed. "Oh, I'm sorry. I'm just so tired and out of it..."

"Maybe you can sleep once we're moving again." She looked at Jenny with a smile dampened by concern. "We've all been through so much dislocation and missed sleep recently."

Jenny nodded. Her young, clear face was masked by dark shadows below her eyes.

Jessica shook her head, pulled her hairpiece loose, and smoothed her gray hair back more tightly into a new ponytail, the wooden pin between her teeth. "There," she said, when she was done. "All better."

The trio rose from the curb, picking up loose items that lay around them, and walked toward the wagon, where the others were gathering.

Ethan Burhans spoke up. "This is where we part, I guess." He looked at Mike and Grandma. "We've sure enjoyed traveling with you for, what, these five, six days. We're a good team. Thank you so much." Mike and Grandma smiled and shook their heads.

"You helped us more than we helped you!" said Mike.

Ethan continued. "The boys tell me that we can get to within a hundred yards of our house with the team hitched, and get everybody up there on foot. Haul the coach up later."

"You'll still have rebuilding to do, I imagine," said Ari sympathetically.

"We have food, hay, clean water, tools, hands—my neighbor's been keeping an eye and a scope on things, too—so we ought to be OK," reflected Ethan. "A roof that don't leak."

"I am so pleased to be going home," sighed Lena somewhat sanctimoniously, and, to no one's surprise, added, "the Lord be praised."

"We'll miss you all," said Grandma. "You've been so helpful, and very nice to spend time with."

"Next time you come visit, we'll show you a nicer time," laughed Lena. "More civilized."

They all chuckled, pleased and embarrassed.

"If we get started now," said Grandma, "with the help of that truck we'll be home late tonight." Fernando, standing beside her, beamed.

"We're going to have to take it very slow," said Daryl. "'Cause we'll have the wagon hitched behind the horse trailer. We still have a lot of rigging to do, and this is going to take time..."

115

"Better than walking," said Grandma. "And we can go all sixty or so miles because the horses can rest the whole way."

Carl whistled at the thought of sixty miles in one evening, truly awed.

"Bit further than sixty, even," guessed Ethan, letting that sink in.

"Are we going to take the Beltway?" asked Jenny anxiously. "Hon said there was trouble in the District, and ..."

"Oh, no, they'd never let us up there with this contraption," said Daryl, nodding up toward the interstate. "Maybe the Burhans can coach us on what way to take."

"Since you've got a motor, you don't have to go bee-line as much," said Ethan. "You should probably get as far west of the interstate as you can, so you get away from the storm damage and traffic. Go up Route 17, maybe..."

"Ah, the storm damage goes a long way west of here," interjected Ari. "We drove through it this morning. Even Charlottesville was awful. You'd add half a day getting around it, even with a truck."

"Maybe y'all should go up Route 1 then," mused Ethan.

"I came down Route 1, and it was fine," said Grandma. "Of course, that was before the storm."

"They've got the Rappahannock bridge open again," said Nate. "Half of downtown's gone but that bridge held and you can drive up on it. That's how we got across."

Ethan laughed. "I thought you rode across the river!"

Carl frowned. "Daddy, the river's full of all kinds of stuff, like trees and barbwire fences."

"How come the horses are so muddy?" Ethan glanced at Celia, who was holding one of the North Swedes by its lead, a big wooden curry brush in her other hand.

"'Cause everything's muddy and silty everywhere you go in town, and we had to scramble across that creek that goes under Carriage Hill 'cause it washed away the road."

"Oh." Ethan scratched his head. "Better take Route 1, even though there may be back-ups and odd checkpoints."

"We'll turn west before the Beltway and stay well away from the District, honey," added Grandma, turning to Jenny and putting her hand on Jenny's arm. "Don't you worry."

116

For a moment, they all surveyed one another, six almost home, eight with more journey still ahead.

"I'm coming with you," Celia suddenly blurted out. Her mother started, her face registering shock.

"What, baby?" asked Ethan, turning to look at Celia in surprise.

"I'm going up to Washington."

"Oh, Celia, no you're not!" exclaimed Lena Burhans. "Don't be silly!"

"Yes, I have to go," cried Celia, tears starting to trickle down her face. "I want to go see someplace else. Someplace big." She threw down the curry brush. "I'm not ready to be Billy Foster's housemother!"

"Billy Foster!" her mother half-laughed, stunned. "Billy *Foster?*"

"Or somebody like that," sobbed Celia. "Or their *housegirl!*"

"You'll never be anyone's housegirl, Celie!" soothed Ethan. "Not a *real* housegirl."

Nate and Carl were frozen, looking at their sister. Jenny was turned away, her face red as the significance of Celia's defiance dawned on her.

"Billy Foster!" marveled Lena.

"I heard you talking with his mother!" countered Celia, wiping her cheeks angrily, tears mixing with road dust. "With *Mother* Foster."

"Ha!" scoffed Lena, thoroughly distracted.

"She could come for a visit," offered Grandma, recollecting their conversation on the interstate. "See what it's like and then come home."

Ethan looked at her with a frown, and glanced back at his incredulous wife. "How would she get home safely?" he wondered aloud. Lena shook her head at him, mouth pursed. He continued, "Perhaps when things are back to normal?"

"We could drive her back," tried Lara helpfully.

"You should probably leave that up to Daryl, Lari," remarked Ari.

"Oh, there are lots of ways to get her back down here safely," said Grandma brightly, glancing ever so briefly into Celia's yearning eyes. "I know people who run barges down the Potomac, for example." She turned to Fernando. "Don't they stop at Widewater Landing?"

"Sure," confirmed Fernando.

"We're in the middle of a disaster!" said Lena Burhans indignantly. "It isn't safe!"

"I'll be just as safe with them as I am with you!" said Celia glumly.

117

"You don't know that," retorted Lena, looking around at all the question-filled faces. "You don't know! It's just *not* going to happen." She picked up the thrown curry brush. "Come on, we have a lot to do."

Celia crumpled down on the brown grass and drying earth, sobbing uncontrollably. Her parents walked toward the grazing horses with the clear intention of hitching them up again. "Come on, Nate," muttered Ethan, glancing at his son as he passed him. Nate stood frozen, looking at Celia. He understood her despair. They had spoken of the future many times.

"Carl, come help with the horses!" called Lena. Carl and Jim both started toward her.

"I can go with her," said Nate. Ethan and Lena froze. "I can make sure she's OK."

Lena let out a raw sigh. "What on earth are you saying, Nate?!"

Nate pointed at Celia. "Look at her! Poor Celie! This is nothing new. She talks about this all the time. You can't force her to stay much longer! She's almost eighteen." He went over to her and reached down a hand. "Come on, Celie. I'll give you a hand up."

She raised her head, grabbed his hand, and allowed herself to be hoisted to a standing position. Her blond hair was across her eyes, dark with dust and tears. There was mud on the hem of her long skirt, and a splash of mud across the patched elbow of her jean jacket. She looked at her parents with defiance, and said nothing.

"They are welcome," said Grandma quietly. Ari met her look with a wry smile, and turned back toward the truck, where Daryl was already pulling out chains and cable.

"Go, then," muttered Lena Burhans. "Go see the world. But you have no money nor anything else you need to go off chasing fun and God knows what else. And your father and I need you every minute we can get you, there's so much work…" She trailed off into disgusted silence, aware once more of her audience of relative strangers.

"They can stay with me for a little while and come back down when it's safe. Your crops are all in, aren't they? And your last hay?" Grandma smiled at Nate and Celia with understanding.

"I still have potatoes," said Lena, shaking her head.

Ethan came back from the direction of the stagecoach. He smiled wearily at his two children. "I guess you're both going." He looked thoughtfully at Nate. "I hope this wasn't all a setup."

"No sir!" erupted Nate in surprise.

"We'll miss you both terribly in this crazy world. You look out for Celie. Don't let her out of your sight." Nate shook his head emphatically, looking a bit dazed at his own outspokenness in this unexpected turn of events. "Couple weeks at most, OK?" Ethan then turned in the direction of Grandma, Mike, and Ari. "You sure they won't be trouble?"

"Oh no, not at all," said Grandma. "I have a big, old house. I'll put them to work." She laughed. "They deserve to see more than Tidewater Virginia, at least once in their lives." A distant gleam sparkled in her eye. "When I was Celia's age, back in, um, the Eighties, I couldn't wait to get away from Washington..."

"Where did you go?" asked Celia shyly, breaking her silence.

"Oh," laughed Grandma. "I took a gap year—two, really—after high school, and traveled and worked all over Europe, India, and Australia!"

"Different times," remarked Ari over a cough. "Puts it into perspective."

Celia stared at Grandma in abject wonder.

"India," she sighed. "Australia."

* * *

They had been on the road for hours now, and the sun had long since set. Without looking at his watch, Mike guessed it was about nine o'clock. From a distance, sitting bundled against the cool air on the roof of the truck, Mike and Lara thought they could see a checkpoint or barricade. There was a glow of orange light around the road, and by its twinkling and occultation, they imagined the presence of people moving around in front of it. There were no flashing lights, however, or bright white floodlights. It looked more like firelight.

"I don't like the look of that," muttered Mike. He leaned down over the driver's side and called in through the open window, "Daryl, you see that ahead?" Daryl was driving, accompanied in the cab by Grandma, Ari, Jessica, and Jenny.

119

Daryl's voice floated up in the affirmative from below. The truck slowed down slightly, its change in motion clicking and vibrating through the linkages of the train it now pulled: the four-horse trailer and the John Deere wagon hitched behind it. They were only moving about fifteen miles per hour, with the truck geared way down. There was little traffic now, with the time near nine o'clock, and the road ahead was empty all the way to the lights.

Indeed, they had made it all the way to Woodbridge without incident, crossing the Occoquan on a pontoon bridge the Army had set up beside the remains of the washed-away 123 bridge, and were nearing the southern edge of Springfield, not far from the old prison at Lorton. It was a desolate area now, apparent even in the darkness. Few people lived here. The suburban developments and malls had been stripped years before, and the land given over to agriculture. The former inhabitants had crowded closer in to the city as energy became more expensive and they lost all motivation to continue living in a risky suburban wasteland of stranded assets and plummeting home values. Only a few of the resourceful ones had remained, aggregating tiny lots into viable homesteads.

The truck-train's passengers were all looking forward to getting into the more populated areas closer to Washington, where there was a semblance of order, police, and street lighting. After so many days on the road, the excitement of reaching home was beginning to build. Leaving an endless series of long, dull Tidewater straightaways, Daryl and Grandma had begun conspiring about the series of zigzags that would take them through the Northern Virginia suburbs to Bethesda and her Chevy Chase home: Old Keene Mill to Backlick; Backlick to Columbia Pike; Columbia Pike to Glebe Road; Glebe to Chain Bridge (still standing); Chain Bridge to MacArthur Boulevard; MacArthur to Dalecarlia Parkway and on up Western Avenue to Chevy Chase, assuming the border checkpoints would let them through.

Mike squinted at the fires ahead, and felt for the rifle, its strap wrapped around the roof rail so it would not fall. Lara was already calling Fernando, who was back in the wagon with Celia and Nate, with a warning to be on their guard.

"We've been awfully lucky so far," she said tensely to Mike. "No trouble, no situations."

Mike nodded in agreement, scanning the roadsides and the way ahead. "You should get down into the cab, maybe." If anyone took a shot at them, she would be exposed, but with her down below, he could lie flat and inconspicuous on the roof between the rails, presenting no silhouette.

"Well, OK," she agreed softly. "Maybe I should get in the horse trailer with a weapon in case somebody comes for that."

"Good idea. It's metal-sided, too. We can stop so you can get in." Mike made ready to lean over the edge toward the open driver's-side window. "You should get Grandma's MAC pistol."

Lara murmured assent in the chilly darkness, and squeezed his forearm. Mike felt her warm breath on the side of his face as she shifted position, preparing to climb off the roof. He paused for a second, pleasantly distracted, and then stuck his head out over the driver's window and called to Daryl. The truck and its train revved down, slowly coming to a creaking halt. Lara quickly climbed down, took the MAC over whispered words, opened the front side-door in the horse trailer ahead of the stalls, and vanished into its murk.

"Hang on," said Mike, now down on Daryl's running board. "Let me go back and talk with them back in the wagon for a sec." He jumped down and jogged back to the wagon.

Nate, Celia, and Fernando were nestled down among the cargo, the men on each side and Celia concealed behind the metal tailgate between two big crates. Each had a weapon. Mike went up to where he thought Fernando would be, on the left side.

"Pssst," he said.

"Psst you," answered Fernando.

"We don't know what's going on up there, but if somebody starts shooting or tries to stop us and it doesn't look like the good guys, we're going to keep going, OK?"

"Yes, boss," answered Fernando.

"You've done some of this stuff before, I guess," laughed Mike nervously.

"Never went looking for it, but sometimes it found me."

"OK." Mike raised his head and started to call out to the others, but Fernando was already sliding back to huddle with them. "OK, good luck," Mike whispered loudly, and ran back up to the truck, swinging up onto the ladder and making himself nearly invisible below the rails. The train restarted its creaky forward progress.

They drove in silent anticipation for several minutes, the orange glow resolving into several small fires on and beside the road. As they got closer, the illusion of people vanished. The road appeared deserted. Mike felt his heartbeat accelerate as he wondered whether this was an ambush. He glanced from side to side into the darkness of the fields and thickets they were passing, preparing to react to any attack, but the darkness remained empty and calm.

They were almost up to the fires now, and he could see that some sort of vehicle, tilted off the road into a ditch, was the main burning object. It first looked like a wagon, but then he saw it was a wood-burner, judging by the size of the dark mass on its bed that he guessed was its boiler, next to the smoldering remains of a cab or cargo. The other fires were along the ditch, where brush had caught flame in a circle perhaps thirty or forty feet across. It looked like it was slowly burning itself out. Beyond a small margin of smoldering grass, there looked to be a marsh, its water reflecting the light. Across the marsh some distance were forest trees, lit dimly in the orange glow.

Daryl kept driving. There was no need to stop and discuss. They all stayed vigilant. The road remained empty, and darkness returned. Lara stayed down in the cab, happy for the warmth and company. Perhaps five minutes passed. Mike was starting to doze, the stress and effort of the long day beginning to overcome him. Then, someone down in the cab jolted him alert with a bang on the metal roof. He opened his eyes wide, tense, trying to see what was going on. The truck's engine was slowing down. Ahead on the road, lit spectral white against the black background, were two people carrying large, bulky packs. They were stopping and turning, gesturing. Then the figures of small children emerged from among their legs. Daryl brought the truck and its train to a rickety stop beside them in the middle of the road.

"Hey!" called Grandma down from the passenger's side window.

The people were putting down their packs, the trio of children huddling behind them.

"Hey," replied a man warily. Mike saw the other was a women.

"That your truck back there burning?" asked Grandma kindly.

"Yes, ma'am," answered the man with some disgust. "Got so hot the whole thing caught fire and we couldn't stop it."

"Where you going to?" Grandma started to open the door, but Mike instinctively groped for his rifle, down alongside his left leg, his senses still attuned to threats and dangers. Daryl switched off the truck's flywheel drive, and silence replaced the whirring, broken only by the tinkling of the open-door alarm and some horse noises from the trailer.

"Frederick, Maryland," he replied.

"That where you live?"

"No, ma'am. Relatives." The woman picked up the smallest child, and there was the sound of tired complaining between the others, who appeared older.

"Are you storm refugees?" asked Grandma, down on the road now.

"Yes," said the woman.

"Where are you coming up from?"

"Burgess."

"Where's that?" Grandma had no idea.

"Southeast of Fredericksburg," said the man. "Seventy, eighty miles down the Northern Neck."

"By the Bay?"

"Yes, just about," said the man. "Bay come up maybe thirty feet. Up all the creeks. And the wind. We lost everything—the house, barn, horses, the vineyard, the hogs and chickens, four acres of topsoil I spent ten years building up…" His voice was like broken bone-ends grinding.

"Well, you can ride with us as far as we're going, Bethesda. That'll get you off these dark roads with your kids." She started to walk back toward the wagon. "There's no room up here, but let's get you up in my hay-wagon back here." The family shouldered their belongings and trudged behind her.

"God bless you, ma'am," said the woman.

"Don't you mention it," said Grandma, her voice blending kindness and fatigue. "We wouldn't leave you out here. Were you going to walk all night?"

The man laughed slightly, his spirits seeming to rise despite everything he must have experienced in the past several days. "We were aiming for a barn or maybe a house where somebody would let us sleep until tomorrow…"

123

Grandma did not answer. The challenges were overwhelming. Mike wondered what they would eat. Did they have any money? How would they travel the remaining distance to Frederick, a farming town in Maryland's rolling countryside way up to the northwest of Washington? Would relatives have the means to come down to get them?

The woman was up in the wagon's bed now, the others making room for them. Her male companion—husband?—lifted each child up to her in turn.

"I'm going back up front now," said Grandma. "We're going to get started."

The man and woman gave her profuse thanks. Grandma smiled at them. "Really, it's OK. Glad to help." She wrinkled a wry smile at the children, now kneeling down in the tight space between cargo and sideboards.

"I'll bet this is a Halloween you'll never forget!"

The man and woman sighed and shook their heads in shared bemusement.

"All tricks and no treats."

16—WORD FROM LOST ARROW

Thursday, November 1st (morning and evening)

Mike knew he had to get up. The day was becoming warm and humid, and by the sounds from the yard and downstairs he could tell that many members of the swollen household were already up and working. Hens were clucking, horses were whinnying to be fed, a cow was lowing, kitchen pots were clanking and rattling, an axe was chopping, and someone was pounding on a metal object. Storm cleanup and repair was in full swing in the compound and around the neighborhood. Roofs needed to be patched, trees trimmed and branches cut up, and greenhouses re-glazed.

He stretched long and luxuriously, and folded his hands under his head, studying the ceiling of his grandmother's guest room, trying to match his memory with its features. It had been several years since his last visit to the grand old house where he had spent much of his childhood. As his eyes ran across the door frame and over the old, comfortable furniture, he swayed suddenly between the primeval sense of security Grandma's home awakened in him, and the bleak recollection of the crisis all around them.

Daryl was still snoring faintly on the other guest bed, breathing deeply and evenly. Mike glanced over at him. He had heard his Blacksburg story in detail in the wagon, and mused now on the trials that all of them had gone through in the past days and weeks. They needed more than a little rest. They needed to sleep for a week. As Mike prepared to swing his legs over the side of the bed, he wondered whether they would ever get that rest.

* * *

"Cumberland's out." Grandma face wrinkled in resigned disgust as she leaned toward the ample alcohol-burning samovar in the center of the table

125

to decant herself another cup of tea. No one replied. Mike entered the dining room, and was greeted by a chorus of murmured hi's and good morning's. Grandma motioned toward one of the few free seats at the table, close to where she was sitting. Her expression brightened slightly. "Here's one helpful grandson," she said softly. Jenny gave his hand a squeeze, and Marcus nodded from across the table.

Mike laughed in mild embarrassment, and took in the unaccustomed sight of almost all of his immediate family, friends, and other household members gathered in one place. "Never expected such an adventure with my own grandmother," he mumbled, eying a big basket of bread and biscuits hungrily.

"We've had more than our fair share of adventures recently," frowned Ari Daniels, "and there will surely be more."

"Cumberland what?" responded Mike to Grandma's earlier comment with a slight delay. He reached for the bread and a bowl of jam.

"The Cumberland Coop is pulling out of the Chevy Chase Market Garden, honey," said Grandma. "I'm out of a job."

"Why?"

Grandma sighed wearily and stirred her tea.

"It's all destroyed," Marcus spoke up. "All the greenhouses busted, trees all over the fields. Harvest ruined."

Mike looked around in surprise. "But why can't it be fixed?"

Grandma shook her head. "It can be, it will be, but *they* don't want to do it. Somebody local's going to take over sooner or later, surely by next planting time, but Cumberland just doesn't have the extra capital. This is pretty far from their home base. This storm was the last straw." She shrugged. "But Washington has to eat. Wish I could come up with the money." She spiked a meaningful glance at Mike.

A child's voice cut happily through the pause, at odds with the adults' gloom.

"Uncle Mike!" exclaimed his nephew Lee, running into the dining room. "Grandma!" Mike turned in his chair to greet him with a big smile. Gliding in behind Lee came Honorée in a long, loose dress, her hair all wild, with Asa on her hip. Mike and Honorée beamed at one another, and she bent down with Asa counterbalanced to give Mike a big kiss on his forehead. Lee was now up in Mike's lap, squirming, the tablecloth starting to reel down off the table under his arm, drawing everything upon it toward the table's edge.

"Lee! Mike!" cried Grandma, grabbing the sliding cloth from across the table. "Look out!"

Everyone gasped, and nothing fell. Lee, oblivious, was asking Mike one question after the next and not waiting for answers. Asa watched Mike from the safety of his mother's hip, shy and quiet. He did not know Mike. Mike noticed his expression, and smiled up at him.

"Who's the little guy?" he smiled, shaking Asa's naked foot with this thumb and index finger. Asa's face clouded with impending tears, and he buried it in his mother's side. "Aw," said Mike.

"He's very fragile," said Honorée softly. "With all this change, and especially since –" and she lowered her voice to lip-reading volume "- Sanna disappeared."

Mike nodded.

"They were really close," added Honorée.

She pulled a chair close to Mike's, and sat down, still holding Asa. Lee, meanwhile, was sitting with delight in Mike's lap, repeating "uncamikedoyouwannaknowsomething?" over and over in his little-boy soprano and trying to turn Mike's head to look at him.

Yet even in this moment of wiggling chaos, Mike noticed that Grandma, Ari, and Lara were re-gathering into a small knot across the table, heads low, returning to what appeared to be an intense conversation. He strained to hear, catching only odd words like "Congress," "Laugherty," and "evacuation." Honorée smiled at his predicament, and, deftly preventing Lee from knocking Mike's tea over, leaned over to him and said with a chuckle, "Lee's absolutely crazy to see you, bro, but he'll have lots of time with you from now on, and maybe they want you over there in that, um, meeting!"

"Maybe you're right," said Mike.

* * *

Ari's voice ran flat as he described what he had read and heard that morning. Mike listened, interested but sleepy and somewhat overwhelmed, distracted by the work going on outside the open dining room windows.

127

Grandma's house lay midway between Connecticut Avenue and Brookville Road, on a shady street of old Victorian, brick, and stucco houses at least a century old. Recent decades had seen an accelerating transformation of the once-affluent neighborhood into an urban village, as garages became (or were restored to) stables and carriage houses, lawns became gardens and livestock yards, and single-family dwellings became teeming apartments. Grandma's house had developed into a compound. The house next door had burned to the ground in a lightning storm twelve years before, leaving an open lot that she and Jack had purchased. It now held a large vegetable garden, some fruit trees, a poultry run and henhouse, and a small cottage built from the original detached two-story garage, where Marcus and his family now lived. On the lot beyond that, closest to Brookville, was an additional house—a medium-sized 20th-century brick colonial—that Grandma also owned, and rented to several families who worked either for her or the Market Garden. In Grandma's main house lived Grandma and now Honorée, Lee, Asa, and Claudia, along with the eight recently arrived travelers, including Mike. Around the three now rather densely inhabited lots was a robust ten-foot-high wall/fence mixing sections of wooden stockade, brick, and wire that had been erected in the years since Jack's passing. Various utility sheds and a couple of rusty shipping containers stood here and there. The whole compound was entered through one main gate that faced south, or alternatively through a small door that opened on a back alley. Since the storm, the gate had been routinely kept closed and locked.

On this balmy late Thursday morning, the outdoor sounds were having a soporific effect on Mike: the hens; the singing of a grinding wheel; the metallic clip of shears; a hammer in the distance; the clatter of a loom; a woman singing. He wished he could go back to bed.

The tone of Grandma's voice brought him out of his reverie. "They should be thinking about how to get the electric power back on, not all that rubbish!"

Ari laughed. "Did you even have electricity to start with?"

Grandma snorted. "Of course. It was on when I left to go down to the Outer Banks. Had been pretty reliable."

"Well, you're all very lucky around here, that I'll say." He leaned back and looked around at the spacious room, and out through the windows toward the lush garden, yellow and gold with autumn beans and squash.

128

"The electricity wasn't cheap, but it worked." She sighed. "But really, it's very disappointing, the way Congress is carrying on." She took in a long breath through her nose, eyes closed, and stared pensively across the big table as she let it slowly back out. "But it's not surprising, especially now."

Ari wrinkled his brow and blinked questioningly at her. "Now? You mean you are suddenly less surprised at the politics than you were before?"

Grandma took a long sip of tea, smiling with a polite shake of her head at Lara, who made to fetch her more from the samovar.

"Of course it's all been getting worse and worse, worse and worse, more and more deadlocked. The Trust and the oligarchs and the Republicans all have their deals, you know. I imagine that the Front has been shaking things up, making the oligarchy uncomfortable, so they've been paying them off. Where do you think Carl Holt gets all his weapons and fancy vehicles? The Fort McMurray radicals probably don't fit into the Trust's or into *some* oligarchs' plans either, but they do into others'…"

Ari nodded, waiting. She went on.

"Meanwhile, there's still this Morales government in the White House… This inconvenient, democratically elected progressive president and her cabinet. How did they pull *that* off, anyway!?" Grandma laughed sarcastically. "Oh, *yes*. There were international observers that time, in '36."

Lara frowned.

"Don't expect them *this* time." She took another drink of tea.

Ari was matter-of-fact: "This may in fact be the last democratically legitimate executive branch under the current republic."

"The First American Republic," mused Grandma.

"They are certainly doing their best in Philadelphia to bring down the curtain on this one," said Ari.

"What *are* they doing?" asked Lara.

"Turmoil," replied Ari. "Laugherty and others have been railing rabidly against the idea of the relief mission. They know that if it happens, as the President apparently announced yesterday afternoon while we were on our home stretch, then their right phalanx will swing to the Front and the moderates might actually warm up to Hedges, and even Laugherty might not be able to steal this election. This republic might actually survive another presidential term! Or," he added grimly, "go to the Front."

"I can't believe they are standing up in Independence Hall and saying these things publicly, with so many poor, desperate refugees protesting right outside," muttered Lara, exasperated. "This is a national disaster that needs immediate action!"

"Most of them are being kept over in New Jersey by the military," remarked Ari. "And the rest at a good distance." He looked at his daughter, his hand on his chin. "And it's a regional disaster, not a national disaster— just one more regional humanitarian disaster among many—but the foreign relations and national election implications are national, I guess. What's more important?"

"I mean, I just can't believe, even after all this, that they are more worried about an election than people's well-being and survival." Outrage was in Lara's eyes.

Grandma cleared her throat. "Looking at it cynically—which they do - the storm refugees and others affected are just a small minority of US citizens, and most in this region are not big Laugherty fans anyway, so he's not too concerned about what they think."

"But..." interjected Ari.

"Wait," said Grandma. "But it's even bigger. I have to explain to you now what I found waiting for me when we got home." She gestured to an old-fashioned manila envelope on a sideboard to her right. "I want Hon and Jenny to hear this. Claudia, too." She turned to Mike. "Do you think you can go upstairs and find them? Maybe see if that Celia can watch the boys?" Then, turning to Ari, she said, "of course, you and your kids can hear this, too."

With a recess abruptly declared, the conversation halted. Ari and Lara exchanged wide-eyed looks of surprised curiosity. Mike stood up, taking a bite of the slice of bread with cheese on it that remained on his plate, and took it into the kitchen. Jenny was in there, talking to their mother.

"Mom, Jen, could you go out there in a minute? Grandma has something she wants to tell us."

Jenny raised her eyebrows. Claudia made a face and shrugged.

"Whatever she says," said Claudia.

"Hey, Jen," added Mike. "Do you know where Hon and her boys are?"

"I'm in here," called Honorée from the pantry, where she was labeling jars. "I heard you." She got up and came into the main kitchen.

"The boys OK for now?" asked Mike.

130

"They're across the yard with Becca and her kids," said Honorée, referring to Marcus' wife.

"Good. I'll go up and get Daryl, and be down in a minute." He yawned. "Some pretty heavy stuff…"

"What is this about?" asked Jenny with a whisper, catching his arm. "Money?"

Mike shook his head. "No idea. Politics, maybe."

"*Politics?*" said Jenny, startled.

"That's what we were talking about," replied Mike. He yawned again, and stretched. "I really have no idea…"

"'Kay. Go get Daryl," said Honorée. "Should I add more tea water?"

"I think it's OK," said Mike. "Later." He turned and jogged across the back hall and up the back stairs to the third floor, where he was sharing the room with Daryl. The room was ajar. For a moment, he wondered whether Daryl had already gone down the front stairs. He pushed the door open. Startled, he stopped. Daryl was sitting in bed, shirtless, leaning back against the headboard. He had his hands clasped behind his head. Sitting cross-legged on the bed was Celia, in a bathrobe she appeared to have borrowed from someone.

"Sorry, I, um, should have knocked," smiled Mike. "Hey! Daryl, this is *our* room," he joked, looking curiously at Celia.

Celia turned pale and jumped up from the bed. "I'm sorry. I'll leave!"

"No, no, no. I was kidding," said Mike with a gesture of denial. "I just came to tell Daryl that we're all waiting in the dining room for Grandma to tell us something and that she sent me up here to get him." He re-directed his words at Daryl. "So, you better hurry. I think she's going to start in a moment."

Daryl looked irritated. "Can this wait? I haven't even gotten dressed."

"Not up to me, man," said Mike. "Urgent." He smiled at Celia. "I know. We're a crazy family." She stared at him with serious eyes.

"What's this about?" asked Daryl, jumping out of bed in what turned out to be shorts.

"I don't know," said Mike. "Something political."

"Oh, God," said Daryl. "I hate politics more than ever now, and I already hated political conversations with your grandmother anyway." He meant to end this sentence in a joking tone, but it came across as petulant and adolescent.

Mike turned quickly to leave. "All right. See you down there, maybe."
He glanced at Celia. "You can come too, if you want. I guess." She stood
in stiff indecision as he left the room. "It's fine, I'm sure..." he said,
plunging into the hall toward the narrow wooden stairs. "Come down, too."

* * *

They had all moved outside by the time the stragglers found their way
down to the dining room. The air was stagnant, and Grandma had called
for a relocation to the big covered porch along the front of the house,
which had looked out onto the street in days before the stockade fence
went up. There, they all felt, it might be a little breezier. They were
disappointed. A mugginess had enveloped Chevy Chase, along with a hint
of thunder weather in the air.

"I hope that everyone's feeling a little better, after so many long and
difficult journeys," said Grandma formally, reverting it seemed to a
professional persona from days gone by. All the recently arrived family
and guests agreed enthusiastically.

Nate Burhans spoke up, to the red-cheeked embarrassment of his sister.
"We sort of stowed away with y'all, but we're very grateful you've let us
come to stay with your family," he announced. Grandma smiled faintly,
and nodded. The rest met this comment with an equivocal silence. Lara,
reluctant to speak out of turn as a guest, aimed friendly looks at the two
siblings.

Grandma coughed and continued. "A few days ago, I was *so* looking
forward to coming home..." She caught herself. "I mean, I certainly *am*
happy to be home, with all of us together again, after so long, and in such
trying times. I was particularly worried about Jenny down there alone in
Fredericksburg, and about Hon and the boys, over in the District,
especially after such troubles even before the storm—*Rhiannon*—came
along..." She pronounced the name of the hurricane in a slow and precise
manner, drawing out its Celtic syllables. Honorée, noting the implied
reference to Sanna's and the van's disappearances, studied the porch's
plank floor. Claudia, whom Grandma had neglectd to mention, pouted in
silence.

"And I am so very grateful to Marcus and Becca and Lon, and to
Fernando's family, and to the other tenants and workers at the Market

Garden for doing so many things to keep this household functioning during my absence." She was answered with polite smiles. "You are all wonderful."

But Grandma's tone was heavy as she spoke these measured words of appreciation, and the perception of this spooled the tension tighter on the porch as her audience listened.

"There are two things that have affected the nature of my homecoming, and I want you to understand them, because they may have some big impacts on the plans of each and every one of us—family and others—quite soon." She looked around for assurance that everyone was listening closely. "The first, of course, is that the Garden is closed until further notice because of the storm, so I don't have the income I thought we could count on." She looked at her hands and paused. "A lot of which was in-kind payment in food. The other, and I won't go into the details because most of you don't need the background and I don't relish the idea of telling the awful story again...the other thing is that I have just suffered a very large financial loss." She closed her eyes and put her hands to her forehead to maintain her composure. This was met with a murmur of expressions of alarm. Honorée came and sat next to Grandma, putting her hand on Grandma's arm.

"Are you feeling OK, Grandma?" she asked with concern.

Grandma took a shaky breath, and let out a long sigh. "Let's keep it at that, but what it means is that many things I had planned to do with our houses and with the White Flint business and replacing the van and the boys' schooling... oh, and knowing we would have all the food, feed, and fuel for the winter we needed... Well, all that's on hold now, out of reach." The expressions of her listeners ranged from solemn to frightened.

"These are making me rethink things," she went on. "Just about everything. I am concerned about our safety here, about our ability to hang on." Grandma smiled wanly at Honorée. "The market stall just isn't enough for us all to live on, and even there we've suffered some setbacks. And we have food stored up here, but I'm not sure it would get us to springtime..." Honorée returned Grandma's look but did not smile. Turning back to the others, Grandma continued. "But then I find this waiting for me upon my return, and, well, now I have even more to process!" She pointed at the manila envelope on the small wicker table in front of her.

"What?" asked Honorée, giving voice to everyone's question.

On the cover of the envelope, hand-written in ink, was the name Florence Trudeau.

"This came for me a few weeks ago, after I had left. Hand-delivered! By whom, I don't know."

She picked it up.

"But I do know who sent it. I don't know him personally, but Jack did. I don't even know his real name. But I do know the name he goes by."

There was considerable suspense as her audience waited, surprised by the odd turn in her monologue. Family members, tenants, and guests alike glanced at one another, mystified.

"It's from Jesus!" said Jenny impulsively. That set the suspense off like a trigger, and for reasons no one could fathom there were several minutes of stifled, hysterical laughter and gasping. Honorée, with tears streaming down her face, held a hand tightly over her mouth. Mike struggled to suppress a senseless grin. Jessica let out a shriek of laughter, and—red-faced—tried and failed to control it. Celia giggled, clueless as to why everyone was cracking up infectiously. Ari surveyed the group with a startled look, eyes darting again and again to the envelope on Grandma's lap. Grandma was a mask of gravity.

"Oh, my lord," gasped Jenny, collapsing into sobs. "Oh, I am *so* sorry!" She struggled to control herself amid her tears. Honorée moved over to comfort her.

The unexpected eruption of stifled emotions came to a quick end.

"I can only imagine where that came from," said Grandma drily. This was met with calmer demeanors. "Things have been awfully serious for a long time." She cracked a wan smile at Jenny. "Jesus? So you think I'm getting envelopes from Jesus now, do you?"

Jenny shook her head and answered with a sob, "I don't know why I said that."

"Maybe we are all hoping for miracles?" said Lara, trying to joke, but her comment landed athwart the conversation, and the tension persisted.

"So... Lost Arrow," said Grandma. There was silence anew. "Lost Arrow was his name... Is his name. I don't know where he got it, or why. He's not a Native American as far as I know. But that's what he's been going by for a long time." She frowned. "He must be in his eighties now... Lost Arrow."

They all stared at Grandma, waiting for her to go on.

"Many years ago, he worked with Jack." She glanced at Nate and Celia. "My late husband," she explained. "They worked together over quite a long time, with a variety of people. And they came up with what were considered very accurate ways of understanding all the crazy changes that the past few decades have seen... Most of my lifetime." She fingered the envelope. "Ways of predicting what was likely to happen next."

"What kinds of crazy changes?" asked Lara.

"Oh, you know, the economy, energy supplies, politics, climate change, water shortages … how they all fit together as a system. How you could explain rapid, complicated shifts, using systems theory."

"This is fascinating," said Ari. "I recently re-read the book he gave me, Flo."

"Yes, yes," said Grandma a trifle abruptly. "I'm not bringing this up for academic reasons, Ari," she said. "We're all still recovering from yesterday's long drive and I'm sure everyone has things to do, so let me get to the point."

She then smiled briefly at him to signal that she wasn't cross. Ari nodded back with slight embarrassment.

"Anyway," she continued. "I hadn't heard from Lost Arrow for years, but I have a great deal of respect for him and his group, and it's funny but I thought about him a few times during my long trip these past few weeks— what he would think about the growing political crisis right now—so it was a remarkable surprise to find a letter from him waiting for me. Hand-delivered, as far as I can tell, by someone in his network! And sent before Hurricane Rhiannon had even taken place!"

Honorée's patience gave way. "Grandma, what does he *say*?" She made to reach for the envelope, but Grandma shooed her hand away.

"All right, all right!" Grandma paused to compose herself. "He basically recommends that I move my family away from here to a safer place because he expects major political changes to start happening, sudden changes, changes that have been building up for a long time, with a lot of turmoil and migration." She looked around. "He doesn't think the DC area is a good place to be, and he seems to be telling me this out of concern for his old colleague's family."

Grandma opened the envelope and pulled out a report printed in the old-fashioned manner on paper. They could see it was perhaps a centimeter thick, with a hand-written letter over it.

"Here's what he says." She put on her reading glasses, and began reading excerpts from the report, where she had made notes.

> *On the verge of the phase transition we have been postulating for years...*
> *It will take a major triggering event, such as a natural disaster, foreign action, or pandemic.*

She looked around at them over her glasses. "We've got two of those right now," she said, and returned to her reading.

> *We have been predicting this for many years, but we systematically underestimated the defensive strength of interests with deep financial, reputational, political, and psychic investments in Phase F3...*

"That's apparently this phase—the phase during which fossil fuels have dominated society and formed the basis of our most powerful institutions," she explained, and read on.

> *The emergence of the Energy Trust and its web of oligarchic and partisan relationships is the example par excellence of this phenomenon. So is the militarization of the Interstate System, as well as the federalization of bioenergy resources and US designs on Canadian fossil energy resources. We have been predicting these developments since the Phase Transition Model was first proposed...*

Grandma stopped, took off her glasses, and looked around. She shook her head. Her audience appeared to have quickly disintegrated into a few rapt listeners and a larger number of fidgety, distracted individuals. She clapped her hands together. Several people jumped. Honorée nodded in mute approval.

"OK. I won't keep reading the report. You can do that yourselves, if you want. I'll get to the point of his letter. Here's what he says. Um." She put the report down on the table and took up the letter.

Florence, you may find this hard to accept because you are a strong, independent, and self-reliant person, and you have probably dealt with the long emergency more successfully than most. Jack always said that about you. But the reason I am concerned is that you and your family are based in the federal capital, where much of the economy is still tied to Phase F3 agencies and institutions, and when that vanishes, it's going to vanish very quickly and the power and economic resources are going to move to other locations—mainly certain state capitals. Unless you have a large farm and a lot of people and weapons, and perhaps you do, the Washington area is not where you should be. There will be conflict and dislocation, and a lot of very aggressive and entitled actors, but the absence of a strong civil society that can govern itself.

From my vantage point in Satan's Kingdom, I have felt this way anyway for quite a while because of the hot and turbulent weather you must deal with in your region, the tropical diseases, and the crime.

"Satan's Kingdom!" burst out Claudia. "What on earth does he mean by that?" Grandma ignored her and read on.

The situation is different now. I cannot reveal to you how I know this, but there are political developments underway that closely match our model, and everyone will know about them fairly soon— this year, anyway, I predict.

Grandma adjusted her glasses, and raised her voice slightly for emphasis.

I strongly advise you to relocate to a place where there are strong traditions of local and state democracy, where the F3 corruption is

137

limited, where there has been less federalization of energy, and where a more resilient society has been and is being invested in. Of course, I am partial to New England, and I know you and Jack have connections here. Plus, there are political developments right now that make New England especially relevant. But there are other places that fit this description—Minnesota, for example - and you know what's best for your extended family.

I know this will be hard to accept—perhaps impossible until the Phase Transition is in full swing—and also very inconvenient and expensive to respond to—but I owe it to Jack to warn you, since he certainly would be warning you himself if he were still with us.

You and I have never met, but Jack was a wonderful friend, and he spoke often of you and your children and grandchildren.

Please, as soon as you can, get to a place where democracy is strong, where the electorate is not bought, where everyone takes shared responsibility for civil order and respectful debate. A place with a future. I am very concerned that where you live now does not have a very safe or secure future, at least until the Phase Transition has run its course.

Your family friend...

Grandma paused dramatically, looking around at all of them.

Lost Arrow
Satan's Kingdom
September 25, 2040

For a heartbeat, there was a startled silence, and then everyone began speaking at the same time. This went on for several minutes. At his side, Jenny was asking Mike lots of questions, none of which he could answer. Ari was bending down, talking inaudibly to Grandma, and Honorée was leaning over to catch what he said. Daryl, Nate, and Celia sat in a huddle on the far side of the porch, Celia wrapping and unwrapping a lock of hair around her index finger as she listened. Lara was looking over at Mike, starting to make her way toward him. Jessica and Claudia, side by side, sat in worried silence, nervously looking around.

Grandma stood up. "Everyone!"

The babble of voices continued unabated.

"Everyone!" She raised her voice, her hand on her forehead. Honorée joined in, motioning with her hands. The talking stopped.

"OK," said Grandma. "There is a lot to think about, and I think that everyone who wants to should read his letter and report, and we'll talk about this, um, maybe later this evening. But I wanted you all to know about this, and about how seriously I take it."

"I don't get it," said Claudia with confused alarm. "Why did you read this? What are you trying to say?!"

"Are you saying we can't stay here?" asked Jenny with exasperation.

Grandma sighed, and a weary burden of responsibility became almost visible over her thin frame. "I'm not saying anything yet, except that I'm worried and that our food and money situation as a household just took an unexpected turn for the worse, and ..."

"We've always been fine!" cried Claudia. "This is our home, and ..."

"*Mother*, let Grandma finish!" interrupted Honorée.

Grandma looked shaky. "I've been on the road for weeks, Claudie, and it's been hard going, and I would love nothing better than to take time off and just relax..."

"I think you've been remarkably tough through it all," interjected Ari pacifically.

"I think we've all been tough, but that's not what I was trying to say!" exclaimed Grandma in frustration.

"So, why are you trying to scare us with this Lost Arrow letter?" said Claudia shrilly, clearly agitated, standing now, her palms to her temples. "I don't remember him at all..."

"No, of course, you were busy raising kids..." replied Grandma, trying to regain the thread. "And I wasn't trying to scare anyone. We just have to take this seriously..."

"We're just fine here!" repeated Claudia, starting to break down.

Honorée put her arm around Claudia's shoulders, helping her to sit down again. "Mother, Mother... Let's just take this one step at a time. You know Grandma's a bit theatrical and maybe this wasn't the right time...

But let's just listen and ... and, you know?" Claudia fended Honorée off, but seemed to calm down nonetheless.

"'We' were always fine because Grandma always figured everything out," whispered Jenny to Mike. "And had lots of money."

Mike looked at her out of the corner of his eye and nodded.

"Well, I appreciate what you shared with us, Florence," said Ari in a quiet, reasonable tone. "Things have really been coming at us this past week, that's for sure, so there's a lot to digest, but –," He looked around. "– some of you may not know that we're continuing north ourselves in a little while."

Mike, who knew this, nodded again. Jenny and Honorée both cocked their heads at Ari in surprise.

Ari shook his head. "It's a long story, but for several compelling reasons we're going to be staying with family in Connecticut or Massachusetts for a while."

"Where Lost Arrow said we should go," said Jenny. "Kind of."

Ari nodded.

"Not staying with us for long?" asked Honorée with visible disappointment. Lara bit her lip. "We would love to have you stay."

Ari shook his head. "No, I'm afraid. Even without Lost Arrow's warning."

Now it was Honorée's turn to briefly look like she might cry, but she composed herself and just frowned.

They all sat in silence for a moment, letting the words sink in and the emotions dissipate.

"Mike, can you come help me with the truck for a few minutes?" asked Daryl, getting up. It was still jerry-hitched to the trailer and wagon, and the whole train stood parked conspicuously in the yard, blocking the driveway.

Everyone else made to stand up and leave.

"So, that's that," said Grandma, exhausted. Addressing everyone, she added, "So, there you are, things to think about, reasons not to get too relaxed, even though we just got here." She sighed and shook her head. "We'll keep working on this, watching the situation. We don't even really know yet how things are around here."

"I do," remarked Honorée. "Just ask mother and me!"

* * *

140

Daryl was napping. Mike changed quietly out of his shorts and T-shirt, and into long pants and a clean shirt, freshly washed by Grandma's staff. He pulled his wallet out of his duffel and stuffed it in his hip pocket. Into his opposite leg pocket he dropped the rolled-up cylinder of his lapscreen. Moving silently, his shoes in one hand and his hat in the other, he glided out the half-open door, and closed it behind him. The hallway was deserted. Thunder rumbled in the distance. Aiming for the side-exit through the stockade, from the rear of the house into the alley behind it, he stole to the back staircase and descended. As he walked past the entrance to the kitchen, Honorée suddenly stepped out in front of him, a case of jam jars in her grip.

He stopped quickly to let her pass.

"Where you going, little bro?" she asked with a curious smile. "It's kind of late." She eyed his clean clothing.

"Oh, is it?" he replied. Glancing at his watch, he answered his own question. "No way, it's only six-thirty!"

"I meant, we're going to have dinner pretty soon, so if you go out now, you may miss it."

"Dinner?" He looked around absently. "Oh, no, don't worry about me." Mike was not hungry.

"You sure?" Honorée looked surprised and concerned. "First night back. All of us together." She smiled hopefully. "Chicken barbeque."

"I'm just going out to see some friends I haven't seen for a really long time," Mike heard himself say.

"Oh, yeah?" said Honorée doubtfully. "Friends?"

Mike felt himself bristling, but fought it. "Yeah, sure. Guys I knew in ROTC."

"So, nobody I know, then?" Honorée fished.

"Uh, nah, probably not," laughed Mike tensely, feigning jocularity.

"Will you be out long?" she asked.

"Couple of hours, maybe," Mike replied. His tone changed. "Look, Hon, Jesus Christ, I need some time of my own. I've been a part of this traveling circus for, gosh, what, three weeks! No breaks!"

Honorée raised her hands, palms out. "Hey, I totally understand. We all need a break." She studied his face.

"OK, so, see you later." He reached one arm around her neck and kissed her on the temple. "It's great to be back."

She laughed, and stood watching as he vanished out the kitchen door.

Mike pushed open the alley door in the stockade fence, and carefully pushed it closed behind him, making sure the heavy latch clicked shut. He looked around in the October dusk. The alley was quiet, and there were few signs of the storm here. It looked to him as it had always looked: all manner of gates and fences among overgrown bushes, shady trees, parked and scrap vehicles, and the odd pile of compost, hay, or wood chips. He felt good to be back in the city where he had been raised. Times were tough but there were so many things to do and people to interact with. He had spent a relatively long run of years in his young life in rural settings, and he was tired of the relentless poverty and grinding agrarian routines.

Turning right, Mike walked quickly toward Connecticut Avenue, zigzagging for several blocks until he found himself on Thornapple Street, heading west. When he reached Connecticut Avenue, the amount of traffic surprised him. Most of it seemed headed out of town, partly because the preponderance of trucks, cars, and wagons were in the northbound lanes, and partly because of the way many of them were loaded, not with the sort of market cargoes one would see on a typical Thursday, but instead with a lot of passengers, baggage, and household items. He found himself trying to recall whether the streets had been so busy when they pulled in during the early morning hours. He had become pretty drowsy up on the roof once they entered Maryland and their security improved. But, no, there had not been much traffic at that hour.

He jogged across the avenue, dodging traffic, and found himself passing a large police guard post on the other side. Several county policemen stood watching him as he completed the crossing. Mike nodded in a friendly manner.

"Lot of traffic," he commented.

"'Specially since noon, sir," replied one of the cops.

"Noon? Something happen then?" asked Mike, alert to this possible distinction.

"The president instructed the Interstate Highways Command to allow refugee movement in all directions, not just returning home," the cop explained.

"Hm," nodded Mike. "Thanks. Do you know why?"

"No idea, sir," said the policeman, shaking his head. "That's just what we heard."

Mike gestured in appreciation and continued down Thornapple Street at a quick walk. Before long, he was approaching the seedy strip of Wisconsin Avenue where it passed through Bethesda. Amid the dark, hulking shapes of former office buildings and cavernous parking garages, where the bygone enterprise of vanished industries like financial services, management consulting, and software design had once flourished, was a thriving souk of street markets, bars, casinos, and brothels. Food carts sold steamed noodles and roasted chicken, filling the air with a greasy, not unpleasant aroma. Once Mike descended into the Woodmont Triangle, the sidewalks became very full, and the traffic in the streets moved slowly. A dissonant mix of barriachi and cydub pounded from the open storefronts in the humid night air. Lightning occasionally flared in the west, outclassing the riot of cheap neon signs, kerosene lamps, and swinging paper lanterns. The thunder was becoming more audible.

Mike almost felt back home again. His teenage years had unfolded in these streets and in nearby sections of suburban Washington. He knew the lay of the land. But like night descending the shabby, frenzied economy of the forever impoverished had settled across the heart of Bethesda, and he knew that no area in the region had been spared, except perhaps a few gated exurbs. Bethesda was not like this back in the early '30s. There were still retail chain stores here then, and fast-food restaurants clinging to a still-affluent clientele. The traffic lights worked. English was still by far the most common language. But although Mike could still thread his way through the crowded streets with confidence, imagining from time to time that he saw familiar faces, his was nonetheless the sense of a visitor's now, encountering this relict of the atrophying global metroplex as he would any other.

Pausing for a moment, Mike pulled his lapscreen out of his leg pocket and studied it. On the map, which oriented automatically to the compass directions where he stood, the path to his destination pulsed softly. He held the lapscreen up in front of his face like a windshield. It became partially translucent. A building two blocks away became shaded in a spectral green color, and arrows circled down to where the entrance would be. He quickly scrolled the lapscreen and thrust it back into his pocket.

In moments, he was admitted through the narrow airlock doors, and found himself in a small, softly lit lobby. The air conditioning nearly took his breath away. There was a woman behind a thick plexiglas window, seated in a swivel chair against a background of large wall screens. She wore a steampunk AR monocle over one eye. Manifold windows on the screens showed a mixture of security camera views, VNET footage, and admin tools.

"I have a reservation," he said.

"Yes," she murmured, gesturing with a tiny thumb-ring bat. "Mister Kendeil, you're all set. Studio Twelve. You have it until three. That's seven hours, just in case." She smiled coyly. A door down the hallway slid open, and dim LED lights brightened, beckoning.

"Can you fix me up?" he asked, laughing at his own nervous anticipation.

"Mm, and what can I help you with?" she asked with a seductive set of her painted lips and eyes.

"L-tropin and Remol," he answered in a practiced tone.

"Normal dose?" she asked.

"Yep."

She smiled again, placing two small mist vials in the window's tray, and popped it over to his side of the counter. He took them in his hand, thanked her, and strode into the interior of the V-tel.

"You're oh-so-welcome," she laughed. "Have a good flight."

* * *

"Did Grandpa Jack also write about these phase transitions?" asked Lara, who had also spent her childhood summers referring to Jack Trudeau as "Grandpa." She was curled up on an old, fraying wicker chaise in a corner of the screened-in section of the porch. Jenny sat cross-legged at her feet. Candles burned on the end-tables and upended barrels scattered around the sitting area. A few late-season moths battered themselves against the screens. Crickets sang their song with a November tempo.

"He did," said Grandma, looking more rested after a long afternoon nap and a quiet evening. "He wasn't as much of a scientist about it all, though. He wasn't the one actually doing the calculating and everything."

"But he believed it, right?" Lara.

"Sure." Grandma laughed. "The basic ideas were hard to understand for most people, unfortunately, but they weren't controversial, at least, not among people with any education or sense..."

"How come I never, *ever* heard of any of this from my teachers, or from national leaders?" Lara was baffled. "I mean, I'm twenty-seven and I somehow missed this. Even when they talked about 'systems thinking'."

Doug Orman, Grandma's neighbor of many years, who had walked over as soon as he heard that she was home, laughed a raucous, sarcastic chortle. "Our so-called national leaders haven't wanted people like you to know anything about such things for years!" He swirled the bourbon he had brought in his glass, and took a sip. "Either to keep you away from challenging their privileges, or because they were terrified of what you might do if you knew the truth and freaked out because they were not doing anything."

Ari nodded soberly.

"It took decades for my dear old party and its leadership to even admit that climate change *might* be happening," said Orman. "That was before you were born..."

"She's not that young!" laughed Grandma.

"I was born in 2012," clarified Lara, curious to hear where Doug was going with this.

"OK, before and a while after..." He continued. "They still haven't admitted that there might be such a thing as goddamned evolution!" He shook his head. "Pennsylvania voters wouldn't let me get away with that horse shit, tell you what. But a lot of states' voters did."

"But that was all a long time ago," said Jenny. "Why doesn't anyone talk about it now?"

"Because we're not even capable of it anymore, given what's distracting everyone," said Ari darkly. "The average person is more concerned about why their hens aren't laying or how they are going to get enough firewood for next winter. There's no demand coming from citizens. Anyway, politicians don't even have the capacity themselves."

"But it sounds like it's going to start mattering," insisted Lara.

Doug Orman laughed. "Shit'll just hit the fan—*is* hitting the fan - never mind whether people are versed in fancy theories or not. They'll just react. They already are. People don't need to know that the acceleration of gravity is 9.8 meters per second squared to know to run when a tree's falling on them." He nodded toward the west. "You see all the refugee traffic on Connecticut Avenue today, by the way?"

The others all shook their heads.

"We haven't been out of the compound since we got here late last night," said Honorée, stepping into their midst after helping with the dishes and kitchen cleanup.

"Why, hello Honorée!" said Doug Orman warmly. "Glad to see they got you out of DC."

"Oh, I owe that to Lon and Marcus," smiled Honorée. "My rescue party."

Daryl appeared in the doorway leading from the living room onto the long porch, looking somewhat dazed from his long nap.

"Hi Daryl," said Grandma. "Did you get some food?"

"Uh, no," said Daryl, rubbing his eyes.

"There's still plenty out in the kitchen," said Honorée helpfully.

"Is Mike still up there?" asked Grandma.

Daryl looked puzzled. "No. I thought he was down here with y'all."

"Mike went out," said Honorée coolly.

"Out?" exclaimed Grandma. "What on earth?" She turned to look at Honorée. "What do you mean, 'out'?"

"He said he was going to see some friends," shrugged Honorée a trifle disingenuously. She knew her brother well. Lara caught the nuance and met her eyes with eyebrows raised. Jenny rubbed her neck and looked at the floor. There was an awkward silence.

"I wish he were here, to hear this conversation," said Grandma crossly.

"Well, I wouldn't worry too much," said Honorée. "He's a big boy now." She smiled ironically.

"Look, he was an enormous help to me during my trip. Couldn't have managed with only Fernando. Once we started our journey back, we needed three pairs of eyes and hands everywhere we went, and that was even before the storm came along." Grandma sighed. "I suppose he needs some time off."

The younger women made wry faces in the dim light. Daryl turned on his heel and went looking for food. Pots clattered in the kitchen. Celia and Nate replaced Daryl in the dark doorway. Grandma waved them toward a sagging, unoccupied loveseat beside her.

"Even us old guys need time off occasionally," joked Doug Orman, attempting to reset the porch atmosphere. He winked at Ari.

"Speak for yourself," stage-muttered Ari.

"What, about not needing time off?" probed Doug, laughing.

"No!" retorted Ari mock-seriously. "About being an old guy."

Everyone laughed.

"Daddy," said Lara, her mind and demeanor far ahead of their repartee, "you were talking before about *enthalapy*, and about why things could suddenly change a lot."

"Enthalpy," he corrected her.

"Yeah," she replied. The group on the porch settled down. "And?"

Ari took a deep breath. "So, I've read many of the books that Lost Arrow based his explanation on. I, um, read his report this afternoon. Of course, I read *Graveyard of Paradigms* when it first came out."

Doug Orman nodded in recognition.

Ari went on. "Even back well before all of you were born –." He looked around at Jenny, Lara, Honorée, Nate, and Celia. "- A community of thinkers and activists were talking about EROEI—we defined that earlier - about how, after oil and gas supplies peaked, it was going to take more and more energy to obtain each new unit of energy, reversing what had triggered the industrial revolution in the first place… Waterpower and coal, and all that. This was a huge break in the trends of more than a century." He took a breath. "Most people, if they paid any attention to this minority view, just thought, oh, we have technology, and that will overcome every challenge. So that was that. And the government and energy companies, and eventually the Energy Trust, all pretty much stayed away from any consideration of this." He took off his glasses and pinched his eyes and the bridge of his nose. "But where Lost Arrow and Jack and many others came in—Greer, Ruppert, Kunstler, Richard Heinberg, Holmgren, Janet Rizzo, the Lakeshore Institute, DMI—was in recognizing that *all* of society was pumped up with cheap energy—embodied energy— dependent on it—and not just inefficient vehicles and buildings and factories. Everything that anyone considered a normal part of modern life—governments, big universities, global aid NGOs, the American Empire, lifestyle trends, consumerism, vacations, popular culture, where people lived, what they expected from life—was all partly a function of a common variable: EROEI. When it went up, society's scale and complexity could grow. When it went down, they shrank. Eventually, anyway."

He leaned back, and took a swig of his bourbon. "Good hootch," he remarked to Doug Orman. Orman grunted.

"There was a nice little book by Mayumi and Sorman and, um, somebody else back then—we were looking at this in the Civil Engineering Department—that looked at society in terms of energetics." He paused, and looked around. "Am I losing anyone?" Lara, Jenny, and Nate were listening intently. Honorée shook her head. Grandma sat as if she were dozing, eyes half closed. Celia looked embarrassed, eyes downcast, but made no move to leave.

"OK," he laughed. "I have to remind myself that not everyone is an engineering grad student!" He went on. "All right. So, yes, that book looked at societies as having energy-based metabolisms, and did a nice job of squashing the argument that higher and higher technology will keep economies strong and prosperous even as energy quantity and quality deteriorate..."

"Look around you," muttered Orman. "Case in point."

"Well," said Ari ironically, looking over at Orman, "with our Energy Trust and the way the oligarchs captured the government in the Twenties, we never even gave technology a chance, did we?" He made a face. "Or science-based policy."

"Spoken like a true engineering professor," laughed Grandma sleepily.

"Hm," said Ari. "OK, one more point, because it's getting late and I think my audience is getting tired."

"No, we're not!" countered Lara. Jenny shook her head in agreement.

Ari smiled at their enthusiasm. "Good. So, here's where Lost Arrow's team came in, with their phase transitions and F2 and F3 phases. You know what a phase is, right? Gas, liquid, solid, melting, freezing, evaporating, condensing, right?" They nodded. "What makes one phase turn into another phase—go through a phase transition—is increasing or decreasing the heat in a material system—all the homogeneous atoms or molecules interacting with each other—that's changing the enthalpy, the total energy in a thermodynamic system, delta H." He took a deep breath and went on. "Around key phase transition temperatures for a given pressure, you increase the energy slightly through heating and—bang!—a liquid becomes a gas, for example. Or you remove energy by cooling and

148

suddenly, like, at zero Celsius, water becomes ice." He looked around, gesturing. "And you all know that water and ice are two very different things. There's no gradual continuum from one to the other. No in-between. It's abrupt. Either-or. That's a phase transition. The structure and behavior of the material utterly changes. That's nature."

Lara shivered in the night air, drawing her shawl more tightly around her slender shoulders, but her attention remained rapt.

"The genius of Lost Arrow and his team at, um, I think they were at MIT at that point, was to take all the math and physics notation—all the concepts—and apply it to society. Society as a material substance! As a system of elements and structures, of phases. They modeled societies. Big structural changes. The industrial revolution. Empires. Economic eras. Dynasties. Levels of government and power structures. And they found that energy—enthalpy—EROEI—explained a great deal. Society as a substance with its own sorts of phases, different from physical materials, more complex, more subtle, many more phase transitions. But following certain regular laws, and more or less predictable, regardless of how much people believed that technology would save them, or how ambitious they were, or how much power they thought they had, or how many people or lands they conquered. We've seen energy draining away from our society for decades now. Everyone has struggled to keep things the same, and to offset the draining-away—the dropping EROEI—by working harder and coming up with more efficient vehicles and planting more energy crops and nationalizing fossil fuels. But, well, it's like what Doug said. Look around, and all we've managed to do is forestall the phase transition a little longer. Our complex institutions are leftovers from a time when EROEI was much greater than it is today. They're overdue for a phase transition."

"But what *IS* the phase transition, Daddy!?" burst out Lara, fascinated and impatient. "What is it?" Jenny giggled at Lara's insistence.

"Yeah, Daniels. Get to the goddamned point!" laughed Doug Orman.

"It could be a lot of things, many things..." said Ari owlishly, looking into the center of the porch.

"No!" laughed Lara. "Why did *Lost Arrow* write to Florence? What phase transition is he thinking about now? Why she should leave Washington?" Lara had no more tolerance for academic meandering.

Ari caught himself, and laughed grimly. "The end of the United States. The end of the First Republic." They hung on his words, silent. "Lost

149

Arrow's simulations have been saying for years that a certain point in the decline of EROEI would be reached where the US Federal government abruptly ceases to function—massive system collapse—despite many people's efforts to keep it all together, with HUGE investments at stake in its survival—because it simply cannot continue functioning from a thermodynamic standpoint. The same thing happened to the Soviet Union." He looked at Celia and Nate. "Ever heard of that?" Celia shook her head. "Huge empire. Massive embodied energy, massive inefficiency. Then, poof. Gone. Even though they had lots of fossil fuels. There was a little violence, and a lot of adjustment all over the world as people and countries got used to the phase transition. But it was surprisingly quiet and quick." He frowned. "But Lost Arrow doesn't think that will be the case here. Too many weapons, too many latent internal migrants, too much dislocation and poverty, and too much real power in the hands of those with the most to lose. The structure will drop down from a federal system to regional confederations of states—Lost Arrow tells us it's already underway—but the old Soviet Union had plenty of food, not much climate change yet, and other factors that look mild compared to where we are."

"Is the Aztlán uprising a sign of the phase transition?" asked Nate.

Ari shrugged. "Maybe. It has been going on a long time. It's certainly there to step in if US federal authority in those states—New Mexico, Arizona, Colorado - fades away." He nodded. "That one sort of reminds me of the Roman Empire, which they also researched..."

"Daddy, forget the Roman Empire for a second," urged Lara with a smile. Others laughed. "Why does the federal government have to fall apart? I mean, it's what holds America together. Um, national defense and things... Why can't it just dissolve the Energy Trust, become more open, support renewables more, like it once did...?" She appealed to the whole group. "That sort of thing?"

Grandma sighed and opened her eyes. "Progressives have been trying to do that for many years, honey. But the oligarchs and their groups control the Energy Trust, which in turn relies on federal government dependency upon it to maintain its own control." She chuckled. "Did that make sense? Anyway, there were times in the past when the people were more powerful, and when sensible government policy was possible, but that all changed when the middle class died. The federal government didn't need the middle class anymore after that. Not for taxes, not for staff, not for political support. Not even for soldiers."

"No more of-the-People, by-the-People, for-the-People," snorted Doug Orman.

"But now, because it has all the energy, the federal government can just go on forever, right?" Nate was struggling to understand.

"That's not what the phase transition theory says," said Ari. "Lost Arrow's saying that the continent-wide federal government and all the departments, agencies, institutions, and habits it's based on will simply run out of gas, so to speak, because the energy needed to keep them running—the staffs, the offices, the transportation networks and vehicles, the Interstate Highways Command, the Energy Trust, all of it—will just hit a point where it takes more energy to keep it all together than the fossil fuel complex produces."

"They should have switched to renewables a long time ago," sighed Jenny.

"No kidding!" said Ari. "Exactly!" He smiled, but then frowned. "But remember that EROEI is quite low for all renewables—most of them come down to solar energy, in the end—so society would have had to undergo a huge transition—a phase transition—in all aspects of life in order to shed embodied energy and live successfully in a new phase." He looked around. "And in a way, most of us have. That's why the middle class disappeared, and why we all live like farmers, tinkers, and day-laborers now." He winked at Celia. "And house mothers and house girls."

Celia twisted her lip and smiled faintly.

"And so what's left has to fall apart before we can go on," said Lara sadly.

"At the federal level, yes," said Ari.

"But," came Grandma's quiet voice from her corner of the porch, "there are many states that have made the transition more successfully. Maryann tells me very encouraging things about the situation in Vermont and Massachusetts. You just don't see it in the DC area because the federal government's so dominant here."

"That's right," said Ari. "You actually do see this in Virginia, in fact. State and local government are less complex, closer to the local level, more face-to-face. Distances are shorter. The problems are less diverse.

Departments are smaller. People know each other. Maybe less corrupt in some places..."

"And," said Daryl (who had returned with a plate of chicken and beans) with dawning understanding, "they are not totally committed to propping up and being propped up by the Energy Trust."

"Bingo," said Ari. "That just postpones the inevitable. Past White House administrations and the Republicans today saw it—see it - as a survival strategy. Well, it's not. It's looking more and more like a suicide strategy."

"It's worse," said Doug Orman in disgust, topping up his scotch. "It's been an ongoing death spiral for years. The black heart of what's left of twentieth-century capitalism—rich, powerful, corrupt, bunkered down— first sacrificed America's position in the world to hang on to their influence, then America's middle class, then any remaining social conscience, then the Bill of Rights and one of the greatest democracies the world has seen... then, relations with Canada." He knocked back a gulp. "Now, they're going to take down the first American republic. They are that short-sighted and self-centered. Shit." He wiped his forehead with a handkerchief. "Won't be the first time that a power elite ate itself rather than yield power."

"But who are they going to give up power to," asked Ari rhetorically. "Ultimately, if they lose control, who steps in?" He opened his hands and looked around, and answered his question right before Doug Orman could respond to the opening. "I'll tell you who. Either the states, or foreign powers. And that's going to depend on where we're talking about."

"That's what I'm worried about," muttered Orman.

"There are a lot of pretty well-armed people who aren't going to let that happen without a fight," said Daryl gloomily. "I know them, and I've seen their weapons."

"That horrid Front," said Lara.

"And all the militias," added Jenny.

"Daryl," said Ari. "I know they gave you a scare, and they have some scary weapons, it's true, but if the federal level doesn't have the power to hold things together—the regular army, the national guard, the SIF, the Interstate Command, the Corps of Engineers—then do you *really* think that a bunch of local irregulars can do it? They barely have enough diesel to get over to the next county, and they don't know anyone there. There's no unified communication and control system. That's what would be lost if the phase transition leads to broad defederalization."

"Mm hm," followed Lara. "I see. If they want to work for anyone, it will have to be the states."

"For better or worse," added Ari. "And that won't necessarily be better. Just different."

"There are plenty of governors and state legislatures I'd trust about as far as I can spit," laughed Doug Orman.

"What if all this is wrong? Just theories?" asked Jenny in a small voice.

"Yeah," shrugged Daryl wearily. "I'll believe all this when I see it. Until then, I'm betting on the USA and all the guys with the guns who are willing to stand up for it."

"Honey," replied Grandma with a yawn, ignoring Daryl and directing her words at Jenny. "I'm afraid it makes too much sense to me, and it's a process that's been at work for a long time, with lots of missed opportunities along the way, and it's just going to have to run its course."

Ari stood up. "Sometimes things have to fall apart in order for a true renewal to take place." His tone was grave and thoughtful. "I just hope things stay civilized, and that we can stay ahead of this wave." He stretched and gave Grandma his hand as she prepared to stand up. "See you all in the morning."

Grandma stood up with a grunt, and smoothed her skirt. "There is still one thing I just don't like about this whole way of seeing things. Never have."

Everyone paused to listen.

"It's so mechanical and predetermined. As if human society were some sort of energy system that just goes up and down based on how easy it is to get energy. Like some sort of fluid. It seems so, well, disappointing. What about honor, and destiny, and refined cultures, and … and progress?" She sighed. "I always liked to think they were safe from the engineers."

"I think a society can still have those things. Think about all the culture from much simpler phases in human history," said Ari.

Grandma laughed. "I suppose you're right."

And most of them went off to bed.

17—DYSFUNCTION AND INJUNCTION

Thursday, November 1st (late at night)

"Steve, we're in recess now." It was Wilder. Steve Johnson patched Wilder over to one of the wallscreens they had unrolled and taped up on the suite's wall.

"I know, boss. We have a C-SPAN feed on the other wall."

"Good. I didn't know if you'd been able to fix that yet." He nodded with relif. "Glad you thought to bring those from the office, when you had th chance." As Rhiannon approached, the evacuation had been abrupt, and no one had expected to reconvene in Philadelphia. Now, the Capitol Police were not letting anyone near Capitol Hill, if you could even get into the city.

Steve nodded. He gave a high sign at Lola across the room. "Um, Jake, can you put on a mike, or just speak a little louder?" They could barely hear Wilder's naturally soft voice over the din in the hall around him.

"I'll speak up," said Wilder more loudly. "This place is a zoo."

Jake Wilder was standing in the middle of the vast floor of the Grand Hall of the National Constitution Center, a short walk from Philadelphia's Independence and Congress Halls. Four hundred and forty-one seats and desks had been hastily assembled to reproduce the floor plan of the House of Representatives' chamber of the US Capitol building in Washington, centering on a podium and raised seats for Speaker Laugherty, the Clerk of the House, the Sergeant at Arms, and the other officers.

It was nearly midnight. The evening before had all been formalities, but it had been business since this morning. The hall was packed. Congresspersons and myriad others streamed and swirled around the crescent of polished oak desks. After Laugherty precipitously announced that the House would be temporarily reassembled in Philadelphia (with the Senate hopefully following suit), congressional managers quickly discovered many difficulties with the venue, from the fact that there was no spectators' gallery to problems with limited bandwidth, parking, air conditioning, and accommodation for the media and the representatives' own staffs. But Laugherty knew how to stage political drama. Philadelphia's Independence Hall was not only the site of the First and Second Continental Congresses, during the American Revolution; both the Declaration of Independence and the US Constitution had been drafted, debated, and signed there. Congress Hall, next door to Independence Hall, was where the US Congress met from 1790 until 1800, as they awaited the construction of Washington, DC. If crisis actions were to be taken in dire times, and the role of the Speaker and his House to appear solidly legitimate to the American People, there was no better location than Independence Mall in Philly! Neither of the venerable old buildings had the seating capacity needed, so the seldom-used NCC had been drafted instead.

"I can't believe there hasn't been a substantive vote yet," said Moriah Oglethorpe, rubbing her eyes. She was standing with Wilder in the Grand Hall. "This has been going on too long."

There had been a long string of procedural votes as various factions jockeyed for advantage and the Democrats and marginal parties fought to defend ground they were about to lose. A fistfight had broken out around ten o'clock as nerves frayed, and representatives from Illinois and Indiana were asked to temporarily leave the hall. Prominent Republican and Front politicians had given one resounding speech after another about national pride, sovereignty, the powers of the Congress, and foreign duplicity.

"And all this," said Lola in disgust, "while there's a food riot this evening in Wilmington and people are shot and killed." She was sitting cross-legged on one of the beds, facing Wilder's magnified image on the wallscreen.

"There was a food riot right over in Camden earlier, Lola," said Linda Shatner quietly. "And Baltimore."

"'K," said Wilder. "Good cue, Lola." He looked at his watch. "Recess ends in about ten minutes. Let's do a status briefing now." He turned to Moriah. "You go first."

Moriah was used to doing this. She ran quickly through the scheduled votes. First, there would be the motion of censure against President Morales for having authorized the foreign relief mission without seeking

155

the approval of Congress. Next was Laugherty's vote to seek an injunction from the Supreme Court enjoining the President from allowing the relief mission to proceed. Neither of these needed similar action by the Senate. After that was another Democratic appropriations bill to authorize emergency money for storm relief and recovery. Wilder was a co-sponsor. This was not expected to pass the House, unless the Democrats agreed to attach a rider finding equivalent savings in other programs that could be cut. They were unanimous in their adamant opposition to this.

"We'll be up all night," muttered Lola, shaking her head sadly. "This has already been a long day." The others looked grimly determined to stick it out.

The sharp rapping of the Speaker's gavel cut suddenly through the babble. The recess was at an end. The noise level dropped, and representatives flowed back toward their seats. Wilder waved at his staff in the hotel suite and sat down at his desk. Moriah walked back to the narrow gallery that had been erected across the rear of the room on raised decking, where she could lean against the railings. From up there, she could see out across the now-federalized Independence Mall, where a massive security cordon had been placed around the NCC. Bright lights on mobile towers cast a stark illumination across barricades, vehicles, and a sea of helmeted riot police. Drones hovered in strategic locations.

Laugherty spoke, indicating that the Clerk of the House would begin with some important news. The Clerk, Helena Rodriguez, walked to the podium with small, quick steps. She spoke in a high-pitched, rushed voice. Representatives and spectators strained to hear. Groans and muttering could be heard as the meaning of her words became clear. Earlier that evening, it appeared, a secret EU Special Forces team had been apprehended outside New York City, in Montclair, New Jersey, operating on the territory of the United States without authorization. They were in jail in Newark. The FBI had suggested that they were studying transportation routes into New York City through the Hudson River tunnels. Ambassadors had been summoned. A presidential complaint was encouraged. "A military incursion," yelled one of the younger Front representatives. "The tip of the iceberg," yelled another. "They're planning their invasion!"

The Speaker's gavel could be heard again, as he pounded it to silence the angry outbursts. They would, he reminded them, be proceeding with the agenda. Heated debate began on the question of censure.

* * *

In the gallery, Moriah leaned back against a railing and took in the scene. Wilder was barely visible, the top of his head appearing occasionally. But her voice was in his ear as they conferred on developments by the minute. Also in their ears was the staff back at the hall. Other Congressional staffers stood with her on the improvised decking, along with media reps and other guests.

Moriah was suddenly aware of a presence to her left. She glanced over, and found to her annoyance that, even as she registered that it was an attractive, stylishly dressed young woman, her own hands were already patting and smoothing the front and sides of her suit and dress—an unconscious habit when confronted by younger women who made her feel frumpy. Which she was not, of course! No one ever said that. But here was this girl. Moriah tutted under her breath and stopped her hands. She stole another sideways glance at her. The girl was very expensively attired. Diamonds hung from her ears and twinkled against her nose. A platinum choker adorned her slender neck. Some oligarch's wife or daughter, perhaps. Not a staffer, certainly. There was something about her that Moriah recalled or was struck by. Some confidence or air of insight. She was just deciding that it wasn't worth spending more time on when the girl turned her head slightly toward Moriah. Their eyes met. The girl smiled for an instant, and then turned back toward the hall. There was nothing polite or reserved about her, nothing patrician. The girl's eyes sparkled with excitement, ambition, hunger. She seemed to have a stake in the outcome of this assembly. Moriah was left with the impression of a fan at a sports championship.

* * *

"Hey, uh, you catching this?" Lola Osmanian waved across Steve Johnson's line of sight, and gestured over at one of the T-pads that lay on

157

the desk. It was cycling through local news and weather channels, in and out of 2D and 3D. "Something big's going on in Center City."

They waved the feed over onto the second wallscreen, overlaying a second Congressional channel. Others in the room glanced over, wondering what she was referring to.

"That stuff over at City Hall is a full-blown riot," breathed Lola, whistling. The House motion was temporarily forgotten. Others walked over to the wallscreen. In vivid ultra-high def, they saw how the areas around Penn Square and Dilworth Plaza, and the side streets in all directions, were jammed with rapidly moving crowds. There were phalanxes of riot police—few in number relative to the protestors—and the smoke of teargas blowing across the crowds. They zoomed in on the protesters, mingling through them in 3Depth for the length of a block. They were mostly ragged, agitated, and male.

"Oh, they do *not* want to be doing this," breathed one of the Rosen staffers, fascinated. "The Philadelphia Six got death row, and that was nothing compared to this."

"This looks like the old videos of the Occupy movement," said Selena with nervous excitement. "Or the 1960s."

"We know where *those* went," sniffed Lola.

"Was anyone following this today? Where did this come from?" Linda Shatner was asking.

"Honey, are you kidding?" laughed Lola ironically. "Our staff alone's got more than a thousand HCE's following news and opinion, but who the hell can make sense of *anything* anymore!?"

"What are they protesting?" asked Moriah from the NCC. "Still about government inaction?"

Doug Dupre had a VRI set on, and was sitting raptly as he steered his engines through a multitude of searches and queries. "Yeah..." he muttered as he worked. "Lot of stuff... Food, want more routes opened up for travel, but it's political too..."

"Do we know this guy?" Steve Johnson waved a pane onto the second wallscreen. "Sash LeTourneau?" A diverse in stylish, rumpled andrometro clothes was seen flanked by KP-toting riot police as he was hustled from a crowd into a waiting van.

"Sure," said Moriah. "Princeton researcher. We've used his institute's stuff. Jake was just saying something about him."

158

"He was just arrested over in Camden for a national security violation," said Steve, studying his T-pad. "It says he's part of a group that called earlier today for the dissolution of the Energy Trust, a declaration of a national state of emergency, and a new American revolution to re-empower ordinary people..."

"Should have done that back when the One Hundred Oligarchs only owned three-quarters of the country," scoffed Lola.

"You're sounding like Bart Ross," reproached Linda Shatner at Lola's sarcasm. Lola laughed darkly and raised her eyebrows.

"There's more," said Steve. "He's been over in New Jersey in these huge refugee camps that have sprung up, giving speeches among the storm refugees and trying to organize them."

"Sounds like sedition... Speaking of which," said Doug, waving a new video pane onto the wallscreen. "Check this out!"

An unsteady aerial feed of lights and buildings swayed on the screen.

"What's that?" asked Steve, squinting. "Where is that?"

"That's the Benjamin Franklin Bridge, going over to Camden, just a little ways from here, few blocks, even closer to Independence Mall," answered Doug. All eyes turned to the pane showing the bridge, the House debate forgotten.

"What's going on?" asked Lola. They were all having trouble making sense of it.

"The police shut the bridge down," said Doug. "I don't know, maybe that's the National Guard. You can see all those people around the entrance to the bridge on the other side, trying to get over to Philly. But see what's going on down beside the bridge? On the right?" He pointed to an area on the New Jersey bank of the Delaware River, where there were clearly thousands of people gathered, and fires brightly burning.

"They're building something in the river!" exclaimed Linda in wonder.

As they watched the aerial video feed, movement was discernible, and the huge crowds seemed to be maneuvering small boats beside some sort of projection into the river, beside the large suspension bridge.

"They're building a pontoon bridge using boats and wood," said Doug. "This is incredible! They must be taking half of Camden apart to do this, with their bare hands!"

"The part of Camden that wasn't already taken apart," muttered Lola.

"This is awful!" cried Linda. "People are going to drown."

"The police are never going to let them get across anyway," said Steve grimly.

"Oh!" said Moriah from the NCC, noticing a sudden change in the larger, sent-to-back pane of activity around the City Hall. "Something's on fire!" In the Grand Hall, as the debate about the censure motion dragged on, and all doubts it would pass were erased, a small knot of people had gathered around Moriah, watching her T-pad intently. Something was indeed on fire near or in the City Hall building. More fire flared in a broad avenue beside it, appearing to set a vehicle alight.

Doug Dupre shifted his attention, reacting to Moriah's exclamation.

"Molotov cocktails," gasped Doug.

Linda Shatner had tears in her eyes, and was becoming agitated. "Oh my God. Unless this stops, a lot of people are going to get hurt."

"Morales federalized Philadelphia already, as a precaution," said Steve.

"Independence Mall," corrected Lola.

"No, the whole of Center City," said Steve. "Jake confirmed it earlier."

"How do we know it was her?" asked Lola.

"Who else can federalize a region?" asked Moriah, in disbelief. "Except the President?"

"Maybe it wasn't her," said Lola. "I can't imagine she would. Maybe she was somehow forced to."

"God knows," said Steve. "Who would force the President's hand on an authorization like this?"

"Well, if Philly's federalized," said Lola, "and the police can act accordingly, then a lot of people are in terrible danger unless they settle down and pull back!"

"What choice do they have left?" asked Moriah quietly from the Grand Hall. "They've lost their homes, everything they own. They lost their rights a long time ago. Now they are fighting for their lives."

The small knot of people around Moriah dissipated as attention returned to the floor debate, which had become more energetic. The diamond-clad young woman was nowhere to be seen.

18—MORE SIGNS OF TROUBLE

Friday, November 2nd (very early in the morning)

Jenny was quietly weeping. Honorée sat next to her on the wicker chaise, hugging her. Daryl sat beside them, his face blank, the T-pad in his hands dark.

"What's happened?" exclaimed Lara with dismay as she returned with several more mugs of tea.

"I'm just so, so sad for all those people," said Jenny with a wrenching sob. She rubbed her bicep across her teary eyes.

"She's sad about Philadelphia," said Honorée, her own eyes tearing up.

"What, about the censure and the injunction resolution?" asked Lara, her instinctive disbelief softened by rising concern. "I mean, that's bad and all, but ..."

"No, Lara," said Daryl bluntly. "There was a massacre."

"What?!" Lara staggered, hastily putting down the mugs before she spilled them.

"The fucking government..." Daryl's tone changed abruptly to rage—perhaps a delayed reaction to both his recent political disillusionment and his unit leader's betrayal—and he spoke in angry gasps. "The fucking government ... just executed hundreds and hundreds of people ... in Philadelphia ... for protesting because they want food, and they want rights, and they want their homes back!"

"Oh my god," said Lara, sitting down. "When?"

"Tonight," said Honorée. "We just saw the news."

"Can you imagine Morales authorizing this?!" asked Daryl. "When she's the one who wants the Chinese and the Europeans to come over here and give us emergency assistance?"

"They will never come now," said Honorée. "No government has the right to do that. They're making it look like a civil war."

161

"They used Hive," said Daryl, quieting down.

"No!" said Lara.

"Do you know what that is?" asked Daryl doubtfully.

"Um, I know it's a deadly mass-kill weapon," said Lara. "OK. No. What is it?"

Daryl looked at his hands. "Mike could tell you more, but it's thousands of tiny drones in a smart swarm that each target one person, ID them, and then shoot them in the head, all in seconds. They drop them from a plane. Go into buildings, into cars, into closets, up your clothes. Then they fly away. Like hornets. That's how the Coahuila revolt was put down." He drew a deep, shuddering yawn. "Never been used in the USA before."

"How many people?" Lara was aghast.

"Officially, or really?"

"Whatever."

"The news said between five hundred and a thousand. But, I mean, there were bodies everywhere, and falling into the river up there."

"I cannot believe that Lucia Morales would order that!" said Honorée. "It's crazy. It goes completely against what she's been saying! Even if someone calls the demonstrations in Philadelphia sedition. They didn't have to do that!"

"Maybe someone else hacked a Hive system—nest—and sent them in," mused Lara.

"Who knows? But now it's done," said Jenny, drying her eyes.

The four of them sat in silence on the porch, letting their thoughts settle, listening to the night sounds. It was well after midnight.

"I don't want to be the one who mentions this to Grandma," said Honorée finally.

"Or my dad," echoed Lara.

"I guess this is what Lost Arrow was talking about, you know, the powers that be going to more and more extremes to keep things they way they are, and them at the top," said Jenny.

Honorée looked slightly askance at her younger sister, for whom politics and ideology had never had much appeal. "Someone has to answer for this," she said, "whatever the reasons."

"Mm," answered Daryl skeptically. "We may never know."

162

A bright flash of lightning illuminated the porch and yard, followed by a rumble of thunder. The humidity had been rising all evening, foretelling a storm. November had just started, but it was still hot and humid enough for summer storms, albeit without the violent fury of June and July weather. Another flash lit the sky, with more thunder. Wind began to rush in the treetops. Soon, raindrops were falling in irregular pulses. Everyone pulled back from the screens, moving cushions and furniture away from the spray. They sat back down to watch the storm, thinking of bed but not yet ready for sleep. The tempest roared.

"Oh!" exclaimed Lara. There was a bright flash, and another. She heard the horses whinny from behind the brick house, where the stable was located. Another brilliant white flash of lightning flooded the compound as the rain started dying down, but then she sensed there was something wrong with the light, something wrong.

"Fire!" shouted Honorée. They all jumped up. Orange light flared up brightly from a corner of the property, behind a large shed that bordered the wooden stockade fence.

"Were we hit?!" Daryl was already running out through the screen door. The rain had diminished to nearly nothing. The fire was already as high as the upper branches of a tree just outside the fence, filling the yard with its vivid glow.

"Wake Fernando!" Grandma screamed from an upper window as she pulled up the sash. "Get Fernando!" Ari and the Burhans siblings were already rushing out of the house, hastily clothed. Lamplight emerged from Fernando's door as he came running out. "Save the buildings!" cried Grandma. "Don't let it leave the fence!"

Lara rushed to help Fernando drag long hoses from a shed and hook them up to a diesel pump. He set to starting the pump, yelling at her to connect one hose to a large rainwater cistern that stood on stout legs beside the barn. She struggled with the weight, but her mind was clearly focused on the objective after many such drills at the stables in Salem. The cock was clearly visible. She ran toward it, shoving the hose's connector into the cock's sleeve. Meanwhile, she heard the horses whinny again, and made a note to go reassure them after the hose was working.

In minutes, the fire appeared to be under control. It stayed on the upper part of the fence, charring an area of wood but not threatening the structure. Daryl climbed onto the roof of a tool shed so he could send the

163

water down the outside of the fence. The flames were gone now. Clouds of steam and smoke swirled around him. The cistern was mercifully full to the brim in the wake of Rhiannon and several thunder storms.

Fernando ran to the alley gate to get around to the outside of the fence so he could throw dirt on the fire and swat any remaining embers with a shovel. When he came to the gate, the hairs on his neck stood up and he stopped abruptly. The gate was open. He looked around wildly, but saw no one. Why was the gate open? He pulled it tight behind him, and ran to the section that had burned. He saw Daryl's head above the fence. The hose had been shut off. Puffs of steam rose from the charred wood. There were no flames or glowing coals. He scuffed dirt up with his shovel and tossed it against the lower part of the fence. In the darkness, he could see little, now that both the storm and the fire had subsided. All the street lamps were out due to the power outage. Honorée came running up behind him with a lantern.

"Thanks," he said, starting to recover from his sudden awakening only fifteen minutes before.

"What's that?" said Honorée, swinging the lantern toward the base of the fence.

They both looked. It was a metal can. Fernando picked it up. It was warm, open, and empty. It reeked of kerosene.

"Oh my lord!" he said. "*Santa María.*"

"It was set!" cried Honorée. "It was arson!"

They both looked around in the darkness, suddenly extremely nervous. "Let's get back into the compound," hissed Fernando, taking her arm. They both moved quickly back to the alley gate, which clicked open as it sensed their identities. They slid in, locking it securely, and met Lara face-to-face in the walkway behind the house. Lara was running.

"The horses. Two of 'em. They're gone!"

19—RETURN TO OLIA SUPERLA

Thursday - Friday, November 1st & 2nd
(from Thursday evening into the early hours of Friday)

It hadn't taken as long as Mike expected. In the cool, quiet, soundproofed interior of the V-tel, it was as if Hurricane Rhiannon had never happened. The storm's sweaty, dusty aftermath was far away, forgettable inside the sturdy old concrete walls. The building's solar power system and its reliance on satnet links lay beyond the reach of the storm.

This did not come without a price, however, he reflected with a mixture of exhilaration and guilt, as he removed his clothes and shoes, and prepared to settle into the stim/sim. Back in the Army, he had had to make do with the smelly but cheap V-tels around the bases—converted mobile homes and motels with unreliable power and loud air conditioners, dirt yards and whorehouses next door. This was a V-tel of a totally different character, catering to the affluent elite of a capital city. Of course, the really rich had their own VNET studios at home, and you could always make do in a private home with your crappy old I-balls, headsets, trode scanners, and bats, but for the drop-dead orgasmic sensuality of the VNET in all its splendor, there was nothing like a high-end V-tel, spiced with the right meds. Yes, it would cost plenty of milscrip, but what the hell? He had been looking forward to this for a long time—all those dusty days on the road contemplating the drab face of RL. The V-tel was fine wine, delectable, ecstasy deferred. He was a cowboy finally arrived in a town of substance, weary from the trail! Time to live like an asteroid miner on Earthleave!

Mike knew he was hooked. With a twinge of shame—quickly pushed away—he recalled that his onlining had been the main reason for his accelerated termination from the Corps. His record was clean, but the

165

health techs knew where he was headed, and the Army doesn't want Vtopians.

Online games had drawn him in as a kid. They had drawn in a lot of other guys, too, he reflected, with the emphasis on *guys*. That's the way it had always been. Back in the illusory order and stability of the Teens and early Twenties, the little kids had always hung out in front of somebody's Xbox or Wii, shooting and building. Teachers and coaches and parents were always chiding them, restricting their screen time, telling them about how, "when they were kids," they played outside in neighborhoods with other kids, built forts, read books. Mike and his online friends just laughed, and pulled all kinds of subterfuge to get online as much as they could, where the real action was: WOW, EVE, Call of Duty, Minecraft, League, Order of Battle, StarCraft. As they got older, some remained power-users while others gravitated toward more balance, or were forced into it by circumstances like abject poverty.

With the worlds of work and education as virtualized as they were, what was wrong with power-users, anyway? They had the best online skills, the sharpest instincts. Employers hardly needed to train them. They were cyberfluent from a young age.

Mike was an early power-user. He largely remembered college as one long Vtopian haze, although he had stuck with Rotsie—oh yeah, it paid his expenses!—and managed to graduate with a tech degree. Somehow, no one thought of him as an onliner, maybe because he had gone on to an Army Corps career after college instead of totally vegging out, but his heart of hearts belonged to Vtopia. Why bother with an RL girlfriend, for example, with all that Vtopia offered? There would always be time for real girls, *later on*. And there was a kind of buzz from balancing on the razor's edge between too-tame and total burnout. The onliners had fallen into the abyss. They were gone. Avatars with no spawn left in RL. But Mike had tasted honeydew and drunk the milk of Paradise, yet managed to stay sane. It was intense, this realization. Intense! He was a Master of Vtopia. He was old and wise enough to laugh at his own fantasies of immortality and invincibility, but, given the drab alternatives, he could not see what purpose abstinence would serve. Some guys he knew took that road. Boy Scouts. Good luck to them, he thought. With the way everything was going, the pleasure of Vtopia might be taken away at any minute anyway. *Un poco de alivio*, the onliners said. A little relief. And they were right. So he spent all the time he could in Vtopia, and didn't worry about it when he couldn't. He'd be back if his luck held.

Securely in the stim/sim, he retrieved the two inhaler vials from the small table at the limit of his reach and huffed them in quick succession. They were big doses, rushy. Mike grinned and shook his head. In seconds, he could already feel his perception of reality shifting. He quickly pulled on the helmet and gloves and willed his way through the V-tel's start-up screen into the lobby of its spawnport. With a deep breath and an involuntary shudder of anticipation, he hung in space a few feet above the deck, looking around, taking in the sights and sounds, stretching his virtual fingers and limbs to adjust and orient. It was moderately busy. Avatars of every imaginable kind moved within his field of vision, nearby and far-off. Thousands. A hologram shimmered ahead of him: "You are now leaving Bethesda/RL." By all the tiers and decks, rising level-upon-level into the deep blue sky, he could tell that this V-tel shared the spawnport with many others. Maybe they were a chain. It didn't matter. He could get back. He had the landmark. Time to fly.

Mike's HUD dropped down, listing messages and past locations and friends. He had not been online in days but it felt like weeks. He flicked his status to "busy," to keep things sane until he had a chance to talk. He first needed to get to Olia. Retainers and officials had been messaging him for weeks about troubles and factions and tensions, and he had been keeping track but had not had the chance to go see for himself. Now he could. There were several ways to get there. He could teleport, which would be instant. But it had been long enough that he felt he should get back his cyber-senses before diving into Olian life, so he started flying at high speed toward the nearest stargate, which his VPS indicated was not far outside the spawnport. He rocketed up from the deck toward a vast arch that led outside, adjusting the music feed to something nice for the journey.

The warm wind whistled. Passing rapidly under the arch, he zipped out into the sunlight of a wide mountain landscape, luscious with forests and sparkling rivers. A yellow sun was near its zenith, a smaller red binary companion beside it. Avatars and interesting aircraft and spacecraft flew in streams above him, following airtracks. He slipped into autopilot, letting it carry him to the gate. As the stargate yawned before him, he felt his velocity slowing. There was a queue. He relaxed and waited. All around him was vivid color, light, fresh air, open space. He watched an immense starship, recently arrived through the stargate, landing on a terrace below a distant mountain pinnacle. Mike did not recognize its design, and idly wondered whether he should. He increased his magnification, inspecting its insignia. He did not recognize the characters. His translator indicated a confederation he had never heard of. Mike laughed. Such was Vtopia. There was always something new. Some things stayed the same, but there was so much growth and novelty, so many surprises. Identities, relationships, power balances, buildings, cities, and whole landscapes and planets came and went with blinding speed. This was the playground of the mind, the garden of the imagination. Nothing was held back by the shabby constraints of RL. Indeed, Mike admitted, the thought of returning to Vtopia was about the only thing that kept him going out in the real world.

Mike's turn at the stargate came quickly. Its capacity was substantial. The gate was suspended between enormous towers perhaps a kilometer apart. Its aperture must have measured 500 meters across. Only the biggest ships could not pass through, but then, most had their own starwarp propulsion and did not need stargates. He felt his body accelerating into the gate. Craft and avatars ahead of him flashed and were gone. Then, with a whirl of light and the tinkle of his cash icon recording the toll, he was snatched from the sunny valley and instantly ejected from a very different stargate orbiting a luminous white and blue planet. It was Olia. Mike heard himself laughing with delight. Ah, Olia Superla, palace planet of the Lyra Asterism, roughly equivalent to what astronomers called Kepler-9d in RL. Its sunlike star, Kepler-9, hung vast and yellow behind him, illuminating the stargate, the planet's dayside, and a variety of craft within Mike's field of view.

Scanning his inventory, Mike picked a sufficiently stylish ship for his arrival, a slim corvette, and rezzed it in space below him. He popped into its bridge cabin, and then called ahead for a landing slot. A bot's voice confirmed the slot. He had about five minutes. That would give him time to check messages and pay some calls. He waved away the "busy" status. In seconds, a call came it. It was Chera. His elegant, tanned face appeared on the cabin's wallscreen.

"Propul Daat!" Chera's tone was formal, friendly yet faintly reproachful. "Welcome home."

"Propul Chera," laughed Mike, "what a pleasure to see you just as I arrive."

"I will come down to the port to meet you," Chera replied. "I'm sure you've seen the messages, but things are tense, and you are returning not a minute too soon."

"Busy, very busy in RL," said Mike, shaking his head in exasperation. "Had important things to sort out. Too much to go into." It was strictly against taboo to reveal any details of real life, and Mike did not plan to, but Chera needed to know that his absence was not fully voluntary. Weak commitment could jeopardize Mike's position in the Asterism—a position he had painstakingly built up over years—but everyone had to vanish from time to time to deal with unavoidable affairs in RL. Even diligent Chera took leave from time to time, though Mike knew nothing about the human behind his avatar.

"Modium is restless, refusing to pay tribute," said Chera. Chera was vice chancellor of Olia's treasury. "This started about a month ago, right around the time you left." Modium was a planet of Kepler-33—a prosperous, vigorous community of builders and engineers.

"Well, they have a credit, don't they?" asked Mike. "What is the rush?"

"They don't anymore," replied Chera flatly. "Her Succulence declared a levy that zeroed all the credits."

"For what?!" exclaimed Mike. He glanced away from the screen for an instant and saw that the corvette was starting the parabolic phase of its descent toward the planet's surface.

"For defense." Chera's face revealed little, but he raised one eyebrow to signal his own doubt.

"I won't even ask who we need to defend ourselves from," sighed Mike, "but what will they do if she tries to enforce this?"

"They are talking about moving."

"Moving?" Mike shook his head. "Where?"

"Some other asterism," said Chera. "Someplace where they feel more appreciated."

"Her Succulence has to accept her limits," said Mike. "Lyra would lose a lot if Modium defected." They had been the main source of Olia's scripts, textures, and weapons for years. "Has she offered to parlay?"

Chera's face stayed deadpan, saying no word, but volumes through his eyes.

169

"And the Supreme Council?" The corvette began vibrating gently as it hit the friction of the upper atmosphere. Heat shields slid down over the bridge windshield and side ports.

More animated in his expression, Chera nodded. "Oh yes. A lot of discussion. Of course, many of them have personal contacts, like Lemmet and Antal Shet. They've been over to Modium several times to buy time and smooth things over..."

"And?" Mike found himself bracing instinctively as the vibration grew.

"And, well, it's the usual self-interest." Chera spread his hands, symbolically distancing himself from such base motives. Antal Shet of course wants to be the next Copulatrix, when the reign of Her Succulence eventually ends."

Mike raised his eyebrows and wrinkled his mouth. "That may be a long time yet."

"Yes," Chera nodded. "So, Shendaal, as usual, wants to be the peacemaker and the arbitrator."

"What a shallow, predictable game," commented Mike. "Always plays the nice guy—everyone's friend—but there's always a hidden agenda."

Chera nodded again. He turned away from his cam, raising his eyes toward an implied window. "I think I can see you now."

Mike noted the deceleration as the heat shields slid back down into the fuselage. He beheld a vast vista of puffy white clouds, with darkened patches of urban and forest terrain glimpsed below. The corvette was leveling out and starting a wide bank to the left.

"I'll come down to meet you," confirmed Chera. "What a pleasure and relief to have you back among your people!"

Mike smiled and nodded with restrained enthusiasm. "Propul! We can continue after I arrive."

"Yes!" The screen clicked off, and Mike stood up, smoothing his tunic and stretching luxuriantly. There was hardly any sense of motion, although the ship had perhaps another thousand meters to descend. It was below the cloud deck now. He glanced around through the wide windshield of the corvette, his hands on the rail, studying the details of the Capital City. The protected Old City, perched on hills surrounding the harbor, looked unchanged. It had been there for more than twenty years, well before Mike came to Olia. He could see its white buildings and winding roads and passages, modeled after Greek island towns.

From the waterfront, the Sea of Languor stretched to the eastern horizon, sparkling in the afternoon sun, which hung huge in the sky because of Olia's very short orbital radius. Its waves were dotted with boats and small, sandy islands. Mike's own villa was located on one such atoll. North, south, and west of the Capital was a diverse patchwork of forests, lakes, and ever-changing sandboxes. In the distance to the north was a vague impression of snowy mountains.

Olia Superla was like many VNET planets, dimensioned to a realistic scale, but with its populations concentrated in a few large cities, since there was no need to produce food, energy, or other resources in the large expanses of a real planet, and since, in Vtopia, there was no shortage of land: as the population grew, new servers were brought online, and new asterisms were conjured into existence with the wave of a bat or neurogesture. The diameters of planets could even be simply expanded, creating more surface. There was always an easy solution to overcrowding. But avatars liked to be close to each other.

Mike had traveled less in Vtopia than many. He had been a young teen when the hypergrid bridges had been fully worked out. Of course, like all of his generation, he had wandered around with turbulent factions and bands of warriors, raided and griefed and trolled and hacked, flown all kinds of craft, built and tunneled, and hung out in the vast variety of clubs and casinos scattered across the metaverse. But then, in pursuit of a girl he was smitten by, he had bonded deeply with a Gorean RP sim he'd nearly forgotten the name of, and tasted VNET social life and responsibilities. It was an idyllic and innocent phase. He was consumed. The girl—a fugitive kajira - left him, but there were others, and he partied in a garden of unearthly delights.

Then, a shopping trip for weapons systems took him to Olia. The level of social development and architectural beauty of Olia was beyond anything he had ever experienced in Vtopia. He also happened to visit when leptopixel technology was starting to appear, and Olia's owners, being tech-savvy, had already implemented it. He was charmed and impressed by the fine details, rich colors, and realistic physics. He was also charmed by its sensuality, and by a series of ladies-in-waiting associated with the Court of the Love Queen, Her Succulence, Annamaris, the Seventh Copulatrix of Olia Superla. So he moved to Olia, and gave up his former sim without a regret. Mike was still in high school at the time. For his fidelity, good sense, and popularity in the court, he was rapidly accepted into Olian society, assuming a succession of more important roles in the military and government as the years passed. He had barely traveled outside of the Lyra Asterism in the time since (which in itself had hundreds of habitable worlds, including a whole complex of earth-like planets orbiting Vega).

Mike's corvette touched down in the center of the Great Plaza, opposite the ceremonial gates of the palace complex, and Mike snapped out of his brief reverie. The engines powered down, and the gangway dropped smoothly from its belly. He saw passers-by gathering to watch him emerge from the ship, and a bot orchestra started playing a rousing reception—a detail probably ordered by Chera. Mike glanced involuntarily around the bridge to see if there was anything he needed to take with him (such a silly habit from RL) and then quickly descended the steps to the gangway. Walking out into the sunshine to smiles and music, he was greeted by Chera with a smart salute. Mike gestured mentally at his HUD and the ship behind him vanished into his inventory.

They flew together up to the veranda of Chera's office, overlooking the Palace, and took seats. Chera was all hasty business, the matter of Modium among the impending crises weighing on his mind.

"The Supreme Council does not meet until Kai-Baal," said Chera.

Mike recalled with an instant's hesitation that that meant Sunday. "That's in two days," he said. "Today's Mok-Baal."

Chera nodded. "But I have requested an audience with Her Succulence as soon as possible."

It was Mike's turn to nod, fighting a feeling of slight fluster and imbalance. "Indeed," he said, trying to sound wise and patient. Really, though, he thought with some frustration, he had been looking forward to his return to Olia as a vacation and a refuge, and it was with some dismay that he felt the urgency of his complex Olian responsibilities closing in upon him already!

"We have much work to do before then—though we don't know yet when the audience will be—and I've drawn up a list of all the Council members and others we'll need to speak with, in advance…"

"I'm sorry," said Mike with distraction, interrupting. "Before when? The Council meeting or the audience?"

172

Chera regarded him skeptically, his face rendered bronze in the late-afternoon sunshine. "The Council meeting, of course." He paused, looking down. "We don't know when the audience will be, of course." He glanced back at Mike. "It could be any minute, at the pleasure of Her Succulence. We must be ready... We must be, ah, *here*."

Mike gave a curt nod, and sat, waiting to hear more.

"Dear Daat," said Chera, changing his tone. "I need you with me on this. This could become a very serious situation if we don't head it off. Do you remember the coup attempt during the Porovalza War?"

Mike remembered it very well. He had hardly slept for a week, and nearly been dishonorably discharged from the Corp of Engineers back in RL.

"That cost Olia a fortune, and we almost lost control of Lyra. But you, I, and, well, really, the whole cabinet were able to stay together and put in the time required to pull Olia back from the brink!" Chera looked at Mike appraisingly. "This sort of effort may be required again."

"Mm," muttered Mike.

"I should ask you, dear Daat, do you know how infrequent and how short your times away from Olia will be in the coming time, now that you have returned home? It would help me to know. For scheduling." He smiled disarmingly.

Chera is worried about my commitment, thought Mike. This is not good.

"Ah, it's hard for me to say right now," replied Mike, thinking disjointedly about his wagon trip of the previous two weeks, about the hurricane, about the uncertainty in Chevy Chase. "It may be hard..."

Chera wrinkled his brow, eyes averted. "So perhaps it is too soon to say that you have returned... To be able to count on you." Chera said this without accusation—he was a pragmatist—but Mike heard his disappointment, or was it merely caution?

"Um, yes, maybe we should let things develop for a few days." Then, impulsively, Mike continued. "I'm in a V-TEL—pretty expensive one—so access is gonna be an issue, and there's been this hurricane and a lot of uncertainty-." He abruptly stopped. Chera's face was a blank, as if he had not heard. "Oh, I am *so* sorry!" Mike had been on the edge of violating that greatest of Vtopian taboos: making excuses (or, worse, complaining) about RL. He bit his tongue.

Chera stood up. "Welcome home," he said, smiling in a slightly deprecating manner. "You have only just arrived. I'm glad we could check in," pronouncing *check* with a hint of sarcasm. "I will inform you about the audience as soon as I hear anything." He cocked his head. "Will you be leaving Olia again now, or returning to your villa?"

"Oh, staying, of course," replied Mike quickly, with a guilty laugh. He waved over the balustrade toward the sea. "I'll be at home." He mustered a relaxed, sincere tone. "I have much catching up to do, and will get back to you as soon as you give me the signal."

"Good. Excellent!" Chera exclaimed. "I hope the wait isn't long." Chera was subtle. The whole damn Olian culture was subtle. 'High-context,' Chera had once called it. It had once felt mysterious and exotic to Mike. Worthwhile. Now he was, what, a little weary of it?

Mike stood up. They both bowed. Then, with a flourish, Mike leapt high into the air and, waving back down at Chera, flew in a wide arc over the Palace, waterfront neighborhoods, and beach, continuing—over the blue, tropical water now—toward the rocky silhouettes of an archipelago on the horizon where his villa lay, a cluster of residential islands named Kalliopea.

Instead of flying straight to his house, located on the largest island of Eufoni, he aimed for the causeway that linked Eufoni with Symfoni and Harmoni. Stretching from the causeway to Eufoni's shore was a broad pier. He landed right where the two joined. Surrounded by the tranquil sea, he started walking toward Eufoni's shore, several hundred meters away. Ahead of him lay the Promenade, the formal park and gardens that lined the waterfront. It was here that couples often walked, and where concerts and dances took place in the pink stone amphitheater embedded in the cliffs. Not far from the amphitheater lay the shady walks and groves of the island's love garden. Mike took a deep breath, enjoying the deepening evening light. Lights twinkled on the islands, hidden among the lush vegetation. There were phosphorescent anibots swimming in the water, and fireflies in the air. Along the Promenade's avenue of stately palms, discrete street lamps were starting to glow. He heard crickets and geckos in the calm air, and somewhere off in the trees he heard girls laughing and bars of piano music.

After busy days in the Capital, and especially after longer absences from Olia, Mike liked to arrive home this way. He liked the gradual reunion, chance meetings with people he knew, and the rich sensual experience of Eufoni's aesthetic cyber-ecology. Olia had strict codes, which Mike had appreciated from the beginning. It created a harmonious, credible natural and cultural appearance. In the gardens of the Promenade, the species and textures were what one would expect on a tropical island. The surroundings were believable, without the usual debris of everything from dinosaurs, misplaced vehicles, billboards, and fun-fair rides to the odd mish-mash of architecture one tended to find in other less-stringent regions of Vtopia.

Mike found himself comparing his return to Eufoni with his first stroll through Chevy Chase only an hour before. He almost staggered at the contrast. The streets and front yards of Chevy Chase were coarse with dust, dry scraps of late-fall vegetation, wind-fallen branches and twigs, horse manure, and trash. Ubiquitous rust-streaked shipping containers were employed here and there as walls and roadblocks. The air smelled of smoke and sawn wood. He did not see a person he knew. Here, in Eufoni, all was clean and pure. Perfect. There was no dust or debris. Residents sat on benches or sauntered along the walkway, nodding at him, or flashing smiles—some shy, some polite, some sultry. In place of an atmosphere of disarray and decline, there was order and beauty. And you could always select a great sound track. It was no surprise how many people preferred to spend more time in Vtopia than they did in RL.

Turning off of the Promenade, Mike headed away from the shore, into the interior. The path was lined with elegant, identical waist-high stone lanterns. He walked past gates leading off into dark gardens, past trellis arches, past tiny boutiques and cafés. The path angled upward, gaining elevation. Peering up through the dark trees, he watched the first stars beginning to twinkle in the deep lavender sky among Olia's necklace of moons, and, lowering his gaze slightly, he saw soft yellow lights glowing in the distant windows of chalets high up among Eufoni's central peaks.

A few more steps, and he was at his own gate. It was all lit up, prepared for his return. He walked under the bamboo arch and into the garden, the laser-red gridlines of the security perimeter shimmering momentarily in the air as he passed through.

"Anyone home?" he called out, striding toward the door.

"Hi, Master Daat," came a musical voice from his right, and Lishus, one of his housegirls, came mincing out of the trees, swinging her long silver hair out of her face, a boy trailing behind.

"Hello, Lishus!" smiled Mike, without breaking stride. "Looking lovely, as always!" Lishus giggled.

From a second-floor balcony, bathed in a halo of his own light, the household's senior guard, Emmet, waved down with a greeting.

"I see you've been building, Emmet," said Mike, gesturing at a newly constructed tower down in one corner of the property.

"And more," replied Emmet.

"I look forward to seeing it all!"

As Mike passed under the ornate stone and wood lintel of his doorway, a figure stepped forward into the foyer, backlit by the gentle torchlight. Mike stopped, smiling in greeting, his breath taken for a heartbeat. He drew himself up, and looked into her eyes. Giannaluna. His bondmistress. There had been a few messages back and forth, but he had not seen her in the flesh since before Head Island. She had also been away in RL for a spell. Oh, Giannaluna. They had been together for years, through absences and uprisings and seductions and all the other turmoil of both Vtopia and RL. His Giannaluna. Mike steered his thoughts away from their love when he was totally in RL. He couldn't bear to torture himself. But she was always his first thought upon returning to Vtopia, and here she was again, standing before him.

"My bondmaster," laughed Giannaluna with delight. She floated to him. They embraced for a long moment. Approving eyes peered in from the garden behind him and from doors further down the corridor.

"My Gianna!" sighed Mike. He held her tight, letting his fingers steal down her sinewy torso.

She pulled back, still holding him, pressing her bare belly against his, and looking into his eyes with her aquamarine cat-pupils narrow and tricky.

"Come."

He went.

20—NIGHT OF FIRE

Friday, November 2nd
(very early and then early in the morning)

Everyone was up. The yard and porches moved with angry, worried adults, groggy children, and excited dogs. A policeman from the checkpoint on Connecticut Avenue came over at Grandma's request, although there was nothing the police could do at this point except take a report and reassure the compound's inhabitants that the law was at least in the neighborhood.

"This looked planned!" exclaimed Ari. He stood on the front steps of the main house, slightly hunched, his hands stuck deep in his pockets. It was not cold, but he shivered slightly in the damp, storm-cooled night air.

Honorée, her eyes flashing with anger, responded with stifled oaths as she paced on the gravel drive below him. Behind Ari, in the dark shadows of the porch, Grandma sat silently in an old, ragged wicker chair, her face drawn and stricken.

"I'll take them back up to bed," said Jenny softly, herding the little boys before her up the steps past Ari. "What time is it?"

Ari glanced at his watch. "One-thirty." Receding thunder rolled somewhere in the eastern distance. Jenny and the boys threaded their ways past Grandma toward the dimly lit doorway. Grandma absently extended her hand as they passed, ruffling their heads.

"The horses was stole," said Asa woozily, without any trace of an 'r'.

"Yes," said Grandma softly. "Don't worry."

"Will they bring them back?" asked Asa, resisting Jenny's gentle tug.

"We'll see," murmured Grandma. "Maybe they just borrowed them." She managed to smile at her grandson.

Jenny and the boys vanished upstairs.

"Bill was loose, but we put him back," called Lon, striding across from the stable with Lara, Fernando, and the police officer close behind him." Grandma got wearily up to meet them.

"So it was Belle and Sherbet?" she queried.

Lara and Fernando nodded in unison. Lon looked at the ground, swearing and shaking his head.

"I got what I needed," said the policeman, putting a slender T-pad back into its holster.

"Thank you for coming," said Honorée, her voice mixing gratitude with ire.

"It's OK, ma'am," he said. "We'll let you know what we find out." He nodded in weary sympathy, glanced around, and quickly left them through the main gate, which now stood open.

"Lon, honey, go close the gate," said Grandma. "Never know what else might go astray at this point."

Lon nodded and jogged off toward the double gate.

"Has anyone talked to Mike yet?" asked Honorée, looking around.

No one responded.

"Where the heck is he when things get even worse all of a sudden?" she asked angrily.

"Hon-" started Grandma.

"No, seriously," said Honorée, her voice becoming shrill. "Where is he?" She stopped as a thought struck her. "And didn't he go out the side door when he left?!"

"That's not quite fair," offered Ari cautiously. Honorée turned to face him, her head cocked in irritation. "Mike," he continued, "has been working like a dog for weeks to get us here. Who expected this?"

"Let's not bicker for no reason," entreated Grandma. "It's bad enough…" She sighed wearily. "I left a message for Mike. He'll call soon. Anyway, what could he have done?"

Honorée's fury passed. She took Lara's hand beside her, and put an arm around Fernando, hugging him sideways. "OK." It was her turn to sigh deeply. She turned her face away. "I remember Sherbet when he was a foal."

"They might very well turn up," said Ari. "They're chipped, right?"

"Are you kidding?" asked Honorée quietly, no longer mad, but grimly serious. "Um, maybe you're right, but the police already have way too

178

much to do just dealing with the storm. We were stuck in DC only a few days ago. No police anywhere in Cathedral Heights. We only saw them at the border." She brought her hand to the side of her face. "And they have to deal with all this cargo traffic…"

"Have you heard anything about your van?" asked Lara, prompted by the thought of cargo.

Honorée was silent for a moment, distracted. "Oh, yes, the police did find it. But Sanna sold it, so there was a record and a new registration. She was on the title. All legal. And anyway, that was before the storm. Before all the craziness." She laughed. "With what we have to deal with now, I hadn't even been thinking about the van…"

"I'm going to make some tea," said Jenny, reappearing. "Anybody want some?" Everyone murmured in the affirmative.

"I'm going to take a walk around the fence and take another look at things," said Fernando. Grandma smiled wanly at him and nodded. Lara handed him the flashlight she was holding.

"I'll join you, said Lon. The two men walked off toward in the dim direction of the brick colonial and kitchen garden. Everyone else went back up onto the lantern-lit porch. Grandma switched off the floodlights above the porch door. The darkened yard reacquired its nighttime quiet.

* * *

The house was soundless when Honorée woke up. Jenny lay fast asleep next to her in the double bed they were sharing. Lee slumbered in the small cot at the foot of their bed, curled up, clutching his bear incongruously named Mister Mutt.

Honorée wondered what had awakened her. Was it time to get up? She lay still, listening. Other than distant street sounds, she registered nothing. It felt like time to get up anyway. She carefully rolled off the bed and stood up, pulling her nightgown straight across her shoulders and throwing on her old brown bathrobe, which hung from the bedpost. She did not want to wake anyone, savoring the thought of having the crowded house to herself for a precious moment.

Slipping out of the bedroom, conscious of the traitorous cracking of her ankle joints and the creaking of the floorboards, she turned right toward the main stairs, and then, thinking again and turning around, went to peep

179

into Mike and Daryl's room to check whether Mike had returned. She tiptoed back along the long, dark corridor. The window at its opposite end admitted only a dull light. The sun was about to rise, promising a hazy, close day.

Coming to the men's bedroom door, she stopped. It was closed. She hesitated. Turning the doorknob might be noisy. She did not want to wake them. Standing there for a few heartbeats, she was deciding to skip it, when the door suddenly opened quietly in front of her. Celia walked through the narrow opening, almost bumping directly into Honorée, nose-to-nose. She uttered a tiny squeak and froze. The two women looked into each other's eyes at close range, astonished. Honorée felt Celia's warm, sleepy breath on her face, and pulled back.

"Sorry!" she said in a hushed voice. "I just wanted to see if Mike was back."

Celia shook her head quickly, eyes downcast. "No," she said. Honorée looked more closely at her. Celia's thick blonde hair was a wild mess around her young face. She was wrapped in a light-colored blanket. There was perspiration on her face. She smelled of bodies and sex. Beyond Celia, in the pale light, Honorée saw Daryl sitting up in bed, his exposed torso naked. Celia squeezed past Honorée into the corridor. Honorée, seeing that the other bed lay empty and still made, muttered "Sorry" and pulled the door shut. She turned. Celia walked silently away from her, her legs slim and quick, and vanished into the bathroom.

Honorée was again alone. "Huh," she said to herself, pondering. She glanced again at the bedroom door, but all was silent inside. This was none of her business, of course. But where was Mike?

She went downstairs.

21—ROUGH EXIT FROM PARADISE

Friday, November 2nd (morning)

The insistent tone eventually pierced Mike's deep, woozy sleep. It sounded and sounded and sounded. Mike coughed and opened his eyes. Vtopia had frozen and the view was 2-D and gray-scaled. Nothing moved except a flashing icon in the upper right corner.

He was in his house, in the great hall. Or had been. The connection was down.

Fighting the temptation to fall asleep again, Mike groggily moved his head. The flat gray image of the hall moved with the helmet. There was no animation, no parallax. Shit, thought Mike through his fog. He raised his hands and flexed his fingers in their gloves. His head hurt. He willed the tone to stop, which it did, only to be replaced by an insistent text and voice message: "Usage fees have exceeded limit. Session terminated at operator's request."

No way, he thought. He hadn't terminated anything. There was plenty in that account.

The message was repeated several times, and then the annoying tone resumed.

Mike pulled off the gloves, and reached for his helmet, but a wave of nausea forced him to lie back in the seat for a moment before continuing. The RDD was really messing with him. Now where the fuck was he? He struggled to recall the details of why he was in this particular V-tel, but the power of the Frame was very strong, and his mind kept going back to his strained conversation with Chera and then the hours of passion he had spent with Giannaluna.

He tried again to remove his helmet, clutching it delicately. He discovered a notice at the bottom of his frozen screen: "17 messages." No

181

access to those now, but he'd take a look when he opened his T-pad, which was in his jacket, hanging from a hook across the tiny, capsule-like room.

The helmet came off. He squinted around the room. The colorful logo of "Woodmont Virtual" was splashed across the walls. That was it. The Frame wobbled. Mike started remembering more: Bethesda, Grandma, the long journey... His heart rose, then sunk. Vtopia and RL battled for control of his brain. He fumbled with the chest harness, and threw it open. Sitting upright, his left arm out to his side, he stepped and rotated clumsily onto his hands and knees on the tile floor. More nausea gripped him, and he retched, a string of thick saliva and suppressed vomit rappelling down onto the white tiles. His bare knee slipped onto something hard and sharp—a piece of grit or glass - that ground piercing pain into the thin skin. He recoiled, his hand slipping onto the warm liquid and sliding abruptly to the side, bringing his averted face down hard against the floor. "Ugh," he grunted, waiting for the wave to subside before he rose back to his knees.

The air near the floor was cool. He looked up, wiping his wet cheek with his forearm. The door to his cell was wide open. Someone had come in while he was away in Vtopia. That was worrisome, and against the usual rules. Why would someone be let in? He crawled the short distance to the door, and pushed it shut. Reaching up to the stim/sim for a handhold, he pulled himself upright and took a deep breath. No nausea. He breathed again. Giannaluna's gorgeous face floated in front of his eyes, too real for RL. He rubbed them. Removing the rest of the harness and sensors, he leaned toward his clothes, and pulled them on. Socks on next, and then he stepped into his shoes.

Just then, the door opened without a knock. It was a man he had not seen before. He was short and broad and dark, of unclear race. He had a pistol in a shoulder holster.

"Sorry to intrude, sir," the man said, not sounding too sorry. "You're all done now."

Mike was taken aback. "Isn't that up to me?"

The man smiled humorlessly. "As long as you pay, we all gonna be fine, but your time's up when you can't pay no more."

"This is on my milscrip account, and there's plenty."

"OK, well, OK," said the man. "That's something you talk about with the front desk. But they send me in here to tell you time up." The man evidently meant to carry out the front desk's instructions, whatever Mike said. Mike looked at him in foggy indignation. The man pointed at the hooks on the wall. "Don't forget that." Mike turned around slowly, holding the stim/sim for balance, and retrieved his jacket. They then walked down the softly lit corridor toward the entrance.

"May I help you?" asked a different pretty girl behind the thick glass. The man stayed by the door to the corridor, watching.

Mike's mouth was dry and gummy. "Yes, I was cut off—kinda jarring—and there shouldn't be any problem with my account."

"Hm, Mr. Kendeil," the girl intoned as she looked at the window that her system opened for her as it sensed his RFID implant. "Hm." She looked up at him with a frown and cocked her head sympathetically. "No, I'm *so* sorry, but you have insufficient funds."

What? Impossible. There was a fortune in that account. A couple months of exit pay. "May I see the bill?"

"Of course," she replied, and gestured at Mike. His T-pad chimed. He pulled it from his leg pocket and opened it. There was a statement from Woodmont Virtual. He rubbed his sore eyes and inspected it. He'd been there for almost fifteen hours. He glanced at the T-pad's clock. It was after nine A.M. That seemed right. He looked at the rate, and felt his blood pressure drop. "Eight-hundred and fifty!" he exclaimed. "What kinda rate is that!?"

The girl looked surprised. "That's our standard rate," she said. "It's been that way for at least a year, when I started."

Mike put his hand to his forehead angrily. "Are you crazy? That's, that's insane." He had never paid rates like that down south. Not even close. There was something fishy with their fees. "People can't afford that!" He lurched toward the counter involuntarily. The man behind him tensed.

"This is what our customers pay," said the girl, with a hint of impatience. "If you-."

Mike cut her off. "All right, forget it. You won't see me here again." He tried to walk proudly, his self-respect intact, but stumbled as he approached the main door to the street, his motor coordination still returning in Vtopia. He caught sight of the man shaking his head at the girl with a knowing look. Descending the steps, and fighting the instinct to fly up into the air, he stumbled again, catching the railing. A hot, muggy sun

183

beat down on his bare head. Gnats swarmed. The street was busy. Clouds of flies danced above the uncollected horse manure in the gutters.

He looked down at his T-pad again, which was still in his hand, and inspected the messages. He squinted in the watery sunshine to identify their sources. There were several from Hon. And one from Myste Rains. Lara! His heart rose and sunk again. He wished he were back in Vtopia, so he could call her and find her there. She was back at the house, of course. Why was she calling him? Was she online now? Hon wasn't, of course. She was probably just trying to track him down because she didn't approve. Hon, always the older sister. He was twenty-eight years old, and in charge of his own life. This was totally normal behavior... But, then again, he had disappeared overnight, with no real explanation. Guilt flickered. They might be worried. There was a lot of shit going on, and Bethesda wasn't safe. But how could he go home now? He cringed at his unaccustomed sense of shame.

Mike caught a glimpse of his own pale face in the V-tel's window. He recoiled for an instant. This wasn't the Daat he knew! But of course it wouldn't be, here in RL... Damn Frame. He looked again. His hair was rumpled and warped from the helmet. His eyes were dark. He was very thirsty, and as the nausea receded, he realized he needed food and hadn't eaten since late yesterday afternoon. Crap. This was always the downside with major Vtopia excursions. RL and your damn body caught up with you, sooner or later. They hadn't figured out how to eat in Vtopia yet. Then again, a normal V-tel usually let you clean up and have a drink and a snack before hitting the streets. A normal V-tel didn't just throw you out...

He looked around. He was on Bethesda Avenue. He peered down the slight grade at the storefronts and stands further along the street. There had to be a cup of something warm and a sandwich or kebab down there. He would rest and rehydrate before going home to face the women. He started walking in that direction, eyes chinked against the sun's glare, legs wobbly.

It took longer than he expected. Many stores and cafés were closed. It was Friday. This was business hours, to be sure. Funny. Yet the sidewalks were crowded.

Finally, after several impossibly long blocks, he came to a small outdoor bodega. There were men sitting drinking beer, and a couple of wan-looking waitresses who looked like they had worked all night. Mike approached and sat down at a table by the street—one with a large parasol to get the strengthening sun off his head. One of the waitresses approached.

"A hot tea, please," croaked Mike, trying without success to sound relaxed and friendly. "And a large drink of water."

The waitress glanced at the small T-pad on her wrist. "I'm sorry, sir, but it's not taking it."

Mike felt the blood drain from his face. How stupid to forget! But it was a jolting confirmation that the situation at the V-tel had not been a dream. "What? How could that be?" He mustered surprise - mortified surprise, knitting his brows and frowning.

The waitress repeated her words. "It's not taking it." She shook her head. "I can't accept your account."

Mike sighed. "OK, do you mind if I sit here while I check something?" He brought his T-pad out. "There's some kind of problem with my account."

She nodded. "I'll be right back, OK?" She walked back toward the kitchen entrance and outdoor bar.

Mike opened his T-pad and selected his account's window. He flipped through various screens with his fingertips. Where was the money? It wasn't in his account. It had all gone to Woodmont Virtual. Mike sat there in stunned silence. This was completely foreign to his experience, even though DC tended to be expensive. He leaned back and looked around. The bodega was in a block that showed little apparent storm damage, apart from drifts of leaves and branches in some places, but then he saw, over in back of the low fence that surrounded the seating area, the debris of a large tent that must have covered part of it. It was scuffed and crumpled.

The waitress was over talking with the men, glancing back at him. Mike followed her with his eyes as she disappeared into the kitchen, re-emerging with a glass of water a moment later.

"You can have this," she said, putting the water down on his table. She did not have to say anything else.

"Thanks," he smiled gratefully, and drank the water quickly. He felt a bit better. He was just about to stand up when he remembered the oily old yuan bill he always kept in the rear slot of his T-pad case.

"Do you take yuan?" he asked.

"I think so," she said. She turned toward the men and called the question over in Spanish. Mike's Spanish was weak but he clearly understood their answer in the affirmative.

"Then I'll have a strong coffee and any kind of food you have!" he exclaimed. She smiled and nodded.

"I will bring you a breakfast burrito and sopapillas with honey, OK?" she asked.

Mike sighed with relief. "Beautiful."

His T-pad vibrated again. Another message.

22—TIPPING POINT

Friday, November 2nd (late morning)

"It's like we're walking around in some kind of, some kind of I-don't-know-what," said Honorée angrily, pacing around the porch. "Like, absolutely clueless, doing what we think is, oh, I don't know, perfectly reasonable, and we keep getting clobbered!"

"Sissy," Jenny begged. "Come sit down and have this tea I made you."

Honorée ignored her, walking up to the ancient metal screen and peering across the yard at the closed gate. "Sanna goes, the van disappears, you get chased home from Fredericksburg, we get chased out of DC, Grandma loses the apple thing, and the Market Garden and White Flint get wrecked, and now we get two horses stolen from right under our noses!" She laughed sarcastically. "Under our noses, with the compound full of people, and armed, even!" Her arm flew up like a bird, flapped around, and then slapped down against her thigh. "A week ago, all I was worried about was whether I had enough mint jelly at the stand, and winter clothes for the boys."

"You were worried about Sanna leaving and where the van was, too," interrupted Jenny softly.

Honorée stared at her in unfocused irritation.

"I mean, things were already..." Jenny stopped, wondering why she was countering her older sister.

"OK, yes," Honorée went on. "It was already getting bad, but look at this!"

Jenny grimaced at Lara, who sat across from her. Lara returned her look with tacit solidarity.

"At this rate," said Honorée, we'll have nothing left at all in another week, and we'll have to go out and beg."

"Not you," said Jenny.

"Huh? What?" Honorée had not been expecting that.

"Not you. You'd scare them into not giving us any money," chided Jenny.

Honorée shook her head with no amusement at all, and turned to leave the porch. "I'm going to go see if Grandma's finished her call." She walked off.

Lara and Jenny were the only ones left on the porch. There had been no sign of anyone else yet, save those working quietly off across the courtyard in the garden and sheds. Lara uncrossed her legs and set her bare feet down on either side of the old, battered chaise. "When I came down here earlier," confided Lara, "your mother was here by herself, and she did not look happy at all."

"Oh, I know," said Jenny. "We're in the same bedroom, and I saw her get up."

"She seemed to have been crying just before I came in."

Jenny nodded. "Yeah, she is afraid we're going to leave."

Lara was silent.

"Mom was never very good with transitions," Jenny added.

"Neither was mine."

"Maybe it's a generational thing," murmured Jenny. "Maybe it's cuz she's lived within about five blocks of here her whole life. And she's from the old times, too."

Lara considered.

"I can't imagine Jessica was very happy to come up here with y'all, either," offered Jenny.

"She got a little upset," agreed Lara, "but it all happened very fast, and Daddy was very definite, and then Mom saw Daryl's picture in the paper and that was that."

Jenny laughed a small, sad laugh. "I don't think *anything* would make it any easier for my mom."

"But nothing's been decided," countered Lara. "I know Florence has shared some worries, but, I mean, there are lots of possibilities."

Jenny shook her head with a hint of sadness. "Things are bad." She frowned. "Not so many possibilities."

Lara waited. Kitchen sounds clattered in the house, and someone descended the creaky back stairs. Roosters off in various directions kept crowing. The cloudy, humid calm had reasserted its grip on the weather.

"This is how bad things are," Jenny related. "Hon told me that they had maybe three-four months of food laid up if all of us were going to eat, visitors not included, of course." She paused, embarrassed. "I didn't mean that the way it sounded."

"Oh," smiled Lara. "I know you didn't!" She reached over and patted Jenny's arm. "We didn't all come here to move in with you!"

"No," said Jenny, serious. "But, you see what I mean? All of our fallbacks—the Garden, horses, the van, the stand at White Flint—they're all suddenly gone, at least for a while!" She put one palm against a cheek, turned her head, removed it, and looked back at Lara. "We always thought we were privileged, with this house and all, even after Grandpa Jack died and even with no father around, but you know, now I know what privilege is after living down in Fredericksburg, and it's not having a house in town and a few horses and wagons. And making *jam*. That just allows you to be a slightly more comfortable pauper - a laborer or a peddler with some extras. No, unless you're an oligarch or big farmer or some sort of professional they need, like a doctor or engineer, privilege comes from one thing." She looked directly at Lara with a disgusted pout. "Land."

They sat there bleakly.

"You know what we are?" continued Jenny rhetorically. "We're leftovers. You and me, we're leftovers. We were raised by people from a time when there were privileged, educated people doing what our parents and grandparents did because there was lots of money around for professors and experts and all sorts of business executives—none of them had a scrap of farmland. But they lived like they did: pretty well."

"So why are we leftovers?" Lara looked confused.

"Because we think we're something, but we're not."

"Don't be silly," said Lara. "You're a good horsewoman. You could be a teacher."

"Mm hm, exactly," replied Jenny. "You're a nurse and a *great* horsewoman. But we have no means. We have to get hired by or married to someone who does." She pouted again and chased loose strands of hair away from her face. "Land. All wealth comes from land, whether it's on Earth, for food, or in space…"

"You can go back down to Fredericksburg once things get back to normal," said Lara. "You have your horse. Doesn't that family still need you?"

"The Ginsberg-Smiths," muttered Jenny. "Yes, they said I should come back as soon as possible. My house was ruined, and poor Portia ..." Jenny fell silent, her eyes tearing.

"What have you heard?" asked Lara. She noticed Jenny's tears. "Oh!" she exclaimed with concern.

"There will be a funeral next week," replied Jenny after a pause and a deep breath. "She's from down near there. Julius messaged me. But I don't see how..." She trailed off.

"Does that make it hard to go back?" asked Lara carefully.

"No, not that," said Jenny quietly. "It's awful, but I have friends there now and the Ginsberg-Smiths said I could live in a room on their land... Not in town... No," she shook her head. "I was there for two years, and it was better than staying here, but it has to lead somewhere, and I'm almost twenty-five now, and down there it's marriage, spinster, or -," she lowered her voice, "- housegirl, like Celia says." She smiled wryly. "Of course, you know all that, growing up down in Roanoke."

"Blacksburg," Lara corrected her. "Until Salem, recently."

"Well, down in Old Virginny, anyway." Jenny grew grave again. "I'm not a Southerner. That I know now for sure." She looked up. "It was fun for a while."

It was Lara's turn to smile. "Not sure I am, either!"

"Which is just as well," added Jenny.

Lara looked at her with her head cocked questioningly to one side.

"Since we're going north now." Jenny completed her thought.

"Maybe," said Lara. "Well, my parents are, true, but let's wait and see."

Ari's voice, chatty and matter-of-fact, echoed out from the kitchen, followed by faint evidence of Honorée's reply.

"I've never been north," said Jenny. "North of Baltimore."

Lara laughed again. "I went to New York once, when I was a kid. On the train."

"I've seen all the movies and pictures," mused Jenny. "But I don't know if I'm a Northerner, either."

"Anyone want coffee?" called Ari across from the kitchen window.

"Coffee?!" answered both women with surprise. "Yes," replied Lara. "Where on earth did you get it?"

* * *

"We're going to have to make this quick," said Grandma, looking out with concern at the leaden sky. The humidity had risen to a boil, and the treetops were starting to move in the faint wind currents ahead of the approaching derecho. "The storm will be here in a couple of hours." She looked around the porch, where a new meeting had been assembled. Her family members were there, minus the little boys and Mike, along with Ari and Lara.

"Where's Mike?" she asked.

"He went to see friends," replied Honorée doubtfully.

"Still?!" exclaimed Grandma, who knew that. "It's almost lunchtime." She looked around. "Is there something somebody's not telling me?"

Honorée and Jenny exchanged looks. "We've called him and messaged him," said Honorée.

"A lot," said Jenny. "So has Lara." She adopted a coy irony. "He was online, but apparently busy."

Lara looked at her nails.

"Mm," said Grandma. "I don't like this. I hope he shows up soon." She scrutinized their faces. "I hope he's OK."

The younger women shrugged or shook their heads, unspoken suspicions poking out from behind their deadpan. Grandma glanced at Claudia, who sat in a corner, uninterested, an unhappy expression on her pale, thin face. "Claudie?"

Claudia shook her head but said nothing.

Grandma was standing, but took her seat now, leaning forward on the wooden chair. She looked around. "All these meetings." She sighed. They all waited expectantly. "So," she started. "I had a long conversation this morning with Maryann." She glanced at Ari, who nodded in encouragement. "Of course, she's been urging me to move up to Vermont for years." She suddenly yawned deeply, stretching her back as she did. "Oh, pardon me! I still have more sleep to catch up on." Although, everyone present thought to themselves how resilient Grandma already appeared, after only a couple of days.

"What did she say?" prompted Honorée. "Or, did you say?"

Grandma glanced at her eldest grandchild. "*We* said, that it makes most sense to go up and spend the winter with them."

191

Her audience murmured, sat up, gasped, or otherwise displayed reactions of interest. They waited for her to go on.

Grandma took her time. She sighed again, and looked around. "I really don't have that much to say. We have a big challenge all of a sudden. How do we live? That wasn't really ever in question before, but, oh, so much has changed in such a short time and I don't really see a lot of options." She glanced over at Honorée. "Hon, I suppose you could get the stall going, but we couldn't really live on that." Honorée shook her head and looked down. "Perhaps I could get my job back at the Market Garden, but there's no guaranty, and that might not be until next spring."

"But what about everything here, everything we have?" Claudia looked incredulous. "Are we going to pack everything up? Are we going to sell this house!?"

Grandma shook her head, with an unusually kind look at Claudia, who tended to irritate her. "Look, honey, it doesn't have to be anything final. We might get up there and find that things down here are getting better by the springtime. We could come back, then. So, I think the best thing is to leave Marcus and Becca here. Maybe Fernando wants to keep his family here, too. They can eat the food, watch the garden and livestock, and keep an eye on things. Fewer mouths, plus outside work. That's worth free rent to me."

Honorée looked skeptical. "Grandma, I don't know them like you do, and I'm worried. Are we just going to show up like refugees and live off their hospitality? Because, then I don't want to go. I refuse to live off of charity."

Grandma shook her head. "They're family. It's not charity. You'll find work. Wouldn't we do the same for them?" She smiled. "Didn't *I* do this for all of us?" Honorée gasped. "I mean," continued Grandma, "you all ended up here!"

Honorée looked indignant. "I was driven here by the storm!" Then she laughed, and quickly added. "Well, so would we be if we went north, but, I mean, we all live in the same city, and you have this extra room, here in Chevy Chase, and it's *temporary*." She stopped.

"All true for Maryann's invitation, too." Grandma.

They all let this sink in. Claudia appeared to stifle a sob. Lara and Ari remained politely silent.

"So, when?" asked Honorée? "And, HOW?"

192

"The train would cost a fortune," added Jenny, who knew about the price of tickets to Fredericksburg.

"I don't think the trains are running this side of Philadelphia, anyway," added Ari.

Grandma looked sideways at Ari. "How far are you taking that cell-electric?"

Ari raised his eyebrows. "All the way to Boston, I think."

Lara looked suspiciously at him. "Did the stripper say Daryl could do that?"

Ari laughed puckishly. "I offered to buy it."

Lara sat back, looking at her father and cocking her head. "You *did*? And what did *he* say?"

"He said, for a price, and I said I'd pay him more if he gave it to us immediately, so we could use it for the drive north. And he said, yeah, he needed the money now more than the truck."

She looked at him with approval.

"Well," he chuckled, looking around. "If we're going to show up somewhere as refugees, we might as well have a way to start making money right away, and what's better than a truck?"

"So, do you think you'd have room?" asked Grandma, frowning.

"Sure. The cab takes five, and there's the bed. Which you can cover."

"But there are, let's see," Grandma counted mentally. "Seven of us Trudeaus and Loportos and Kendeils!"

"Aw, we'll make it work. Go slow. Take breaks."

"We could pull my wagon behind it," said Grandma tentatively. "Then we could take luggage along."

"Sure," said Ari. He pointed at Grandma. "Which you'll want to have because it could be a source of income, too."

"What, sell all our things?!" gasped Honorée. "We hardly will *have* anything to begin with."

Ari looked at her blankly.

"I said we could take luggage along," explained Grandma, smiling faintly at Ari and then at Honorée, "and you said that would be a source of income too."

Ari laughed. "I meant the wagon, for hauling." He looked at Honorée. "Not the clothes for selling."

Honorée relaxed a notch and returned Grandma's faint smile. "Oh."

"Wow, a truck," breathed Jenny. "Ari, how fast would that get us up to New England?"

"Why," said Ari, in a tone usually reserved for miracles and surprises, "I bet we could make it to Boston in three or four days!"

There was a pause as they all considered this remarkable possibility. A low rumble of thunder muttered in the west.

"Three or four days," repeated Jenny in moderate awe.

"Ari," said Grandma softly, walking over to where Ari was seated. "My dear old friend. You really are here at the right moment, with the right vehicle." She hugged him. "But wouldn't Vermont be out of your way?"

Ari's smile faded, and he replied with a serious tone. "Given what has just happened, I don't think it's wise or even possible to go up I-95 through Maryland or New Jersey. If it's not outright dangerous, it's slow and congested on the interstate. And, off the interstate up there, well ..." He looked around. "You'd probably be taking a lot of risks."

"What about beyond New York?" Honorée's curiosity was overriding her general mood of irritation.

"You mean up in New England?" asked Ari. "There's no storm damage there. The roads are open. I hear even the secondary roads are pretty safe... So, yeah, we'd go through there from the west, cross the Hudson somewhere, drop you off, and keep going to Boston."

A sudden gust of wind roiled up dust and leaves in the yard, wracking wind chimes and causing the sprung screen door of the porch to swing open and then slam shut.

"When?" asked Honorée, repeating her earlier question.

Grandma and Ari looked appraisingly at one another. "Tomorrow?" asked Grandma rhetorically.

Ari shrugged. "Sure."

Honorée laughed in disbelief. "*Tomorrow*?" Jenny smiled at the adventurous decisiveness of it. Claudia held her face in her hands.

Grandma pondered. "Hm. All we're taking are clothes, food, some loose things, tools, weapons... All of our large belongings stay right here. There's nothing to close down. Everyone else will still be here, as usual."

"We have to take winter clothes," reminded Honorée. She looked frazzled. "I have to go back to my apartment!"

"Ask the boys to take you back there," said Grandma. "That ought to work fine. Move everything out of there and terminate your lease. Take

Mike and Nate and Daryl, too." She turned toward Ari. "And maybe you can take this truck."

Ari nodded.

"*If* we can enter the District again, that is," frowned Honorée. "Anyway, I already gave notice, as you suggested, but it was already too late to avoid paying rent for this month."

"I think you'll be able to get back in," said Grandma.

"We'll help," said Lara. "Just put us to work."

23—WHISPERED WORDS

Friday, November 2nd (afternoon)

"Are you gonna order anything else?"

"Mm?" asked Mike, starting. He realized he was falling asleep and that someone was speaking to him. He opened his eyes. The bodega waitress was looking at him with impatience.

"You gonna order anything else? Because we're gonna be closing soon and putting things away 'cause of the *dérécho.*"

Mike looked groggily around. He had not been paying attention to the weather, but the morning's hazy sunshine had given way to a cloudier sky and a gusty breeze. "OK. A medium maté." He still had tab credit left over from the yuan bill. She nodded and walked briskly off toward the kitchen. Others were starting to take down umbrellas and put away tables and chairs.

He had to do something. He couldn't loiter in the Woodmont Triangle much longer, storm or no storm. He had no money, for one thing, and he knew he wouldn't get another autopayment for about two months. He was going to have to find a job, fast.

And the others would be pretty pissed off at him by now. He wondered what they were up to. He'd only listened to one message—from Hon—and was not inclined to listen to any more. This was going to be humiliating. But he had to go back to Grandma's, and soon, especially with bad weather coming.

The waitress bustled back, with the maté in a disposable paper cup. "You gotta pay now. We are closing."

Mike smiled broadly at her. "You saved my life. Thanks. Just keep the rest of the yuan."

She gave him a dour, resigned look, gathered up the used cup and plate, and hurried away. Mike watched her go. Pretty young. Nice ass. A little fleshy. Too real. Too human. He sighed. Not his type.

This sent his thoughts back to his biggest problem: how the hell was he supposed to get back to Olia now? He had just reappeared after a long and problematic absence. Chera was pissy about it. A crisis was brewing and he had responsibilities. And Giannaluna had been so happy to see him and had reminded him intensely of all the good things that came with bondmasterhood. Now he was sitting in a crappy bodega on a dusty street in RL with no cash, zero status, and no convenient way to get quickly online again. Kind of a come-down for the 'Hero of the Lyra Asterism,' he thought with disgust.

He sipped the maté. You know, he thought, I am starting to feel OK again.

He glanced at his watch. One-thirty. He inspected its fading band and scratched crystal. The watch hadn't failed him through all his years in the Corps of Engineers. He picked at a smudge of green paint on the glass. Must have come from Grandma's wagon. This thought sent a new twinge of guilt through him.

"Well," he muttered, lost for an instant in consideration of his next conversation with Grandma, and then looking around in surreptitious embarrassment in case someone had heard him. No one had. His attention returned to the watch. What he then found himself thinking about were the trendy, colorful smart watches, ear buds, and glasses that everyone wore when he was a child. What had happened to them? Everyone still had T-pads and lapscreens and all sorts of VRI headsets and other mobile devices, albeit mostly old and beat-up. There were wireless networks everywhere. But all those little jewel-like gadgets seemed to have disappeared from everyday life. Surely not from distant, exotic places like China or Germany or Northern California, of course, but they had vanished from Mike's everyday, anyway. Maybe they just weren't durable enough to hold up these days. Mike did not know.

The thought crept into Mike's mind that all the little smart watches, buds, and glasses had surely vanished because you didn't need them anymore: the com feed and sound track just went into your head by themselves. This was The Frame talking: forgetting which reality one was in. After a moment of confusion, Mike shook it off. He was back in RL.

There *was* an RL. In RL, you needed some kind of device to connect with wifi networks. In Vtopia, you *were* the wifi network. Duh. And he did *not* need another episode of RDD. It had been hard to shake last time.

A long, roaring, rising-and-then-subsiding whip of wind lashed Bethesda. The air was briefly full of dust and bits of trash. Mike squinted and closed his mouth tightly until it had passed. The air was quiet again. Mike got ready to get up. The street was languid. Pedestrians were around, but there was little traffic. Many stores remained closed. This was a puzzle Mike had no answer to. It was—he had to think—Friday. Then, in the distance—in no particular direction—if he concentrated he could detect what sounded like traffic or construction: engines, rumbling vehicles, men shouting. It sounded like it might be coming from Wisconsin Avenue. Mike stood. He would find out soon enough, he figured.

Lost in thought, he wandered slowly back up Bethesda Avenue. He'd have to wait until the evening for some VNET, if he was lucky. The rig would be decidedly simpler than a V-tel: a headset, an I-ball, a bat. He could hang out in Grandma's barn, after dinner: narrow-band, low-touch, low-rez, and privacy not assured. Oh, well.

"Hey, you're Honorée Loporto's brother, aren't you?" A skinny semi-crazed-looking guy stood in the middle of the sidewalk, blocking Mike's path. The sidewalk necked down between a shop's doorway and an old tree grating that now supported a horse trough. Addressed this way, Mike couldn't squeeze past him without appearing odd or rude. He stopped.

"Yep." Mike was neutral, careful. He waited. This guy had a good memory. Mike hadn't been around Bethesda for a long time.

"I'm the mighty Grack, brah. Work in the markets." Grackle smiled and pushed his knuckles toward Mike, anticipating a mid-air bump of greeting. Mike kept his hands in his pockets. Grackle laughed ingratiatingly and retracted the fist-bump with a "Boom!"

"Uh, huh," said Mike.

"How she doin'?" asked Grackle.

"'Bout the same as a lot of people right now," replied Mike.

Grackle took his streetjive down a few notches. "She's a good lady. Nice. I was really sorry to hear about all that shit with her girlfriend and the van, and now White Flint is a shee-ambles…"

Mike found himself listening to Grackle with more regard.

"So, you say hi to her from Grackle, OK?" He held his thumb up. "Gonna come up roses, brah. Sun'll come out tomorrow. Bet ya bottom dollah. You say that, tell her I see her at the market when we're all on our feet again, *wakatta*?"

Mike nodded noncommittally.

"If anybody's left!" added Grackle.

Mike knitted his brow. "Left?"

"With so many folks leaving," explained Grackle. His thumbs-up rotated into a thataway-thumb.

"Oh, yeah?"

"Wagonloads, brah. Busloads. Like, ever'body decided it was time to spread their wagons and fly." Grackle laughed at his own pun. "Yeah."

"Huh," answered Mike, thinking that image over. "Yeah, well, thanks, I'll tell Hon."

"You do me a fine thing," smiled Grackle, already moving. "You say, see ya soon, Ms. Loporto. Now, I gotta get out of the bad weather comin'." With a cheerful wave he was gone, crossing the street toward a parking lot and Arlington Road beyond with a rapid, bouncing gait.

Mike watched him go, and continued his walk back to Grandma's house.

* * *

The sight that met Mike's eyes when he reached Connecticut Avenue about ten minutes later caused him to stop in wonder. He was back at the Thornapple Street crossing, beside the county police post. As far as his eyes could see—looking southeast down toward Chevy Chase Circle and the District line, and then northwest toward Kensington—he saw a slow column of dense traffic, all headed outbound from the city. Wagons, trucks, cars, vans, buses, carriages, motorcycles with trailers—every kind of vehicle imaginable, all with as many passengers as they could carry— were crawling away from Washington, D.C.

Mike rubbed his unshaven chin. Had it been like this when he crossed the Avenue the night before? There *had* been a lot of traffic. *Maybe* this much. Maybe he had not been paying attention, eager to dive into Vtopia.

Observing his surprise, one of the county police officers remarked, "Lot of traffic."

199

Mike nodded. "I was here yesterday. How long's this been going on?" "Couple of days, now," said the policeman.

"Don't look like they're planning to come back anytime soon," mused Mike aloud.

"No, dudn't look like it," replied the policeman. "Nope."

"What you think's doing this?" asked Mike, feeling disoriented. "The storm?"

An older policeman sitting on his motorcycle answered. "Hurricane seems to be what set it off, but there's been rioting and shooting downtown, and reports of fever." He jangled the keys on his belt nervously. "Looks like the same idea got around very quickly, and a lotta people had it at the same time."

The policemen looked glum.

Mike nodded. "Weird." They nodded. "You guys have a good one." He set off across Connecticut Avenue, jogging between a large wain and an old biodiesel van as they inched forward.

* * *

The alley that led to Grandma's rear gate was a gallery of contrasting projects and priorities. Pot-holed and barely paved, it was somewhat narrow, running mid-block along the back walls and fences of the big consolidated house-compounds that fronted Thornapple Street and the next street over. There were piles of branches and other storm waste everywhere, signs of the ongoing cleanup. Beside gates there were piles and bins of the sorts of things that normal life revolved around: mulch, compost, sawdust, sand, wood chips, lumber, bricks. You could tell who had chickens or goats from the smell and from the sounds from just over the wall. Mike did not see any signs of departure here. The alley was quiet and domestic.

He saw Grandma's house ahead. He assumed the gate would be locked. As he drew close, he reached into his leg pocket to fish out his T-pad. He'd call Jenny. She'd be the least hard on him. Or what about Lara? No, he'd feel chagrin with her. He stopped, and was just about ready to speak into the T-pad when he heard low voices from the other side of the gate, which was really a door in the high plank fence. He paused, trying to hear who was speaking. Maybe he didn't have to call Jen after all. He strained to distinguish the words and voices. He heard a woman's voice, and the lower tones of a man's, neither of which he recognized. Mike looked around, wondering for a moment whether they were coming from a neighboring house, but no, they were clearly coming from the other side of Grandma's back fence. Then, he recognized the woman's voice. It was Celia, in a hoarse whisper that sounded angry and defensive.

"No, he did not!" she insisted.

The man's voice rumbled in tones he could not resolve into words.

"No, he didn't!" She laughed angrily. "It's my life, *Nate*, not yours." So the other speaker was her brother Nate. Now Mike was very curious. He held his breath, listening intently.

Rumble rumble rumble, went Nate.

"It worked out for..." Mike could not clearly hear the rest of her sentence.

"It's not just about mother," said Nate in slow, crisp syllables for once. "Or father. It's about our whole family!" Celia said something in reply. "We're a household," Nate continued. "We all have to work. Together!"

"I *want* to go with him," said Celia in frustration. "It's up to me."

"Jesus Christ, Celie," said Nate. "Jesus!"

They paused. Mike wondered how long this would go on. He needed to sit down. His mouth was dry and sticky. He needed to take a leak. He still wasn't completely himself. Should he knock?

A silence hung for a moment. Then he sensed that Celia was crying in low sobs. The gate moved against its latch, perhaps because someone was leaning against it. OK. Mike needed to come in. The conversation sounded like it was over. Waiting for a few more heartbeats, Mike took a breath, and then knocked sharply on the gate.

"Hey, it's Mike. Can anyone in there let me in?"

"Mike?" It was Nate's voice.

"Yeah. Nate?" Mike pretended to be surprised.

"Yeah. Just a second." Nate fumbled with the gate's latch handle. The door opened. Mike looked at Nate. Celia was gone.

"Hey Nate," smiled Mike sheepishly.

"Hey Mike," said Nate, surprised and curious. "Come on in."

"Yes, *get* in here," said Honorée from just above them as she pulled up the sash of a second-floor window. "Where in God's name have *you* been, Michael Lambert Kendeil!? We have been so worried about you!"

201

Mike squinted up at his big sister, grinning and scratching his head. "Uh," he said. "Nowhere." He and Nate caught one another's expressions, and suddenly laughed together in spontaneous sister-bedeviled brotherhood.

* * *

Mike took another long drink of water, his butt resting back against the counter. The rain and wind rattled the windows, even though the shutters were closed.

"What the hell, Mike?" Honorée was pacing around the kitchen, distractedly putting things away. "Where were you?"

"Seeing friends," he answered, looking into the cup.

"What friends? Why now?"

"I just got back."

"I just wished you had waited, told us…" Honorée was not so much angry now, as she was frustrated and off balance.

Mike sensed the shift. He went over to her and tried to grab her hand, which she pulled away. "Hon, OK, I'm sorry. Just slow down for a second," he said, apology in his tone. "OK, I should have told you, so you wouldn't worry."

Honorée stopped and, looking down, pinched her temples with her thumb and index finger. She sighed. "I know you all had a rough journey, but things have been pretty rough up here, too." She glanced askance at him, dry-eyed but her chin quivering. "It's not just me… Everyone's worried. Poor Grandma." She composed herself. "I need to tell you. We're leaving."

Mike blinked and shook his head, starting to laugh and then suppressing it. "Leaving?"

Honorée nodded. "I don't know if I have the energy to go into all of it right now, but Grandma's been talking with Maryann and with all of us— *see* why I wanted you around!?—and, well…" She threw up her hands. "We're all going to Vermont for the winter."

"Wow." Mike looked stunned. He shook his head again. "Why?!"

Honorée shook her head and shrugged. "No food, no money, no safety, no jobs, no stall, looting, fever… *Oh!*" She abruptly looked at him, straightening up. "You don't know!"

His stunned look returned as he looked at her again. "Know what?"

"We were hit last night by arson and horse thieves!"

"What?" Mike glanced around the room in guilty amazement, and then back at his sister.

"*See* why you need to stick around!" She took his hands. "We were all caught by surprise—you would have been, too—but you just don't know what's going to happen next."

"I don't see anything burned…" began Mike.

"No, it was just a little fire on the fence around the side, but while everyone was putting it out, someone managed to take two horses. Out the back gate."

"No!" Mike was shocked and angry. "Who? The back gate?"

"Belle and Sherbet. The two mares."

They both stood in silence for a moment.

"Jesus," said Mike. "That hurts. Probably halfway to Baltimore by now."

Honorée shrugged. "They were troded, of course, but the police can't be everywhere."

"They can extract trodes, too." Mike corrected himself. "I mean, chips."

"Yuck," said Honorée. "Anyway, there's DNA too, but only if the police actually have a reason to suspect them. And there are so many anonymous horses around." She rubbed her eyes. "Grandma spent a lot of money on them, especially Belle."

"Probably hitched up to one of the wagons going out Connecticut Avenue."

"What wagons?" asked Honorée.

"Oh, here's something *you* don't know," said Mike without irony. "Last night, and today as well, the Avenue is packed with cars, trucks, and wagons heading west, out of the city. A lot of people are leaving."

"Hm," said Honorée, nodding. "Probably for the same reasons we are."

She let her hands drop, and then glanced behind her as the kitchen door opened and Jenny came in. Mike rinsed out the cup and put it on the drying rack.

"You should wash that," said Jenny to her brother, reproachfully.

"Oh, Jenny, shush," said Honorée. "Not now."

"Did he explain where he went?" Jenny persisted, her eyebrows raised, not addressing Mike directly.

Both Mike and Honorée laughed in the same instant. "Oh, for Christ's sake, Jenny!" said Honorée. "Yes, yes, yes. Been there and done that. Time to move on." She turned to confront her younger sister, who stood looking at both of them with a mixture of indignation and confusion on her face. "You and I have to get upstairs now and start working on the towels and linens." She hustled Jenny out of the room.

Mike stood watching mutely as they left the room. He was exhausted. He needed a nap. Somehow, he sensed he would not get one anytime soon.

24—MISSED CHANCES

Friday, November 2nd (late afternoon)

"Daddy, why aren't Europe or China in this situation?" asked Lara. As they worked, Ari and Lara were talking about the House resolution to seek an injunction and the riot in Philadelphia the previous evening. The news had been full of polemics on these topics all day. "Why does America seem so, so stuck?"

"Honey, aren't you going to pull back on that thing first?" Ari pointed to the lever by her elbow. She returned her attention to the center bar, and slowly pulled the yellow lever into a horizontal position. It was stiff and she had to pull hard.

"This thing probably hasn't been off the wagon since before Grandma's trip," she remarked, grunting. The end of the bar came loose. With Ari holding the other end, they stepped over the traces and whippletrees, now lying on the ground, and laid it down beside them.

"There," said Ari.

"We always take them off when the wagons aren't being used," said Lara. "At the end of every day."

"How come?" Ari did not know much about harnesses and draft rigs.

Lara shrugged. "Cuz you don't know what sort of tack the wagon's going to need the next day. Maybe it's one horse. Maybe a team. Maybe oxen…" She gestured over at the truck, parked across the yard. "Maybe you're going to hitch it up behind another wagon, or a truck, like we're doing. Plus, you want to keep them clean and dry. Greased."

Her father nodded. "Makes sense."

She pointed down toward his left. "You can start detaching the traces now. " He leaned over and started to unscrew a metal collar that covered a pin. "I'm going to go get the hitching bar." She started toward the truck. "I hope it fits."

"To answer your question…" called Ari.

She stopped and turned back to face him. "Oh, right." She waited.

"Well, it's a long story…" he started.

"Daddy!" Lara exclaimed in mock impatience.

"No, no," he protested, "I'll tell you. OK, in a nutshell, they freed themselves from fossil fuels—especially natural gas—and we didn't, and we were captured in our own trap." He waved her toward the truck. "Go get the bar and I'll tell you more." She walked on quick, agile legs over to the cell-electric and rummaged around in the wide utility compartment above the rear bumper, returning carefully with a hollow metal bar with a square cross-section and various holes and flanges, about three meters long.

Ari took one end. "Surprisingly light," he remarked. They maneuvered it into a compatible slot in the front end of the wagon, at the same height as the axles, well below the footboard. Spring-loaded pins clicked shut. The hitching bar now stuck out from the wagon, cantilevered over the gravel driveway.

Lara wiggled it tentatively. It only moved slightly in its socket. She pushed harder on it. The wagon's front wheels started to turn. "Good," she said. She returned her attention to her father. "Tell me the story."

Ari was only too happy to. Being a professor of many years, he had grown to enjoy professing, and had too little opportunity these days to practice it. What frustrated him, moreover, was that most of the adults he knew, whether of his own or younger generations, seemed to have little or no interest in most of the things he found interesting: history, politics, technology, science. Lara's blossoming curiosity delighted him. Florence's always had. Jenny appeared promising. Nate might also have the spark; Ari wondered whether he would be continuing with them up north.

He started gathering up the traces. "To really understand it all, you have to go back to the Green Teens."

Lara walked around the hitching bar and went to work on the left-side traces and their whippletree. "The Green Teens," she repeated. "Sounds so romantic, like, a bygone era."

Ari leaned back against the wagon's side. "It *is* a bygone era. But it didn't feel very romantic at the time. We were terribly busy back then having and raising you all, of course. Compared to today, things were easy then, but there was a lot of uncertainty. The economy wasn't very good.

206

There was a financial crash back in 2008, and a depression that followed. Constant turbulence. War in the Middle East."

Lara sat down on a large box to rest a moment and listen. "I don't remember any of that."

"No, you were a baby, a toddler." Ari had a distant look.

"I was one year old," mused Lara. "In 2013."

Ari nodded in recollection, and continued. "But then things gradually got better. There was a lot of enthusiasm for renewable energy—wind, solar, bioenergy—and a lot of hope for better days, for climate solutions. The really big climate problems hadn't emerged yet, and there were still a lot of deniers, although more and more was starting to happen. America was still without a doubt the most powerful country in the world." He stopped and rubbed his eyes. "But a piece that most people kept forgetting back then, aside from a few economists, was that the middle class was collapsing well before the Green Teens. Huge debts. All the supposed prosperity and progress looked good, and gave the politicians something to try to claim credit for, but it wasn't leading America back toward where it had come from. All the profit went into fewer and fewer pockets."

"Oh yes." said Lara, nodding. "I remember the pictures and videos of all those students occupying cities and marching on the oligarchs. The Ninety-niners, or something like that."

Ari squinted, looking off through the trees toward the sun as it set amid the ragged clouds of the fading storm. "Mm. That was right before you were born. That was nothing, really. Just a tantrum." He chuckled. "And they didn't use the term oligarchs in those days, either."

"What did they call them?" asked Lara.

"Oh, I don't know. CEOs and bank presidents, I guess. The One Percent. People thought of them as rich, but nonetheless basically as ordinary people that were just like them... Just much richer."

"What was a see-oh?" asked Lara.

Ari nodded, amused. "C-E-O. A Chief Executive Officer," he said.

"Military officers?" asked Lara, puzzled.

Ari chuckled. "No, business executives. Bosses. People who worked for the oligarchs, running companies." He shook his head in amazement. "It really was a different time, wasn't it?!"

"Daddy," said Lara seriously. "So, it sounds like the Green Teens were, um, positive, and we all know that they were followed shortly by

207

Sanderborough in 2021, which was tragic and everything—I remember that all very well—but that was *nineteen* years ago. Why has everything remained so messed up? Why is everyone so poor? Why do most people have to ride around on horses and work on the land when foreigners are exploring the Moon and Mars, and the Chinese live in huge modern ecocities and live longer than Americans? Why is all the spaceflight reality 3V in other languages with English simtrans? Why do we have to pay so much for the satnet, which is run by foreigners?" She paused breathlessly. "And why is the world trying to help us after this hurricane, and we're not letting them?"

Ari watched her passionate questioning with a mixture of fascination and apprehension.

"Why did everything that the Green Teens supposedly advanced stop working?" she added.

"OK. Whew," said Ari. "Lots of questions." He scratched his neck. "All of this story starts and ends with one word. Do you know what that word is?"

"Greed?" Lara asked. She looked at him expectantly.

"Greed!" laughed Ari. "No. Gas. Natural gas. Like I started to say before."

Lara furrowed her brow and cocked her head. "Ah ha, OK. Gas." She nodded. "Say more."

Mike and Jenny were walking toward the bed of the wagon, carrying ropes and a huge, rolled-up tarp. They veered toward Ari and Lara, curious.

Ari sighed. "You know the Energy Trust?"

"Who doesn't?" laughed Lara scornfully.

"So," said Ari, "back in the Green Teens the other thing that was happening was the gas boom. Fracking. Huge amounts of cheap gas all over. Exporting it to the rest of the world, where it was more expensive. That boom was rolling by the time you were born, and kept going well after Sanderborough, even with some bumps in the road. A few people got extremely rich—your oligarchs—and the renewable energy investment stopped because it became too expensive. Couldn't complete with the cheap gas. The coal burning stopped, too, thank God. Oil slowed down, taking the wind out of the Albertans' sails, but saving their oil sands for later, when they became much more valuable." He looked around, including Jenny and Mike in his oratory. "I know all about that because my research had to do with renewables, and the money for that just stopped. Gas for heating. Gas for vehicles. Gas to generate electricity." Ari suddenly looked weary. "Gas everywhere. Subsidized by the government for national security and economic recovery. Which, by the way, made us look more and more like Russia, and less and less like the countries in Europe we used to have a society sort of like. Look at Russia. Instead of the Energy Trust, they have Gazprom, but the two countries are virtually identical today—industrially, socially, politically ... agriculturally. Religiously!" He laughed. "That is something that would have been unimaginable back in the Cold War! US-Russian convergence!"

"The Cold War?" asked Lara.

"Oh no!" laughed Ari in mock despair. "No time for that tonight as well." He smiled at Lara in reassurance. "I'll tell you about that tomorrow. 'Course you can look it up. Cold War."

"So gas kind of postponed things?" asked Jenny.

"Yes, well, that's not all," replied Ari. He considered. "You see, the gas was so cheap it stopped all real modernization in American, most investments in sustainability and resilience. In efficiency. In renewable energy. In railroads." He held up his right index finger. "But! And this is the thing. It made it possible for the gas oligarchs to buy the US government completely. Gas was domestic, so the people getting rich were right here. No Arab oil sheikhs. No OPEC. No foreign oil companies. No complicated refineries. Just lots and lots of money going to a few good old boys. Who promptly purchased the Congress, the White House, the government departments, the universities. Remember, most everyone else was already pretty poor in those days to begin with."

"I thought the US government nationalized the fossil fuel industry when national security was threatened, and set up the Energy Trust to run it?" wondered Mike aloud.

"Oh, no," said Ari. "Oh, no no no no no. It was the other way around. National security was just a pretext. It almost always is. No, the ET did not only acquire the gas wells and pipelines and ports and coal mines and oil refineries, most of which were bankrupt or even closed... The oligarchs acquired the US government, and the rest of us in the bargain. Our blind dependency, with no one in government or academia to stand up for us, has made them rich beyond the most fertile imagination, and put America's development on the back burner." Ari laughed at his unintended pun. "A gas burner, of course." No one laughed back.

The conversation went on like this for a while longer. While Mike wandered off, looking for something he said he had misplaced, Lara and Jenny pumped Ari with questions, trying to improve their own understandings of history, and rummaging through their own memories for shreds of personal experience. They spoke of gas and oil and EROEI and Lost Arrow and the Trust and Rhiannon and President Morales and OSCIA.

"Dad," said Lara. "What's OSCIA again?"

"Hm, OSCIA," said Ari. "That one really gets my blood pressure up." He quickly explained. The Oil Sands Co-Management Initiative Act had the stamp of the Homelanders and conservative Republicans, although there were Democrats who had aligned themselves with this as well. President Morales had castigated it from the earliest days of its mention, and declared over and over that it would die a veto's death on her desk. The media and the public had been oddly apathetic about it. Perhaps few people took it fully seriously, concerned as they were with their daily struggles. Or perhaps vengeful sentiments were more widespread than many let on.

OSCIA was a measure of the desperation filling America. It would authorize the use of both diplomacy and military force if necessary to compel Canada to sell the US nearly all exportable oil production from the vast fields of Alberta at deeply discounted prices. Chapter 6 of the half-century-old North American Free Trade Agreement (NAFTA), also known as the Proportional Sharing Clauses, commited Canada to steadily export oil and gas south to the US until reserves were exhausted. The share lay at about thirty percent now, and was declining. Most of the rising balance went to China, which was always able to outbid the US and had long been active in taking equity positions in Canadian energy companies and then sending all of their output to Asia, where they could use it as an economic and political weapon, because even with the widespread use of renewable energy, there were always critical needs for fossil fuels. Plus, Canadians urgently needed energy, too, and relied on a share of this. But the US Energy Trust and the oligarchy wanted every drop of it now because of the enormous shortfalls in the US and the fact that the collapse of the dollar had priced US buyers out of world markets. Civilians had fallen back on "other arrangements," but the US military and government still needed fossil fuels. The development, construction, operation, and maintenance of renewable energy systems still was not free from fossil-fuel dependency.

In a nutshell, explained Ari, the only foreign oil America could now afford was the oil it could take by force by invading its neighbors. Of course, everyone knew this after what had happened in Mexico and Venezuela... and the threats were even more naked now. In fact, this situation had been coming on for so long that most people were inured—habituated—despite the enormity of it. Most parts of the country had been thoroughly unprepared for the grim realities of true energy scarcity and the profound economic crisis that unfolded. So here they were now: contemplating burning the forests up and invading no better a neighbor any country could have to capture its remaining oil. Where, wondered Ari, would the energy come from next, after these impulsive, destructive measures? Could the Energy Trust's endless promises of clean coal and new nuclear energy be believed? How long would this take to develop? How much would it cost? Who would pay? Better alternatives were staring them in the face, long in use in forward-thinking places, blossoming among the grass roots. What would it eventually take to break the forces of Conventionalism and isolationism in Washington? Or, more fundamentally, to temper the government's determination to use its control of the fossil fuel infrastructure to maintain central control of the country, rather than allowing the rising trend of power decentralization driven by increasing local energy and food self-reliance to run its natural course, and attract the domestic and foreign capital it deserved?

Of course, reflected Ari, the Fort McMurray Declaration a year earlier was a major culprit in the latest developments. It emboldened the separatists in Alberta, and their allies in Congress. Ari described Fort McMurray as a deal with the devil for Alberta's premier and his government. Perhaps in the short run it meant revenues and political clout vis-à-vis Ottawa, but what guarantee was there that Alberta would be granted exit and statehood, and what other battles would it have win in order to join the USA as the 51st state? Whatever its longer-term impacts, the Fort McMurray Declaration had so far made OSCIA seem almost sensible by comparison.

Mike, Lara, and Jenny listened in fascination. But this all had to come to a pause sooner or later, and it did when Honorée called out "Ten minutes 'til dinner!" at which point they all jumped up and focused on finishing some of the things they had set out to do before the subjects of politics and history captured them, as politics and history can do.

211

25—NOWHERE TO HIDE

Friday, November 2nd (late evening)

Avoiding the porch and the kitchen, Mike walked silent as a shade out through the front door and onto the lawn, and headed toward the smaller brick house at the eastern end of the compound, hoping it would be unoccupied. But, as he approached, he could see members of Fernando's family through the first-floor windows. Damn. There would be no sneaking into its upstairs rooms tonight. He looked around in frustration, a headset in his hand. Marcus and Becca were in the little cottage—the carriage house. And the main house was ablaze with light and activity as his family packed for the following day's departure. Frustrated, Mike loitered in the shadows, examining his options. He had been away from Olia all day. Messages had come that he'd been unable to respond to. What were people saying about him at this point? "Shit," he muttered. At odds with both RL and Vtopia, at the same time. There was nowhere that wasn't pissed off with him.

Bill uttered a nicker in his stall. Mike's ears pricked up. Belle and the other mare were gone. That meant that part of the stable was now unoccupied. The stable surely picked up the main house's wifi. Without a second's hesitation, Mike set off toward the stable, dark in its rear corner of the property. Anticipation rose in his heart—the anticipation of impending relief and satisfied curiosity. He walked up to the stable, and quietly opened the door. A hinge creaked. Bill's stall was immediately to his left. "Hey Bill," he whispered, to reassure the horse. Bill snorted and clicked the boards with his hoof. Beyond Bill's stall were the Lanc team's stalls. No noises came from their quarter.

With the door open, standing on the threshold, Mike paused. His hackles rose. Something was odd. He heard something sliding against boards. Dread froze his breathing. He backed away, getting ready to fight or run. There was a creak and a huffing sound somewhere to his right, in pitch-dark shadows. A muffled girl's voice suddenly cried out, gasping. There were more thumps, and a man's low moan.

"What the hell!" A bright light sprayed Mike from behind. He spun around, blinded. There were one or two men standing there in the darkness, their flashlights directed at his face. "Mike, is that you?" Fernando started laughing, and lowered his light.

26—ON A FINE FRENZY

Friday, November 2nd (night)

Pulling the hotel room door firmly closed behind him, Prokop Vulk called on the lights and kicked off his shoes. He glanced in the tiny refrigerator to confirm that Suzanna had added the six-pack of beer he'd ordered. He was beat. He went over to the window, switched off the rattling air conditioner, and opened a pane. He hung his jacket on the closet door's hook and removed his tie. Then, irritated with himself for the unnecessary motion, he reopened the refrigerator and withdrew a beer, which he popped open cautiously to prevent an explosion of released gas and spray. Vulk hated unnecessary motion. He liked to plan every physical movement, every comment he uttered. Eliminating waste was like an obsession for him.

He sat down on the bed, leaned back against the oversized pillows and headboard, and took a drink of the beer. It was good: some local Philadelphia ale named "Old Drexler". Thank God for craft brews. That was something the Long Emergency had not stamped out, yet. Far from it. And just when they were needed most.

Vulk listened. His hotel was close to the river. He could hear sirens and the distant rhythm of chants or beats—he couldn't tell—but it was clear that the protests were still going on across the river, despite the heavy-handed action of the riot police in Philadelphia the night before. That wouldn't stop the pathetic buggers. Vulk laughed ironically to himself. It just confirmed their worst fears. Whether they swung partisan or Homeland Front, they would only fight harder. They had little to lose, and a lot to gain. The mayor of Philadelphia was a fool. So were the trigger-happy Congressional Guards. The Hive system was theirs. They put the mayor up to this, Vulk figured. The mayor's got an election on Tuesday to worry about. Last thing he needs now is to look weak on law and order. So

214

he clamps down. Peace again in the City of Brotherly Love. The rioters aren't his constituents, anyway. Bunch of refugees from Jersey and Delaware. But the people in the streets and across the river and pretty much everywhere else aren't stupid. Poor, hungry, and displaced, maybe, but not stupid. They know what's up. This has been going on for generations, Vulk reflected. If he didn't have his fancy staff position working for Speaker Laugherty, he might be out there too, helping to turn centuries of American expansionism, military dominance, weapon worship, and sheer badassedness in upon itself.

Or maybe not. No. He would play it safer. Not fall on his sword. Things were going to get crazier and crazier for a long while before all of these kinks and contradictions were worked through. Before America or some combination of its parts agreed on what kind of civilization they were going to be. Perhaps he'd go back to Minnesota. Or even go stay with relatives in Slovakia. He could afford it. Not now, though. He fortunately *did* have a decent Capitol Hill staff job, and he had no plans to leave anytime soon. Indeed, it might very well get him into the White House, the way things were looking. It just might, goddamit! Suzanna seemed to think so. That was her wishful thinking talking, her vivid ambition, of course, but her enthusiasm was starting to grow on Vulk. And he couldn't think of any reason not to bring her along. She was presentable, fashionable, and did just what he liked. It was a business arrangement, of course. No strings attached you couldn't easily clip. She seemed perfectly happy with this. He'd adorn her, set her up. She'd be a reflection of his focus, his drive, his … potency. His Court Concubine, while he attended to his Prince, a modern Macchiavelli…

Vulk looked at his watch. Suzanna wasn't due back from the hotel gym for another half-hour. He swore impatiently. He wanted her right now.

His thoughts turned to Martin Laugherty. Ah, Martin Laugherty. Vulk had worked for Laugherty for twelve years. He had originally been doing campaign strategy and media relations in Chicago for both Republicans and Democrats, and his contacts there had recommended him to Laugherty when Laugherty was only a second-term representative. Laugherty had been a steady meal ticket ever since. Vulk didn't always like him. They were extremely different people. But he respected him. Nobody could work the crowds like Laugherty, and nobody could play the left off against the right like Laugherty.

Right now, however, Laugherty was making Vulk nervous. He was in a frenzy. Vulk had never seen him like this. Events were developing by the hour now. The special Philadelphia session had only opened yesterday. They had already censured Morales. Today had been full of press conferences and debates about the injunction. What would Saturday hold? Last-minute partisan campaign promises and threats? An attempt to get OSCIA through? More appropriations for storm relief and recovery were certainly on the agenda, but with what money, and with whose blessings? Perhaps some benevolent oligarch would announce a "gift" to the Congress for storm recovery—a little aid to make the Republicans look good and head off any foreign aid. Better the oligarch you know than the oligarch you don't. Ha. Saturday would be interesting indeed. Then, the whole thing was scheduled to wind down by Sunday at noon so people could get home to their districts. The election was on Tuesday, he kept repeating to himself. Tuesday!

One thing Vulk knew was that he had a breakfast meeting with Laugherty at five o'clock. Five A.M. Less than seven hours away. Laugherty had something up his sleeve he wanted to share. He wanted to get more verification first, he had said. Which he was possibly getting up in the Sky Suite right now, where Vulk had just left him in the company of a couple of Republican congressmen, the Florida Homelander Senger, and a few guys from the Energy Trust, GasGen, and AnthraCor, who were paying for the room and the snacks.

Since before they arrived in Philly, Laugherty had been alternately morose, maniacally optimistic, and furious at Morales and her administration. He was larger than life. Laugherty had always been prone to extremes in private, with a tendency for mood swings. Vulk wasn't like this at all. In this, they complemented each other. Vulk provided the structure, the careful analysis, the strategy, the sequencing. He left nothing to chance. Laugherty was chance incarnate. He was intuitive beyond anything Vulk had ever experienced before, and could deploy public empathy and charisma that literally moved mountains—most recently an entire range of low hills in the Macoupin-Clay-Union Basin back in Illinois that had rapidly vanished as part of a massive overburden removal and on-site coal gasification project Laugherty had secured approval for. Three towns had to be transferred, and part of a state forest sacrificed. But

216

Laugherty did that stuff in his sleep. He was just like that. Which was why he was Speaker of the House.

Vulk finished his first beer and tossed the can toward the recycling basket. It hit the lip, spun, and crackled metallically against the wall, leaving a wet mark on the drab wallpaper. He swore and opened another one, zoning out for a moment and staring at the mark. He probably should check the news. He always should probably check the news. No. Screw that. He would know the latest soon enough. If the Supreme Court had ruled on the injunction, somebody'd be calling him already. The staff were working 24-7 at the Springfield office, with the Capitol Hill office still closed and the election Tuesday, and the Chicago office was without a doubt still open at that moment as well.

Vulk figured the SCOTUS would rule in favor of the injunction. They'd come down on partisan lines. Five to four. But even one of the Democrats might go with the majority. The CU and the EU (in other words, Greater Germany) were pretty scary for most people these days. They had not been making overt threats, but their military strength and soft power were the story of the day all over the world as extreme weather events followed each other in rapid succession and about half of the Earth's population struggled amid grinding conflicts to either find a new place to live or completely change the way they produced food. What had Americans even more on edge was the fact that China and the EU by now had almost completely decarbonized their economies, while the US (along with Russia, Australia, and many other countries) continued to muddle along in their coal and natural gas dependency. The CU and the EU wanted this stopped. Compounding this gap were China's and Europe's accumulating accomplishments in space, which not only promised huge economic gains, but had clear military implications.

In the current climate, armed foreigners bearing gifts, descending from the sky in the latest transports and helicopters, was about the last thing that true patriots—especially Republican and Homelander politicians - wanted to see. As he took a long draft of the Old Drexler, he imagined hundreds of mud-covered refugees with their makeshift wagons and ludicrous sect attire staring at the heavens as dozens of all-electric podcopters silently descended like UFOs from an EU mothership, looming like a vast swan over the Delmarva Peninsula. If images of that got around, it would so traumatize *or* inspire people that they'd never vote Republican again, either way. Best to keep them feeling safe and hopeless as long as possible! That's what their ET clients jokingly reminded him on a regular basis. Safe and hopeless. Hm. Was that a stable state?

Vulk pondered the presidential censure for a moment. The censure was just a symbolic gesture. Morales did not have to do anything about that. It had no teeth. It came as no surprise. It was just grist for the election mill. It must have felt good to the Congress members who had voted for it, and was one more thing they could hold up in last-minute campaigning in their districts, but there was no action item there to worry about. That was done.

Alberto Senger. Vulk had wondered why Laugherty had to bring Senger into the conversation winding down upstairs. It was always dangerous to include Front people in face-to-face meetings with anyone from Big Fossil or the ET. The Trust leadership and their oligarch patrons were justifiably nervous about the Front. Some, like Holt, were strongly pro-fossil. To them, it meant a viable national defense, and continued energy self-sufficiency. It was a pretext for pushing ahead with the Fort McMurray process and OSCIA. It offered access to the concentrated Federal power that would be needed to crush the Aztlán movement, which Morales was afraid to do. She was so compromised on the Latino side anyway. Without Latino moderates, she never would have been elected. Vulk sighed. It was horrifically complex. Senger himself was a Latino— one of the social conservatives who sided with the Front. Aztlan was a weird beast. In some ways, it was the Southwest's version of the Front. They were against Federal power. They were against Anglos, too, although seemingly not for racial or ethnic reasons, but simply because the Republicans were the gringo party, and the Republicans—the Grand Old Party of the Union - were against any secession, by definition.

Laugherty had brought Senger to reassure the ET and Big Fossil guys that he could sway the Front—that he had the pro-fossil phalanx of the Front in his pocket. Holt had sent Senger, along with his apparently sincere apologies that he couldn't be there. The fact that Senger was a Latino only helped. The ET and oligarchs appeared to be largely agnostic about Aztlan secession. They had no fossil fuels down there. They would still be a captive US export market. Leland Guch, one of the most powerful oligarchs, had famously remarked from his fabled stronghold in Casper, Wyoming that Aztlan was all just a romantic movement anyway, and that a national government in Phoenix would be even easier to manipulate than

218

the federal government in Washington. Guch had said he thought a dissected USA would suit him best as five or six separate nations, as long as all the coal, gas, and oil ended up in the one he remained based in, which prompted pundits to call his suggestion "gucheymandering."

Senger had been sitting next to Vulk on the sofa upstairs earlier. Vulk had watched him out of the corner of his eye, wondering. Senger had been silent much of the time, smiling, nodding, appearing friendly and relaxed. He was youngish—in his late thirties, perhaps—and sporty and tanned looking, with smooth, well-fed cheeks. Vulk should have done his due diligence, but Holt's decision to send Senger came at the last minute. He wondered where Senger's sentiments really lay. Senger was, Vulk vaguely recalled, a businessman and landowner in North Florida, where a lot of the displaced people and capital from the sunken keys and South Florida had fled. Was he just another baby oligarch, unprincipled, content to keep things going the way they were? Or was he an idealist?

The Front had its share of idealists, too—right-leaning puritans who were fundamentally anti-fossil, anti-VNET, and anti-oligarchy, along with their ultrapatriotism and isolationism. Libertarians, really. "Liber-talibans," Laugherty jokingly called them. The kind who embraced the simple life, self-reliance, rugged individualism—as long as everyone else embraced these values, too, and at gunpoint, if necessary. They envisioned a better world, but their "better world" was a medieval world of small freeholders, mandatory church every day of the week, closed borders, and neither fossil-energy oligarchy nor the modern mixed-market SHE-WEBS and spacefaring economy of China and the EU.

These were the kind of Front adherents that the Republican Party was justifiably scared of. They were drawing growing support among evangelicals and the rural poor. How much of the Front's total base they represented, no one could really be sure yet. This election would be an indicator. Was this Senger's crowd? Vulk pondered this question. He hoped not. He hoped Senger was a realist, which, despite his Homeland Front affiliation, would put him squarely in with most Republicans. The Republican Party, Vulk had long since concluded, occupied the only realistic position in America today. Counterbalancing the wacko liber-taliban wing of the Front were all the liberal Democrats, with their pathetic nostalgia for a middle class and for social welfare programs, and their touching optimism about renewable energy and ecological restoration. That train left the station a long time ago. Those options were gone. The Dems were living in the past. Keeping everyone fed and keeping America sovereign were about central authority, a properly tiered society, and enough of a national defense to dissuade foreign powers from meddling in America's internal affairs. There was no room for dangerous utopian dreams in the status quo. And the Republic Party alone had the common sense and leadership experience to maintain the right balance.

Anyway, thought Vulk, polishing off his second beer and glancing at his watch again, climate change would eventually catch up with and overwhelm the CU and the EU, despite all their exemplary measures, and America, with fossil energy, diverse agricultural zones, a large northern neighbor to annex, fewer people, secure borders, and plenty of land high above the rising sea level, would inevitably find itself back in an advantageous position. All they had to do was to stay the course, stay strong, take no chances, and wait it out in one piece. America's comeback would occur when everyone else had been beaten down to worse circumstances. As the historians liked to say, the Twenty-second Century will be a new American century, just like the Twentieth had been. The Twenty-first was just a temporary adjustment. The race would not be to the swift, nor the sure of foot, but to the best endowed. It was only a matter of time.

The door lock jangled and Suzanna came walking in.

27—A BIG DAY AHEAD

Friday, November 2nd (late night)

"Big day tomorrow," said Wilder, stretching his arms and back, and taking a deep breath of the cool, humid night air.

"How so?" asked Moriah. She looked at him curiously. They were standing outside the National Constitution Center in a gaggle of other representatives and staffers, waiting for their secure shuttle back to the hotel. It was almost midnight. "How could anything top the past two days?" Moriah wrinkled her studious brow, trying to think what else might remain on the busy agenda.

"I think Laugherty will make sure we adjourn." He glanced at her confidentially. "And I think we're going to hear from the Supreme Court."

"Already?" Moriah sounded doubtful.

"Yep." Wilder nodded. "I have it on reliable authority that the Justices have already been in a marathon session since last night, with a few hours off for naps, and are aiming to have this question resolved pronto, partly because of the humanitarian need, and partly because they feel it should not be left until after the election."

Moriah nodded. "The human part makes sense, but I don't follow you about the election. Morales will still be president on Wednesday."

Another armored bus arrived. Moriah and Wilder looked around, but its display read "Michigan," so they went back to talking.

"It's all imminent. If she had formally issued the request, the Europeans and Chinese could have been here by yesterday. The word is, she'll do it. Maybe she's also waiting to hear what the SCOTUS says, which puts even more pressure on them. I don't think she'd jump the gun at this point."

"And what a mess it would be if the relief mission got underway and aid started actually reaching people, and then the Court declared it illegal. People would riot."

"They're rioting already," Wilder pointed out.

"Yes," said Moriah a bit breathlessly. "I mean, how awful it would be." She shook her head, glancing around at the waiting crowd. Another bus was pulling up. It wasn't theirs.

"The President's between a rock and a hard place," said Wilder in a low tone. "There is going to be a lot of trouble in the destination states if the relief mission is prevented but nothing equivalent is done by the US government and states."

Moriah looked at him quizzically. "Not to mention trouble in the storm's path, no?"

Wilder looked at his legislative director appraisingly for a long instant. "If the USG and richer states don't start moving the relief effort a lot faster, there's going to be a migration away from the storm's path like no migration this country has seen in a long time. It's simply about water, food, and shelter. That will send out huge ripples…"

He was being evasive. "Can you say more about what ripples you're referring to?" Moriah asked, frowning at him.

"Well," said Wilder, dodging her point, "anyway, allowing China and the EU to chip in would take that, um, risk away…"

"So, how do you think the Court will rule?"

"That," smiled Wilder ruefully, "is exactly why I think tomorrow will be a big day."

"But what do you *think*?" laughed Moriah in faint frustration. She waited. He said nothing. "OK, *I* think they will allow it. I just do. Now, what's your opinion?"

Wilder shook his head and shrugged. "Even though I'm usually willing to disclose my bets, I have absolutely no idea in this case. It truly could go either way." He sighed. "There."

The Vermont van appeared. Wilder and Moriah moved toward the curb, signaling to the guards that they were next. They were the only two members of the delegation still at the NCC. Wilder's phone rang just as the door opened. He answered as they entered the van and took a seat.

"Hi, baby," said Christine's voice into Wilder's ear.

"Hi," he laughed in relief. "How are you?"

"Fine. Tired. You OK?"

"Long day in session," he said as the door closed and the van pulled away from the bus stop. "I'm in a van going back to the hotel."

"Wow. Late," she said. "How did everything go? I heard about the censure and the request for an injunction."

"Yeah, lots of grandstanding," said Wilder, smiling. "Oh, the indignation and high moralistic dunder. Nothing accomplished that will actually help anyone, even people in acute need. Of course."

"Mm," said Christine.

"The Red Cross, Rotary, the evangelical churches," continued Wilder, "have each put more resources into relief than the USG, but it's band-aids, and to think what the Trust could contribute if it wanted to..." His voice trailed off. "It makes no sense. That would win hearts and minds more than shutting down a foreign relief mission would."

"Yes, it would," she agreed.

"By the way, did you get any of that supposed derecho up there earlier?"

"No," she said. "I think it was forecast this morning, but never came through."

"OK, just wondering. We had a bit of wind and rain, but they were making a big deal about it earlier, and it never seemed to amount to much." He yawned. "Good thing for all the people in refugee camps and on the road."

"Yes." Christine paused. "Honey?" she asked. "I actually called to let you know something else..."

"Oh?" Wilder was relieved to move to another topic. "Hope it's something good!"

"My aunt Florence is coming up to stay with us for the winter. Mom's really excited."

"That's nice," said Wilder. He had met Grandma many times. An interesting, well-informed woman. "Sorry I never got all the way down to DC to see her this time. Is she OK?"

"She's OK, but she's bringing her whole family up—you know, Honorée, Mike, Jenny, all of them—because the food and jobs situation has gotten so bad they're afraid they won't be able to hold out until next growing season."

"Bingo," said Wilder.

"Huh?" Christine sounded a note of surprise at this odd response.

"I said bingo, Chris. Migration is starting to get personal, tangible. I'll tell you what I mean when I see you." He laughed.

"Oh," she responded with a mystified laugh. "OK." Her tone became firmer. "So, when will I see you?"

"I think we'll be finished tomorrow, and we might be able to catch a night train. Otherwise, we'll leave Sunday morning." He paused, glancing for confirmation at Moriah, who often knew more about logistics than he did. Moriah raised her eyebrows and nodded. "Anyway, that's the plan. But all the schedules are messed up, being right here on the edge of the area the storm destroyed, so I can't exactly predict what will happen." The thought of train schedules drew Wilder's attention back to Grandma and her clan. "What about Florence? How are they traveling?"

"Not by train," answered Christine. "Someone they know is driving north in a truck. They're catching a ride."

"Another family migrating?" asked Wilder.

"Hm, don't know," replied Christine.

"I wonder," said Wilder. "Anyway, I'll call you one way or the other."

"'K," said Christine. "Sleep tight. I hope tomorrow works out well."

"'Night, sweetheart."

"'Night. I love you."

"Love you, too, Chris."

28—REJECTION IN VTOPIA

Saturday, November 3rd (very early morning)

"Zap!"

The security system propelled Mike backwards through the air for about five meters with a brilliant blue explosion of sparks. The red gridlines of the security box briefly flickered, encompassing the government offices and extending right out to the edge of the Great Plaza. Pedestrians and ailestrians paused to stare. He stood up, wondering what to do next. His chat box was filled with text from his repeated attempts to enter: "Daat Sulanra, your security access privileges have been suspended by order of the Supreme Netmagister."

"Fuck." Mike stood up. Chera had not answered his messages. Nor had Lemmet, Shet, Emmet, or a half-dozen other friends and officials he had contacted. Of course, you never could be sure whether people were inworld, or AFK, or otherwise out of the loop, but the silence was disconcerting. This was the confirmation of a greater rejection he had been fearing all day long. He felt devastated, sick. This was not how things were supposed to go for him in Vtopia. Things always worked out in Vtopia.

An even greater terror started rising in him. Giannaluna. She had been messaging him since yesterday morning. A little while ago, he had replied, but hadn't heard back. Where was she? He glanced at his inbox. Nothing. He selected his villa and initiated a TP. The system paused, his view went dark, and then he felt the momentary transmission. No time for flying or strolling through Eufoni's flowered alleys today.

"Zap!" It happened again. Mike rezzed outside his own gate, banned from his villa's grounds by his own security grid. This was as far as he could go. What the hell was happening?! Gianna wouldn't have done this. The villa was a senior government official's estate. He had paid for some of it, but Her Succulence's Government had paid for the rest, provided the

225

staff, and authorized his access to this upper-level neighborhood, "The Peak," where only the demi-aristocracy and higher castes could live. Chera and the Supreme Council were behind this. Was this permanent? Was it a kind of temporary suspension, a warning?

Mike stood back, looking around. He felt a panic rising. His eye caught movement up near the house. Someone was coming, walking silently down the path toward him. It was Lishus. She came up opposite him, just on the other side of the roofed gate, with a sad look on her face. Her small blue unicorn followed a few paces behind, its horn downcast.

"Master," she frowned, her head down, not meeting his eyes.

"Lishus, what's going on?!"

"We cannot leave. You cannot enter. We have been told to wait."

"Who? Who said this?"

"Master Chera," said Lishus.

"What else? How long?"

She shook her elfin head slowly from side to side, her long silver hair flowing in a wave. "We have not been told."

"Did he say why?"

"No."

Mike swore. Lishus reacted with a delicate gasp.

"I am so sorry this has happened to you, to us…" said Mike. "It's all my fault. I've been… I've been away too much."

"Oh," she said with a tiny voice, making no attempt to disagree.

"RL. I've had so much to do, been taken away…"

Tears fell from the tip of her perfect, honey-tanned nose.

"RL has taken over my life!" He was filled with remorse.

"Master Daat," said Lishus softly, "please don't worry about me, about the house staff. We know things have been happening that affect us here." Mike listened to her with surprise, hearing a different persona, a deeper character behind the simple housegirl she had always been to him. "Our people live in RL, too. Our bodies. Emmet has lost his home and family in RL to… to troubles. He should tell you himself. He has been away a lot. He was afraid you would be angry, would lose faith in *him*." She looked into his eyes. "We understand."

Mike sobbed out loud. The shock, his anguish, and her compassion took him. He reached out to hug her, unthinking, and was abruptly zapped back by the security grid.

"Oh!" she cried. "Poor Master Daat!"

"Don't worry. Don't worry," he muttered, suppressing the temptation to cry. "And Gianna? Where's Gianna?"

"I have not seen her since yesterday," said Lishus. "I don't know. Have you messaged her?"

"Of course," he replied. "A bunch of times... Let me see." He scanned his HUD to find when he had last sent a message from his lapscreen. It had been several hours.

"I have to go," said Lishus. "RL." She bobbed a small, awkward curtsy.

Mike bowed low to her. "Bye, Lishus."

"Take care," she said, blowing him a heart-shaped kiss, which glided through the air until it landed on his forehead with the tinkle of a little bell. "Everything will be OK. See you soon." Her avatar evaporated with a shimmer. Her unicorn just disappeared artlessly.

Mike looked up at the house, wondering if anyone else was in. He glanced up and down the sloping path, seeing no one. Nothing moved except the slight swaying of the vegetation in the afternoon trade winds, and the occasional electric flash of a hummingbot among the foliage. His HUD indicated that it was nearly five a.m. in Chevy Chase, and since he was not in a stim/sim, he remained aware of his body's surroundings, ensconced in the wagon's cab, the night air a bit chilly and damp. Five a.m. Shit. They would be leaving for New England in a few hours. At least he could doze in the truck once they got started. There were enough drivers that he could fend off a stint until later in the day. But he needed to finish up in Olia—make some progress—and he felt the time pressure.

Calling up his message window, he composed a short message to Giannaluna, explaining his predicament, asking her what she knew and when they could meet. He told her he would be traveling again, but that they could message for the few days it took to get to a stable RL environment again. They would figure out what to do. He apologized profusely for his suspension, and asked her forgiveness for the embarrassment it might have caused her, as the bondmistress of a dishonored high-ranking official. Mike felt her love was real, but knew how proudly and jealously she prized her social status. They had met when he was a still a young Knight of the Asterism, and she a courtier in the House of the Seventh Copulatrix. They had climbed the ladder together.

227

Shaking off this painful recollection, he finished the message, and hit send. His HUD icon spun as the message processed. Then a text flashed back at him. "User account terminated at user's request. No forwarding account specified."

Oh my God! thought Mike in panicked agitation. *Oh my God!* He tried again, fingers trembling. The same text was displayed again. Her profile had been deleted. Emails bounced. Giannaluna Infinita did not exist anymore.

Avacide!

29—RUMORS FROM THE STATES

Saturday, November 3rd (early morning)

In the hotel's all-night coffee shop, a few early patrons quietly ate, and the faint sound of ceramic cups and plates could be heard from the kitchen. Laugherty was already sitting in a side booth looking at a menu when Vulk walked in. Vulk nodded across the tables at Laugherty and went over to join him. An armed guard by the entrance followed Vulk with his eyes.

Laugherty smiled sleepily, still in the part of the circadian cycle when he would normally be asleep. "This is the time of the day I like," he said. "I can go into a coffee shop and nobody knows who I am, or doesn't care."

"All the gawkers and paparazzi are still asleep," replied Vulk. "Do you do this often?" He raised his eyebrows inquiringly.

Laugherty laughed. He was, as they both knew very well, not a morning person. Not under normal circumstances, anyway. There had been a lot of early mornings recently, however. These were not normal circumstances.

The waitress brought over a pot of coffee and filled both cups.

"This is truly retro," commented Laugherty. "Is that really coffee?"

The waitress nervously smiled. "The hotel makes sure it is."

"Very impressed, miss," said Laugherty. "We picked the right place."

The waitress nodded, smiled again, and skittered away. Laugherty's and Vulk's eyes met in brief mock puzzlement, and then each took a long, appreciative drink of coffee.

"So, how did the meeting last night end up?" asked Vulk.

"Dang, Prokop, you missed the best part. We painted the town red."

Vulk arched his eyebrows, and took another long drink. Laugherty chuckled.

"Nah," he resumed. "No bar-hopping. Same old shit. You know. Reassuring the corporate execs, making sure the 'garchs get the right

229

signals. Keep supporting us and your money will be safe. Keep supporting us and the country will be safe. Safe and hopeless."

Vulk listened, slightly surprised at Laugherty's sarcastic tone. This was not usually his style. "You could go Democrat, you know," he joked. "And not have to put up with that any more... You could pull a Bart Ross."

"What, and get Illinois to secede?" Laugherty chuckled. "Nah, I don't mind. It's a tough job but somebody's gotta do it."

"And that Senger guy? R-FL." Vulk had become very curious about Senger's leanings. "Any read on him?"

"I think he's in Holt's camp pretty firmly..." mused Laugherty.

"You sure? I started wondering whether he was an idealist. A closet renewables guy."

Laugherty tapped his cup. He shook his head. "I don't think so."

Vulk waited.

"Wanna know why?"

"Why?"

"He owns about half of Pomonico Gas."

"He does?" Vulk was bemused. "I didn't find that in his profile."

"Shells. Relatives. Fronts. But he does." Laugherty sounded very certain. "Has a big fat ET contract."

"Ah, OK. That pretty much settles it." Vulk was satisfied. He went on. "So, Martin, you said you had some news."

"Yes." Laugherty straightened up a little. "Yep, I could'a let you sleep a little longer, and I didn't drag you down here for chit-chat at five a.m." He sat back, and glanced around. Lowering his voice slightly, he spoke in a more businesslike tone. "Yesterday evening, one of my state government sources told me that there's some funny business going on. There is apparently a group of governors putting pressure on Morales to permit the EU-China relief mission, no matter what. No matter what's legal."

"Who?" asked Vulk. "How do you know?" Not that he was surprised. The states were bearing the brunt.

"Not totally sure which governors, but it's pretty easy to guess it's the Dems and independents, and also that they are all in the East somewhere. Northeast, probably. I'm not gonna speculate—I wanna know more - but if we brainstormed I'm sure we'd be 90 percent accurate."

"Um, no," said Vulk. "I mean, who told you?"

230

"That's not important right now," replied Laugherty. "Let's just say that this is a very reliable source."

"OK," said Vulk, his curiosity unsatisfied. "So, what are they threatening to do?"

"Why do you say 'threatening'?" asked Laugherty. "I didn't say that." He looked at Vulk with a slightly suspicious frown.

Vulk looked straight back at him. He laughed humorlessly. "Look, I know nothing about this, but when do people ever put pressure on someone—*especially* a politician—without brandishing carrots and sticks?"

Laugherty relaxed. "OK. Maybe. Anyway, I don't know what the threats are—my source didn't—but it's apparently a big deal and there's a lot in play. Some kind of ultimatum or, yeah, well, maybe, threat. I'm going to try to find out more. We may find out quickly enough in the public domain, the way events are moving so fast."

"Is that all your source said?" It all sounded very vague and unspecific. Vulk's inclination was to dismiss it. "The election's three days away. All kinds of silly rumors can get started."

"There were a few more details," said Laugherty. "This part is what makes me think we have to be particularly watchful and ready for anything." He looked to the right and left, and lowered his head and voice so that Vulk could barely hear him. "First, we know the Europeans are keeping their aircraft and crews in constant readiness. The cargoes are all on board. There has been no de-escalation. Second, in a dozen Northeastern states, there are extensive state militia and National Guard movements. Nothing announced, nothing jumping out at you, but they have called up reserves and are moving a lot of guys and vehicles around. We'll know more soon."

Vulk took this information with furrowed brows and a look of slight disbelief.

"Third, they appear to be reinforcing their staff at border crossings."

"Staff?" Vulk was momentarily baffled.

"Personnel! People!" Laugherty spoke up with impatience. "Soldiers. State police."

"OK. Border crossings with Canada?" Vulk was jumping to no assumptions or conclusions.

"No! Inter-state borders. Like Connecticut-New York and Connecticut-Massachusetts. And not just interstate highways. Smaller roads."

"Maybe it's just because state borders have welcome centers and rest stops and that sort of thing, and storm refugees are bunching up there, so they have to send more police. Or food vendors..." Vulk was reluctant to uncritically adopt Laugherty's alarm.

Laugherty laughed out loud. "Rest stops!? Are you kidding? When was the last time you stopped at a highway rest stop for a coffee and doughnut?!" He shook his head.

"I meant that there's usually a lot of parking, open space, in places like that."

"Uh-huh," grunted Laugherty. "Well, look, we don't really know anything, but if Morales is about to cave, or there's some secret deal being hatched—especially with foreign powers in the picture - we have to get all our eyes and ears out there, and be ready for anything."

"I'll get on it, boss," said Vulk. "We have a lot of sources we can tap."

Laugherty was playing with his spoon and cup. He was silent for a short moment. Then he spoke. "Whatever happens, the public is going to look to whomever seems to be in charge. Will that be the White House, the Congress, or the Courts?"

"Or, as you seem to be suggesting, the state governors..."

Laugherty nodded. "Yes, them as well." He leaned back. "Another thing I do know is that only Congress has the right to regulate interstate commerce, including travel, and no president or governor has the power to undo that. Article I, Section 8, Clause 3."

"You know your Constitution, sir," said Vulk.

"Never know, might need to actually use it sometime!"

They both chuckled. Vulk glanced at the wall clock across the coffee shop. It was about 5:45 a.m. "Too late to go back to sleep for a few minutes," muttered Vulk. "It's going to be a busy day. Might as well get ahead of it." He waved at the waitress again, to order food.

"Oh, damn, there was one more thing!" Laugherty pointed for emphasis. "Which you may not know about."

"What?" Vulk looked at him apprehensively.

"Aztlan is now in open revolt. They are boycotting the election, and have declared a republic!"

"Jesus," said Vulk, rubbing his jaw. "Any violence?"

232

"Pretty restrained so far. Federal agencies and the Guard chain of command have refused to go along, of course. Pretty much a standoff."

"One more situation for the President to go fix," laughed Vulk. "How could *anyone* covet her position?" He looked at Laugherty in pretend dismay. "Oh, I am *so* sorry! You do!" They both smiled wearily.

30—A SENSE OF EVAPORATION

Saturday, November 3rd (afternoon)

Lara felt OK now—really comfortable, in fact. She lay back against the bags and relaxed in the autumn sunshine, luxuriating in the warmth and feeling a little drowsy from the rhythmic swaying of the wagon. Through half-open eyelids, she watched Daryl and Celia snuggled up beside one another, their backs against cargo stowed in the front part of the bed. Celia was wearing a bright, flowing poncho someone had given her—Hon?—and had braided her hair. She had coaled her eyes, and looked fashionable. In fact, Celia was more relaxed and light-hearted than Lara had ever seen her. She mused on their first meeting by the highway overpass in Fredericksburg, Celia glum and veiled. And then the scene with her parents. And then Nate's dismay when Celia announced she was not returning to her parents' home. Celia was one teenager in revolt, thought Lara. How sad her parents must feel. Yet she was not exactly running away. They knew where to find her. Who knew what the future held? Celia might get tired of Daryl and hate New England, and end up on a slow train south before anyone had gotten used to her being away…

Am I running away, wondered Lara? Not really. She was with her parents and Daryl. *They* were running away, that was certain. She felt OK about it now. It seemed unremarkable, logical. Her ire about her father's Holocaust analogies had faded. The dislocation of leaving had quickly become routine. This perplexed her mildly. With very little planning or warning, she was walking away from her life in Salem, her nursing and horsework jobs, some of her things, her small social circle, everything that was most familiar to her, and just *taking off.* Wow. I should be feeling more strongly about this, she insisted to herself. What about Ginny? Ginny was still living in their tiny apartment. Another friend would presumably move in to take over Lara's room. She and Ginny had hastily hugged the morning they left, with Ginny moving back over from her parents' house where she had stayed while Lara's family were visiting, those few days. They'd both cried quick tears and promised to stay in touch and maybe Lara would be back before too long and Ginny was always welcome to come up and visit. There had been no discussion of exactly why the Daniels were leaving, no comments about Daryl's "wanted" status. It was just family business. Hard to say. Ginny had asked no questions. Maybe this was the key, the key to the times. No one needed to know any more, or ask any more questions. Things were just unraveling in the way they needed to. They had all the answers, as unsatisfactory as some were. But, my God, I've known Ginny since middle school, Lara realized! It was all like smoke, dust, mist...

It was this image that brought Lara's latest dream back to her. They had all gotten up early for their departure, but even earlier, in the darkness before dawn, Lara had been awakened abruptly by a sound that fused dream with reality. In her dream, Lara discovered she was evaporating. Others knew this. In one scene, she was in a waiting room, where her four grandparents all sat together on benches. They were sad she was evaporating, but accepted it with disapproving resignation. "You're all dead," she told them resentfully. "You evaporated, too!" But they shook their heads. No, they had not evaporated as she was doing. They had been good and solid even after death, heavy and substantial. "Red-blooded Americans," her mother's father had said incongruously to the others' nods. None of them had evaporated. So why was Lara evaporating like this? Could it be stopped?

In the dream, she looked down at her own hands and arms. They were already a bit hazy around the edges, starting to sublime away. She sobbed. Lara was proud of her lean, tanned hands and arms. She hadn't had many boyfriends since high school, but the ones she had had were always complementing her on her arms, and she had often noted with relief the fact that her mother still had slender arms with no hanging wobble. Ginny had always been complimentary about her arms (and other parts of her body) too, and their brief fling had been more a guilty body-ego trip for Lara than a serious exploration. They'd pulled apart awkwardly and stayed apartment-mates, Ginny eyeing Lara's physique secretly without further incident. But now Lara's lovely arms were evaporating and soon the rest of her would, too! The sobbing grew louder, a series of stifled moans and coughs. Evaporation made her feel so desolate, so insubstantial. And then she woke up, the sobbing in her ears, only to discover it wasn't she who was sobbing, but rather Claudia through the bedroom wall. Claudia had been crying quite a bit. She was inconsolable about leaving Chevy Chase.

Lara had lain in bed for a few more minutes, listening to Claudia and digesting her odd dream, and then had jumped up to face several hours of road-food prep and last-minute packing so they could be on the road by late morning.

Now, she inspected her hands and arms again. In the bright sunlight, they looked nice and solid. No traces of evaporation. Unreasonably, Lara reflected that any evaporation would first be noticeable in bright light, before you could see it at lower light levels, and then shook off that silly notion. But the odd subject of evaporation remained on her mind. Perhaps it was all about how her life up until the present was evaporating... To condense again as what, she wondered?

"Isn't it nice?" said Jenny quietly, and a bit sadly, Lara thought.

"Mm, the sunshine," said Lara. "No humidity. That's a relief." She smiled at Jenny in a sisterly way. "You've been through a lot in a short time, huh?"

Jenny's eyes teared up, and she looked down at the floorboards. She nodded.

"One week ago today, the storm!" Lara marveled at the events since the previous Saturday.

Jenny brushed away her tears with the backs of her hands and took a deep, trembling breath. She smiled at Lara. "Everything changed for me. Well, no, not everything. My future." She dabbed her eyes again. "Portia's got no future now."

Under a deep blue sky full of clean, white clouds, they sat quietly, rocking with the wagon's motion. Daryl, Celia, and Mike shared the wagon's ample, moderately loaded bed with them (with Mike sprawled on top of the wagon's folded canopy, mouth agape, sound asleep). Claudia and Jessica sat up on the bench in the wagon's cab, looking at the back of the truck. Grandma, Ari, Honorée, and her two boys occupied the two rows of seats in the truck's cab. The truck's covered storage bay was full of cargo.

Another broad vista of rolling Western Maryland landscape unfolded before them: golden fields of stubble, muddy paddocks, hedgerows, haystacks scattered to dry out, whole hillsides of stripped suburbs with nothing left but concrete pads and nameless deconstructed cul-de-sacs. They were making good time, well past Frederick now, bumping along in the cratered left lane of US 15 at nearly 50 kph. The Pennsylvania border lay close ahead. It was early afternoon. At breakfast, Grandma had declared they would be in Harrisburg, Pennsylvania's capital, by nightfall. The prospect of this ambitious achievement was met with a mixture of wonder and skepticism. Yet they were already more than halfway, and at this rate would be in Harrisburg in little more than two hours.

Harrisburg was nearly due north of Washington, and about 150 km away as the crow flew. In the old days, such a trip as theirs would have skipped Pennsylvania entirely, angling eastward past Baltimore and up through New Jersey. But today's detour was deemed necessary in order to steer clear of the areas directly affected by the hurricane. Damaged roads and bridges, military checkpoints, large numbers of refugees, and the petty criminality of dislocation were all good reasons to first loop west, and then come east again further north. No one had any objections. The speed of the truck gave them the luxury to choose an indirect route.

Ever since they left Washington, merging onto Interstate 270 from the Beltway, the right lane had been solid vehicles: wagons, carts, ancient fuel-burners and newer electrics, most of them pulling trailers, overloaded with passengers of all ages, baggage, fuel cans, dilapidated solar panels, cages of chickens and geese, expertly balancing goats, cats, potted plants, disassembled sheds and fencing, small boats, agricultural implements, tools, giant bundles, food, lumber, furniture, rolled carpets and blankets, and every other sort of evidence of rural migration. Behind the slowest vehicles, relegated to the weed-clotted shoulder, walked horses, cattle, and dogs. Their own truck was moving too fast for conversations with the other vehicles, but many looks were met and returned as they sailed by, traveling the same road—just faster. As the day passed, Lara had become increasingly curious about the other travelers. Their license plates came from all over. Were most of them fleeing the storm's immediate destruction of property and livelihoods, or were they on the move for other reasons?

The traffic began to slow. Lara, Jenny, and the others sensed it, and looked around more alertly. At first, it was almost imperceptible, but then the traffic in the fast lane began to alternately surge and brake as the flow

237

became choppy. After a long downhill coast, they came to a definite halt. Vehicles squeaked and rattled to a stop around them. The road noise calmed.

Jenny was inspecting her T-pad. "We're at the border," she announced.

"I wonder why it's so slow?" asked Lara. She messaged this question to her father in the truck's driver's seat just ahead.

"They might be asking a lot of questions," came the message back from Ari. "Doing searches, maybe."

Lara stood up, holding the sidewall in case the wagon started moving again. She leaned out and peered ahead of the truck. They were on a long, level straightaway. The four-lane highway was a parking lot of shabby vehicles as far as she could see. Less than a mile ahead, she could discern the shapes of towers, flags, and some sort of building. That must be the border.

"We'll be lucky to get acrosst," said a toothless old man from a wagon beside them in the right lane. Lara looked at him, taken slightly aback. Why would there be a problem? He smiled at her. The man was sitting on an ancient lawn chair atop a bed full of crates and chests. The legs of the chair were tied to the crates with electrical cord. Around on the crates sat numerous blond children, grooming each other's hair like monkeys. On the driver's bench sat several adults.

"Where ya goin'?" the old man asked.

"New England," said Lara. She decided he looked OK, and smiled back.

"Pretty girl like you'll have a better life up there, praise God," said the man. "Yes, yes, we all will. If we live to see it!" He grinned and coughed.

"Where are you going," asked Jenny?

"Canandaigua, New York," said the man clearly and firmly. "We left Lu-ray, Virginia two day ago, and been drivin' sunce."

"Did Luray get hit bad by the storm?" asked Jenny.

"Not the wind, miss, thanks to the Blue Ridge, but the rain come upon us like Perdition." The children stopped talking and all looked over at Lara and Jenny. "We lost twenty acre topsoil to the river, right down to clay and bedrock. Lost the barn t'uh river, too." He pronounced "river" like "ru'vuh" with an old-fashioned Shenandoah accent.

"You know anybody up in, um, where you're going?" Lara had not caught the pronunciation of Canandaigua the first time.

238

The man nodded. "My brother's family, yes." He waved around the wagon. "These all his grand-nieces and nephews." The children peered inscrutably.

"That's a long way, huh?" remarked Jenny. "How long will that take?" She glanced at the two-horse team drawing the wagon.

"Could take a month," nodded the man, speaking almost as if to himself. "Said it could take a whole month."

"Why aren't you staying in Luray?" asked Jenny. "I've been to Luray. It's nice."

The old man sighed and laughed. "W'all been talking about leaving for ye-uhs. Weather's too unreliable. Never know what'll grow and what won't. Not enough money to build greenhouses. New parasites on the animals whole time. But you know, you talk and talk and don't do nothin', 'cept when you have to. Sunce last week, we got no winter feed for the livestock and no cash to buy more. And there's fever comin', they say. My brother, bless him and dang him." The man laughed sheepishly. "He up and joined the Amish years and years ago, and they have all the food and feed they need. Now they need more hands." He laughed again, and clenched his arm. "I'm just the muscle they're a-looking for!"

Jenny and Lara laughed, impressed with the man's good humor.

"Are others leaving Luray, too?" asked Lara, her curiosity growing.

"Oh, a few. Here and here. The dirt farmers," said the man. He gestured toward the carriage behind them, pulled by four dusty Belgians. "Some not so poor, too, but fed up, like our neighbors down Egypt Bend Road there." He waved at the woman driving the carriage, who nodded back. "Them that's left buy the land and the animals and add them to what they got and maybe they can make a go of it then."

The vehicles around them all crept forward and stopped again. This kept happening every few minutes. They crawled closer to the border. There was no traffic over on the southbound side of the highway.

Lara heard voices ahead, and looked down the narrow passage between the lanes. Two Maryland state troopers were walking along, speaking up to the drivers on either side of them.

"Please have identification ready, folks," said one as they came abreast. "We're sorry this is taking so long, but as of this morning, Pennsylvania is requiring transit visas for non-residents." A muttering arose from everyone in earshot.

239

"They can't do that!" exclaimed the woman driving the Belgians, poking the side of the napping man on the bench beside her.

"Pennsylvania Governor's orders, ma'am," said one of the troopers. "It's out of Maryland's hands."

"As of when?" the woman asked, disgusted. "We were here last month and there was nothing of the kind."

"As of this morning, ma'am. As I said."

The other trooper spoke up. "The length of the visa will depend on whether your vehicle is motorized or not."

"What if we're staying in Pennsylvania?" asked another driver.

"You'll have to ask the Pennsylvania State Police, sir," replied the trooper. "I'm not in a position to tell you." The troopers continued walking.

"Transit visa!" said Jenny. "What's that?"

"I, I don't know," answered Lara, shaking her head. She opened a video channel to her father.

"A transit visa is permission to cross the state within a given amount of time," said Ari, wrinkling his brows and frowning. "Very strange. Never heard of that within the US before."

"Is that allowed?" asked Lara.

"Probably not," replied Ari. "I think the Constitution prohibits this!"

"I hope they let us through," said Lara.

"We're not staying, and this truck will make sure we're out pretty quick," said Daryl.

"Hope you're right," said Ari, hearing Daryl's voice but unable to see him.

In the relative quiet, as they waited, a whisper arose, seemingly coming from all directions at once, becoming louder and louder. Mike, awake now, was the first to react.

"Hey, everyone's on the same channel. Listen!" They could hear a voice, a speech, emerging from scores and then hundreds of mobile devices all around them. Mike reached for the lapscreen in his leg pocket. Jenny, Lara, and Daryl followed suit. The whisper rose to an audible voice, the voice of Speaker of the House Martin Laugherty.

"Not another campaign speech!" laughed Daryl, suddenly falling silent as he realized this was not a campaign speech. They all listened attentively, wondering why so many other people were doing the same.

"...cooperate with the wise decision of the Court," Laugherty was saying, surrounded by dozens of sober-faced Congressional colleagues. "Never in American history has a president entered into this kind of agreement with a foreign power without the advice and consent of the United States Congress, especially that of our friends in the Senate, as stipulated in Article II, Section 2, paragraph 2 of the Constitution." Intimating a wink, Laugherty continued, "We hope to hear from our Senate friends shortly on this matter. In the meantime, we are extremely gratified that the Supreme Court Justices have shown the prudence to bring the kettle back from the edge of its boil, as my grandma used to say, and restore some due process to this certainly urgent matter. This great nation has all the resources it needs to look after the needs of everyone who is faced with unexpected adversity, even when the weather acts up, as it has done throughout history, and sufficient resources are being marshaled now to make sure that this happens, I have been assured." He smiled generously. "Under these circumstances, as the Justices have implied in their decision, there is certainly no call to jeopardize the sovereignty and security of these United States by inviting in thousands of armed troops representing foreign powers to do the work that Americans can, should, and will do. I am therefore confident that I speak not only for myself, nor only for my party—the majority party in *both* houses of Congress—but for *all* of the American people when I say that the *precautionary* injunction against the Chinese and European relief intervention, just handed down by the United States Supreme Court, was precisely the right decision, and puts us all back on that even keel of democracy, checks and balances, and Constitutional government that distinguishes our *Homeland* as the world's longest functioning democracy, where there is no room for rogue executives, unilateral power plays, or private dealings with *never disinterested* foreign powers!" Laugherty briefly paused for applause.

"It *is* another campaign speech, after all," whispered Daryl scornfully.

"No, it's more than that," said Ari over Lara's T-pad. "Listen!"

Laugherty continued, sounding decidedly presidential. "Later today, when the business of the House of Representatives concludes here in Philadelphia, I will meet with Congressional and industry leaders to resume coordination of the raising of funds from many sources, public and private, to ensure that any remaining problems caused by Hurricane

241

Rhiannon are properly addressed in the affected areas. Tuesday is indeed election day, and I, like you, will take a moment to exercise my right and fulfill my obligation as an American citizen to visit the polls and vote, but aside from that, we plan to stay hard at work until recovery from this hurricane becomes a distant memory." He raised his hand and waved gallantly at the audience and cameras. "Thank you, God bless you, and God bless the United States of America!"

The program quickly reverted to the news studio, where eloquent, stylish commentators stepped in to discuss the Speaker's speech to the media. The whisper faded from the surrounding traffic, and the passengers of Ari's truck and Grandma's wagon found themselves as they were, waiting for forward motion in the bright sunshine.

Lara spoke into her T-pad. "Daddy, can I come up and sit with y'all up there?"

"Of course," said Ari. Lara jumped quickly down from the wagon and jogged along the right side of the truck, swinging up its rungs into the front seat beside Grandma.

"Hi!" she said breathlessly, and her greeting was returned. "Oh! It's nice to be able to look ahead again." She scanned the series of vehicles beyond the front of the truck, which were starting to roll forward again. "We don't have too far to go now, do we?"

"Mm, no," said Ari, releasing the brake. "Here we go." The truck accelerated and they rolled several lengths before coming to a new stop.

"So, what was that all about?" asked Lara, looking at Ari and Grandma.

"The Supreme Court granted Laugherty his injunction, to forbid Morales from allowing EU and Chinese relief flights to land here and provide food, water, shelter, and medical help to all the people affected by the storm." Ari's tone was ironic.

"But isn't it desperately needed?" Lara was incredulous.

"Of course," said Ari dryly.

"For reasons that are completely beyond me," said Grandma wearily, "the government is not getting these things into the storm zone very quickly, and people are suffering as a result."

"The ones who can't leave," said Ari. "Of course, all the people leaving are causing more emergency problems, too. Like all this." He gestured at the highway and vehicles around them.

"But why? Why can't the government do what it takes?" asked Lara. "They can operate the Interstates, and the railroads, and all the mines and wells."

Ari and Grandma were silent.

"Do you think they are doing it on purpose? For some reason they won't admit publicly?" Lara frowned angrily.

"Now, what might that reason be, I wonder," asked Ari sarcastically.

"Laugherty's going to win the election anyway, at this rate, so voter suppression in the storm zone can't be the main reason," mused Grandma aloud.

"I think it's a lot simpler than that," said Ari, easing the truck forward a few more lengths. "I think that it's just the combination of the Republicans having painted themselves into a corner on this issue, politically and emotionally, so they don't want to jeopardize their lead in the election or give the Front more ammo, along with the fact that the government's very low on cash, low on personnel, unable to borrow, and needing to safeguard resources far away from the storm zone to maintain order there, and keep the Trust and the oligarchs happy."

"Maybe too many government people have underestimated the severity of the damage," suggested Lara.

"No, I don't think they have," said Grandma, "but then there's also the fact that a lot of the troops and trucks and helicopters don't belong to the federal government. They belong to the Energy Trust."

"Aren't they really the same?" asked Lara, her head cocked to one side.

"I guess this is the part when we get to find out whether they are, or aren't," said Ari. Peering ahead, he exclaimed, "Hey, we only have few ahead of us now."

The length of the queue had quickly become much shorter, as the traffic disgorged into an old toll plaza located immediately across the state line, splitting two lanes and a shoulder into eight lanes. A faded sign in the highway's median, a meter deep in dry weeds, announced, "Welcome to Pennsylvania, The Keystone State." Each toll booth had become a border-control checkpoint. The toll plaza looked like it had not been used in a very long time. There did not seem to be any electricity; none of the signs or stop lights was illuminated. The windows of the booths were broken or covered with old, warped plywood. On the booths on the left were signs so sun-bleached that it was only with difficulty that the ancient letters "E-ZPass" could still be discerned.

They drove forward slowly. Ahead of them was a large, flat-bed trailer with Maryland plates, pulled by an ancient diesel pickup. The vehicle, passengers, and cargo were almost monochrome—a pile of dusty grays, peeling black paint, tans, and greasy browns. Several state troopers stood around the vehicle, looking at and under it. The driver had gotten out and appeared to be arguing with a state police officer. He waved his hands around and pulled off his cap. Ari and Lara leaned closer to their respective open windows to hear what he was saying.

"Three days!" yelled the man. "Three days?" The troopers appeared to be confirming this. One attached a sticker to the pickup's windshield. Other troopers, armed with automatic rifles, moved closer, tense and watchful. The man jumped back into the driver's seat and slowly accelerated away from the toll both. Ari pulled into the booth, looking around vigilantly to make sure Grandma's wagon would clear the bollards and low concrete walls.

"Hello," he said to the state trooper.

The police officer gave no greeting and, face blank, said, "With a motorized vehicle, as a non-resident you have three days within which you must exit the Commonwealth of Pennsylvania. If you have a destination within the Commonwealth, you must register with the state police within twenty-four hours of arrival, or you will be considered to be at large on an expired transit visa."

"That shouldn't be a problem," said Ari with forced cheer. "We are just on our way through. Is this, um, normal?"

"No, sir. Since this morning."

"May I ask why? The highway is backed up for miles and miles." Ari gestured behind him.

"Governor's orders," said the trooper in a clipped, tired voice. "We are collecting data and processing migrants."

"But can you tell me why? How on earth could you prevent people from staying in Pennsylvania? I mean, people have family. Not everyone is a storm migrant. That's temporary. There's trade, tourism…"

"Tourism, sir?" The trooper's face was deadpan.

Ari was apparently not going to get a satisfactory answer. "Does this cost anything?" he asked, changing the subject.

"There is no fee," said the trooper. Ari watched another state policemen place a sticker on his windshield, surely containing a chip.

"But you can go freely to any other state, so why impose this on non-residents?"

"Sir, you are going to have to move along now, so the next vehicle can enter this lane." He stepped back and motioned at the next driver with the upheld fingers of his gloved right hand. Then, leaning briefly back toward Ari, he added, "Not any other state, sir. Try getting into New York. Least that's what I heard this morning." He turned away.

Ari drove out of the toll booth. It was as if the world had suddenly changed. As they proceeded through the converging lanes of the toll plaza's obverse side, they fell silent, looking around. Beside the administrative building astride the median of the plaza were as many as a hundred troops in riot gear, resting and talking in small groups. A large Stirling generator on skids hummed softly nearby, its enormous parabolic dish aligned with the afternoon sun. A Pennsylvania National Guard helicopter sat on a dirt lot over beyond the right-hand shoulder. In the middle of the plaza, a tractor was dragging a fallen horse, apparently dead, across the lanes, out of the way of the traffic, leaving a wet mark and clumps of droppings on the dry pavement. Right where the lanes merged into two again, a large, temporary sign had been painted across what was once a billboard: "NOTICE - After 3 pm, all northbound non-motorized vehicles issued transit visas must exit the roadway at the Gettysburg Migrant Camp for overnight accommodation. Violators may be fined and/or have transit visas revoked."

"Seems harsh," muttered Ari, glancing at his watch. It was nearly three o'clock. They drove on for a couple of kilometers, quiet, each lost in thought. The boys awoke from naps snuggled against their mother in the cab's rear seat, and Honorée herself awakened. Lara found herself playing a finger game with Asa, who was suddenly silly and vivacious. The cab was filled with children's laughter, amusing Grandma, who smiled, the tensed muscles in her face relaxing.

Before long, they came to a highway exit for Gettysburg. There were signs for the Gettysburg Battlefield Monument. The state police had set up a makeshift checkpoint, and were waving most animal-drawn traffic and a few slower motor vehicles off the highway onto the exit ramp. "Three o'clock!" said Lara. "They were serious." The line of wagons and carts

245

mounted the ramp and crossed over the highway, bound for a large camp they could see from the truck. There were hundreds and hundreds of vehicles, tarps, and tents in long rows encamped across a large sloping field. Smoke rose from a central kitchen, fluttering away in the breeze like flags. They could see many people walking around. A few observation drones hovered high above the corners of the expansive field, where paddocks had been cordoned off for animals. There was a high fence around the camp.

The police signaled their truck through the checkpoint, and Ari accelerated onto the uncrowded road surface. "We'll definitely be in Harrisburg by nightfall now." He smiled at Grandma. Lara closed her window as the cool wind filled the cab. Grandma lay her head back against the headrest and closed her eyes. The highway snaked its way across the countryside, generally straight, trending north by northeast. Settlements became denser as they approached the outer villages surrounding Harrisburg's stockade. Despite well-kept farms here and there, there was a general air of neglect. As they passed a line of oxcarts carrying heaps of pumpkins and squash, the vast hulk of a logistics warehouse or box store complex appeared along the highway to their right. It seemed a kilometer long, the siding that had not been stripped flapping loose in long, buckling festoons. Several stories high, the building sagged at its corners, and the roof had caved in. Around the building was a thick growth of sumacs and other bushes and small trees. In large letters, above an entrance, remained the truncated text "WAG-."

"America was not built to last," said Ari.

For a moment, no one spoke. Then Grandma opened her eyes and tutted in irritation. "How can you say that, Ari?"

"Look at that." He gestured at the ruin.

"That's just a building, Ari," said Grandma dismissively. "Nothing money couldn't fix."

"It's a symbol of much more. I'm just saying. Things, institutions, lives, cities, landscapes—all thrown up fast so someone could make a buck or spend a buck quickly. No commitment. And this is what we end up with."

Grandma laughed angrily. "You say that almost as if you liked the thought."

Ari was taken aback by her irritation. "I think I'm just observing facts. Of course I don't like it!"

Grandma pointed at a large, neat farm just ahead, over to their left, with dozens of yellow haystacks and colorful hex signs on the gables of its big, whitewashed barns. "That looks built to last, Ari." Lara nodded in agreement.

"That's probably Amish," countered Ari. "Pennsylvania Dutch."

"Well, isn't that American? Part of America?" asked Grandma pertly.

"Well, no, not really..."

"Of course it is," said Grandma. "As American as you or me." She pursed her mouth and stared straight ahead.

"That would be there whether there was an America or not," said Ari.

"Oh, for Christ's sake," said Grandma angrily. "I love you, Ari, you're a wonderful old friend, but sometimes you sound so dismal and fateful and *knowing*, you know... I think you like to wallow in it. America's as built to last as any country... People and families are built to last."

Ari looked hurt, and absently probed at something between his teeth with his tongue. Lara watched them, fascinated. She had never seen Grandma and her father fight, and she felt an odd sympathy with Grandma's retorts. She recalled her own reaction to her father's Holocaust fixation.

"Maybe we're talking about different things, Florence," said Ari finally.

"What buildings were you talking about?" laughed Grandma sarcastically. "I didn't see any others."

"No, look," said Ari. "A nation, a political system, a story of nationhood—of course it isn't buildings. Take those first things away, and for a while all the people and physical things remain the same. But that warehouse was built because of an America that's gone, and you don't see any new ones popping up to replace it. The America that built the economy that built that warehouse was not built to last. What remains, including that Amish barn, keeps on going if its resilient, but it becomes part of something new."

"That's because of the Long Emergency, Ari. No money for that part of the economy, the part that relied on consumer spending and on cheap energy. The warehouses and box stores declined. But this is still America. How could it be anything different?" Grandma almost shouted her question.

"So, good! Yes." Ari smiled, eyes on the road. "So, we need to define what America is. Is it a culture that goes on and on, or is it a political system, a constitutional order, which can fall apart, like that warehouse?" He glanced at her, face open and inquiring, but quickly withdrew his smile when he saw her angry mien.

"It's a lot of things," said Grandma, exasperated.

"Because having to get a transit visa at the PA border definitely ain't the America I used to know. Nor are mandatory migrant camps. All the collapsing infrastructure is certainly a reflection of a bad economy, which we know has been going on for a long time." He slowed down as traffic backed up ahead. "But what first caused the bad economy is now apparently causing something deeper, some erosion of what America is all about. Freedom, equality, democracy. If you think—" He turned toward her again, but fell silent when he saw that her eyes were filled with tears, and her mouth an angry grimace.

"I am so dreadfully *sick* of all this," muttered Grandma, wiping away her tears. "We had so much to be thankful for, so much prosperity once, and so many stupid people have just gambled it away, and you, *you*!" She turned on Ari with a sob. "You just act as if it were all some sort of destiny happening to someone else, some kind of intellectual exercise!" She mimicked him. "Oh my, America wasn't built to last. *Oh, well*." She drew in a shaky breath. "Well, America was once, a long time ago, the most powerful, hopeful, generous country on earth—America did good in the world and at home. It wasn't perfect, but it was a damn sight better than this!" Grandma burst out crying, stunning everyone in the cab, none of whom had ever seen her in this state before.

"Oh, Grandma," said Honorée, leaning forward and putting her hand on Grandma's shoulder.

"Can we stop?" asked Grandma. "I need some air. I think I'll get back in the wagon with Claudie and Jessica."

In silence, Ari pulled carefully over onto the shoulder, and decelerated to a stop. Grandma squeezed past Lara and jumped down, walking unsteadily back to the wagon's cab rungs, where she vanished up into its cab. Ari started up again and accelerated back to their previous speed. Conversation remained stilled. A thin veil of low cloud passed across the sky, reducing the afternoon light level and turning the sky a uniform light gray. The dark skyscrapers of Harrisburg appeared over the horizon ahead.

31—A FUTILE THOUGH PRINCIPLED GESTURE

Saturday, November 3rd (evening)

"Do you want another one, Jake?" Linda Shatner stooped slightly to offer him the plate of pizza slices.

"Oh, no thanks, Linda. I'm good." Wilder smiled, and then turned back to his T-pad. Across the hotel room, Steve Johnson was doing the same, headset obscuring his eyes.

"I agree that we should leave first thing," Steve was saying. He scanned the train schedules. "Without the trains coming up from the south right now, there's less to choose from. Wait. We could take this one and change in New York." His avatar pointed at a row in the timetable. Wilder could see this on his own screen, in 2D.

"OK," said Wilder. "Book it for all of us. It's just as well that we're getting out early. Nothing sane is going to happen during the remaining day."

"Has Laugherty said when he'll adjourn?" asked Mary Worthington.

"Noon," replied Lola Osmanian.

"So, we won't miss much," confirmed Wilder. By their nods, the others confirmed this impression.

"You want to know the latest polls on secession?" asked Mary.

"I had almost forgotten about that," said Lola, laughing. "Wishful thinking…"

"Yes," said Wilder. "What have you seen?"

"Fifty-two for, forty-one against, seven undecided." Mary looked at them all expectantly.

"Hm," replied Steve. "Sounds like a landslide. Never polled at those levels before. How recent is this?"

"Yesterday," said Mary. "Wanna hear the breakdowns?"

They nodded.

249

"Women are fifty-four percent for, men only fifty-fifty. Non-white are fifty-five for. First Nations are the same as women." She studied her T-pad. "Here's a weird one. Republicans are in a dead heat, split forty-seven to forty-seven. But the few Front voters in Vermont are predictably strongly against: fifty-nine percent against. POGM is of course ninety-five percent for."

"What?!" giggled Lola. "Five percent of POGM voters are against secession?! Very logical."

Mary shrugged. "Margin of error."

"It should pass," said Wilder. "I'm glad I'm not Jeanne Remington!" They all chuckled wryly. "But then what?"

"Canada here we come," said Lola. "I mean, could we *really* survive on our own?!"

"Is everyone OK for food for the time being?" called out Linda. A few voices answered in the affirmative.

"I'm going to go to bed pretty soon," said Wilder. "I'm worn out. It's almost ten." He glanced around at Steve Johnson. "Steve, before we all disappear, you and Moriah and I need to go over the day's stats."

Steve nodded.

"And check in with Howard's people about the press conference on Monday."

"Yup."

Wilder stood up and stretched. Steve remained focused on his headset, listening attentively, facing off into space.

"Hey, there's something going on," he said suddenly. "Lola, can you turn that screen's volume up?"

Lola waved a hand within the largest wallscreen's control space. The sound swelled from its quiet background murmur. Conversation subsided as tired eyes were turned toward its display, which showed GNN's 24-7 newsroom feed. The regular programming was being interrupted in order to broadcast a message from President Morales.

"A new White House statement," paraphrased Mary from the banner. Everyone in the room froze and watched in apprehension as the White House Press Secretary Sora Rimena walked into view and took her position behind the podium. A slight, pale woman with a mass of dark hair, she looked small and nervous behind the podium—quite different from her normally assertive, even pugnacious character.

"That's Camp David!" whispered Moriah. "I recognize that wallpaper."

"So they're already up and operating back there, and not in Colorado any longer," remarked Wilder. "That was fast."

"We don't know if the President is there," muttered Lola.

Sora Rimena began to speak. "Ladies and gentlemen of the media, fellow Americans," she intoned formally, "at nine o'clock this evening, President Lucia Morales, in her capacity as Commander-in-Chief of the United States Armed Forces, instructed our military to facilitate in all necessary ways the orderly, peaceful delivery by Chinese and European Union units of relief supplies to the areas most severely affected by Hurricane Rhiannon one week ago. This joint operation, led by the United States with logistical and emergency response support by a coalition of friendly nations, will commence immediately. By this time tomorrow, we anticipate that delivery of potable water, food, medical supplies, and medical and humanitarian services will have substantially increased in the affected zones, in New Jersey, Delaware, Pennsylvania, Maryland, Virginia, and parts of North Carolina and West Virginia, as well as in states to the north, where many refugees are heading or have arrived."

The news feed across the bottom of the screen read: "3 million storm refugees now traveling west and north from zone—Number to grow to 7 million by next weekend."

Sora Rimena took a deep breath, shakily sipped a glass of water, and continued. "President Morales and her cabinet will continually monitor the efficacy of and need for this joint operation, and curtail it when appropriate, in consultation with members of Congress and with our allies in the field. In conclusion, the President wishes to recognize that, on many occasions during the history of our great nation, the United States has provided assistance in times of need when called upon by other nations, and it is with both pride in our generous history and gratitude in our hearts that we welcome the assistance of our friends in our time of need. Thank you."

There was a babble of voices as the few journalists in the press room at Camp David attempted to pose questions, but without even meeting their eyes Sora Rimena turned and left the room. With the empty podium still on the screen, the surprised voices of newsroom commentators cut in to begin the clamorous mass-media sensemaking of what they had just heard.

Lola dipped the volume. After a second of stunned silence, everyone began talking, a scene surely playing out in millions of wallscreen-equipped rooms across the country and world.

"She's defying the injunction!" gasped Mary Worthington.

"She can do that," said Wilder. "She's the Commander-in-Chief."

"It's now per definition illegal!" cried Lola. "She's got balls!"

"How many divisions has the Pope got, asked Stalin," marveled Moriah Oglethorpe, always the historian. "How many divisions does Martin Laugherty have?!"

"She's putting human needs above politics," said Mary quietly. "She's brave."

"I don't think a US president has *ever* gone against a SCOTUS injunction like this," breathed Moriah."

"What happens next?" asked Wilder, one hand on his head, the other holding his T-pad, which was already buzzing.

"I really don't know," answered Moriah. "Do you mean, procedurally or in real life, um, I mean," she laughed nervously, "as the constitutional crisis unfolds?"

"Both," said Wilder, glancing down at the list of who was trying to reach him. "All."

"OK," said Moriah. "It's one branch against another, so I think the first step would be to examine the authority question in front of the Senate Judiciary Committee...Um." She paused, one palm against her cheek. "Then, if Congress or the Court wanted to contest the President's actions, I think the full Senate would serve as the jury, like in an impeachment trial... The Chief Justice would preside—not Hedges, which makes sense. Except that the Supreme Court is a party to the dispute, sooo... maybe not! And anyway, the House would have to draw up articles of impeachment before sending them to the Senate." She laughed with embarrassment. "And this isn't necessarily impeachment anyway, but rather the question of defiance of an injunction, of bypassing an appeal and due process. I really don't know. I have to go study this. Talk with the AG. Because, really, this is a new situation..."

"This is when ya wish ya had a king to knock some heads together," cracked Lola Osmanian. "Break the three-way tie."

"Vermont may be looking for a king pretty soon at this rate," laughed Wilder ironically.

"Or queen," interjected Lola.

"Yeah, Queen Lola," said Linda with a look of mock astonishment. "Long may she wave, er, reign."

Lola laughed a little too uproariously.

"Moriah, thanks," said Wilder. "This may be how it all plays out, and I can't even imagine how this is going to affect the election now, but hungry, sick, displaced people can't wait. The legal process could take weeks or months. People need help now. Are they to be sacrificed for legal rigor and purity?"

"But Jake," said Mary. "Needy people aside, this is about a president defying the Supreme Court and Congress and admitting the armed forces of foreign countries into the US, albeit for a good cause. This is treason to a lot of people."

"They're not the ones starving and living under a tarp," sniffed Lola. "Having just lost everything."

"It really pits different perspectives and interests against one another," sighed Moriah.

"Guys, there's more coming," said Steve, waving up the volume again. They all stopped and stared at the screen. The banner and the newscaster were both reporting that House Speaker Martin Laugherty would be speaking to the press at eleven p.m. That was in nearly an hour.

"I'm going to take a nap," said Lola. "This is gonna be a long night." She nodded toward one of the suite's bedrooms. "I'll just use the sofa in there." She went in and closed the door behind her.

32—GOOD MORNING AMERICA, HOW ARE YOU?

Saturday, November 3rd (evening and late at night)

A big fire was crackling, and the crowd sitting around it had grown to perhaps a hundred. A few were dancing. The beer and moonshine had come out, and the smell of weed drifted in the air. Jenny and Lara were watching from the open tailgate of Grandma's wagon, close enough to enjoy the music, but far enough back to avoid the smoke as it ranged around, and to be able to talk above the rowdy singing.

"'Cause I'm as free as a bird now!" howled the crowd. "And this bird you cannot change!" There were gales of laughter, and silhouetted figures who jumped up to join the actual musicians with their swaying flourishes of air guitar.

"I can't believe how many old songs they know," said Jenny. "'The City of New Orleans,' 'Sweet Home Alabama', 'Who'll Stop the Rain?'"

Lara laughed. "'If I Had a Hammer" was one. And 'Ramblin' Man'. 'Proud Mary.' There are so many of them!"

"I know," said Jenny. "In Fredericksburg we had a tea house where they used to play all those old folk songs, although the Triple-C used to raid them all the time for playing devil music."

Lara laughed in recollection of a similar tea house in Roanoke.

The impromptu band of guitars, drums, violins, horns, a flute, and a cello was now nearly a dozen players strong, and despite having played for a couple of hours already, they looked like they could hold up all night.

Honorée and Ari joined them out of the dusk, and the women scooted sideways to accommodate them on the tailgate.

"The boys are *finally* asleep," said Honorée, looking exhausted, "and Grandma has taken over the front seat of the truck and is snoring like a trooper."

"Over all this noise!?" exclaimed Jenny. "And I thought Grandma would enjoy all the old songs."

"If you're tired enough," said Ari, "anything's possible. Where's Daryl?"

"He's over there by the fire with Celia and Mike," said Lara.

"And the ladies?" asked Ari.

"In the wagon's cab, still." Lara gestured over her shoulder. "They went back up there after dinner."

Their truck and wagon were in the motor vehicles section of the travelers' camp that had grown up over the previous week in the open land between the rail yard and Wildwood Lake, on the northwestern edge of Harrisburg. The motor vehicles section felt more comfortable and secure than the sprawling manure-strewn animal-draft and walker camp they had entered through, possibly because the motor crowd was somewhat upscale, and possibly because it was more orderly and cleaner underfoot. The entire encampment was relatively well-organized, between the efforts of the state police, the National Guard, the Red Cross, and the churches. Food was simple and limited, so travelers needed to rely on food they had with them as well, but security was good, and there was plenty of clean water.

The mood had been upbeat since Grandma & Co. arrived earlier in the evening. There was a crazed, almost festive atmosphere, which seemed to get rowdier with every new item of news that emerged about the developing national political drama. Whether people agreed or disagreed with Morales' move to support the foreign relief mission, they reacted with a growing sense of anticipation and excitement. When Laugherty had angrily denounced it an hour later, and announced the formation of a joint Congressional-Supreme Court "Crisis Group" to examine the situation and coordinate their response, people reacted with cheers, toasts, and laughs of scorn and derision. It was, reflected Ari and Lara in conversation during a late dinner, as if people understood what was at stake but had completely lost faith in the ability of the Federal Government to serve the public interest. State governments were laboring to deal with the storm and the refugees, but Congress and to some extent Morales herself were engaged in rhetorical games and a continual puppet-dance for the Energy Trust and Oligarchs.

"The Feds are dead!" a drunken young man with a long beard and straw hat had yelled during an early music break. "God save America!"

255

"Eat th' awligarchs!" screamed a merry girl, revealing her Baltimore origins.

A family came strolling by, looking at all the different vehicles: a man, three women, some young girls and boys. One girl was carrying a frightened-looking cat.

"Evening," nodded the man. The family paused in its stride. "That's a fine wagon."

"Thanks," said Honorée. "It's my grandmother's."

"We had a similar one once," said the man. "John Deere." One of the girls took his hand and tried to pull him onward.

"She looks like she's in a hurry," smiled Jenny. The girl made a face and stopped pulling.

"We're not going anywhere until tomorrow morning, anyway, honey," laughed the man.

"Where are you headed?" asked Lara. "You sound like you're from Virginia."

"Just south of. Greensboro," said the eldest of the three women.

"We were down in North Carolina barely two weeks ago," said Lara.

"Did you get hit by the storm?" asked the man.

"No, but our friends here did," said Lara, glancing at the others. Jenny and Honorée nodded in confirmation.

"Terrible, terrible hurricane," said the man. "Just awful."

"Is that why you're traveling?" asked Lara.

"Greensboro wasn't hit too bad—few trees down, lots of rain—no... We just don't like the way things have gone, so we're trying someplace new. This just finally did it." The man made a that's-that expression and grinned at the women.

"Much work in Greensboro?" asked Ari, curious but trying not to pry.

"Plenty of work. People just can't pay me with anything but food, feed, and livestock."

"Hens," laughed one of the women, quietly.

"What do you do?" asked Ari.

"We're vets," said the man, nodding at the older woman.

"I bet that will travel well," said Lara. "We were always short of vets at the horse draft center."

"We hope so," said the woman.

"Where are you headed," asked Ari.

256

"New Hampshire," said the man.

That elicited an animated response from everyone seated on the wagon's tailgate.

"We're going to Vermont," said Jenny. "Well, some of us."

"Some of us are going to Boston," explained Ari.

"No kidding," said the man. "Where in Vermont?"

"The south. Southeast," said Honorée. "Windham County." She glanced at Jenny for confirmation.

The vets shook their heads. "Never heard of that," said the man. We're going to Manchester. They are advertising for vets, and they pay cash. And have top technology. It's an entire clinic."

"Hard currency," said the woman. "Euros and Canadians." Then, in slight embarrassment, she added, "I mean, we could get by with hens and that sort of thing ourselves, but two of our kids need operations and you just can't ever get enough cash together for that anymore."

They fell silent. The vets offered no more details, and no one asked for them.

"You know anyone up there?" Ari probed.

"Nobody!" The older woman laughed. "Not a blessed soul."

"Wow," said Jenny. "That's a big step."

"We've had enough of Greensboro," said one of the younger women.

"I didn't," said the girl cradling the cat. She frowned.

The woman vet stroked her hair. "I know. Poor Sarah. But you'll make new friends."

"We're not into the Commonwealth of Christians," said the woman in a dismissive drawl. "W'all are just *not* into all that."

"And in Greensboro," said the man, "you just have to be Triple-C."

"We actually had people stop calling us because they wanted their horses treated by 'Christian' veterinarians!" The woman shook her head. "Don't think the animals cared one way or the other! I don't believe Genesis says anything about what religion the beasts of the field are!"

"We started looking into this months ago," continued the man. "The storm came at the time of our trip by pure coincidence." He looked around at the camp. "We didn't expect to have so much company on the road."

"There's a new storm coming," said the oldest boy.

"Really?!" said Ari. "I hadn't noticed that. That must be brand-new news."

257

"Hurricane Sulis," said the boy.

"Sulis?" repeated Ari. "That's a new one."

"She was an ancient Celtic goddess who punished criminals and carried out curses." The boy stood shyly, a bit uncertain but proud to show what he knew.

"Well!" said Ari, impressed. "I hope this hurricane sticks to the criminals and leaves ordinary people alone."

"Like Martin Laugherty," said Honorée sourly. "And all those damn Front people." She didn't care what the passing family might think. But they laughed quietly in response.

"You know," said Ari. "Vermont might be a separate country by the time we all get there."

The vets and their companions nodded. They knew about the secession referendum.

"Of course, they've tried that before, so you never know if it'll work this time." Ari shrugged.

The family visited with them a little longer, sitting beside the wagon and on the tailgate, comparing notes about the trip ahead, accepting pieces of apple pie they had baked before leaving Chevy Chase. Toward the children's bed time, with increasingly spirited music in the background, all said farewell, vaguely promising to look one another up once they made it to New England.

"Nice people," commented Ari as they vanished among the dark cars and trucks. "Smart people."

* * *

The din when the next major story emerged, toward midnight, was considerable—singing, strumming, rebel yells, laughter, spirited conversation—but as the import of the news spread through the crowd, the noise level dropped abruptly. Many fell silent, listening to the polyphonic murmur from the fleet of mobile devices scattered across the acreage. This time, it was not a political leader's voice, but rather a popular newscaster— a woman well-known for her many years with GNN and the BBC before that.

With a sober voice, she explained the stunning turn of events. Fearing for the security of the country, and unconvinced of the necessity of foreign help on the scale the President had ordered, the Joint Chiefs of Staff had, with the help of members of the Homeland Security Council and the National Security Council, prevailed upon the Unified Combatant Command to stand down, remove their forces from presidential command, and act in accordance with the Supreme Court's injunction. The President was under house arrest at Camp David, guarded by a company of U.S. Marines. One small, sad item that emerged from this drama was the news that the commander of Marine Security Company Camp David, a decorated colonel, had handed over command of the company to his executive officer when the controversial order came down from UCC, saluted the flag, walked off into the autumn-dappled woods, and blown his brains out.

"This is a mutiny," said one man, standing near the wagon's tailgate. He turned up the volume in his own truck's cab. The newscaster had finished speaking, and others were speculating about whether this was indeed a military coup.

Arguments were breaking out near the fire. Lara heard Daryl's angry voice in the babble. There was a scuffle. The festive mood was gone, replaced by something just as electric, but dangerous and unpredictable.

"That fucking president has been leading us in the wrong direction for years, and this time she had to be stopped!" shouted one agitated man.

"People need *help!*" another pleaded. "People are running out of *everything!*"

A woman was sobbing as she walked by. A man swore in disgust.

"This is very bad," said Ari quietly. "The emotions, the pent-up fears and resentments that this is going to unleash…"

"What's going on?" came Grandma's message on Honorée's T-pad, which was strapped to her wrist. "Where are you?" She had apparently been awakened by the commotion.

"We're back here on the tailgate, Grandma," said Honorée. "The President has been arrested."

"*What*?!" exclaimed Grandma. "That's terrible! Where is she?"

"Camp David," replied Honorée.

"Is she OK?" asked Grandma.

"We don't know," came back the reply.

"Has she made any statements?" Grandma's voice was urgent.

"No," said Honorée.

"Has the whole executive branch sided with the junta?" probed Grandma, sounding less groggy now.

"Junta?" laughed Honorée in surprise. "What's that?"

"Old term for non-democratic leadership. Wait. I'm coming back to you." Grandma paused. "Don't worry, Hon. I'll lock the boys in, and leave my PDA on for them." Honorée nodded as Grandma signed off. In moments, she stood beside them.

"Come on up here," said Ari. He stood up to give Grandma a hand. In the distance, a gunshot cracked. "Maybe we should raise the tailgate and secure things a little," said Ari. "I don't like the mood that's brewing." The music had stopped, and the vehicles and avenues around them echoed with hushed conversations and the occasional flare-up of an argument or oath. Daryl, Celia, and Mike returned from the fire.

"Some guy over there said that Morales was dead," announced Daryl with a breathless tone.

Ari shook his head. "Now how could he know that?" he asked. "And how crazy would that be?"

Daryl shrugged.

"He said his brother was a marine," said Mike doubtfully.

"So are thousands of people's brothers and sisters," retorted Ari. "Rumors are going to spread like a wildfire now that it's not clear who's in charge." He looked around. "Anything can happen now."

"I think it's pretty clear who's in charge now," said Daryl sanctimoniously.

Ari and Grandma both looked at Daryl with a mixture of disbelief and apprehension.

"Who?" asked Ari.

"Laugherty and the Justices," said Daryl cleverly.

Grandma laughed mirthlessly. "We'll see about that."

"What?" Daryl was irritated. "It's, um, not that I agree with them, but they have the Pentagon on their side, and what can an old lady locked up in Thurmont, Maryland do against three branches of government?"

"Daryl, that's only two branches. The military reports to the President... Or should."

"That's what I frickin' mean!" shouted Daryl, unreasonable in his agitation, swept up the currents of the moment. Celia, by his side, recoiled and looked him in surprise.

"Daryl," said Ari softly with a supplicating gesture. "What I mean is, you don't know where the military will continue to stand in this. And they can call the shots. President Morales has more powers than you think, and God knows where this whole thing might go…"

"Mm hm," said Daryl sarcastically, unmoved.

"The sooner we can get back on the road and out of PA, the better," said Grandma. "I am very scared of the ripples that this may send out."

"What do you mean?" asked Jenny, her worried face tense. "Like, what?"

Grandma took Ari's hand and held it up. "Earlier today, I snapped at Ari because he made some remark about America not being built to last that I took as fatalistic and negative." She smiled at Ari in the darkness. "Sorry, Ari." She turned back to face the group. "I was talking about America as a culture—rich, complex, vast—while he was talking about political institutions, I think." Ari nodded. "A culture can last and last. But maybe Ari's right about political institutions. They can seem strong for generations, and then suddenly change, or vanish. What's going on now has never happened in our history. God knows what it might unleash. There are so, so, *so* many scores to settle, and unrealized hopes and dreams looking for a way forward. So much misery and fear. So, when things come unstuck, well, you just don't know how they will come together again. And then there was all that Lost Arrow talk about energy and phase changes…"

"Do you mean violence?" asked Jenny.

"Oh, honey," Grandma stroked Jenny's cheek. "Not necessarily. Maybe, in some places. But, you know, shortages, routes getting blocked, more migrants, new laws, suspicious police, problems with money. Lots of inconveniences and injustices. I don't know…"

Some music started up again, by the dying fire. A man was slowly strumming a guitar, and a few voices picked up the lyrics and sang sweetly.

"Listen," said Grandma. "Like a bridge over troubled water." She started to softly hum. The others smiled in silence, too young to know the words. Ari blushed in the darkness, recognizing the lyrics, but no singer himself. The song gently flowed like a breeze across the dark encampment.

I'm on your side
When times get rough
And friends just can't be found
Like a bridge over troubled water
I will lay me down...

The man in the truck beside them, a heavyset black man, got back out of his cab and stood beside the wagon's bed, listening. There were women's and children's voices behind him in the dim truck. Lara glanced at his face, anonymous in the darkness. In the flickering firelight, she saw tears falling down his cheeks.

When the song ended, there was a scattered applause and many sighs and quiet expressions of appreciation. At long last, after such an emotional day, it seemed the camp was finally settling down and falling asleep, although many tense conversations were sure to continue through the night.

The man beside them spoke, lost in thought, emotional, almost oracular. "People may say I'm a naïve old fool, and what's going on now surely ain't very healthy, but I have a deep abiding belief in the goodness and the creativity and the strength of the American people, and believe that the mess we're going through now is a sign of how tangled up the government's gotten with the oligarchs, and of how weak our democracy has become, and of the terrible things that are testing us now, but we'll find our way out, yes we will, in towns and counties and states, until the right way of running this nation is found again, and then we'll all come together again in a new Second Republic...Mm hmm. Well, the First Republic is dead now, anyway. But look at all the old nations on their third, fourth, and fifth republics." He laughed sadly. "This one was gettin' all worn out anyway after so much use."

"And abuse," said Grandma, with what sounded like a suppressed sob, although, in the darkness, Jenny and Lara could not be sure.

33—AN IMPRESSION OF CONTROL

Sunday, November 4th (early morning)

"They're saying now that we'll be back in the Capitol by a week from tomorrow, sir," said Bob Peyton. "I got a message from Ms. Rodriguez' office last night. The streets are being cleared and the power is back on. Total security has been re-established." Laugherty nodded with split attention. Laugherty was on his cellphone, taking in some other conversation, but Vulk saw he had absorbed Peyton's news. Laugherty touched Peyton on the shoulder, shooing him away in a commanding, let's-talk-when-I'm-off-the-phone manner. Peyton bowed and backed off, turning his eyes toward the breakfast table, across the big conference room.

Vulk watched Peyton as he retreated from Laugherty's tall frame, eyes level with Laugherty's shoulders. Vulk had never liked Peyton. Where Laugherty had found him, Vulk couldn't really recall. It was before Vulk's time, somewhere in Chicago. Some campaign volunteer. Peyton was efficient at all the gopher tasks that Laugherty threw at him, following Laugherty around like a pet coyote, cringing and smiling. Vulk had tried to fire him several times. But Laugherty had warned him off. And Peyton kept his nose out of the most obvious trouble. Sharon Denny thought that Peyton was one of Laugherty's rumored illegitimate children, a theory others on his staff shared. Vulk wondered. He could not see even the remotest genotypic similarity.

Vulk's sideways look followed Peyton across the room, silhouetted against the scarlet panorama of Philadelphia's dawn through the large windows behind him. They were high up in the Burj al Sadaaqah Hotel, nearly six hundred meters over the dilapidated city, and well-protected from its riffraff. Fog, mixed with wisps of darker smoke, lay across Philly - the ground fog of autumn. The Delaware River was only a vague trough in the fog, swinging in its bight around Center City. Far to the southwest, he

263

could see the crimson towers of the crippled Delaware Memorial Bridge, its distressed cables and plates invisible at this distance. At a right-angle, to the southeast, he could see the pink sparkle of ascending sunlight on the surface of the Atlantic. The day before, he mused, these would not have been visible at six-thirty in the morning, because the clocks had only reverted to Eastern Standard Time a few hours before. Now, it was sunrise already.

Some of the members of the new Crisis Group were apparently not aware of this, Vulk guessed. Perhaps they were already up, running around in a hurry in their hotel rooms, throwing on their clothes, shaving hastily. It was already past six-thirty. The meeting was supposed to be underway. Laugherty, always punctual, stood by his chair, still talking on the phone, scanning the room. This was not an auspicious start to what was only the second meeting of the Crisis Group, and its first quorum. If they couldn't fucking get EST right, reflected Vulk, how were they supposed to run the country in a crisis? Where were the grownups?

The military representatives were grownups, Vulk noted. The Joint Chiefs were all in place, seated at the table by their name cards. Behind their sector of the table loomed a busy staff of senior officers and civilians, T-pads and lapscreens at full parade. Where attendance was not yet complete were the sections reserved for the Congressional leadership and the Supreme Court Justices. Of the latter, two Justices were not yet in place. Around Laugherty, just in front of where Vulk sat, the seats of the House majority leader, the House minority leader, the President Pro Tem of the Senate, and the Senate minority leader were all still empty. So was a seat conspicuously marked 'Vice-President of the United States." Most of the selected House and Senate committee chairs seemed to have arrived. Seated near the table were also a host of high-ranking civil servants from State, Treasury, Defense, other departments, and the intelligence agencies. Although this was a closed-door meeting, with no media or public present, there were, due to presumed necessity, a lot of people in the room. Vulk wondered whether this was in fact a good idea. How much of the Crisis Group's deliberations could be kept secret, exposed to this large congregation?

The bustle and conversation in the hall leading from the elevators suggested the imminent arrival of more Crisis Group members. The big room was quickly filling up now, and there was an air of expectation.

As Vulk went for a refill of coffee from a nearby table, the room suddenly echoed with the rapping of a gavel. As third in line in the leadership of the federal government behind the President and Vice-President, Laugherty was calling the meeting to order. He remained standing, banging the gavel on the elegant wood table, looking around the room with a soft smile and hard eyes.

"Ladies, gentlemen, fellow patriots, we are gathered here in a moment of dire threat to lead our country away from the brink of delinquent leadership and Constitutional crisis." He banged again and waited for the remaining talk to subside. The room became silent. Latecomers took their remaining seats at the oceanic table. Laugherty resumed. "Twenty-seven of us from different branches of government, all appointed or elected national leaders, have been selected to ensure that our nation can smoothly transition from one fully legitimate Executive Branch administration to the next, following Tuesday's election. It was decided one day ago through expeditiously arranged and highly confidential and complex consultations that the current administration, under the leadership of President Lucia Morales, had failed. This decision has been explained in writing, and communicated publicly, by the Supreme Court. As far as I am concerned, this matter is not in dispute, and although the current situation has come as a shock to us all and will certainly occupy the work of political scientists and constitutional scholars for a generation, we are not going to debate it here. The Crisis Group is here to govern, *not* examine the reasons or arguments for its own existence. So that is what we will do." Laugherty fell silent, his face grim, and looked out across the room from one side to the other. Faces were stony. Eyes gave nothing away. There was a faint background of whispers, no doubt remarking on how presidential Laugherty appeared.

"So," continued Laugherty, "I am going to turn in a moment to the Clerk for a reading of the agenda that has been prepared, which will be followed by a situation briefing by the director of the Defense Intelligence Agency."

That's because the Director of National Intelligence refused and then resigned, thought Vulk.

"But first, I ask all of you join me in the Pledge of Allegiance," finished Laugherty.

265

There was a rumble as everyone in the room arose to recite the Pledge, turning to find where the Stars and Stripes was hoisted, fumbling with their right hands across their hearts.

I pledge allegiance to the Flag, they said in unison with the cadence of a dirge, *of the United States of America, and to the Republic for which it stands, one Nation under God, indivisible* –

Vulk listened ironically for the strident voices among them who substituted 'indivisible' with 'invincible,' the Homeland Front's alternative wording.

- with liberty and justice for all.

As the crowd sat down again, Laugherty beckoned to a woman in uniform near him, and introduced the Chief of Chaplains of the United States Navy, who would give a benediction.

Jesus Christ, thought Vulk. All this pomp and rigmarole! They had so many practical things to attend to: urgent, desperate things. Not to mention a time limit of ten A.M., by when they would have to adjourn so that they could get over to the National Constitution Center and adjourn the session of the House of Representatives, after which they would all bolt home from Philly. It was crazy, and would be laughable were it not such a serious situation. They were operating off the map now. There was nothing in the Constitution about this procedure. They were inventing it as they went along. Which meant that some people accepted its legitimacy while others were in doubt or outright opposition. Nothing was certain now. This development could go anywhere. So pledges and benedictions, titles and uniforms were even more important now because of the legitimacy they symbolized. People clung to them. But without a Constitution in full force, they camouflaged clay feet. God help this country make it through this one, Vulk found himself praying.

And then an unaccustomed feeling stirred in his gut like a stowaway: fear. Prokop Vulk was suddenly afraid that something—some bizarre twist—might change all of their destinies, and divert Laugherty and his loyal staff from their anticipated ascension to the White House—an eventuality that everyone had been taking for granted for months now. Laugherty had been performing policy *gymnastics* with the Front to ensure they would conquer the White House. Vulk could not see exactly *how* this might fail. But here they were, inventing a new governmental order on the fly—who exactly *was* in charge, and under *whose* authority?—and when invention takes over, certainty flees. On top of everything else, there were all these vast numbers of people moving away from the storm's track - giving up on other places where they had been eking out a living, and moving. Some were violent, defiant. There had been riots. But most were just moving—glumly, slowly, almost aimlessly, it seemed. They were restless in a way they had not been before. It wasn't a revolution. It was more like a collective capitulation to an arrangement that, in the end, everyone agreed had failed. Where would this leave the political parties? The Trust? The oligarch's markets and bases of power? And yet, it was barely even being mentioned as the meeting unfolded. Something was not right. Vulk unclenched his sweaty palms and glanced around to see whether others were also feeling it. Sharon Denny met his look with a tense, doubtful look of her own.

Three hours raced by. Many spoke, and detail upon detail cascaded onto the decorated shoulders of the Crisis Group and the officials who now worked for it. Vice-President Hedges had still not been located, even though it was known he had survived the storm, and the speculation was that he was in hiding in his home state of New York. Scores of foreign governments had issued condemnations of the 'coup,' as they were calling it. China and the Europeans had lodged formal complaints, summoning US ambassadors to their foreign ministries and insisting on proceeding with their suspended disaster relief. They spoke of a humanitarian crisis. US leaders must not be sidetracked by internecine politics, said the complaints from Beijing, Brussels, Berlin, and Delhi. Above all, they emphasized, there must *not* be violence. They would not stand for violence. The world situation was already far too precarious. Their forces and those under the United Nations were stretched thin. The US must not join the ranks of failing states, they maintained. Democracy must be fully restored, and as soon as possible.

Many US governors and state legislators across the continent were in dismay, caught between their own discomfort with this unprecedented move by national politicians and civil servants they didn't trust, and the outcry from their constituents that a storm affecting only a small portion of the nation's population and landmass not be allowed to distract and compromise the entire nation. And a regional crisis it really was, except that the news was emerging that storm-related migration had now expanded to more than seven million people across eight states, and—

along with the fact that this was an enormous number of people—it was not entirely clear why many of them were on the move, because they were leaving areas where storm damage had been slight. Even stranger, there were reports of migrations in parts of the country far from any hurricane risk.

There were public protests, critical articles in the media, and sermons in churches and synagogues demanding that President Morales be reinstated. In desperate defiance, a dozen or so people, holding hands in a circle, set themselves on fire in front of the regional Interstate Highways Command building in St. Louis, Missouri.

Some staunch Republican governors and prominent oligarchs had meanwhile sent messages of support and encouragement to the Crisis Group. This was the right move for the nation, they said. We are on your team. Stay the course. Meanwhile, three of the nation's leading evangelical Christian clergymen issued a joint statement from Fort Collins, Colorado in which they expressed cautious optimism that this might in fact reflect a kind of divine intervention by which militant atheists and secular partisans could be removed from the White House ahead of schedule, and said they were relieved that the Crisis Group appeared to have a strongly Christian composition. They asked their congregations to pray for the Crisis Group.

A range of other matters swirled around the Crisis Group as well. Hurricane Sulis, the nineteenth named storm of the 2040 hurricane season, had reached Category Four and was steaming slowly but steadily toward the tip of Florida. The Aztlan uprising was entering its second week. A coal slurry pipeline in Indiana had collapsed, flooding several square kilometers with toxic fluids. And there was more…

The Burj, an unlikely gift to the American people from Arab nations in the wake of the Sanderborough catastrophe, caught the morning sun and flamed like a torch over Philadelphia. As the morning progressed, the fog evaporated, and a glorious blue autumn sky arched over the troubled land. A 'nine-eleven' day, the locals called it (although most could not recall why), dawning clear, crisp, and tranquil, yet latent with long odds growing shorter.

Some time in the morning's agenda had been devoted to matters of Crisis Group governance and process. There was majority agreement that the Crisis Group's mandate should be limited to the time interval from Tuesday's election to the presidential inauguration at the end of the third week in January, a period of roughly eleven weeks. The legislators in the room cautiously advocated for the assignment of full executive powers to the Crisis Group, including the authorization of all legislation, but the Joint Chiefs and judges pushed back. The Chief Justice drily but forcefully argued that foxes should not be left in charge of the hens, and that the Crisis Group needed to be on constant guard against usurping the checks and balances of republican government. A vote was taken, and the Crisis Group agreed by a thin majority to limit its enactment of Congressional bills to only those laws and appropriations "as are essential to the functioning of government and national security in the immediate term." There would be no long-term policy innovation by the CG, as more and more speakers were now referring to it.

Some asked whether, given the extraordinary circumstances, the new president could be inaugurated immediately following the election, but there was extreme discomfort among the Justices and many senior military officers with any further deviations from the Constitution, and the date of Inauguration Day was stipulated in the Constitution's Twentieth Amendment. The House Minority leader, Paul Carter-Wilson, who was a staunch Democrat and supporter of Morales, and who must have overcome considerable personal revulsion to attend this meeting, went so far as to raise the possibility of postponing Tuesday's election for several months "until things settled down," prompting a howl of protest from the Constitutionalists in the room, as Vulk had begun to think of them. This was quickly shot down. Yet his gamer's mind immediately became fascinated by the possible motives behind such a proposal. Perhaps it was sheer naiveté, but Carter-Wilson was pretty wily. Perhaps it was a way to provoke a cleavage in the Crisis Group, hampering its effectiveness so the Morales-Hedges forces could regroup. Maybe it was an attempt to give the Crisis Group more rope by which to hang itself, thereby discrediting the Republican-Homeland Front quasi-coalition and returning the electoral advantage to the Democrats, independents, and small parties. But Carter-Wilson's proposal went no further.

How exactly, wondered Vulk, could the other branches of government depose an errant—even treasonous—president, other than through impeachment? What if, as the Crisis Group had claimed, the need to rein in the president was extremely urgent? He pulled out his lap screen and did some quick research, realizing that he should have done this already. He found that the Twentieth Amendment to the U.S. Constitution was clear about situations where a president had died, and that the Twenty-fifth Amendment made reference to a president's being "removed," voluntarily resigning, or being incapacitated. The Twenty-fifth also explained how a Vice-President along with a majority of members of the Cabinet and/or Congress could declare that the President is "unable to discharge the powers and duties of his office," and thereby depose him or her. The Vice-President had to be part of the process. The President could disagree and fight back. A two-thirds vote of the Congress could ultimately resolve the matter, and put the Vice-President in charge. But there was no guidance for situations where the Vice-President refused to take part in the process. Nor was there guidance about how to define "unable to discharge the powers and duties." Did ignoring a—let's face it—politically motivated injunction (Vulk was no Pollyanna) in order to let more-or-less friendly nations assist the U.S. government with disaster relief constitute "unable to discharge the powers and duties"? In whose opinion? The Supreme Court's? Some Congressional staff had been saying that this was, in the end, about policy, and that the SCOTUS needed to stay away from micromanaging policy. That was the President's job. But here they were now, with everyone all hyped up about national security, the President under arrest, the VP missing in action, a Crisis Group formed to supposedly run the country for a short period, and millions of people on the move and in urgent need of help. Although certainly no one in *this* room needed help, thought Vulk. Everyone here had a full stomach, mobility, and a safe harbor to go home to. No one here had to fear hunger or poverty through the approaching winter. No one here had lost all they had. But somewhere out there to the east and south, not far from the Burj, and warmed by the same sun that was brightening their conference room, were a lot of people with very little hope. What should the Crisis Group do to restore it? Or was this not really a priority?

Three different interpretations of the Crisis Group's role seemed to materialize for Vulk as the morning's fog dissipated.

One—adopted by a small minority of legislators and one or two military chiefs—saw the nation in a worsening existential crisis, and wanted the Crisis Group to assume extraordinary powers, suspend democracy, and place the country under martial law. This should have already happened months or years before, they argued. It was high time!

270

These included Homeland Front sympathizers. They had a hard time articulating precisely why this was necessary. But they had clearly felt this way for a long time, and had been looking for an excuse. They were adamant, and knew what they wanted to do. The proverbial hammer that sees all problems as nails? Vulk dubbed them The Authoritarians.

Others railed against this with utmost passion and indignation; the problem, they said, was the failure of a president to carry out her duties legally, but the nation was not under attack or embroiled in civil war, the Aztlan uprising was of limited regional scope, and so were the effects of Hurricane Rhiannon. Our democratic legislative branch is working just fine, they asserted. Moreover, they pleaded, most states were operating normally and did not need the Federal government to step in and take over. This view—Vulk's Constitutionalists—wanted to keep the Crisis Group on track to sunset by Inauguration Day, deviate in as few ways as possible from the Constitution, and basically function as a placeholder for a normal Executive Branch. This point of view seemed to infuse most if not all of the Supreme Court justices. Laugherty, trying to appear above the fray, nonetheless sided with this point of view.

But a third position showed its face as well: Policy Opportunists. A loose coalition of primarily legislators argued that there was a lot of important legislation that had become stalled during Morales' presidency, including Forsa and OSCIA, but was sure to pass as soon as the White House changed parties, and with Morales gone now, why wait? Why subject the nation to even more delays in implementing policies that were urgently needed? Why subordinate practical needs to "proceduralism"? Expeditious moves in above all energy and natural resource policy could be justified by the need to stimulate an economy that could power the recovery from the hurricane, and stop all the migration—get people to go back to their farms and start working again. And these bills, they asserted, were critical for rebuilding national strength and prestige anyway, storm or no storm, so that foreign powers would mind their own business and stop interfering in American domestic affairs.

Florida Congressman Elijah Semmel, one of the members of the CG, stood up during one of the debates about procedure and, in an outraged tone, added to the drama: "This nation is in trouble, and my state may be in even more trouble with a new hurricane out there in the Atlantic looking our way, so more than the usual dose of medicine is warranted at this time.

Hell, the patient may die while we sit here deciding just how alive she gets to be while in our care!" There were scattered laughs. "Ladies and gentlemen, we have beheld a downward spiral in this great nation during years of liberal indecision and stalemate and fiscal mismanagement, and now we have a whole series of democratically grounded, future-oriented, national-security-boosting bills ready to roll out the gates. My party has soldiered on tirelessly to move these planks into position, despite a flagrantly, treasonously incompetent Presidency. Please, *please* screw on your heads tightly and understand that we cannot delay, we *must* not delay! This is a historic opportunity!"

These pyrotechnics were met by dry silences from the military and judicial sectors. Vulk watched in veiled bemusement. It was clear that the Opportunists were mostly legislators, the Authoritarians were mostly military and Homeland Front, and the Constitutionalists were mostly judges. This did not seem very surprising. Not surprising either was the hazy influence of the Energy Trust and its necklace of oligarchs behind both the impetuosity of the Opportunists and the rigidity of the Authoritarians. But what was unsettling to Vulk was the low level of understanding and regard in which the three apparent factions held each other. Where was the rallying around national unity in this time of need? But even with a President deposed, things were almost back to factional business-as-usual. It was all about turf and special interests. Around the table sat three camps, bunkered down in their own distinct cultures, beholden to their own constituents and patrons, ordinarily buffered from one another by a White House administration and the ornate layout of Imperial Washington's Mall and avenues, but now thrown together in the same arena. And skepticism and mistrust reigned.

As they moved through the parts of the agenda they had time for, debating procedure and top-line matters, tiers emerged from the basic design of the CG: an executive committee of nine and a 'troika' of three who would organize the continuing agenda, set priorities, make simple decisions, and streamline what many feared was already becoming a cumbersome instrument of government. Votes were hastily taken. Laugherty, of course, was elected a member of the troika. A delicate rock-paper-scissors balance arose among Authoritarian, Constitutionalist, and Opportunist positions, to the point where Laugherty himself joked that these would form the new party system that emerged if they decided to scrap the Presidency altogether and move to a parliamentary system with a prime minister; he called the positions 'Hawks,' 'Minimalists,' and 'Cowboys.'

No one laughed. Vulk thought that many people's facial expressions revealed far more queasiness than amusement. As the morning's meeting lurched along, he felt an increasing unrest himself. His fingers fiddled nervously with the stitching of his leather T-pad cover. Were they governing, or playing at governing? They had certainly taken a serious step with the arrest of the President, and they *thought* they were governing—they were all Very Serious People - but no one had elected them for *this*. The People had in fact not yet spoken. The sooner they could all make it through Tuesday's election and count the votes, the better, he thought. Otherwise, Vulk was afraid that a fateful assumption might be put to the test: the assumption that the nation would *allow* the CG to govern. For all that had happened during its turbulent history, thought Vulk, the USA had been able to operate under one single constitutional order for two-hundred and fifty-one years, without interruption. It was a world record. It was essentially the only system of authority the nation had known. It had been challenged, bent, ignored, weakened, and re-invented all along, but it had usually been followed in most ways, and the CG expected the nation to keep following it, even with the CG temporarily—or so they said—at the helm.

Could the CG count on the nation to do this?

34—RUMORS FROM THE BORDERS

Sunday, November 4th, late morning

"Wouldn't you know it," said the plump woman with a kind laugh. Christine smiled politely, and took another sip of her tea. What *was* her name? Christine could not remember. It was embarrassing. There had been quite a few newcomers to the congregation in recent months, many of them fresh arrivals to the area, between refugees and Vermonters retreating home. This woman had become active quickly. She was already volunteering with the Altar Guild. Betty? Or Berta? Christine did not know, and it was stressing her. Her cup rattled on her saucer. She laughed nervously.

A distraction conveniently presented itself. Mrs. Heller was coming down the stairs into the Undercroft, and appeared to need assistance on the lower steps, where the bannister ended prematurely.

"Oh!" exclaimed Christine. "I'll just..." She smiled and gestured as she drew away toward the stairwell, setting her teacup on a cart in passing. The others smiled and nodded. "I'm coming, Mrs. Heller," she called, moving quickly toward the elderly woman standing cliff-hung above the final slopes. Several other churchgoers were right behind Christine, bustling to help Mrs. Heller land. Mrs. Heller's face rose above the scrum of Samaritans, an unsteady blend of gratitude and indignation. Up the dim stairway above her waited the shadowy outlines of others trying to reach the Undercroft for their customary tea and snacks after the ten o'clock service.

There wasn't much Christine could (or needed to) do. Helping hands escorted Mrs. Heller down. She debouched into the better-lit function room, and the congestion above her cleared. As Christine turned to retrieve her tea, a familiar voice called down to her from the stairs. She looked. It was her old friend Sue Bailey. They both waved.

"I didn't think you were here today," said Sue breathlessly as she caught up with Christine. "Didn't see you when we were sitting down."

274

"I snuck in a few minutes late," admitted Christine with a guilty smile. "We got a late start this morning, and the horses spent most of the ride protesting against the rain." A series of heavy downpours had started in the early hours, and even as they spoke, the roar of more rain could be heard above the chatter of conversation.

"Oh, is Jake back?" asked Sue.

"Jake? No, he's on his way back from the emergency Congress in Philly today." She glanced at her watch. "I think his train leaves in less than an hour."

"Oh, 'cuz you said 'We'," Sue explained.

"Oh." Christine caught her assumption. "Oh, no. Jessamyn and the girls and me." She nodded her head over toward the tea table, where Jessamyn was talking with someone and the girls were loading up on crackers and jam. "Jessa and the girls are staying with me this weekend. Chris has been called up by the Guard and he's over in Bennington, at the border."

Sue frowned. "Seems like everyone is being called up. Dave is scheduled to go up to Burlington tomorrow."

"Is he still flying?" Christine sipped the rest of what had quickly become cold tea.

"He's not flight-certified because he hasn't done enough training, but he can navigate and do other things." She shrugged. "We've barely had time to talk about it. He's been in the fields fifteen hours a day for weeks. And I've been in the kitchen and barns…"

"At least you have lots of helpers, even when he's away." Christine smiled. "Or?"

Sue laughed wearily. "Yeah, most of them now. Leah and Justin are still only ten, though." She rolled her eyes. Sue and David Bailey had seven children, all of whom worked in some capacity on their large farm up the valley from Christine's parents' house. "Our hands are what I'm worried about. Everyone's still around, but Jason—you know, the red-head—is one of the new sheriff's deputies that have been called up—hundreds of them— and we might lose him part of the time."

"We're going to have—or need!—lots of helpers soon," said Christine with a nervous laugh.

"You are?" asked Sue. "Why?"

"My mother's whole family…"

275

"What?" Sue indicated that she could not clearly hear what Christine was saying. Someone from the vestry was making an announcement across the room, and the noise level was swelling. Christine stepped around a corner, away from the Undercroft and into the hallway that led to the Choir Room, beckoning for Sue to follow her. Once in the corner's sound-shadow, they both smiled in relief.

"So what were you saying about your mother?" Sue looked concerned. "Is she OK?"

"OK? Oh, sorry, no, nothing to do with my mother directly. No." Christine took a breath. "My mother's sister Florence and her whole family are moving up here—something like six or eight of them. Four generations. Things are not going well down in Washington and they are already on the way."

"Oh, no," said Sue with alarm. "Were they affected by the hurricane?"

"Yes, well, indirectly, I gather. Everyone's OK. But it's not a good situation." She lowered her voice. "I don't think they have enough to eat for the winter."

"Isn't that awful," said Sue. She shook her head. "Dave knows someone with the same thing going on."

"So some of them may have to stay with us. We have room. Jessa is helping me clean up and put stuff away."

"Can they be helpful? I mean, what can they do? You know, city people..." Sue revealed her farmer's mentality without reservation.

"I don't think that's a problem," said Christine. "I think they're pretty much like us." She chuckled. "It's going to be interesting having so much family around, through."

Sue nodded. "Oh yes, know what that's like." They both laughed. "But, you know, it may be hard to know what to do with people who have been, well, forced. You know, tensions, regrets..."

Christine shook her head and shrugged. "Cross that bridge when we come to it. First we have to just get everyone settled with a bed to sleep in." They both glanced back into the Undercroft, which was starting to empty. "Want more tea?"

Sue nodded. They both walked back to the table and refilled their cups from the nearly empty teapot.

"Mother's excited," said Christine. "She's close to her sister. Everyone says she's a good person, though I don't really know my aunt very well, not since I was little..." She glanced at her watch involuntarily. "Jake has met her many times, down south. He likes her."

"I don't know *what* I'd do if I suddenly had that many more mouths to feed," said Sue with a tone that Christine found a little disapproving. "Especially with it suddenly being so hard to get a lot of things that come up from Mass and Connecticut, with their states of emergency. I was just looking for spices and rice the other day, and I couldn't find..."

"They'll be feeding their *own* mouths pretty quickly, I would think!" retorted Christine. "Most of them aren't *babies*." She looked at Sue askance. "Jake says there's a labor shortage, with all the new people. He says there's good land sitting idle, greenhouses to build, and lots to do. My aunt was running big greenhouses in Washington..."

"Well, there you *go*," said Sue with a skeptical laugh.

"No," said Christine with an emphatic smile and wider eyes. "I'm really *not* worried! My cousin Claudia's daughter is apparently very good with horses, and her brother was in the Army until recently."

Sue put her hand on Christine's arm. "*Sorry* to sound like I'm pooh-poohing. You know your family. But with Dave's call-up I've been hearing all sorts of things about what's going on at the borders. Most of these poor people don't have families to come stay with." It was her turn to lower her voice. "Did you know that more than five-thousand people arrived at the border on 91 yesterday—in only one day - and that they're not letting most of them in? They are sending some to a whole new camp the State's setting up on the old Yankee nuclear plant grounds. Under guard! The rest have to stay in Massachusetts. Which I'm sure Mass isn't very happy about."

"No!" answered Christine. "*Really?*"

"Yes," said Sue. "The migrant camp at the Visitor's Center is full. I know because the Myrick men have been down there doing construction all week, and you know what *else* Dave said?" Sue started whispering.

"What?" Christine lowered her head to hear better.

"There's Chinese and European relief supplies coming down there from Quebec—the Guard is letting it through at Highgate—even though they're not supposed to. To feed them."

"Who's not supposed to?" Christine looked confused.

Sue turned her head and looked sidelong at Christine. "I thought *your* man was the national politician and *mine* was the dirt farmer!"

"Oh, I'm sorry, I mean, I know about the relief standoff, but it's only about troops, not about supplies. If they're just being shipped in from Canada..."

Now Sue looked confused. "Oh. I see. No foreign troops, but, supplies are OK?"

Christine frowned doubtfully. "At least, I think so..."

Sue corrected herself, falling into a whisper again. "But there *are* foreign troops. Dave said he saw foreign trucks on the interstate yesterday, a whole column, driving south."

"*Really!*" Christine looked shocked. "I thought this was what all the fuss was about in Philadelphia the past couple of days. The President was locked up because she allowed it. A total no-no. And the Guard is just *doing* it? Maybe they're only Canadian trucks..."

Sue frowned and knitted her eyebrows. "I *think* so. Dave wouldn't make it up... He *never* makes anything up."

"Are you *sure*?"

Sue nodded uncertainly.

"Oh my *God*," said Christine. "I'll have to ask Jake about this." She shook her head slowly, the fingers of one hand to her chin. "Oh my God. I wonder if my aunt and her family will have any trouble getting in. Isn't it all crazy?"

They stood in silence for a short moment, finishing their tea and reconnecting with the scene around them.

"Well, it's good that Jake and your mother like them," resumed Sue, in a noncommittal tone. "And they're family..." Her eye caught something behind Christine. "Oops. I have to go. Dave's making eyes at me." She flashed a lippy smile across the room at her husband, who stood surrounded by children and teenagers in raincoats. He gave her a dour look back. "Bye. Let's talk during the week."

"Yes," said Christine, glancing around for Jessamyn. "Let's."

Seeing her opportunity, Jessamyn glided over to Christine, trailing her youngest girl, who was holding Jessamyn's index finger and pulling in the other direction.

"Chrissy," said Jessamyn in her careful, pursed-lipped manner. "We ought to leave."

Christine's eyes, following Sue's departure through the ground-level door, shifted to the large window beside it. The window framed a background of trees tossing in the rain and wind.

"Is this the new hurricane?" asked Christine absently.

"Oh, no, it couldn't possibly be," replied Jessamyn with a tone of authority. "That's still way down in the Gulf." She pulled on her coat, and turned to her girls to supervise their coat-dressing. Christine realized she needed to go back upstairs to retrieve her own raincoat, but for a moment could not tear her glassy stare away from the fluttering trees. Under heavy, gray skies, the trunks heaved—maples, white pines, birch trees—their burnt-off summer green mixed with the dismal yellows of autumn. The downpour intensifed, drumming like some enormous machine on the roof above the entrance. It felt like the whole church was vibrating. The rain turned the playground outside into a boiling kettle of gravel and mud.

"I hope the roads don't wash out again," said Christine, re-emerging from her reverie.

"They will if we don't get moving!" said Jessamyn illogically.

"I just can't stop thinking about Aunt Florence and everyone, out in weather like this."

Jessamyn was buttoning up her youngest's coat. "Well, they're in a truck, anyway." Her tone betrayed a lack of enthusiasm for their impending arrival.

"Of course, I know that," said Christine, now fully present again, and ready to re-engage with her bossy little sister. "But half of them are out in the back of Aunt Florence's open wagon, right?" She flashed her eyes at Jessamyn. "Would *you* like to trade places with them? And have your girls along for the fun of it?!"

"*I* wouldn't put myself in such a situation in the *first* place," said Jessamyn dismissively.

Christine laughed drily. "Oh you wouldn't, would you? Do you think they *chose* this? You never know what's just ahead," she said. "There but for the grace of God…"

Jessamyn was silent, but her buttoning fingers spoke eloquently.

"Anyway," said Christine, "it's still going to take them a few days, and I pray that they don't run into any trouble."

"So do I," said Jessamyn.

"And have better weather."

"Yes," said Jessamyn.

35—THE LAST DELEGATION

Sunday, November 4th (afternoon)

Their train had left Philadelphia late, and was now somewhere between Trenton and Newark, New Jersey. It kept slowing down due to storm-related precautions. Track had been partially undermined in places and maximum allowed speeds had been reduced, even for maglevs that did not directly contact the track. Debris lay near the rail line, but had been cleaned off the track itself. The stations they passed were in varying states of damage. The platform roofs in Trenton, for instance, had been blown off their supports, but the station appeared to be operating normally.

The Vermont delegation and staff filled nearly a third of the car - both Rosen's and Wilder's staffers. There was a murmur of conversation. A few worked quietly. Most were still buzzing with adrenalin from the past several days, trying to make sense of it all.

Wilder had excused himself from meetings for a half-hour in order to take a nap. He felt exhausted. Yet he could not sleep, so he rested—eyes closed, ear-buds in—in his first-class seat by the window. Princeton. They had flashed past it a few minutes before. As if looking down a long tunnel into the distant past, a memory of his conversation on the northbound train with the Princeton professor Sash LeTourneau returned to him, and he realized with a shiver that it had only been a couple of weeks before. LeTourneau was supposed to be in Europe by now, or almost there. It felt like years had passed. What had they discussed? Mutual concerns. Concerns that had felt urgent then—about electoral politics, about civil rights and liberties, about what *might* happen - but which now, in today's context, could only be remembered as trivial, preliminary, downgraded by new developments. What a difference two weeks could make.

Did it all come down to the storm, he wondered. Hurricane Rihanna, er, Rhiannon. It was certainly a destructive hurricane, a terrifying hurricane, but there had been others. He'd seen the statistics. This was a bad one. But no, maybe he wasn't fully grasping what was different about this hurricane because he had not experienced it directly, or personally visited the areas affected. He'd seen the media footage, of course—the floods, the shattered houses, the acres of mud and debris—but you saw that on VNET all the time, all over the world. The cyclones in Australia, river floods in Central Europe, swamped Asian coastlines. The fires in Siberia. The dust storms in India. Maybe he needed to see it all with his own eyes, smell it, touch it. He opened one eye and glanced eastward from his seat, across the flat, cultivated landscape of New Jersey toward the eastern half of the state that the storm had plundered. As the scenery sped by, he saw a few branches down, a blown-over fence, missing shingles on roofs, standing water. Traversing a village center with the blink of an eye, he registered military vehicles, people standing in a long line, and the collapsed bleachers of a ball field. Maybe there *was* more he could see with his own eyes if he looked carefully. He realized that their route was taking them closer to the coast as it approached New York. The Big Apple had been spared the worst of the storm, but not northern New Jersey. Why had he been so unobservant on the way down? Perhaps it was due to his intense conversation with Howard Rosen about Vermont's domestic affairs.

Then they were abruptly out of the village and crossing open ground - the sense of speed reduced against the backdrop of a more distant horizon. In the fading light of the November afternoon, under ashen clouds, he saw vast tatters of what might have been hoophouses draped in a poplar windbreak. He saw the soaked remains of haystacks scattered across muddy earth. Then they passed acres of punctured green houses. People stood or worked here and there with shovels and axes. Wilder saw few motorized construction or farming vehicles. Then the train slowed as they crossed a bridge, and he gaped down into an eroded, debris-choked channel, amazed that the flood that passed through it had failed to take out the bridge.

The storm had clearly left many traces. But was the hurricane the single source of the intensifying political and refugee crisis, or was there some other cause? A conspiracy? A movement? The arrival of a new paradigm?

The stage had been set, of course. Foreign powers, fearful of what America was becoming, had been pressuring it to accept redevelopment assistance—"constructive engagement," they called it. That had quickly morphed into an offer of disaster relief. There was already explosive antipathy toward Morales among Republicans and Front people, and her defiance and arrest, although unprecedented, were logical escalations of this that seized upon new circumstances. Things were as they were. But what was really driving all of this movement of people, of evacuations and exodus? It did not entirely make sense to Wilder. Why now? Why so precipitously?

He ceased his surreptitious scan of the countryside, removed his earbuds, and stretched. Moriah smiled at him from across the aisle. He scowled at her with mock suspicion, and then grinned. Had she been watching him while he pretended to sleep? Waiting to pounce as soon as he awakened, ahead of anyone else? Ah, the houndedness of public service... Yet he didn't mind being watched by Moriah. Despite her sober manner and scholarly demeanor, she was one of the best-looking women in his staff, and she was single of late. And, Wilder suspected that she fancied him, concealed beneath her accustomed layer of professional protocol. Lola was larger-than-life, all flouncy and perfumed, and with a partner and kids. Mary was severe and efficient—an old-fashioned Yankee - and married to a farmer woman up in the Northeast Kingdom whom Wilder had never met. Selena was coltish and rangy, and way too young. Linda was bubbly-cute, and—Wilder suspected—quietly together with Steve. There were others up in the Burlington office and down in DC. But Moriah stood out. He stretched again, regarding her through half-closed eyes: her pale, clear skin; her wavy brown hair; her lithe figure leaning back against the edge of the seat as she half-sat on the armrest. He indulged in an instant of secret appreciation. He was Christine's, *of course*, but there was no harm in looking.

"Welcome back, Congressman," said Moriah. "Did that rest help?"

Wilder sat up and gathered himself. He disliked being formally addressed by his staff, though he knew she was jesting. "Please, Dr. Oglethorpe! Jake!" he laughed. "Hi." He took a deep breath. "I guess it helped, although I never really slept."

"Mind if I join you?" she asked.

"Of course not," Wilder said, hoping he did not sound too eager. "Here, let me get this stuff out of the way." He moved his small briefcase and T-pad from the vacant seat on his left to his seat-back tray. Moriah sat down beside him.

"I want you to see this," she said, all business, positioning her T-pad on the armrest between them. Her finger flicked quickly through a few selections. Aerial OS-drone video footage of an enormous traffic backup swung into view, near a river and bridge. The highway was solid with stopped traffic as far as they could see to the west.

"Where is this?" Wilder asked.

"The George Washington Bridge. About an hour ago." He nodded. "See. There's Fort Lee. They are all trying to cross into New York State. Something like 150,000 people, just in this backup." She zoomed in. "That's bad enough. But here's what I wanted you to see." The fuzzy vehicles and crowds near a toll plaza resolved quickly into fine details. They could see individual people, and almost see the expressions on their faces.

Wilder shook his head, watching closely. "Jesus." There was a riot underway. Without the benefit of audio, and with the slight shakiness that came from a video zoom from hundreds of meters, they could nonetheless clearly see people running, a line of riot police forming, puffs of smoke or tear gas, and the queue of traffic becoming ragged as vehicles broke ranks to get away from the disturbance.

"People's impatience boiling over," commented Lola, leaning over from the seat behind them. "They must have been waiting for hours. Days, even."

"No, it's more than that," said Moriah.

"Huh?" asked Wilder. "How?"

"New York was closing that border crossing when this was shot," explained Moriah. "They're dealing with complete chaos. Too many people, camps full, gridlock, health emergencies and horses collapsing along—I don't know—thirty, forty kilometers of highway. New Jersey can't deal with it to begin with, so a lot of people are in pretty bad shape by the time they get to the New York border. Then it just gets worse."

Wilder listened in quiet alarm.

She continued. "It's a bottleneck. These refugees aren't going to take any of the tunnels into Manhattan—they are just passing the City, up 95 -

and it's a long detour up the Hudson to the Tappan Zee Bridge, so they have been putting more and more pressure on the GW Bridge."

"It looks like it's raining," said Wilder, inspecting the video. "See how dark the pavement is."

"I believe it is raining," said Moriah. She glanced outside. "Not here yet, though. An hour ago my sister said it was pouring in Barre."

Wilder followed her glance. There were no raindrops yet on the windows of their train.

"What I don't get is why this is getting so out of control," said Lola in exasperation. "People stand to lose everything they leave behind. They're part of communities. There are supposedly enough relief supplies starting to get through. Why...?" She shook her head. "What the hell?!"

"Lola," said Wilder, twisting to look back up at her, "this is now an avalanche. What started it almost doesn't matter now, because it's generating its own weather. People have already lost everything, and I don't think for a second that enough relief is getting through. Not yet. Plus, what, are states like New York and PA equipped to handle all of this when it's beyond any scenario they trained or prepared for?"

"It's like a leap-frog chain reaction," said Moriah. "The people from the really, really destroyed areas spread out first, filling up the camps and consuming the supplies on hand—the places just west of Washington, west of Baltimore, or what we saw in Camden. Then the second concentric tier of people where the damage wasn't quite as bad start realizing that they don't have enough food or feed, the electricity will be down a long time, they can't run their farms, or get fuel. Their first perimeter of retreat is already full of the worst-hit. So they keep going, leaping the frog. Maybe convincing or dislodging even more people as they pass through." She paused for breath. "And then there's this talk now about fever."

"What?!" Wilder looked at her sharply. "That's the first I've heard of that."

"I've got Selena trying to confirm this, but that's the rumor as of this morning. Some kind of flu or livestock-transmitted virus. Reported in Delaware and Maryland. So..." Moriah looked up at Lola. "So, this has got to be just one more thing people are thinking about as they pull out the truck or wagon and tell the family to start packing." Then she turned and drew back to address them both. "And remember, we are only talking about a fraction of the population in these areas. Maybe only ten, fifteen

284

percent. Twenty in some. Everyone else is hunkered down and toughing it out. And of course they need help."

"Awful," said Lola.

"So this really is a perfect storm-on-top-of-a-storm," muttered Wilder.

"Yeah," said Lola. "And talk about disconnect. They were standing up there at the podium this morning acting like everything was under control and no foreign help was needed, all sanctimonious, when a refugee crisis and civil disorder is unfolding right under their noses. So ignorant…"

"Fiddling while Rome burns," said Wilder. "Our fine brothers and sisters of the permanent Congressional red-black coalition."

Lola shook her head in disgust and rubbed her neck. "And I don't even know who's in charge of DRR now, since the coup. Is it still Quinlan? Is the CG even paying attention to DRR, or are they still all wrapped up in figuring themselves out?"

"The latter," said Wilder.

The train started slowing down, disturbing the maglev's silky smoothness. They all glanced out the window. "A station so soon?" asked Moriah in surprise.

Wilder shook his head. He had done this trip weekly for six years. "Couldn't be, yet." The train decelerated more quickly, its landing wheels singing as they extended onto the rails, and came to a stop on a long curve between scrubby woods and the stripped carcass of a suburban neighborhood.

"Well," said Lola.

"When's our connection in New York?" asked Wilder.

"Six-thirty-four," sang Linda from two seats ahead of them.

Wilder adjusted his glasses and squinted at his HUD. "We should be OK, then." Lola and Moriah made doubtful faces. "I mean, that's not for two hours."

There was a momentary silence until Moriah broke it. "I wonder who used to live there?" she asked, looking out the window across the pattern of cul-de-sacs, berms, and concrete pads stretching down the weedy slope toward a row of trees about a quarter-mile away that likely defined a road.

"I did," laughed Lola.

"Did you grow up in Jersey?" asked Moriah in surprise.

"Yes, I did," Lola confirmed. "I'm joking about right here. We lived up north of Paramus. In beautiful Montvale, near the Hudson. But, well, it coulda been a place like this."

"You ever go back?" asked Wilder.

"To what?" asked Lola. "My whole family moved to Vermont after I got a job there, and I heard it's all ag land there now. Orchards."

The train moved ahead perhaps a hundred meters, and then inexplicably stopped again. No announcement came from the PA system.

"This is worrisome," said Moriah.

"Hey, it's Jersey!" wisecracked Lola.

"So, what's the latest on the injunction and the President?" asked Wilder, hand moving unconsciously toward his T-pad. "Any developments?"

Moriah sat up a little straighter, waving her hair away from her face with her right hand. She patted her T-pad.

"No significant pings since we left the NCC," she said. "Morales hasn't made a statement. Hasn't filed a countersuit or legal appeal. No word from the AG, who as far as I know is with her. Um..." She cocked her head and went on. "The national reaction is mixed. We know about the refugees. Protests in a few cities. The world is up in arms, of course. Now, it's a race to Tuesday, and we'll see what happens then."

Wilder nodded and took a deep breath.

"Oh," she added. "And that hurricane. Sulis. It looks like it's getting very powerful, and they are saying it will come ashore in Florida close to Miami."

"Great," said Wilder wearily. "As if one perfect storm weren't already enough."

"Tea?" called someone from up the aisle.

"Sure," said Wilder.

"I'll get it." Moriah jumped up. "Funny, we're still stopped."

The train sat idle, silent. After a moment, as Moriah's retreating figure vanished from Wilder's view beyond the curtain separating first from business class, the announcement came. A woman's voice explained that there were "track and station delays" ahead and that the train would resume its motion very shortly. No other information was given.

"Track and station delays," said Wilder. Lola sniffed in response. "That's kinda vague," he added.

286

They both sighed.

"Pretty tough few days," said Wilder.

"Yup," she said.

"You guys held up beautifully," he said. "I couldn't imagine working with a better team."

Lola smiled at him from a tired face. She looked like she might cry, but held back.

He eyed her askance, changing the subject. "You think the secessionists will win on Tuesday?"

She nodded and dabbed her nose with a handkerchief.

"You looking forward to that?" he asked.

"Nope."

"You think it'll lead to something with teeth?" he continued his probing.

She nodded again. "Well, yes, something. But things could turn out a lot of different ways and I'm no history expert like Moriah or Mary, so I'm not gonna speculate beyond a simple yes-vote."

"Smart," he said.

"I do think that we haven't seen the last of the Morales presidency," she offered.

"How so?" he asked.

"She's the President, for Christ's sake," she said, regaining some of her usual forcefulness. "Some CG doesn't just decide for itself that they're going to bypass the U.S. Constitution, and toss her out. We haven't heard anything from her, but I'll bet there are a *lot* of people both out there and inside the government who don't agree with what just happened, and regardless of who wins on Tuesday, they're gonna work to see that she completes her term."

"What would the purpose be?" asked Wilder, curious where Lola was going with this.

"Tea," said Moriah, sliding back into the seat with three cups.

"Moriah, thanks. Hey, listen to Lola for a second," said Wilder. He nodded at Lola so she would continue.

"No, well, I, I just think that there are a lot of unknowns and a lot of forces at work. That CG came out of nowhere—who expected that?!—but we all know that there are other things going on behind the scenes."

Wilder nodded. "You're surely right." He glanced a question mark at Moriah.

Taking her cue, she responded, "Well, I didn't hear the first part of what you were both talking about, but I agree with the last part."

"Funny that Hedges has been so invisible," said Wilder.

"Ya think?!" laughed Lola in mock disbelief. "As soon as he appears, they are going to arrest him, too."

"Why?" asked Wilder quietly. "He's not charged with anything. He didn't defy the injunction. He's supposed to be in charge now, or at least a key player in the deposition machinery."

Lola considered this. "I see your point. But as soon as he refused to carry out any part of his legal role, the CG could nab him with the same justification it used for Morales. Plus, whatever he does, he legitimizes what the CG stands for: he's either collaborating or encouraging them to exercise authority. Better stay well out of it. Force them to remain irregular, unconstitutional. Don't give 'em either chance."

Wilder nodded but did not say anything.

"Now that the horse has bolted," said Moriah, "I wonder whether anything is going to get back to normal after the election."

"Normal?" asked Lola. "What's that?"

"Um, a democratic republic?" countered Moriah. "I think that's what the CG is promising."

"Ha," sniffed Lola. "*So* Twentieth Century."

"It may be very challenging," said Wilder, "especially if this storm-driven crisis gives Laugherty's 'Hawks' more ammo to use in calling for martial law and a state of emergency. After that, it could play out any number of ways." He set his mouth. "Which we are going to have to map out and game-play as soon as we see the election results."

"Is anything uncertain at this point?" asked Lola. "Don't we pretty much know?"

Wilder looked at her blankly. "Nothing is given," he said cryptically. Lola pouted at him.

"Well, a lot's at stake and I think things will move toward a resolution more quickly than most people suspect," said Moriah. "It's not like the Universe is going to wait around for the CG to get its act together. The CG might wind up getting bypassed altogether!"

288

"That sounds ominous," said Lola. "Not if they can help it. They're some pretty powerful boys and girls...well, mostly boys..." She glanced at Wilder for his reaction.

Wilder looked down, and then away - out the window at the stalled landscape beyond the bot- and drone-patrolled security fence that skirted the high-speed railway line. "I didn't tell you this," he said quietly, "but I think the states might start playing a bigger role than people expect, once they figure out what to do with this big surge of refugees."

They digested that for a heartbeat.

"Well, if the PGM gets its win on Tuesday, then we might just be the last Vermont delegation to the United States Congress," said Lola.

"But also the first diplomatic mission to Washington," laughed Wilder. "We'd do just fine."

"We speak the language fluently, and understand the culture," smiled Moriah.

"You understand the culture?!" laughed Lola incredulously. "It totally baffles me, I gotta tell ya." They all chuckled wearily.

Then, the PA system hissed on again, and a new announcement by the same female voice sounded throughout the acoustically damped car: "Ladies and gentlemen, TransRail apologizes for this inconvenience, but there appear to be administrative difficulties in crossing the state line from New Jersey into New York. We will be able to start moving again when these have been resolved. This may take a few minutes. In the meantime, please visit the Café Car and Club Car as our guests. Vouchers have been issued to all passengers. We will let you know as soon as the situation has been cleared up."

No new estimated time of arrival at New York's Pennsylvania Station was specified.

"Cheer up," laughed Lola. "At least we're going home, and I'm gonna walk to Vermont from New York if I have to!"

"I hope we have other ways of getting home," said Wilder. "Like a train."

36—SCRANTON, PENNSYLVANIA

Sunday, November 4th (early evening)

Grandma lay dozing in the driver's seat, her head back against the headrest. She had driven the final twenty or so kilometers to Scranton. Now, the truck and its trailer stood parked in their spot in the rocky camp the Pennsylvania Citizens' Militia had established on the eastern side of Interstate 81, up on a mesa of ancient mine tailings and slag. It was already dark, and a cold rain was falling through the gusty night.

Honorée hunched over her T-pad, navigating the State of New York site, trying to find the pages about transit bonds. They had been hearing about these all day long as they traveled up through eastern Pennsylvania, maintaining a steady pace in the left lane of the highway as it rose and fell over the long ridges of the Pocono Mountains. There was a lot of traffic, but it flowed. The roadway was generally unaffected by the hurricane, although at several points the big highway bridges were out for reasons of general disrepair and they had to descend onto narrow mountain roads and twist around until the detours took them back up onto I-81 North.

There. In seconds she found it. "New York State Travel Restrictions and Transit." There was some explanatory text, a video, and yesterday's date. This was brand-new. She squinted at the page. Sure enough, out-of-state vehicles entering New York had to take out a bond, and they would only get the money refunded upon exiting the state within forty-eight hours or being granted permission to stay longer through work, family connections, or other "valid criteria".

She swore under her breath as she scrolled through a table of transit bond prices that varied by vehicle type, state of origin, anticipated length of stay, and point of entry. They were not cheap! Where they planned to enter (Port Jervis), for two days in the state (the minimum), a motor vehicle with a trailer and a total of four axles (like theirs) needed to pay

$2000. It was only $200 if they entered New York up I-99, somewhere to the west. Honorée reflected over how this was creating incentives to take certain crossings and not others. There was some state government logic to it. Why did their route have to be so expensive? But there was nowhere else they could cross into New York without getting way off track. They would have to pay. Good thing that there was still a reasonable balance in Grandma's household account, which Honorée had access to. They might need quite a bit of it to get to Vermont. She went ahead and purchased the transit bond.

When the confirmation came, Honorée put the T-pad away in the glove compartment—she loved that old term for the storage compartment in the dash—and sat back for a moment in the darkness of the cab. Her grandmother's deep, regular breathing lent a quiet rhythm to the closed compartment. She could not hear any of the others; they were back behind the wagon, preparing dinner and unwinding under the large tarps they had strung up beside the bed.

The relative silence of the cab, her sleeping grandmother, and the evening's autumnal damp put Honorée into such a mood of sadness-seeded reflection that it surprised her. The recent weeks had been busy, chaotic, and demanding. With two young children, she had hardly paused to contemplate her circumstances, yet life had swept her along from Sanna's sudden departure and the theft of the van to the storm, its aftermath, her move to Grandma's house, the arrival of all the others, and then the hasty departure from Chevy Chase two days before. Most of the meager contents of her Mount Saint Alban apartment were still stacked on the floor of Grandma's living room, and the last rent only just paid. She hadn't even had time to cancel her stall contract at White Flint, although all that was left there—she assumed—was a pile of shelves and wooden crates damaged by water and wind. Her market neighbor, Mary, would wonder where she had vanished to. She didn't even know Mary's last name. They had worked the market side-by-side for two years. They weren't friends. But there was another human tie that had been clipped, just like that! Really odd. As if the world she now inhabited was moving, like an iceberg pulling away from the shore, changing the landscape as it drifted. And that Grackle. Weird man, but funny and, she had finally realized, kind. Mike had seen him walking through Bethesda. She hoped he would find a safer, happier life. Though maybe he was already as safe and happy as he wanted to be.

Was she safe and happy, wondered Honorée? She didn't really know. She was so busy and tired that she felt like a spectator, watching the continually re-rendering scenes around their traveling party—scenes of countrysides and towns, travelers and state police, camp workers and suspicious locals. She felt safe enough in the company of her family and friends, despite the sometimes menacing atmosphere they journeyed through. Well, no, it was seldom menacing. Wearying, perhaps, or hopeless, but no one had threatened them. On the interstates and in the camps, there was order and security. Maybe if she were traveling alone, she would feel differently. But she did feel safe. Happy? Honorée didn't really even know what that meant anymore. Comfortable, sure. Light-hearted when she joked with Jenny or Lara, of course. Optimistic? Nothing there. Happy? Well, maybe there would be time for that in Vermont.

Coming out of her reverie, Honorée looked out around the field of view the truck's windshield afforded her. Like the camp in Harrisburg the night before, they had been directed to a section reserved for motorized vehicles. This seemed to make sense. Motor vehicles didn't need feed, and they didn't poop. No paddocks were needed, or hitching rails, or haycribs. Motor vehicles needed heavier-duty roads, and could not tolerate mud as deep. They could be parked closer together. There were a lot of differences. The motor section didn't stink as much, either. She was happy about that.

There were old trucks parked to her left and right—cabs dark and empty—and in front of her was a gravel access road and then another row of parked vehicles, noses in, with their passengers camping and cooking immediately behind them, along the road. Several parties had built fires—you could buy firewood at the main office by the entrance—and there were quite a few people milling around or sitting on tailgates. Regarding their dark silhouettes, bobbing shadows, and firelit faces, she was reminded of beach parties down at Head Island when she was a child. This put her in a nostalgic frame of mind. Separated from the damp night and blazing fires in her muffled cab, she watched and grew mesmerized. Her eyes fixed on a young woman who, unlike most, was not moving, but instead leaning against the open tailgate of a trailer directly ahead of Honorée, perhaps fifteen meters away. She was thin and pretty, with her hair pinned up on her head in a big pile, and she wore a heavy work jacket that was too big for her. Across her front was a small child in a cloth wrap, bundled in a wool cap and thick sweater. She stood quietly, gazing into the fire, swiveling almost imperceptibly first one direction and then the other as she rocked the child. Honorée watched her for several minutes—another mother on the move with a small child—and wondered about her origin, her destination, her reasons for traveling. The girl—because that's what she looked like, practically—appeared lost in thought, frozen in the moment.

Then, out of the corner of her left eye, Honorée noticed movement, and saw a large man moving with determination in what appeared to be the girl's direction. He had a long, dark jacket on—down to his knees—and heavy black boots. A hood from a lighter jacket underneath was half-drawn around his head. Honorée saw a long knife on his belt, almost a sword, and an empty holster. In the spatter of firelight and shadow, she could not see the details of his face or hands, but he looked sort of militant or martial in his garb and bearing. In that moment, she realized that at least three of the trucks ahead of her were part of the same group, as were the twenty or thirty people behind them, including the girl. There were similarities in their dress—heavy, almost military—and their trucks had flags and banners flapping limply in the rainy breeze, although Honorée could not discern their patterns.

The man stopped by the women, and seemed to say something to her. She did not turn her head or gaze, but her mouth formed a brief reply. The man spoke again, his hands moving in emphasis. She continued to look at the fire and rock the child. The man became more agitated, bending over her, speaking just loud enough for Honorée to detect the sound in the cab. She opened the passenger-side window a crack to hear what he was nearly shouting by this point. The skinny girl shrugged, her face still toward the fire, and held the child closer. The man, realized Honorée, was probably twice the girl's size and weight—sexual dimorphism, as she recalled from her studies of anatomy and biology. He put his hand on her forearm, and started to close his fingers.

"No way, Andy!" the girl spat, turning to look at him in defiance and pulling away. Honorée opened the window a little more. A fine spay of drizzle came in against her hand and cheek. The man started yelling at the girl, his hands slicing the air above her. At that instant, a group of their

293

companions suddenly crowded around them, effectively moving the man back a few steps and circling the young woman protectively. Honorée lost sight of her. She could see the man's head above the interveners. Huh, she thought, and wondered what it was all about. She could speculate, but unless she went over to them she would never know. Of course she would never walk over. She was only mildly curious about who they were and where they were headed, one group among the thousands she had passed in two days on the road. They'll be in a new place, soon. New neighbors or new nuisances, who knew? Bringing something, leaving something else. Just like her own party. This was really big, Honorée realized. Huge. Everything was shifting. There would be stories about all this movement of people. She made a note to pay more attention, find out more about what was going on.

"Knock knock," said Jenny, appearing at the door. Honorée started.

"Who's there?" murmured Grandma from her slumber.

"Dinner," said Jenny.

"Dinner who?" murmured Grandma again, a bit mechanically. Jenny giggled. Honorée smiled at her automatic responses.

"Dinner gonna get cold if you don't come now," answered Jenny. Grandma nodded, eyes closed, and then appeared to lapse back into a deeper sleep.

"I'll be right there," said Honorée to Jenny. She turned to her grandmother and smoothed the gray hair along her face. "Wake up, Grandma. Dinnertime." Grandma opened her eyes.

"Oh," she said, and swallowed. She looked into Honorée's eyes.

"Hi," said Honorée.

"Oh, I had the funniest dream," breathed Grandma, turning her head and sitting up. She took a deep breath, shivered, and looked at Honorée with awakening eyes.

"You did?"

"Yes," laughed Grandma softly. "You were in it. You were a baby. We were all at home waiting for Jack to come home with some sort of gift, some kind of surprise..." She rubbed her eyes, and then gazed off into space.

"Oh?" said Honorée.

Grandma nodded. "Funny. We kept waiting and waiting... And then, here I am!"

37—DRINKS AT THE FALK

Sunday, November 4th (late at night)

"Claire's got us booked into a hotel, The Falk," said Linda above the rising chatter as the train entered the tunnel. "It's two blocks from the station."

"How are we getting there?" asked Wilder, doing a quick count of his and Rosen's staffs.

"Claire said there's no point trying to drive it in a van or taxi. It's literally across and down West 32nd Street a long block. She said it's packed with people, gridlocked."

"We're supposed to just walk out into the city and find our own way?" Wilder was apprehensive. Once upon a time, this would not have fazed him, but he now understood how public office attracted big risks, and he had his staff to worry about as well.

"No," said Linda anxiously. "The police will have a guard, and we're not the only Congressional group on this train, so the police are going to be escorting quite a few of us down to the The Falk and another hotel. Claire said they might close off the street temporarily."

Wilder frowned and rubbed his eyes. "OK." He realized he sounded off.

"This was all put together pretty hastily…" said Linda.

"Oh, Claire's done a great job," said Wilder. "I'm not upset with her or anyone else."

Linda smiled in relief. "I'll brief everyone else, so there's no confusion. Oh, when we get off the train, we have to look for a plainclothes police officer with a sign that says 'Putney'."

"Putney?" Wilder looked at her in mild confusion.

"They said it wouldn't be safe to use anything that linked us to a state or Congress, or your real name, in case the wrong people saw it. Troublemakers."

Wilder knitted his brows. "OK, if that's what they want to do, they know their city better than I do."

"Claire really stressed how crazy everything is getting, Jake," said Linda. "It's a very unpredictable situation."

He nodded. Linda stood up and turned to the occupants of the next seat ahead of Wilder.

The train was late, very late. It was nearly midnight. In a halting fashion, with long spells of immobility, the maglev train had crept toward Manhattan. Occasionally it would accelerate to normal cruising speed, eliciting cheers onboard, only to slow to a stop within minutes. After vague announcements in the beginning about delays and rerouting, the PA system had fallen silent. Everyone could access the VNET and see for themselves what lay ahead: huge backups, riots at the state borders, diverted trains, cancelled trains, overfilled stations, and thousands upon thousands of migrants who had planned to bypass New York City but were now crowding into its boroughs for the night. Add to them the earlier wave of storm refugees from New Jersey who had fled north, and it was a recipe for disorder.

The photos and videos were riveting. People were clearly getting desperate, and the attempts by the New York authorities to impose order and see to travelers' needs were insufficient. Many travelers had not brought along enough to eat, so a large part of job of the New York State Agency of Disaster Preparedness involved getting food and water to the many stranded vehicles and impromptu camps clotting the highways and bridges around New York City.

There was one short video that Wilder watched several times, deep in thought. A huge military transport ship flying the flag of the EU was in the new ocean lock at the mouth of the Hudson, and several more lay offshore, awaiting their turn. It was high tide, and the level of the Atlantic was a good two meters above the gated river's surface. It looked like the ships were about to plunge downhill through the massive sluice into New York Harbor.

"Pennsylvania Station, Pennsylvania Station," said the steward's voice over the loudspeaker. "This is now the final destination of this train. Please

296

prepare your baggage and personal belongings for disembarkation at New York City's Pennsylvania Station." The loudspeaker clicked several times. The voice returned: "Thank you for traveling with us today. We apologize for the delays and hope that you can now continue safely to your final destination. Pennsylvania Station, on the left side of the train!"

The train was moving slowly now, swaying and rattling on its wheels. Wilder and his colleagues were all standing up, gathering their bags and T-pads and overcoats. The aisles were full, people ducking to avoid the baggage racks and bracing themselves as the train decelerated to its final halt. The doors opened with a hiss. Then they were all crowding down the aisle and out the door onto the aged platform, the air muggy and warm, the lighting harsh after the muted first-class railroad car.

"There's Putney!" called Moriah, pointing toward a cluster of young men down the platform by the humming engine and the ramp leading up into the station. The Vermont staff moved quickly in their direction. Linda Shatner hurried to get there first, assuming the role of travel coordinator, and spoke with the men. Wilder walked toward them, pulling his suitcase, his coat over his arm. Then they were moving quickly through the teeming station, which seemed to be full of people who had just gotten off trains but had nowhere to go. People stood in lines or sat on their suitcases in corners and along walls. It was noisy and close. The lighting now seemed dim, as if a brown-out were in progress.

Then they were in a passage with shops and kiosks on either side - some open, some closed—and after a moment were ascending an escalator toward the smell of open air. A cool breeze flowed down into their faces. Then off the escalator they stepped, onto a sidewalk under a high roof, and the lights and tall buildings and dense traffic of New York City were all around them—a honking, yelling, clattering sea of pedicabs, bicycles, motorbikes, carts, Lancs, wagons, cell-electrics, and pedestrians heaving like surf up and down Seventh Avenue. A steady rain slanted down among the towers and skywalks above them. Before them a channel opened, walled-in by a flying wedge of young policemen who swept the public off the sidewalk and the Avenue before them. Above their heads buzzed a flock of crowd-control dronecopters, Tasers ready. Staying close together, Wilder and his staff followed the policemen's lead and strode ahead, off the curb and into the street.

"Fuck the rich!" yelled unseen faces somewhere outside their cordon. "Look at them, off their train and into the streets with the rest of us!"

"The sidewalks are for everyone!" said a woman indignantly from somewhere behind the cordon. "Not just for oligarchs!" Others jeered and laughed. Wilder caught the eye of a dark teenager grinning at them from between police officers. The boy said something over his shoulder to a companion and then blew Wilder an insulting kiss.

There was clearly some hostility toward well-dressed people getting off a restricted, first-class train on a night like this, whether they were or, as the case may be, were not oligarchs. News seemed to have spread of the trains' distress.

The Vermont group was making good progress down the block. "It's just up there, sir," said a police captain jogging beside Wilder and Moriah. "On the right."

"We sure appreciate this," puffed Wilder. "We weren't sure what we would find when we got to the city."

"Express orders of Mayor Ashanti," said the captain. "There are delegations from a half-dozen states stranded here tonight, along with all the travelers, and the Mayor said, keep 'em safe and make 'em feel welcome."

Wilder laughed, struggling to keep his rolling suitcase's wheels level and looking forward to reaching the end of this unexpected gauntlet. He glanced around at his colleagues ahead and to his sides. Everyone looked harried as they maintained their brisk pace. Lola, tired and irritated, was perspiring and clutched her belongings in her arms as the bag over her shoulder swung uncontrollably. A row of policemen brought up the rear, some walking backwards, surveying the crowds that closed in their wake, weapons drawn.

"In we go!" said Linda Shatner, a few steps ahead of Wilder. Her hair was wet and windblown. The group bustled through the revolving door and the open door beside it, emerging from the tension and damp into a large, brightly lit lobby. The Hotel Falk was a relic of the mid-1900s, with a lobby decorated with gold-plated chandeliers, tall mirrors, taller golden faux-columns between them, and chrome and glass trim everywhere it would fit. The floors were a creamy marble that could well have come from the quarries of Vermont. Dotted around like islands were sofa quadrangles, with ample black lacquered coffee tables in their centers and potted palms at their corners. Each island of this archipelago appeared to have become an impromptu staging area for groups of travelers, including the marooned Congressional delegations just ushered over from the train station: Massachusetts, Rhode Island, New Hampshire, and now, Vermont. People were taking off wet jackets, putting down bags, wiping their faces, and sending emissaries over to the check-in counter to sort out rooms. Representatives of Mayor Ashanti's office were here and there, trying to be helpful. Where was Maine? It was rumored that they had chartered a plane and flown home. Maine was certainly farther away from Philadelphia than the core New England states. Connecticut? Their own official motorcade had already picked them up at Penn Station for the short drive north.

"Oh, it's hitting me now, finally." Moriah stood looking at Wilder, a little bedraggled, and dabbed the rain off her face with a kerchief. "I'm exhausted!"

"It's been a long day," agreed Steve Johnson. "Thought we'd be home by now."

"OK, OK, no meetings now," said Lola with a grumpy frown. "At least we're somewhere safe and warm. Whaddaya say we get some sleep and regroup tomorrow AM?"

"Oh my God, Lola," laughed Mary. "Do you really think anybody wants to start working again now?" She touched her temple and looked into her HUD. "It's midnight!"

"Well, just in case ya did," muttered Lola.

Linda came back over from the counter. "All set." Their respective T-pads would show them the way to their assigned rooms. "Anybody want a nightcap?" There was a general chuckle. Linda looked around at them. "I'm serious. Quick drink before bed?"

Moriah shook her head and declined with an apology. Lola only snorted. The two of them started off toward the elevator.

"Yeah, maybe," said Steve. "OK." He grinned at Linda.

Wilder nodded. "Sure. Why not?" Perhaps they would get talking with some of the other New England delegations and find out what was going on with all the traffic and border backups. The explanations he had managed to obtain so far fell short. It was late now, but he made a note to message the Governor when he went to his room.

"I'll come," said Mary, and Selena and Doug nodded.

"Good," said Linda. "Cuz I'm going to need your help making sense of the news I just heard that, first, there are no trains moving in New York or New England tonight into tomorrow until - I don't know - whenever, and, second, that new hurricane, Sulis, is following the same track as Rhiannon and is already a Category 4."

Her colleagues looked at her in tired surprise.

"Maybe someone can come down tomorrow and get us." suggested Wilder. "We don't necessarily have to take the train." Then his demeanor darkened. "And we don't want to be sitting here in New York if Sulis decides to head this way."

Mary chuckled. "Funny how out of the habit folks are, driving down. We're only four hours from the Vermont border in the fast lane." She cocked her head. "Well, that is, if you could still drive as fast as you used to be able to."

Wilder nodded. There were many good reasons why folks had fallen out of the habit, of course.

The others were already walking toward the lobby bar, which seemed to be doing a brisk business and attracting fragments of other delegations. Linda turned and looked back over her shoulder at Wilder and Mary.

"Coming?"

38—KINGSTON, NEW YORK

They had been driving slowly for many hours in bumper-to-bumper traffic, crossing a high country of ragged forests, vast clearcuts, and the harsh landscapes of a triple violation: ancient coal mining, more recent gas fracking, and the most recent stripping of forests for biomass fuel. There was little agriculture, and the population was clustered in small villages invisible from the highway. Abandoned commercial centers stood like empty cartons on rocky prominences. The names sounded grandiose and biblical: Lord's Valley, Promised Land, New Found Land, Grand Army, Tabernacle, Arc, Mount Storm. Indeed, the main economic activity left in this region appeared to be tending flocks. Lara and Jenny, in the wagon's cab with Lee as their ward, had never seen so many sheep and goats in their lives.

"Seep, seep!" yelled Lee again and again, giggling at the girls' amusement, until they decided it was time to settle him down a little.

"Lee," said Lara, "do you know why they let the goats live with the sheep out on the mountainsides?"

"Why?" asked Lee, suddenly bashful at being asked a serious question by a grown-up lady he barely knew.

"Is this a joke?" giggled Jenny, unsure of Lara's tone.

"Not at all!" said Lara, shooting an absolutely earnest look at Jenny, and then turning back to Lee. "Here's why. The goats guard the sheep. If mean coyotes come into the pasture to try to eat the sheep, the poor sheep just stand there and don't know what to do, but the big, brave goats run at the coyotes and chase them away!" Lara held up her extended index fingers on either side of her head to simulate a goat's horns. "And they ring the transmitter bells around their necks so the shepherds hear a signal and wake up to come help."

"No!" giggled Jenny.

"Yes!" insisted Lara.

"I want to be a goat, too!" said Lee. He tried to imitate Lara.

"Here," she said, putting his hands and fingers in the correct position. "There!"

"I'm a goat, I'm a goat, I'm a goat!" laughed Lee. Lara and Jenny both smiled at the energetic little boy.

"You know, I think we're finally starting to go downhill now," said Jenny, scanning the land ahead. "We are supposed to leave these mountains eventually, right?"

Lara nodded. "Yeah, I think so. I mean, we have to, eventually. Don't we have to cross the Hudson River?" She looked at Jenny and smiled at her own geographic ignorance. "That's in a valley, right?"

Jenny reached for her T-pad. "If the Hudson River weren't in a valley, um, I don't know where it would be! On a ridge?" They both laughed. "OK, look." She flicked her fingers around on the pad. "Well, we have to cross the Delaware River Valley first. That's pretty far down there. Then we go up again and then ... um, down into the Hudson Valley!" She held up the T-pad so Lara could see it.

"Whew. Long way," commented Lara. "Is the Delaware River the border?"

"The New York border?" asked Jenny.

"Yes," said Lara, and Jenny nodded in confirmation. "Another state," reflected Lara, "which I will be visiting for the first time."

Lee grew quiet and continued to watch pastures and woods pass by. He started to doze, and snuggled up against Jenny's side to nap. Jenny flipped idly through news stories and articles on her T-pad. Lara looked out the window. They passed a group of men watching the heavy traffic on the interstate highway from a small bluff beyond the security fence. There were five or six of them, dressed in military surplus clothing, with a couple of horses, a motorcycle, and an old Jeep behind them. They were far enough off that Lara couldn't be sure, but one of them seemed to be looking right at her. The others also appeared to be looking closely at people and vehicles in the passing procession. They made Lara nervous. She fought the thought. Why be scared of the odd rural men along a highway? They were shepherds, or farmers. But she was glad for the protection that Interstate 84's security systems afforded them. They were in unknown, fairly desolate country now, far from towns with their stockades and law and order. She shivered, and looked away from the men as they fell behind her.

Time passed. The wagon crunched along on the pitted, shattered highway. Lara leaned back against her seat and closed her eyes. The light, misty rain gradually stopped, and although the sky remained gray, the warmth of the autumn sun could be felt through the clouds. In the stuffy cab, Lara fell asleep.

* * *

A change in the wagon's rhythm awakened Lara. With a stiff neck and the sensation of drool on her lip, Lara struggled to come to. "Where are we?" she asked, groggily. The others were asleep, Jenny lying back in the corner, against the door, with Lee on the seat between them, face buried in Jenny's thick sweater. Lara pulled herself upright, willing herself awake. They were in heavy, slow traffic, on a long downhill straightaway. High, dark cliffs rose up to the left of the highway. It was cloudy and gray, and raining again. She reached down under the seat, found the water bottle she had stashed there, and took a long drink to wash away the bad taste in her mouth. She pulled her small rolled-up lapscreen from her jacket pocket and opened it, clicking its central seam so it would stay unrolled.

She called her father, up ahead in the truck. "Daddy?"

"Hi baby," Ari's calm voice replied, as his image appeared.

"Where are we?" she asked.

"We're just about in Port Jervis."

"The border?"

"Yes, the border."

"How are you guys?"

"Oh, I think we're fine," he said. Something in his face told her something wasn't fine.

"Uh huh, good," she answered. "We've all been asleep back here."

"I think Honorée really appreciated that," he smiled. "She's been asleep here in the back seat for hours."

"Who's driving?" Lara asked.

"Daryl," said Ari. He tilted his T-pad so that Lara could see along the front seat, with Daryl waving from the driver's seat, Celia beside him, and

303

Ari apparently in the right-hand passenger's seat. She got a quick, shadowy glimpse of Honorée and Grandma asleep in the back seat.

"'K," said Lara. "Are we going to take a break soon? I know I'd like that." She needed a toilet stop pretty badly.

"In about ten minutes, we're going to get off the Interstate and take a different route north. Route 209. Take a look on your map. We can take a break then." Lara heard a murmur of affirmation in the background.

"Whew, thanks," she said. "I'm sure I'm not the only one."

"Hey, take a look at the news," said Ari. "The Front is holding a campaign march in Washington." He slipped a link to her. She opened it. There was a very recent video of thousands of uniformed marchers information coming up one of Washington's avenues. They were carrying shovels and weapons.

"That's a new insignia, as far as I can remember," said Ari. Lara looked closer. At intervals, the Front marchers carried waist-high banners that spanned the avenue, with depictions of rifles and shovels and the words 'Defend and Rebuild' in red, white, and blue. Many marchers carried similar flags. There were thousands and thousands of them—men and women, and teenagers. There were riders mounted on horses, and black and red trucks with a military appearance, as well as articulated ATVs with prominent coil-gun gun mounts, although the guns had been removed. Yet alongside the parade route, there were few spectators, and the quick looks Lara got of the surroundings showed the same landscape of storm debris and damaged buildings she had seen in Chevy Chase. Only a few police were in evidence.

"Ugh," she said. "I wonder if there are people there from the Blacksburg Guard."

"Got out of Washington just in time," laughed Ari grimly. "They're coming after us."

Daryl said something in the background that sounded like an objection.

"Just kidding!" said Ari quickly.

"They're not as strong in the CG as they were in the Congress," said Grandma faintly off-camera. "This is a show of force."

"Yes," said Ari thoughtfully. "Sort of like, we'll get the votes, so don't forget us, because we can out-do your extra-democratic methods with extra-democratic methods of our own."

"Daddy, how many of them are there, really?" asked Lara.

304

"Front members?" asked Ari.

"Yes," she nodded.

"Look, what, maybe a tenth of the voters.. Maybe fifteen percent. But they always have the potential to split and disable the Republican Party, like the old Tea Party movement, and in some states they're nearly fifty percent." Ari scratched his head. "Of course, they're big in the military, the police, veterans, the Oath Keepers…"

"They look very organized and disciplined and, well, *clean*, marching through Washington like that," said Jenny.

"Yeah," said Ari. "That's what they want voters to think today, and tomorrow, especially. Clean things up. Toss out the corrupt politicians on both sides, the partisans and secessionists *and* the Oligarchs and their Trust puppets, and clean house. But you know who they really are, right?"

"Right," mused Lara, feeling overwhelmed by circumstances that felt way beyond anyone's ability to fix or control.

"Hey, I think I can see our exit," said Ari.

Lara, in the driver's seat, leaned over to try to see around the right-rear corner of the truck. Nothing yet. Daryl signaled to start the process of getting over into the right lane - a maneuver that could take minutes because of the slow, dense non-motor traffic. They decelerated with a slight lurch. Jenny and Lee began to stir.

"So," said Ari for the benefit of all, "when we get off I-84, we'll be in the Pennsylvania town of Matamoras. We'll cross the Delaware River on Route 209, and drive right into and through Port Jervis, New York. Because the border runs right down the center of the river, we'll go through the border check on the Port Jervis side. It looks like it's a pretty quick and calm checkpoint right now. Don't seem to be big backups there. This may be because people feel safer on the interstates and are heading further east as well. It's the same New York transit bond as the I-84 exit, so no saving there, but I do think we'll get through faster."

Jenny was awake now, listening. Lara had placed her T-pad up on the wagon's dashboard and toggled the cam to wide-angle. "Is the Interstate really safer?" asked Jenny apprehensively.

"You have to go through the Catskills and through a lot of small, poor communities up 209, as far as I can tell, so we'll have to be on our guard between stockades, but I don't think it's any more dangerous than anything we've already seen," said Ari. "Uh, I'm not hearing about trouble in the travel reports."

The passengers in the wagon's cab were quiet as they worked their way over into the exit lane and down the ramp onto a road paralleling the highway. Several abandoned wagons stood in the weedy verge beside the shoulder. They turned nearly 360 degrees as they followed the clover-leaf, dropping about ten meters, and passed through an open checkpoint manned by a half-dozen Interstate Highways Command troops who simply watched and scanned the traffic as it rolled by. The exiting traffic was light. The ramp then merged with a road that turned out to be US 209 and US 6—"Grand Army Highway." This took them north under I-84 and into Matamoras, a fading, depopulated border town of stripped shopping plazas and rows of rusty shipping containers. The bridge to Port Jervis lay only a kilometer or two ahead. But several large, newly painted billboards on either side of the road advertised a diner in the center of Port Jervis on Route 209 itself—Kingston Avenue—that was 'family-owned since 1966' and offered 'diner delights, home-made pies, and hot breakfast all day.'

Jenny lit up, and switched on Lara's T-pad's audio. "Grandma, can we stop there for lunch?" Lara added her encouragement. They were tired of rice, lentils, beans, and that awful leftover chicken jerky that had been one of Grandma's staples on her long trip. There was muffled conversation up in the truck's cab. After a moment, Ari's voice came back. "OK, I guess so." Lara was surprised at his lack of enthusiasm. What could be wrong with that? Maybe it was money, but this was lunch, not a big meal. And they needed to keep their spirits up. They were under a lot of strain.

"Thanks," said Jenny and Lara in unison.

"What's a die-nuh?" asked Lee, wide-eyed.

"Yummy food," said Jenny, nuzzling Lee none-to-nose. "Pie."

Lee giggled and squirmed to get loose.

They drove for several minutes, and did not slow down until the start of the bridge. Near the bank of the river, beside the road, was a large rambling Victorian house with the sign 'State Lion Adult Entertainment' printed in huge letters across the side, decorated with lions rampant and the silhouettes of dancing women. Beside it was a saloon advertising 'Road Snacks' and 'Strong Waters.' Both establishments were doing a brisk business.

They came to the bridge. The dark waters of the broad Delaware flowed swiftly below it. On the other side of the ancient box truss was a picturesque town of steeples and old brick chimneys, framed by autumn-hued hills. 'Now Leaving the Commonwealth of Pennsylvania,' a sign read. They advanced in stop-start traffic.

Down the other side of the two-lane road came a heavily loaded wagon, with what looked like several threadbare families aboard. The driver was cursing loudly, his face twisted with anger. Three women sat beside him on the bench, their faces turned away or down in embarrassment. "God damn New York!" he shouted at the waiting vehicles, "God damn those fuckers! Two grand to cross and I was fucking born in Ellenville! They've got no right to do this!" He evidently could not or did not want to pay for the transit bond. He drove the draft horses hard, pushing them to step faster. The women beside him reached for the reins, and they struggled. The horses started to slow down as the wagon came abreast. Lara's eyes briefly met the man's furious stare. And then they were gone, clip-clopping back into Matamoras.

The border crossing was efficient. On the Port Jervis side, a large space had been opened up, and a lane set aside for pre-purchased bonds. Vehicles flowed smoothly through. The New York State Police were not doing searches or asking many questions—just making sure that the money had been paid and the bond posted. They keyed off the aptitar that had posted the bond (Honorée's), not the vehicle, so no stickers or RFID tags were needed. "You're all traveling together as a group, right?" asked the state trooper as he inspected the names of their group.

"Right," said Daryl out through his window.

"OK, stay together, exit before the deadline, and you'll be good to go." The trooper waved them on. Into Port Jervis they cruised, leaving behind a complex scene of stopped vehicles, arguments about transit bonds, rebuffed vehicles, and a large official presence.

"That was easy," said Lara. Jenny nodded. They looked out the windows at a town that seemed to have a lot of life left in it.

"This is nice - nicer than what I've seen in Virginia or Pennsylvania," said Jenny. "Hey, look, there's the diner."

Down the straight main street on the right-hand side was a large parking lot, and—set back behind an array of parked vehicles—was a shiny metal diner from the mid-twentieth century. It was busy. Outside on both sides were large tents with picnic benches under them, and behind one of them was a large, smoky outdoor barbecue pit. Above the diner's roof leaned a large, faded sign with the name, 'Old Village Diner.'

They eased into the parking lot and found a place along one side where their long truck-wagon train could be parked. Everyone was out in seconds, eager to stand up and stretch legs after a long morning on the road. Ari and Jessica stepped quickly toward an outdoor latrine and row of outhouses set up near what now could be identified as a biergarten tent. Grandma followed stiff-legged, leaning on Claudia's arm for support. Lara stretched and smiled, hugging Jenny and Honorée as they came near her beside the wagon. Asa, released, ran around with Lee, happy to be reunited. Mike hung over the side of the bed above Lara, looking groggy and red-eyed.

"Ow!" shouted Lara with a gasp, jumping away from the hub of the wagon wheel she had just leaned back against. "That's hot!" She turned around, flinging one hand back to touch the small of her back that had just been burned, and inspecting the wagon's wheel. Smoke rose faintly from the hub.

"Your jacket's been branded!" said Jenny. "Like a steer!" Lara stood in momentary shock, rubbing her back.

"God, it looks like a 'C' on your jacket, right in the middle," said Honorée.

Mike was looking down at the hub from above. "It's starting to burn," he said. "Seizing. Bearing's probably going."

Lara nodded. "God, the wagon's not made for this kind of endless, motorized driving, is it? That could have caught on fire!" Everyone moved in to take a closer look. Wisps of acrid smoke rose from the hub. Paint near the hub was bubbled and discolored, and there was a faint hissing if one held one's ear close.

"Isn't that weird?" said Daryl, walking up with Celia. He spat on the hub and it sizzled. "With all the tech on this wagon—you know, re-gen brakes and stuff—you'd think this wouldn't happen."

"The re-gen's only on the front wheels," said Lara, who had seen similar wagons in Virginia. "These wheels free-wheel, except for of course having disk brakes."

Jenny looked at Lara with respect for her animal traction knowledge.

"We can't just leave this," said Daryl. He squatted down, looking under the wagon. "There's another wheel. I wonder if the whole hub comes off and gets replaced."

"Let's get some lunch and tea and pie and let it cool down," said Honorée, "and let's hear what Grandma and Ari have to say. Grandma will know. It's not going to get any hotter now." There was general agreement with this, so after locking doors and taking a quick look around, the group walked over to the Old Village Diner and in through its main door.

A bustling, harried-looking woman in her sixties greeted them. "How many in your party?" The air was warm and fragrant with the smells of bacon, bread, and muffins.

"Twelve," said Grandma.

The woman looked at them, counting to herself. "We can squeeze you all in if you wait ten minutes. Those boys need high chairs?" Honorée nodded. "OK. I'm awfully sorry about the wait but we have been nothing but packed for days now, with all these folks traveling."

"Good for business?" asked Ari.

"Oh, my goodness, yes," said the woman. "We've been near to shutting down for years now, but this will get us well into next year. Can't barely get the food we need right now! Scouring the countryside." She called over her shoulder to a waitress as she passed. "Next group for sixteen and fifteen is waiting now." She turned back toward them. "You can wait down under the garden tent and we'll call you over the speaker."

They all went back outside and sat at some free picnic tables. Country music played over the sound system. The floor of the 'garden tent' was dust and mud where the sagging, dark-stained canvass tent had leaked. The picnic tables were weathered, splintered, and pocked with carved initials\. The barbecue smelled delicious.

"Dad, are those New York flags?" asked Lara, pointing toward a row of flags hanging out over the road they had just left, and a similar one waving over the entrance to the diner.

"Hm, I'm not sure," said Ari, inspecting the flags. There was an elaborate coat-of-arms on a background of gold, with two standing female figures, and the words 'Excelsior' emblazoned below them.

"That's not the official state flag, although it's close," said an older heavyset men from a table nearby, overhearing them. "That's the flag of the Empire State People's Militia."

"What's that?" asked Ari. "National guard?"

"Nossir," said the man. "Volunteer citizen militia. When you see those flags, you know you're gonna get help if you need it. See that guy in the car over there?" He pointed across the parking lot toward an old electric standing beside a fence, with a figure dimly visible inside. They glanced over and nodded. "He's ESPM. Making sure that nothing gets out of hand here at the Old Village. If he needs backup, they'll be here in a minute. And you don't see any beggars around here, either, do you?"

"What kind of outta hand?" asked Mike.

"I can hear you're all from the south," remarked the man, ignoring Mike's question.

"Well, Maryland, if you call that south," replied Mike. "I guess I might sound more southern because I've been in the Army for a while, down in the Deep South."

The man laughed. "Yes, I do consider Maryland south, matter fact!"

"We're from Virginia," volunteered Ari. "The real south, not like those wannabees in Maryland." Everyone laughed.

"So, what are you worried about here, getting out of hand?" probed Grandma.

"Ma'am, this business moves a lot of money, 'cluding cash—even more now that all you people are on the road—and it's hard-earned, honest money made by decent people doing a good job. She pays her taxes to the town, the school district, and the state, and makes voluntary contributions to the ESPM, too. Those taxes are needed to keep the community together, civilized society. There are a lot of people who'd like to take that money, the easy way, the dishonest way, and the People's Militia is there to make sure they don't."

Ari's curiosity was piqued. This was not anything that the Home Guard back in Blacksburg did. The Home Guard trained for civil defense and natural disasters, not police work. "Isn't that what the police do?" he asked.

"They work together," said the man. "Keeping an eye on small businesses and communities lets the town and state police tackle the bigger and badder stuff, especially with all this migration going on. And the New York Guard protects the borders, civil defense, that sort of thing."

"I'll bet they all have their hands full," said Ari respectfully.

The man nodded and grunted. "You know how many migrants crossed into New York since the storm?"

"How many?" asked Grandma, Ari, and Lara in unison.

"About a million and a half," the man said. "Half a million just in the City. You should see the camp just down the road from here... Well, you will see it you're headed north." He shook his head. "Terrible." He pointed with his thumb back toward the diner. "Part of what they're making in that kitchen and barbecue grills for the camp, all donated food."

"Gillespie, party of four!" called out a voice from the outdoor loudspeaker.

The man got up. "That's us." The women with him, who had been talking in low voices to one another, smiled in a polite, neutral fashion and got up as well. "Have a good rest of your trip," said the man. "Where are you headed, by the way?"

"Vermont," said Grandma weakly.

"Beg pardon?" the man said.

"Vermont," she repeated, more loudly this time.

"Very nice up there," said the man. "Long way still. Travel safe!"

They all thanked him, and continued waiting for a few more minutes. Their call came moments later. Into the busy, noisy diner they plunged for the kind of hot, satisfying meal they had not had since leaving Chevy Chase.

* * *

"Wow, I can't even turn it!" Lara stepped back from the jacked-up wheel, huffing from the exertion. Pulling as hard as she could, she was still unable to rotate the wheel. Mike and Daryl grabbed opposite sides—one lifting, one pushing down—and only managed to turn it slowly, the metal rasping against metal. "We must have driven for miles like that!" she said.

"Horrible," said Grandma, resting on an old concrete block near the parked vehicles. "Mm hm." She pointed toward the rear of the wagon. "The lug wrench is in the same box where you found the jack." Mike was already rummaging around for it, his arm up to his shoulder in the tailgate compartment. He found it, and after a short while they had the wheels switched and the damaged wheel placed under the wagon's bed in the cage

311

that had held the spare. Before long, they were cautiously maneuvering the truck and wagon out of the crowded parking lot.

Ari drove. Lara and Jenny joined him in the front seat. For a change, Daryl and Celia got the truck's rear seat. "Daddy," asked Lara as they waited to pull out onto Route 209, "is Florence OK? She seems awfully tired?" She glanced apologetically at Jenny, Grandma's own grand-child. "I mean, what do *you* think?"

Jenny was silent, frowning. "I'm not sure," said Ari, "but she's worried about herself. She told me she's more chronically tired than she's ever been before—you know what an energetic woman she is—and has a vague sense that one side of her body is weaker than the other."

"God, Daddy, that sounds like a stroke, some sort of paralysis..."

"I know, I know," he interjected. "I told her she should be scanned." He accelerated onto the road.

"Of course she should!" exclaimed Lara. "I mean, that's one of the first things you learn about strokes..."

"Well, she said she'd have it looked into once she gets to Vermont, and later she told me she felt all right."

Lara rolled her eyes. "It could be days and days. We don't know." She fell silent.

"I'll talk to her," said Jenny. "She can be stubborn." She smiled hopefully.

"Oh, God, look at that," said Ari, pointing off to the right of the road. Perhaps two hundred meters beyond the diner's parking lot was a vast lot of a different kind. Beyond a sign indicating the Neversink Fair Grounds and a farmers' market was a huge traveler's camp. The instant impression was mud, dust, smoke, ragged people, and acre upon acre of carts, grimy trucks, draft animals, green tarps, and tents. New York Guard trucks and Red Cross trailers set off the gray-brown expanse with pixels of brighter color. All manner of vehicles were parked along the sidewalk beside the camp, looking newly arrived and teeming with people of all ages.

"There must be fifty-thousand people in that camp," said Ari slowly. He braked hard for a motorcycle that turned abruptly across their lane and shot into the camp. "Idiot." They drove on, watching the camp in silence for several minutes until it was behind them.

"Wow," said Jenny. "I'm glad we didn't stay there."

312

"Mm," replied Ari in agreement. "That's a lot of people to settle. I wonder how long they can keep that up?"

"Who?" asked Lara.

"The State of New York," said Ari. "Society. Food's scarce and expensive, and things are already hard enough without having to run such big camps."

They were now driving through the old town center of Port Jervis.

"This must have been a grand town for much of its history," remarked Ari. "Look at those stone buildings and old Victorians." They looked around at the ornate 19th-century architecture, much of it well-preserved. Port Jervis had a busy, nearly prosperous air. There were a lot of people on the streets, looking adequately dressed and well-fed. The sidewalks were swept, and chickens were kept off the roads by coops and fencing. The old houses were patched with the lighter hue of new lumber and siding. Autumn crops hung on in kitchen gardens—squashes, beans, pumpkins, raspberries—benefitting from the remaining weeks of frost-free weather.

"They're cute," said Jenny, smiling at a troop of young children emerging from an elementary school two by two, hand in hand. Suddenly, her smile turned to an expression of horror. "Oh, God, what's that?"

They all looked where Jenny was staring aghast, with utterances of dismay. A body hung with a rope around its neck from a large tree in a park right beside the school. Below it was a large plywood sign with the words, 'Yankees Rule!'

"Oh, no," said Lara. "Isn't that awful! I thought we were getting away from that sort of thing, and now it looks like they hate southerners!"

"I thought that man outside the diner was a little scary," affirmed Jenney, "going on like that about where we were from and about that militia."

Lara glanced back at Daryl, who was staring with a shocked expression at the hanged figure. But Ari started chuckling, and then burst out laughing. They all stared at him as if he had lost his mind.

"Daddy!" cried Lara.

"Yankees rule," laughed Ari hysterically, fighting for breath. "Now I get it. Oh, haven't we just been completely worn down by crisis and want, these past few weeks, and everyone around us..." They were frozen in silence, waiting for him to explain. "Yankees!" He fought to stop his laughter, gasping and glancing around at them with an air of expectation.

"Yankees?" No one responded. "The New York Yankees! The World Series!" Expressions of comprehension dawned on their faces. "Baseball!" Daryl snorted a laugh and wrinkled his lips. Jenny giggled. Celia looked at them blankly.

Lara smiled. "Ha. Well, that's a relief. We thought you had gone crazy!" They looked more closely at the effigy as they drove past it. It was indeed a dummy dressed in a baseball uniform, with a gray and red colors and 'DC' in fancy script across the shirt-front.

"The Denver Cardinals," laughed Ari. "That's right. I heard something about that. Played all the games in Denver because New York was messed up, and delayed it by a week. I think they just finished playing yesterday."

"Who won?" asked Lara.

"Yankees," said Daryl, who had quickly turned to his lapscreen. "They won five out of seven," he read. "Yep, finished yesterday. Started a week late."

"Wow," said Jenny, marveling.

"I know, right?" said Lara. "To have time to think about such things..."

"It's a good sign," said Ari. "I haven't thought about pro sports in years."

Lara laughed. "Did you ever!?"

"Well, sometimes," said Ari with mock indignation. "Of course, I was always more interested in the sports you kids were playing. Meant more to me."

"And I guess Virginia's not really into pro baseball," said Daryl, "or pro anything these days."

Ari nodded. "What do you know?" he mused. "The New York Yankees..."

* * *

As the afternoon wore on, they drew closer to Kingston. Mindful of the overheated right-side wagon wheel, they stopped regularly to grease the wheels and let them cool, and maintained a speed of no more than forty kilometers per hour. Their road wound around in a long valley that angled toward the northeast, through sweet Catskill country of old farm houses and pastures and orchards and berry runs—a well-watered, food-producing

314

region. There were piles of apples and pumpkins everywhere, and roadside cider presses selling new sweet and hard cider. Along some stretches the farms and villages were run-down and depleted. Along others were signs of care and prosperity. The road was good: well-maintained, although reduced to gravel in many places where asphalt paving had been discontinued years before. When they slowed down to pass through the centers of villages, with names like Wurtsboro and Wawarsing, people stopped to look at them with curiosity but no ragged children ran out to beg and no hostile words were called. There was no evidence of the CCC or Plain Word either. Did these people even go to church, Jenny wondered aloud.

By five-thirty, after a final merge onto a major road heading due east, they drove into the fine old Dutch town of Kingston, on its bluffs overlooking the Hudson River. Traffic into the town through the big west-facing stockade checkpoint was fairly light. The militiamen manning the checkpoint instructed them how to get to the travelers' camp. The weather had cleared, evening was falling, and an autumn chill was settling in. "Tomorrow, we'll be in Massachusetts," said Ari to his companions in the truck's cab as they drove into Kingston, "and, if all goes well, in Vermont the day after." He peered at the road, glancing repeatedly at the parade of bright little arrows on the truck's screen. "Girls," he said to Lara and Jenny, who were still up in the front seat with him, "see if you can spot the sign to the camp as we come down this hill."

"What are you looking for?" asked Lara.

"Albany Avenue," said Ari, "but it seems to have a different name at first. Lincoln Park! Yes, that's what they said back there." He pointed at a small, inconspicuous sign. "We need to follow that." Ignoring the insistent little GPS arrows, he turned left onto a road that headed north. "Wait... wait...Yes! Albany Avenue." They were almost at their destination.

* * *

It was really late, but Honorée was having trouble falling asleep. She was so grateful for the help she was getting from Jenny and Lara, and even from Jessica and Claudia, in watching her boys, but they were restless and bored on the long journey, and as their mother she still bore the brunt of it. And when others took them, she still worried and could not relax. Sanna had not been the nurturing type—Honorée should have paid more attention to that trait early on—but being an adult she was competent enough at caring for the boys for long periods. Lara and Jenny were younger, with less childcare experience (although Jenny had certainly gained some in Fredericksburg), and tended to burn out faster. Well, these conditions—from truck cab to wagon bed to wagon cab to camp, over and over—were not easy for anyone. But now, with the boys asleep in the wagon's bed alongside Jenny and Lara, and the truck's front seat all to herself, Honorée still could not relax enough to fall asleep.

She fought against an interminable state of worry, uncertainty, and apprehension. There was Grandma's lethargy. And the wagon wheel. And she had kept it to herself but she was finding herself becoming increasingly irritated with both Daryl and her own mother, for completely different ❙ reasons, and in their close quarters could not shake this. Worst of all, she had absolutely no idea what life held for her, or any of them, in Vermont. She did not know her relatives well enough to just call them or viz-IT them, and Grandma had not been very forthcoming with introductions— she really should have!—so Honorée had decided to just wait and see. And wonder, and worry. Of course, she had skills. She knew nutrition and food chemistry. She was a good jam and jelly maker. She was pretty good at caramels, too, and at honey sweets. Hm. So were a lot of other people. Wait and see, wait and see. Ugh. There was nothing she could do now. Except sleep. Which she couldn't.

She sat up. What time was it? The digital clock on the truck's screen indicated 1:23 A.M. She sighed, and pulled her blankets tighter to her chin against the night's chill. She could see the area around the front of the truck. They were parked facing a small, sloping meadow where, at a distance, tents were pitched. The bulk of the camp was behind her. It was very dark, but she could see a couple of campfires still burning here and there. Firewood was in short supply at this camp, but some travelers had surely brought their own, or pooled firewood with neighbors. She watched a campfire sparkle and flicker, almost imperceptibly losing brightness as it burned down. Figures eclipsed it, and then sparks leapt into the air as someone put it out. The darkness grew more complete. Honorée closed her eyes.

39—ELECTION DAY

Tuesday, November 6th (early morning to evening)

Dawn stole in from the east, lighting Honorée's cab first. It was a clear, yellow dawn. The meadow's dark grays and browns were frosted with dew. A thin mist lay on the lower ground beyond the meadow. Honorée looked at the clock, which read six-twenty. She had another half-hour to sleep before everyone started getting up and banging around. She was in the breakfast crew today. She shut her eyes, determined to grab a final morsel of sleep. Something caused her to open them again. A figure was moving toward the truck, staggering slightly and carrying a tarp. She watched in apprehension. Who was out like this so early? Then she realized it was Mike. What on earth? He seemed to be limping. His path would take him past the truck on the driver's side, where she lay. She opened the window. For a second, Mike noticed nothing as he shuffled along, and then he drew himself up in surprise and stared at her.

"Good morning," said Honorée hoarsely.

"Morning," Mike mumbled.

"Where are you coming back from?" she demanded, lapsing easily into big-sister authority.

"Uh, nothing," said Mike.

"Nothing? Don't you mean 'nowhere'?" She said this with utter doubt. Then she noticed blood on his trousers, midway down his leg. "Oh my God, is that blood?"

Mike looked blearily down at his dirty gray canvas pants. "Yuh."

"Why are you bleeding?!" Honorée pulled herself up and opened the truck's door, feeling for her boots beneath the steering wheel. She teetered between concern and disapproval. "Are you OK?"

Mike stepped back as the door opened. He stared at the ground with bloodshot eyes. "A rat."

317

"A rat?! What? What do you mean, a rat?"

"Or something," Mike mumbled slowly. His odd expression and slow responses made Honorée suspect he was on some drug.

"Something?"

Mike took a deep breath. "Yeah. Raccoon. Er, maybe a coyote."

"Jesus, Mike. We have to get it looked at. Where is it?" She was searching around his trouser leg for a tear or bite mark. The blood was fresh, smelling ripely of iron. She got out of the truck. "Come back here and sit down." She beckoned him toward their camp kitchen behind the wagon, ancient folding aluminum lawn chairs scattered around, pulling the blanket around her shoulders for warmth in the chill of sunrise. Mike followed her numbly and sat down. She pulled up his right pant leg. In the muscle of his calf was a cluster of bloody puncture wounds. It looked like some animal with sharp but short teeth had chewed on him, biting more than once. The bleeding had stopped, but it would need cleaning and disinfection.

"Mike, what on earth? How did this happen?"

He shook his head and put his hands over his face. Honorée saw he had bloody scratches on the back of one hand as well. "I don't know."

"What were you doing?" Her voice softened as she grasped his dismay. "Hunting?" A mild joke seemed appropriate after her sharp, accusatory questions.

Instead of laughing, Mike began to quietly, woozily sob. Honorée looked at him in surprise. She put her blanket around his shoulders, and grabbed a heavy work jacket that Daryl had hung from the tailgate which she pulled on herself. There was still no one around. The dewy tent up in the wagon's bed displayed no movement. Somewhere nearby, a door creaked open and a horse whinnied.

Honorée brought Mike a bottle of water from the truck. "Here, drink this. We'll get the stove started in a second, for tea." She pulled up a chair in front of Mike's. "What were you doing? What do you remember?"

With difficulty, tears streaming down his face, Mike spoke. His words were vague and full of self-reproach. "I was in Vtopia... Olia... I haven't seen Gianna for days and days, no messages..." Honorée watched and listened, her hand on his knee, trying to grasp what he was saying and shaking her head at his apparent dependency on some alternate life somewhere in the world of the VNET.

318

"Do you know what bit you?"

"Oh, I don't know… Out in the woods, under the tarp…The drugs and the headset take you far away…And then, ow! It hurt so much!" He sobbed and took a weepy breath. "I must'a yelled. It went away." Honorée saw in her mind some animal so emboldened by the torpor of this human that it actually started trying to eat his leg! Oh, the extremes to which the VNET and its cybertropic drugs could reduce people to physical lassitude, forgetting their real existence!

"Who's already up so early?" called Ari as he emerged from the wagon's cab, hobbling toward them on stiff legs. Honorée stood up. Mike wiped his face with his sleeve and let the blanket slide down to cover his blood-stained pants.

"Mike and me," said Honorée.

"Good morning to you both," said Ari, considering the puff of condensation that emerged with his expelled breath. "Happy Election Day. Wow, it's cold up here in New York State in the early morning! No frost, though." He stopped when he reached them, and looked at them curiously. "Everything OK?"

"OK," said Honorée. "I couldn't sleep last night." She gestured toward Mike. "Neither could Mike." Mike slumped down in the chair, looking at the ground.

Ari nodded, casting off any trace of suspicion. "I hope it's nothing serious," he said. "You can sleep on the road." He stretched. "We should be there tomorrow, eh?"

They nodded.

"Or maybe the next day, anyway." Ari pointed across the service road. "Off to the men's room," he said, and hobbled away toward the latrine enclosure.

"You should go get changed and washed," said Honorée in a whisper. "And stop all this late-night VNET stuff."

"It's over," said Mike dismally.

"What's over?" said Honorée, torn between hope and disbelief that Mike might be voluntarily ending his VNET obsession.

"I can't go back to Olia now. I've screwed up my duties. I'm away too much. People have no faith in me. I've got no cred. I've lost all of my privileges." He buried his head in his hands.

"Mike, how could you possibly live fully in this world and fully in that one, too? A world is a total commitment, and, um, *this* one is where your body lives, and things here are very, very difficult these days…"

"But it was all so beautiful," said Mike, weeping. "I was so happy, once."

Honorée came up behind Mike and wrapped his head and shoulders in a hug. "Mikey, listen, you've gotta stop this. You've got all of this real, living world—and all of us—to lose, and in exchange for what? Cartoon people who don't love you, who use you, and then just disappear?" She looked around at the countryside in the brightening morning sunlight. "We're just more real, that's all. The problems here are worse because they're real problems, and you can't ignore them. Which is what all those onliners do. I don't want you to spend your life as an onliner. Look what it does to people."

"I know," he sniffed, sounding less drugged. The cybertropics were wearing off. "I'm so sorry…"

Jenny appeared, a big floppy yellow wool cap on her head and a green poncho over her sweater that was tied with a black sash around her waist. She mumbled a greeting and staggered around in her oversized boots gathering together kitchen utensils and stove components.

"Hi Jenny," said Honorée. "You look like the Jamaican flag."

"Tea in a moment," she mumbled groggily, and wandered off toward the front of the wagon to find a water jug.

"Mike, go take a shower, *please*, before they get busy," said Honorée. "Clean out that wound. With soap. We're going to have to get over to the clinic tent right away to get you some meds for infection. What if the animal was rabid? Like, a rabid fox or raccoon?"

Mike stood up, wondering where he had left his duffle bag. "OK," he answered. Honorée began gathering up damp things from the ground and cleaning up the meal area. She flicked the night's slugs off the metal bowls and plates. Mike found his bag and stood with his eyes closed, letting the sun warm his face.

"Go!" Honorée shooed, seeing him still there. "Take a hot shower. They have them here. We're paying for it! When you get back, breakfast will be ready."

* * *

"I'm not surprised," said Ari, hands on the wheel and eyes on the crowded road ahead. "They didn't expect much of a turnout for this election. People don't believe in them anymore. At least federal elections."

"But GNN is saying it will be less than twenty percent," said Lara in disgust.

Ari shrugged. "I'm not surprised."

"It's awful," said Jessica, who was sitting with Ari and Lara in the front of the truck. "So apathetic." She looked around. "I voted absentee, of course."

"Looks like Laugherty will get around 60 percent," said Daryl in the back seat, scanning his T-pad. "That's no surprise, either. All bullshit. Who even gives a shit anymore?"

"Has anyone heard anything about Hedges?" asked Ari. "And I care, by the way."

"He held a press conference in New York City just a little while ago," said Daryl with a smirk. "All about new beginnings and America's deepest truths."

"Thank goodness that he's back out in public again, so we know he's alive," said Jessica.

Ari glanced at her thoughtfully and nodded. "Yes, alive, but I doubt he'd risk leaving New York at the moment."

"He doesn't stand a chance," said Daryl dismissively.

"No," said Ari. "Although he might stand more of a chance if people in the East hadn't been so disturbed by the hurricane."

"Does he have more support in the East?" asked Lara.

"Oh, yes," said Ari. "Traditional Democratic strongholds. Not where the Trust and the oligarchs dominate, or in Front country. They hate him."

"Remember Bobby Pierce?" asked Daryl. "Yeah, sure you do." He exchanged glances with his family. "Mention Hedges and he'd go apeshit."

"I didn't know anyone who supported Hedges," said Celia, speaking up for the first time anyone could remember in a conversation like this. They all looked at her with a mixture of surprise and encouragement.

"No?" asked Jessica.

"No, ma'am," said Celia. "I worked Tuesdays after school as a housegirl for a big farmer, in laundry, and they-all called Anthony Hedges the Vice-Devil-doer."

"He doesn't have much charisma…" remarked Jessica.

"Anthony Hedges is a decorated U.S. Marine colonel, for God's sake," said Ari, irritated. "He has a law degree from Stanford, and ran USAID for five years before they closed it down. He also ran DRR for nearly ten, and then got elected to the Senate." He glared at all of them. "Seems he got pretty far with the little *charisma* he had."

"Daddy, it's OK," said Lara, alarmed. Jessica turned bright red, set her mouth, and said nothing. Ari fixed his eyes on the road. They drove in a tense silence for several minutes.

"My dad cares an awful lot about this election, about politics," said Lara apologetically to Celia, who had retreated deeper into the back seat.

"Hm," muttered Ari. Lara smiled and put her arms around her parent's shoulders.

It was turning into a sunny, warm day. They had gotten an early start from the camp in Kingston, and crossed the Kingston-Rhinecliff Bridge over the Hudson before the fog had finished lifting from the river. They were out of the major migrant traffic flows now, cutting cross-country, west-to-east, and all the traffic they now encountered was local—most of it animal-drawn or human-powered. Following Route 199, they briefly paralleled the mighty river, and then veered east again as they passed through the village of Red Hook. This was homespun, populated, lively country. There was an air of busy-ness in the villages and along the country roads. The land was worked intensively. Everywhere they looked there were paddocks, cow barns, hay barns, enormous hayricks, fields of stubble, bee hives, greenhouses, vineyards, orchards, and all sorts of vendors and stores. They saw breweries, machine shops, and a regional airport with brightly painted small planes. There were inns, pubs, diners, and cafés. There were old churches that seemed well-maintained, although they saw none of the evangelical billboards or sidewalk pulpits that adorned the churches back home.

Along both sides of the Hudson ran trains, and they saw local passenger and freight trains, not only higher-class maglevs. The river itself contained many sailboats, as well as barges loaded with produce headed downriver toward New York City.

"There's money around here," said Ari, breaking the silence. "I wonder why." Indeed, the landscape had a degree of modest prosperity and orderliness that they were not accustomed to.

"It's nice," said Jessica.

322

"Maybe they trade with Canada up here," said Ari. "And, oh, of course: New York City needs food and this must be where they get some of it from."

"Food producers down in New Jersey must have been hit badly by the storm, too," offered Lara.

"Good point," said Ari. "Even more business for these folks up here."

"There are more motor vehicles around here, too," said Daryl. "We just passed a truck almost like this one."

"Yeah, I saw," said Ari. "Well, there's always been a lot of technology, and lots of manufacturing in these parts—the Hudson Valley, around New York, New England. Machinery, chemicals, materials, weapons, instruments, textiles, all sorts of things. Looks like they're managing to salvage some of it."

"I hope Vermont's like that," said Lara. "It means jobs."

"Maybe it's because they still have a real middle class here," said Ari. "Remember what Lost Arrow said? A middle class with savings and ambitions and needs means economic drive."

"They're into politics around here, too," commented Lara. "Look at all the campaign signs on the lawns and trees." Indeed, the variety of printed and hand-lettered signs revealed a diverse field of candidates in local and state elections.

They drove for a few minutes, slowing down for an enormous hay wain. It finally turned off the main road, and they accelerated up a slight hill.

"You know," said Ari quietly, turning his head briefly back toward Celia. "They don't allow people to work as housegirls up here." Celia looked at him in shy surprise. "Or in New England, as far as I know."

"Goodness," she said. "How can that be?"

"The law says that people have to be paid for their work," said Ari. "Without delay, and be free to quit when they want."

They all let that sink in.

"I never said I'd a-wanted to be a housegirl," said Celia.

"I know!" said Ari, chuckling. "You made that pretty clear to your mother!"

Celia blushed.

"Daddy, what's the difference? How does it work?" asked Lara.

"The concept of a Southern-style housegirl doesn't exist," said Ari. "Back home, and even more so in the Deep South, you know, a housegirl is a girl who leaves her own family, saving them the money of supporting her, and works for a wealthy family until she gets married, and gets paid her lump-sum bond based on the number of months or years she worked there. It's a way to save, in theory. If she has enough of a bond, she can cash it in to go study or start a business. Although that's a big if."

Celia shook her head. "That never happens in real life. The family's always got some reason or excuse. When housegirls get married they're lucky if they get any bond at all. And the family men are always making the girls pregnant, and then nobody wants to marry them, and they don't get their bond if that happens…"

"The courts are not very supportive of housegirls," said Jessica disapprovingly. "That was every mother's nightmare in Blacksburg." She looked at Lara and laughed. "Remember when I told you that, if you didn't study and take your nursing exam, you'd wind up a housegirl?"

"You didn't tell me, Mother," said Lara with chagrin. "You screamed it at me, and locked yourself in your room for the rest of the evening until Daddy came home." They all laughed in surprise, except for Jessica and Lara.

"That tells you how much I cared about you, Lara," said Jessica. "You were running wild for a while there."

"I *never* ran wild!" laughed Lara. "*Me*?!" She turned around toward Daryl with an exaggerated questioning expression. "Seriously! Daryl?"

"She was pretty tame," said Daryl. "Compared to me. Studious."

"Well, OK," said Jessica. "She wasn't as bad. And still isn't."

They all laughed.

"Anyway," said Ari, "nobody has to worry about that up here."

"Why?" asked Lara. "How?"

"It's the law. You work, you get paid. Cash. Promptly and regularly."

"That's really great," said Lara. "Modern."

Ari slowed down. "I'm going to stop at this farm stand up here, and ask for some advice."

"Oh?" asked Lara.

"Yes." Ari pointed at the truck's screen. "See this north-south road? That's the old Taconic State Parkway. See this other one to the east? That's Route 22. See, it runs along the Massachusetts border." Lara and Daryl studied the screen. "They both take us where we want to go, but I want to find out about the traffic and the condition."

"I'll come in with you," said Lara. They got out of the truck.

Moments later, they were back, along with a sack of apples and some dark-brown doughnuts which the farm boy said were called 'cider doughnuts'.

"The man said we would be better off on the Taconic State Parkway," said Ari to the others. "He said, if you're motorized, you can go faster. Pavement's in better condition. Fewer villages and other kinds of congestion. He also said that there had been some washouts recently on 22."

"Well, then," said Jessica. They started off. In minutes, they were leaving Route 199 and ascending the on-ramp of the Taconic State Parkway. Its two northbound lanes were empty. The road was like a tunnel, with no shoulders, and trees and bushes growing close beside and above the roadway. They passed a sign that stated, in large white letters, "Motor Vehicles Only."

"I'm not sure I like this," said Lara. "It's so closed in."

"The surface is in amazingly good condition," said Ari. "I don't think I've ever been on a highway so good. We're going almost sixty kilometers an hour, and it's smooth as glass."

"Slow down, Daddy!" exclaimed Lara. "They're texting me from the wagon!"

"Oh my goodness, you're right," said Ari, slowing to a more moderate forty-to-fifty kph. "Sorry."

"This is fast enough," said Jessica. "We'll nearly be in Vermont this evening at this pace."

Ari was inspecting the road surface as they drove. "It's some kind of continuously reinforced polyconcrete." The civil engineer was coming to life in him. "I remember hearing about this years ago."

After a few kilometers, vehicles appeared on the other side of the parkway, headed south. They were military trucks, in a convoy, lights on. Everyone watched them with curiosity. The first several trucks had the names and markings of the New York Guard. Then came at least a dozen trucks that were discretely marked on the doors with "Canada" and small maple leaf flags. Bringing up the rear were more New York vehicles: cargo trucks, buses, jeeps, and articulated Chafer fighting vehicles.

"Interesting," said Ari. This was met with a few nods and grunts of agreement. "I hope there aren't EU and Chinese trucks driving around these here hills as well," he remarked.

"Why?" Lara asked. "Do you mean, um…?"

"It's what just brought down President Morales," said Daryl bluntly. "Duh."

"I mean, of course I knew that," Lara retorted.

"I can see why the military likes to use this road," said Ari after a pause. "Looks like they're the only ones who do." He glanced at the map on the screen, which was slowly scrolling as their position moved. "This is a funny old highway, isn't it? It's not an interstate. The lanes are narrow and there are no shoulders. But it seems to have been placed in the middle of empty country, and then nothing was allowed to develop along it."

"It's a *park*way, Daddy," said Lara, smiling impishly. "A park."

"I suppose it is," Ari said, musing over the conditions that, once upon a time, gave state road administrators and civil engineers the luxury to plan and build a highway as if it were a work of art or public monument, yet functional at the same time. To be able to conceive and complete projects like that, instead of just maintaining and repairing what was already there, must have been intoxicating.

The Taconic State Parkway continued north, rising and falling as it rode the eastern edge of the Hudson Valley. The vegetation alongside the parkway was thick and neglected, growing out into the right lane in many places. But the pavement remained of a consistently high quality. On and on they drove. The few farms and places of commerce they passed were dismal and abandoned. They saw no villages, no homes. The parkway itself indeed seemed to have been built through a thinly settled, heavily forested hinterland—even in the days of its prime. They passed grazing herds of deer, families of wild turkeys, two foxes playing in a meadow, and scores of woodchucks and rabbits foraging by the road's edge. The woodchucks seemed to be in the habit of standing erect by the road like sentinels to watch them as they passed.

Then, after perhaps an hour, they started seeing signs for a village named Chatham, and then they abruptly arrived in a little settlement where Route 295 intersected the parkway.

"This is where we get off the Taconic State Parkway," said Ari. "We take 295 east from here."

326

"Can we take a rest stop?" asked Jessica.

"Sure," said Ari. "I was thinking that would be a good idea, myself." He steered the truck with its wagon/trailer into a large gravel lot at the crossroads. There were quite a few people about. Diagonally across the intersection was a group of military trucks taking a break. Stationed around the settlement were a number of food vendors operating out of small covered wagons, with smoke rising from their grills. A variety of vehicles stood parked. Not far from where the truck came to a stop was a taquería operating out of an old Lanc. They were doing a good business. Smoke rose lazily from its chimney into the balmy early-November air.

"It's still early, we had a good breakfast, so I vote we skip buying any food here and keep going until it's lunchtime," said Ari. His cab-mates nodded in affirmation. They knew how scarce money was. "By lunch, I figure we'll be in Pittsfield, Massachusetts."

"Yay," said Jenny.

"I hear it's the pits," said Ari.

"Oh, that's too bad," said Jessica. She climbed out of the truck and set off toward a general store that appeared to have outhouses behind it.

"The pits!" laughed Ari. "Get it? Pittsfield?" This was met by groans and a few deadpan stares. "Oh, come on, everyone. We have to keep our spirits up." As he said that, he saw Grandma walking over to the taco stand. He watched her. She seemed to be carrying on a conversation as she waited for her order. The man behind the counter handed her a hot tea, which she paid for. They continued talking. Then, after gestures of thanks, Grandma started walking directly toward the truck's cab.

"Ari," said Grandma, "I said I'd take the next shift at the wheel, but I think it's better for you or maybe Daryl or Mike to drive for the next stretch, until we're well into Massachusetts."

"Oh, sure," said Ari. "That's fine with me. I still feel fresh and alert. But why? Did they say something over there?" Curiosity lit Ari's face. Grandma sat down on the step below the front passenger door, and took a careful sip of her tea.

"Yes," she said. "The taco man noticed us—big group, out of state, slow-moving motor vehicle—and he told me that there's been trouble up 295 recently. A robbery. A car-jacking. In the mountains."

Ari frowned.

"He said it's a pretty desolate area now, near the Massachusetts border. Not many people living up there anymore. Most of the traffic goes down Interstate 90 instead, with all the Federal security, you know…"

"That's pretty far out of our way," said Ari. "With a truck, we can drive through the mountains on 295 quickly." He rubbed his jaw. "Remember that stretch in Prince William County, coming into DC?"

"On Halloween night? When we found that wood-burner on fire?" She nodded. "Of course I remember! That was only a week ago."

"My God," said Ari. "You're right. Seems like months. Anyway, we were lucky there weren't any problems, but remember how we had Mike up on the roof and the wagon bunkered down?"

"Yes," she said.

"In broad daylight, moving fast, we should be all right like that again, with the right precautions," he continued, nodding as if to stoke his own conviction.

"Hm," she said. She glanced at the taco stand. "It's hard to really know the threat level…" She looked back around at Ari. "What do we lose by taking I-90 and then coming up, um, what, I-91 from the south?"

Ari was flicking around on the truck's screen as she said this. "Well, we get into a lot of congestion at the Massachusetts border, and it looks like I-91 is very congested as well. It probably adds a half-day…"

Grandma sighed. "Well, we've made it this far with no problems," she muttered.

"Anyway," said Ari, looking around the little crossroads commercial development, "there's no stockade here, and yet people apparently feel safe enough to do business here."

She nodded. "Ok, then."

In a few minutes, toilet breaks and seat reassignments had been completed, and they set off. They were now only about twenty kilometers from the Massachusetts border. Ari drove, with Grandma and Lara up front with him—Lara by the door with Grandma's MAC-C22. Honorée and the boys sat together in the relative safety of the truck's rear seat. Mike stationed himself with Jenny back in the wagon's bed with Grandma's AK, cargo redistributed to create a rampart. Daryl and Celia sat in the wagon's cab, with Mike's pistol by Daryl's side. Claudia and Jessica climbed into the truck's cargo bay with the food and luggage, preferring its poor lighting and lack of ventilation to any action they might see up the road.

The road wound through long curves as they crossed under I-90—the New York State Thruway—and slowly gained elevation. Ari explained that these low mountains were called the Taconics, and were geologically distinct from the Berkshire Mountains ahead. The day remained sunny and fairly warm—a touch of Indian Summer. The valleys they navigated were quiet and scenic—a land of isolated hill farms and abandoned vacation homes and motels. The road was narrow, and its condition poor. Traffic was very light. Low, steep hills rose around them, their slopes covered with thick yellowing forests and neglected pastures. The further they drove, the more it felt like a borderland, where things ended before they would begin again.

They passed through a crossroads village named Canaan, perhaps ten kilometers from the Massachusetts border. Half of its old wooden clapboard houses were unoccupied, their porch roofs collapsing from rot, and saplings sprouting from walls and doorways. There were no political campaign signs. But old recreational signs appeared advertising a Queechy Lake not far ahead. They drove through a shallow pass. The road divided, with Route 295 taking the right fork. On their right-hand side, a rather large, once-elegant country house with several outbuildings sat vacant behind a dry-stacked stone wall.

"What's this about?" wondered Ari aloud as he peered at a stopped horsecart still some distance ahead. Talking stopped and the mood grew watchful. Lara texted alerts back to the wagon. Ari slowed down to cautiously pass. Ahead, right in the middle of the eastbound lane, a high cart loaded with pumpkins was stopped. A couple of pumpkins lay broken on the road behind it. A boy no older than fourteen or fifteen stood beside it, looking at the truck out of the corner of his eye. He appeared to be alone.

"No," said Ari shaking his head. "This looks weird."

"Why?" Honorée was leaning forward, inspecting the scene.

"What would a kid be doing hauling a load of pumpkins all by himself toward Massachusetts, where I'm sure they have all the pumpkins they need at the moment?" said Grandma skeptically. "It feels like a setup."

The boy half-heartedly waved at them, his thin face drawn.

"Can we see anything wrong with the cart, boy, or horse?" asked Ari. The replies were all negative. "OK, look around, and I'll keep going."

By this point, they had slowed to almost a walk. As they came level with the boy, he stepped hesitantly toward them, making eye contact, his hand still waving as if he had forgotten to switch it off. "You OK?" called Grandma from the truck's window, more to provoke a reaction than anything else. The boy said nothing, but just as they passed him, he suddenly looked up the road. From both sides, a dozen boys stepped out from the dark eaves of the forest that crowded the road.

"Let's go!" shouted Ari, stepping on the truck's accelerator. Their speed leapt higher under the torque of the electric motor, and continued climbing. The boys moved menacingly toward the truck, but backed off quickly as it shot past, much larger and heavier than they were. One of them threw something that glanced off the side of the wagon with a metallic bang. No shots were fired. Looking back, they saw the boys closing ranks across the otherwise deserted road.

"Good God," said Ari with a disbelieving laugh. "What was all that about?"

"They're probably used to robbing wagons," said Grandma. "Or scaring them, anyway."

"The boy looked so unsure," said Lara. "Reluctant."

Ari shook his head. "I really don't know what they were thinking."

"We're lucky it wasn't anything worse," said Honorée from the back seat. That drew silence from the others for a moment.

"Not a place to spend any more time than we need to," said Ari. At a good clip, Ari piloted the truck and its wagon across a flat basin of land that emerged between a series of large ponds and Queechy Lake, and then started up the final grade that would take them to the state border. The ascending road led through a narrow gap between higher hills. The air was becoming close, and a line of darkening clouds over the lowlands behind them suggested an impending rain storm.

Ahead was a simple, lightly manned border crossing. This was clearly a place where little through-traffic crossed. On the New York side, a few state police in a booth scanned passing vehicles and checked out-of-state vehicles out of the transit bond system. Their refund, they were told, "would come in a few days." Passing on to the Massachusetts checkpoint, they waited behind only a few vehicles. Just ahead of them was a luxurious, low-slung electric roadster with New York plates.

"Would you look at that," remarked Ari.

330

Grandma smiled. "Very nice."

"Used to be lots of cars like that on the road," said Ari. Grandma nodded.

"How old do you suppose that is?" asked Lara.

"Ten, fifteen years," said Ari. "It's a Galvano. Italian. See the little gamma in the middle there?"

They admired the car, magnificent in its style and frivolity, and a sharp contrast to the world it passed through.

"Bet the police wouldn't mind an upgrade to their cars," said Ari. "Look at those old junkers." He nodded toward the cluster of aging Massachusetts state police turbodiesels parked beside the checkpoint.

At the Massachusetts check point, the police had a lot of questions. Where were they coming from? Were they all members of one family? Where were they going? How quickly? Where did they plan to exit the state? How many nights did they plan to spend in the state? Could they feed themselves? All of the information was recorded. Several state troopers circled the truck and wagon a few times with scanners and IR cameras, collecting biometrics and vehicle data. Another looked around in the wagon's bed, and elicited gasps of surprise from Claudia and Jessica when he clambered up into the truck's cargo space.

Compared to their two previous experiences crossing state borders, this was relaxed and relatively friendly. There was no talk of visas or bonds. Lara and Jenny hung out by the truck's cab, marveling at the thoroughness of the check.

"Good thing there's not much traffic," commented Jenny in a manner that could be interpreted as either sarcastic or flirtatious. "Or we'd be backed up for hours."

"You think we're being too thorough?" asked one of the senior officers in an accent the women could barely understand.

Jenny laughed in slight embarrassment. "Oh, no."

The officer nodded. "I didn't think so." He laughed. "We have the luxury here of being thorough. Most of the big roads down south are mobbed. They'd trade places with us in a second."

Ari overheard. "How long has this been going on?"

"The migration? Since last Thursday. Been more and more every day." He turned away, spoke briefly to another trooper, and turned to face them again. "You're good to go."

"Thanks," said Ari.

The state police officer smiled at Jenny and Lara. "Welcome to Massachusetts."

"You know, by the way, some kids tried to rob us a few kilometers back," said Ari, pointing back over his shoulder with his thumb. "I know it's not your jurisdiction."

"With a pumpkin cart?" asked the officer with a look of amused disgust.

Ari nodded.

"Ah, Jesus, those Canaan boys." He took his hat off and rubbed his forehead. "Somebody ought to go down there and knock some heads together." He turned toward the New York checkpoint, which only lay about twenty meters away. "Hey Larry!" he called. One of the New York troopers turned around. "Those kids are down there with the pumpkin cart again."

The New York trooper shook his head. "Christ. We'll send a car down."

Ari was about to get back into the truck, but he stopped suddenly in his tracks and turned back toward the policemen. "No visas or bonds?"

"Nope," said the senior officer. "They've been talkin' about it, but nothin' yet."

Ari grinned. "Thanks for keeping things simple."

"Well, I don't know," said the officer. "I heard they might even close the border, so you might be lucky, getting through like you are."

"Close the border?" asked Grandma. "Are you serious?"

"I'm just telling you what the politicians are saying," said the police officer. "I just take orders."

"Good grief," said Grandma. "I've never heard of such a thing!" She looked at Ari and the others in dismay. Ari shrugged and frowned.

Everyone took their places and the truck and wagon pulled away.

"Maryann texted me a couple of minutes ago," said Grandma, seated beside Honorée.

"Oh?" Honorée was giving the boys a snack of crackers to tide them over until they could make a real lunch stop.

"Jake's still stuck down in New York City," she said.

"Oh really?" said Ari without removing his eyes from the road. They were just passing a large blue sign, decorated with state bird and state flower, welcoming them to the Commonwealth of Massachusetts.

"He was supposed to be out by yesterday, but there are no trains, and the state only just sent a van down to pick them all up." Grandma was already composing a reply. "I wonder why it took them so long?" She read several other messages and scanned the news. "Mm hm. Hedges is taking a beating, except in a few states like the ones around here." She studied her lapscreen. She clucked. "Morales is reportedly 'not cooperating' so they still have her locked up. Isn't that awful?" She sat up. "This is interesting. Looks like the Vermont referendum will choose secession. Heading toward about 55%. That will make things very interesting just in time for our arrival. But... um, their incumbent Republican governor Remington seems to be headed for an easy victory..."

"Grandma," said Honorée, "you seem a lot perkier than you did the last few days." Her grandmother was indeed talking more and displaying more energy.

"I can't imagine why," Grandma said dryly. "I've been on the road for weeks and weeks. Surprised it hasn't killed me."

"Does one side still feel weak compared to the other?" asked Honorée.

Grandma rubbed her right arm. "No... No, I'm not sure. I still feel a bit numb on the left side of my tongue. Isn't *that* strange?" Honorée nodded in agreement, concerned. Grandma looked back at her screen.

"Did you know there's a secession referendum in Washington State, too?" continued Grandma. "And in North Dakota? Though it doesn't look like they'll pass. And California is voting on whether to keep or scrap their special independent observer status in the UN. Oh, this is *worrisome*. 'Widespread accusations of voter suppression and voting fraud across nation.' I'm shocked, shocked!" She laughed sarcastically. "Who could possibly be surprised at that? It's been getting worse, year after year. But of course we banned the international observers this time..."

In what seemed like only a brief while, they began to see signs of denser settlement as they reached the outskirts of Pittsfield, Massachusetts. The old city lay in a broad valley, with the shapes of higher mountains to the north, dominated by the summit of Mount Greylock, the highest in the state. They were entering the Berkshires now. Pittsfield gave a mixed impression. There appeared to be areas of small industry and new construction mixed with old collapsing mills and warehouses beyond repair. They passed through a checkerboard of variety. Thunder boomed as the afternoon storm closed in behind them.

"Maybe we should stop for some food, once we're in the center," suggested Ari. "Can anyone tell if this town has a stockade?"

Suddenly, the truck started vibrating in an odd way, and Ari sensed a difference in the steering and acceleration. "What's that?" he said sharply.

"What?" Lara and Grandma were looking around, trying to identify the change. They sensed it too. Then their phones and T-pads were ringing, and they heard Mike yelling for Ari to stop the truck. They pulled over beside a vast, overgrown factory lot, just as the first raindrops were hitting the windscreen, and jumped down from the truck to see what the matter was.

"We're screwed!" said Mike, already on the ground by the wagon's left-rear wheel. Smoke and steam were rising from the hub, and the tire was flat and deformed. "This is totally frozen. I was falling asleep, not really paying attention, and the next thing I knew we were driving a couple of blocks just dragging the wheel!"

"Oh," said Grandma in disgust. "We don't have another." The spare was already on the right-rear wheel. She stood looking at the ground, fingers tapping her chin. Honorée brought her a hooded jacket and told her to put it on or she'd get soaked. Grandma remained frozen in thought for a moment more. The others were retreating to the cabs and truck's cargo space to escape the quickly intensifying rain shower. Grandma walked stiffly back to the truck's cab and got in. They were all damp, and the atmosphere in the cab was clammy now.

"Damn," said Ari. "And I've been trying to keep the speed down the whole time…"

"I suppose the wagon's just not designed for higher speeds for long periods of time," said Grandma. She turned to Ari. "We'll have to take off the bed, and leave it."

"Take off the bed? How's that work?" asked Ari, puzzled.

"You unbolt the bed with the rear axle from the cab. What's left is a limber, with the cab up on top. The limber and its cab can be bolted to short beds, long beds, hayrakes, planters, cultivators, sawmills, whatever. Pretty versatile. If we unbolt the bed, the only cargo space left on the limber will be a very short cantilever bed about a meter and a half long, sticking out behind the cab. We'll have to move everything else into the truck, or up on top of the cab." She squinted and wrinkled her face into a frown. "We can leave the limber hitched to the truck the way it is."

"Is it hard to do?" asked Ari.

"Not really," said Grandma. "But it'll take time. There are a lot of stiff bolts to remove. Luckily, I do have a long wrench for them, and a handle extension."

"I've seen it done, Daddy," said Lara.

"Granted, we're going to all be a bit more crowded together, because we lose the wagon's bed for passengers."

"Aw, we're not that far from Vermont now," said Ari. "What if this had happened in Pennsylvania?"

Grandma only shook her head. "I hope we can leave it here for a while, and come back to get it." She looked doubtful.

They waited for about twenty minutes as the heavy downpour passed over them, pounding the truck mercilessly. The streets started to flood, and the air was filled with blowing mist. An open flash flood drain nearby that had been dry and empty only moments before filled with rushing, muddy brown water. When the rain had stopped, they got out again to detach the wagon's bed. This proved to be a long and arduous process. There were dozens of large bolts to unscrew and pins to remove, and many of them were frozen and needed to be attacked with a heavy hammer before they relented. Mike, Daryl, Lara, and Jenny took turns beating on the handle of the wrench to crack the nuts open. Everyone had a series of snacks that amounted to a late lunch. By the time they had the bolts removed, the bed emptied and dismounted, the license plate transferred to the limber, the wiring switched to the limber's own rear lights, and the cargo redistributed to the truck and limited areas on the limber, the November dusk was settling. Ari looked at his watch. It was nearly five o'clock. The town of Greenfield was not far—no more than three hours' driving—and they knew there were large traveler's camps there beside the interstate highway. Greenfield was also only a short distance from the Vermont border, too— perhaps another thirty kilometers. They decided to make for Greenfield.

"It sounds like a better place to be stuck than Pittsfield," said Jenny, looking with skepticism at the dark buildings and darker alleys that surrounded them. "Greener pastures are better than pits." Lara laughed nervously.

A few bypassers had stopped to speak with them during their delay. They were polite and curious, but said little. This was not a busy part of town. The street remained largely deserted by both vehicles and pedestrians most of the time. There were no street lights or electric lighting in the buildings near them. At one point, a man on an old shaggy pony had ridden by, staring at them sidelong but making no conversation. As darkness fell, even fewer people passed them.

"I guess it will just have to sit there for a while," said Grandma sourly, looking at the wagon's bed, which they had pushed and dragged onto the crumbling sidewalk. "I suppose I should leave a note on it." She called out to Jenny, "Jenny, honey, could you get a pen and a piece of paper, unless there's a spare RFID sticky note in the glove compartment?" The others were picking up all remaining odds and ends, and tying the cargo down on the little chest-high shelf on the limber, behind the cab, which was all that was left of the wagon's ample bed.

It was Lara who first noticed something odd about the figure who had appeared by the truck, but before she realized it was not one of them, the situation changed abruptly for the worse.

"Everybody down!" a man barked. "Face-down, hands and legs out." Another figure quickly moved to kick Ari's legs out from under him and he collapsed onto his belly with a painful grunt.

"Daddy!" Lara screamed. The second figure ran straight at her, and she threw herself down in compliance. She thought she saw a third figure also running among them as Grandma, Honorée, Claudia, and Jessica all suddenly found themselves cowering on the wet, grimy ground in the darkness. But without a pause, metered in pounding heartbeats, the situation continued to evolve rapidly. The third figure ran toward Mike, who had been standing by the limber. He appeared to stoop, obeying the order, but then suddenly—so fast Lara could only guess at what was really happening—he swung his arms up in a wide arc and Lara heard a crackling sound like a walnut in a nutcracker, a shrill scream, and several pops of an automatic weapon. She threw her arms over her head and lay still, hoping she would not be hit by something or someone, trying to make sense of what was happening. Then everything was quiet, and she felt someone taking her arm and helping her up. They were all getting up. The wagon's cab lights and headlights were turned on, and a moment later, the truck's brighter lights came on.

"There were only three, I think," shouted Daryl, panting. "I don't think they were armed, either!" Two remained with them. One lay still on the ground, a dark, shiny liquid pooling around his head. The other crouched on the ground, moaning horribly. The third figure appeared to have fled.

"What did you do?!" gasped Lara to Mike and Daryl.

"I got him with the wrench," said Mike, his voice unsteady. "Somewhere in the face."

"Oh, God," said Lara.

"I was in the truck," said Daryl proudly, "and the AK happened to be right near me."

"We are damn lucky they weren't armed, or more in number," said Ari shakily. "We should have been paying closer attention. We don't know this place!"

"Well, I'm not going to worry about should have and might have," said Honorée loudly. "I'm just glad that Mike and Daryl had their wits about them and acted so fast!" She went over to Mike and gave him a quick hug. "My little Army brother." Mike suppressed a sob. Jenny also hugged him.

"Yes, of course," said Ari, his tone less reproachful.

"Good boys," said Grandma, holding onto Jenny for support and taking deep breaths from the shock.

"We should get out of here," said Daryl. They got into their vehicles, more crowded now, and prepared to set off for Greenfield.

"Daddy, shouldn't we call the police?" asked Lara, still reeling from what had just happened. "There are two men lying in the street right down next to us!"

"And do what?" asked Ari, upset. "Waste time here telling the same story over and over? It wouldn't change anything. Think of what those guys might have done to us, wanted to do to us! Highwaymen. The police have their hands full. We did them a favor." He started the truck. They drove in stunned silence for a few minutes.

"Lara, why don't you turn on the truck's radio?" suggested Ari, eager to put the assault behind them, and the cab was soon filled with voices and music as they passed through the center of Pittsfield and started winding their way eastward on State Route 9, the 'Berkshire Trail.'

The election was continuing its ponderous westward unfurling as they drove and listened, their heartbeats gradually returning to normal. The polls in some parts of Maine would soon be closing. It was only midafternoon on the West Coast. The Republicans and Homeland Front were doing well, gaining in many states. Laugherty would surely win. A storm surge from Hurricane Sulis was washing across most of southern Florida, closing polls early, but people had seen it coming, voted early, and evacuated. Participation in the election was nonetheless terribly low—even lower in the states still reeling from Hurricane Rhiannon. Some commentators were calling this a "mass endorsement of the status quo" while others were calling it the end of democracy in America. Laugherty's supporters were celebrating his certain win in scornful jubilation. "There's no law says you have to vote," said one woman in an interview as she cut hair only a block from a polling station outside Chicago, "and I never have. Don't make me no difference." Meanwhile, others protested in major cities, playing cat-and-mouse with companies of riot police, asserting their right to free speech and imploring the nation to get out and vote.

"This election is just disgusting," said Honorée from the back seat. "At least Lucia Morales had the power of the veto for most of her term. Now it's going to be full speed ahead for OSCIA, Forsa, and all those other awful bills the red-black bloc is going to pass. When is this madness ever going to end?"

"Oh, it will," said Grandma with a tired yawn.

"It will, huh?" said Honorée. "Grandma, I love you, but don't you feel any urgency? Things have been getting worse and worse for years! When do we hit bottom?"

"We will," said Grandma.

"Oh, stop it!" said Honorée in frustration. "In anyone's lifetime?"

"In someone's lifetime," said Grandma.

Honorée rolled her eyes and sat back against the rear seat.

"I think we're going to see a lot of new things, very quickly," said Ari. "Much more and different than we expect." He looked around. "It's in the air. Doesn't everyone feel it?"

40—FROM THE DEVIL'S WATCHTOWER

Tuesday, November 6th (night)

"Heh heh," laughed Manny quietly. He took another appreciative swig of the brown ale, and wiped the foam from his mustache. "This just gets better and better."

"Farmer Brown?" Lost Arrow was standing, hands in his pockets as he looked west.

"No, Boncoeur's," said Manny. "Want one?" He had several more bottles like it in his backpack.

"Sure," Lost Arrow replied. He accepted the freshly opened bottle. "Thanks."

"I tasted their first batch," said Manny. "Ten years ago, must 'a been."

Lost Arrow nodded in the darkness. They were both silent for a moment. The air was still, and through it could clearly be heard the distant din of motor sounds, chopping and banging, occasional back-up horns, snatches of music, horses' whinnies and other evidence of the large number of people in the valley barely a mile to the west.

"Got a front-row seat," said Manny.

"Well, except this is only one of thousands of stages," said Lost Arrow. "Hundreds, anyway."

"Yeah, OK. But it's our own local show," said Manny. He got out of his chair and stood up. "More fires tonight," he remarked, and sniffed. "Little bit of a temperature inversion, too."

"I was just thinking that," replied Lost Arrow.

"Bernardston never had it so good," said Manny sarcastically.

"Mm," said Lost Arrow. "Annie Rexford said they've been posting sentries around the farmhouse since last Friday, and they've still had things stolen."

"Doug told me that with the new camp on Charity Farm, plus the camps across the line at the Visitor's Center and Yankee, there's upwards of forty thousand refugees between here and Greenfield."

Lost Arrow sighed. "So I'm hearing."

The crazed-bee sound of a volocopter buzzed in the air nearby, and then they caught sight of its dark shape moving against the stars and then campfires as it dipped below their eye level.

"Media again?" Manny peered to see if he could spot any identification. Its lack of illumination gave it away as a drone.

"No," said Lost Arrow, watching it through night glasses. "MassDOT."

When its sound had faded away, they both sat down again in the old wooden Adirondack chairs atop their gneiss ledge, and contemplated the night and its doings. They were on a small rocky prominence at the summit of Huckle Hill, almost two hundred meters above the surface of the Connecticut River immediately to their east. Buried in deep woods, unvisited, unobserved, they could look out across miles of hills and forests to the west, south, and east. To the north, the hills became higher beyond the Vermont border. To the east, they could look down onto the scattered lights of the quiet hamlet of Northfield, which remained tranquil this evening because the 181st Infantry Regiment of the Massachusetts Army National Guard had walled it off from the traveling multitudes. Together with their counterparts in New Hampshire, just to the north on the eastern side of the Connecticut River, they were steering all refugee traffic away from the smaller border crossings and toward the seething kettle of Interstate 91.

"'Nother beer?" asked Manny in a comradely manner.

"No thanks, Manny," answered Lost Arrow. "Not finished with my first one yet. Damn fine, though." A barred owl posed its eternal questions off in the pitch-black woods somewhere. A puff of breeze sighed through the stand of stunted white pines that shared their overlook. He shivered and reached for his wool vest, inside his own backpack. "Getting colder."

"They don't know how lucky they've been until now, those refugees," said Manny. "Even with all that rain, it's stayed pretty warm."

"Mm hm," grunted Lost Arrow. "If warm is lucky."

"Know what I'm worried about?" asked Manny.

"The storm?"

340

Manny nodded. "Yuh." He took a drink. "Gonna be nice next couple days, Indian summer weather maybe, but they're saying the steering currents such as they are right now are going to send that Sulis right up the Hudson or Connecticut River. Which is good for everyone got hit by Rhiannon, but I-95, I-93, I-91 and I-87 are where all the refugees are, and they ain't movin' particularly fast."

"We always said it would all come apart during hurricane season, didn't we?" Lost Arrow laughed mirthlessly.

"I believe we did," said Manny. "Er, you did. UNH 2015."

"That far back?!" Lost Arrow shook his head in wonder. "I was thinking maybe Wuppertal in '21."

"No, U of New Hampshire was the first simulation. With those New Zealanders."

"Guess so," said Lost Arrow. "Whatever. Like anyone paid any attention."

"Well, now we know how Cassandra felt," said Manny.

"A day early and a dollar long," laughed Lost Arrow.

"You heard from your lady friend?" asked Manny.

"Not heard," said Lost Arrow, "since before she left. But..." He opened his T-pad and fiddled with it for a moment. "Here is where she is." He showed Manny the screen. A blue pin floated above a winding valley some leagues to the southwest of their hilltop.

Manny squinted. "Where's that, North Adams?"

"No, southeast of there, coming up toward Shelburne Falls the back way."

"She send you a track?"

"No, but she apparently brought my letter with her," chuckled Lost Arrow, "with the RFID tag in it."

Manny smiled and nodded, impressed. "A wise precaution. Are you going to try and meet her?"

Lost Arrow shook his head. "No, no need. She's heading for her sister's up near Brattleboro anyway, so there'll be plenty of time to visit. Not unless she has trouble down there –." He nodded westward. "- And then I'll try to help out, if I can."

"I got to know Jack pretty well," said Manny. "Especially when he was at MIT. We did some resilience stuff together down in New York after that storm Sandy, in fact. More than twenty-five years ago. But I don't ever recall meeting his wife."

"She was pretty busy with her own career back then," replied Lost Arrow. "High up in the State Department for a couple of administrations."

"Oh, OK," said Manny. "That explains it."

"I never met her either," said Lost Arrow. "Not face-to-face."

"No kidding!" Manny reacted with surprise. "Never? Always thought you had. 'Specially after Jack was shot. And the way you contacted her recently."

"Nope. No, Jack made me promise I'd fill her in if I ever thought things were going critical, if he wasn't around to do it himself, that is. Glad I was around myself, and remembered." He gave a little ironic chuckle. "And glad we're still doing this work, have our eye on the ball, and have contacts in the state capitals…"

"Didn't you go to the funeral?" asked Manny, still musing over the fact that Lost Arrow had never met Grandma.

"Didn't have a public funeral."

"You know, you're right!" said Manny. "I had forgotten that. I guess I would have gone, too, if they had had."

"No, just a private family service, as soon as they brought his body home. I was expecting a funeral, and then, bang! Buried, over, and done with. Just like that." Lost Arrow scratched his head. "His body was sent home after Europol did an autopsy."

"Very sad," said Manny in subdued sympathy. "His speech at Davos made a big impression and was reported in the media, and a lot of politicians expressed agreement."

"Yeah. The pinnacle of his career. Couple years after *Graveyard* came out."

"Very tragic for everyone," mused Manny. "Ever figure out who did it, exactly?"

Even though they were ostensibly alone on their wooded hilltop, Lost Arrow lowered his voice. "No, not that I know, anyway… The Front? The Trust? Some oligarch? He was stepping on a lot of toes, although he was dead right. And then *dead* dead…"

"Crappin' on a lot of doorsteps," agreed Manny.

"Well, you can't suppress system truth forever," said Lost Arrow. "Systems are pretty good that way. People, you can shut them up. Systems? They speak volumes."

"Yup," grunted Manny. "Well, we might have our chance to meet her soon, I guess," said Manny. "And her family. And maybe hear the rest of the tale." And then he took another hearty quaff of his Boncoeur's Brown Ale.

"I'm wondering how they're going to get across the border," said Lost Arrow quietly.

"People were still crossing this evening," said Manny.

"Mm, yes," said Lost Arrow, "but the election is going the way everyone expected, and the governors may make their move within a day or two."

"They might squeeze across tomorrow," offered Manny. " On 91?"

"The waits can be up to five or six hours," said Lost Arrow. "I don't know. They'll be lucky."

"Do they know about any of the secret routes?" asked Manny.

"No idea," said Lost Arrow. "I imagine Florence is in touch with her sister. Don't know what they know."

"Well," grunted Manny, "they can always drive over here and hike in on the ridge trail. Get their truck later. There won't be any patrols down on Pond Road."

Lost Arrow nodded in the darkness.

The night was moonless, the moon having set shortly after sunset. Consequently, the black, clear sky offered a stunning display of stars and a section of the Milky Way. The two men leaned back, quietly contemplating the sparkling vault of heaven, as they often did on clear nights in every season. Noises and faint light continued to emanate from the busy valley below. A spray of meteors flashed above the western horizon. To the south, the unusual sight of not one but several aircrafts' lights signaled their approach to the airport at Hartford, Connecticut.

"Feels like the world is getting ready to turn," said Lost Arrow.

"Turns around once a day," chuckled Manny. "Been doin' that long as I can remember."

Lost Arrow laughed. "Not like this, my friend. Not like this."

"You may just be right about that," said Manny. "Finally! We were startin' to lose faith in ya!"

"A broken clock's right twice every day," laughed Lost Arrow. "Yeah, sure. Predicting the demise of Phase F3 has been a pretty unconvincing business for a long time. Darn thing kept discovering new ways of prolonging itself. Generations have been paying the price. The oilygarchs just got stronger, more concentrated. America turned out to have about the strongest immunity to revolution of any society in history. Baffled the rest of the world, as they went off into the future. But here we are, on the threshold of, well, *something*. We're hearing it from all over now…"

Manny cupped his ear and listened with exaggerated expectancy. "OK, I'm waitin' for it… I'm waitin'…"

"Oh, screw you, y'old bugger," said Lost Arrow. "You just wait."

Manny let out a cackle. "I just wanna make sure I can still get decent beer on the other side of this, uh, *threshold*."

"Oh, no. Won't be any of that," said Lost Arrow.

"Well, then, it'll never happen," said Manny. "People won't stand for it."

"It's out of our hands now," said Lost Arrow. "Like climate change. Nobody can change it. Not Laugherty, not Leland Guch, not Lucia Morales, not Jerry Hannity, not Europe or China… And certainly not the Trinity of Fort Collins!"

"We will know in the morning, sir," said Manny, getting up with a groan. "Time to head back?"

"I think that's a good idea," said Lost Arrow.

With the ledge, trees, and trail visible in the starshine to the unaided eye, they were able to navigate off the summit and down into the dense forest of Satan's Kingdom before they turned on their ancient headlamps. They then walked wordlessly along the worn, familiar trail for about fifteen minutes, swinging left and right among the towering pines and hemlocks, and carefully descending the rocky terrain. Ahead between the tree trunks, set deep in a mossy glen, twinkled the play of firelight through the windows of a cabin. They made for the light, and let themselves in through the thick, rough-hewn door to join the lively company of the others.

41—ELECTION NIGHT

Tuesday, November 6th (night)

"USA! USA! USA!" the crowd chanted with manic, substance-enhanced enthusiasm as Martin and Joyce Laugherty took the stage, followed by their five grown children and a photogenic bouquet of spouses and grandchildren. "USA! USA!" Then followed Laugherty's vice-presidential running mate Trinna Ghoshal and her multiracial retinue of family members. "Laugh-Er-Tee! Laugh-Er-Tee!" screamed the election night revelers. "Marty and Trinna, sittin' in a tree! Marty and Trinna, Vic-Tor-Ee!" They packed the Grand Ballroom of the Chicago Renaissance, and overflowed into every available meeting room, restaurant, and suite in the elegant hotelplex. More and more kept flooding in: campaign workers, friends, relatives, colleagues, oligarchs—dressed in their party finery, luxury cars and aeros left in the care of fawning valets. Access to the hotel was tightly restricted. Only authorized guests were allowed in, but the Laugherty-Ghoshal campaign had made sure there were thousands of them. Bands played on every floor. Champagne flowed like the delight it adorned. The atmosphere was raucous and wild, an electoral celebration beyond anything the Republicans could recall. Laugherty's victory was not unexpected—this was not a closely contested election—but all the tension and uncertainty of the previous week seemed to be discharging through some kind of mass cathartic release, now that the election had received tentative certification by the Federal Elections Commission. The Laugherty-Ghoshal team had been staying out of sight in their suites, letting the excitement swell, but now they were appearing before their adoring supporters and the world media, and the mood was one of ecstasy.

Laugherty and Ghoshal ran—skipped—to the podium, holding their clenched fists aloft together in a victory salute. Their families jogged in behind them, fanning across the stage.

345

"My friends!" yelled Laugherty into a hovering dronemike that darted left and right to stay stationed in front of his chin. This elicited a loud response. "My good friends!" The crowd boomed its wild approval back at him. He tried again a few more times, laughing and imploring them to quiet down so he could speak. After long minutes of crackling applause, they finally yielded.

"My friends," Laugherty started. "Here we are, still together, at the end of one road and the beginning of a new one!" Applause... "Thank you, thank you, thank you for all of your hard work and support! For your faith and determination!" The audience shouted its mutual thanks back at him. He remembered Trinna Ghoshal at his side, and raised their clasped hands again in a gesture of victory. "We are both so thankful for your efforts, we just don't know what to say!"

"You always know what to say!" yelled someone in the audience near the stage, setting off a wave of laughter.

"Not this time," intoned Laugherty, sensing his opening. "I'm speechless. NO! I'm not!" Laughs. "I *do* have something important to say, to share with everyone here, and everyone out there around the world, around the USA, around Chicagoland, who's listening." The election night revelers held their breaths. Multitudes of tiny lenses focused on their new President-elect from AR glasses, T-pads, cellphones and a vast array of other devices. The media watched raptly. Martin Laugherty held a dramatic pause.

"America is back!" he exhaled into the expectant silence. The audience exploded in roaring call-and-response.

"Yes, we are!"

"America is BACK!" he shouted.

"YES WE ARE!"

"AMERICA IS BAAAACK!" Laugherty was on fire, grinning and waving and pointing in all directions. "God love us, we're back!"

"YES WE ARE!" thundered the crowd, breaking into a rhythmic repetition of these three monosyllables, clapping, stamping. "YES WE ARE!" The whole building started to vibrate with the insistent beat. It was simply a fact, a fact they had waited for, for so long. America was back. Back on top, back on its game, back at the center of things, back from decline and self-doubt, back from Sanderborough, back from the loss of its military bases, back from humiliations on land, at sea, and in space over the past two decades. And America was back from everything negative that the Morales administration and those bastards with the Coalition for Renewal were responsible for. Baaaaaack!!

"It's morning in America!" shouted Laugherty, eliciting cheers with this age-old Republican victory cry. "It's morning again! Wake up world, it's morning, we're back, we're smellin' the coffee, and we're comin' to eat your breakfast!"

As the clapping and wild cheering reached their crescendo, flocks of red, white, and blue balloons were unleashed from the rafters and fell swirling into the dancing, gyrating crowd along with streamers and the flash of disco lights. A big band picked up the beat and swung into the ancient classic "Back in the Saddle Again," cleaned up for the family-values sensitivities among segments of Laugherty-Ghoshal supporters. The politicians and their families cleared off the stage, yielding to a high-stepping floor show as it took over the program for a party expected to rock all night. Then it was off to bed for most of the politicos after several extremely long, crazy days, including the exhausted Mr. Laugherty, arm-in-arm with Mrs. Laugherty, and the bachelorette Ms. Ghoshal, looking overwhelmed, having experienced nothing this momentous in her relatively short life except perhaps the moment six years before when she was crowned Miss Oklahoma and accepted into the Navy Seals training program on the same day.

42—SUDDEN URGENCY

Tuesday, November 6th (night)

"It's really dark in these valleys," said Jenny quietly. It was one of the first comments anyone had made since they started ascending from the valley where Pittsfield lay, after a hasty rest stop. "You just don't see a light anywhere."

"Nothing but woods," agreed Ari. He glanced back at Jenny's girlish face—pale in the low light of the cab.

"No other traffic," said Lara somberly. "And this road is so washed out in some places. Maybe we should have gone a different way."

"We'll be through here before too long," said Ari hopefully from behind the wheel. "Not more than another half-hour, I'd guess."

"Charlemont 10 km," read Jenny from an old, worn road sign as they passed it.

"Hope we haven't gone too far and that's in Canada," said Ari with a worried look. The others gasped and looked at him with concern. "Nah, I was only kidding," he continued. No one laughed or cracked a smile. His lame attempt at levity fell flat amidst the tension that had seized them since their incident in Pittsfield.

"Any more news about the election?" asked Jessica from the back seat.

"Um, well, Laugherty and Ghoshal are having a big party in Chicago and an even bigger one in Vtopia," said Daryl, who was studying his T-pad. "Hedges still hasn't conceded but it's all over now. Ha. Get this. Only 18% of the electorate voted. Looks like 56% of that for Laugherty now. That's gone up. Um..." He continued to scan. "So he's in with under ten percent of eligible voters behind him."

"That's what I call no mandate," sighed Ari. "Although that's probably a hair over ten percent, to be fair." The others glanced at him blankly.

"Fifty-six percent of eighteen," he explained after a pause. There was no reaction. He went back to studying the road.

"Looks like they did pass a secession resolution in Vermont," said Daryl after a moment. "The governor got re-elected. She doesn't like it, but says she will formally call for a state convention to draw up articles of secession, because the people of Vermont have spoken."

Ari whistled. "That is serious business."

"The secession resolution passed in North Dakota, too," continued Daryl. "Hey, wow!" He fell silent and looked closely at his screen. "The CG just announced that Laugherty's out."

"What?" asked Lara in surprise. There were several gasps. "Out of what?"

"Is Morales back?" asked Ari in confusion as he navigated past a fallen tree protruding into the road.

"No," said Daryl. "Looks like the CG has disqualified him because he's the President-Elect now. Conflict of interest. Needs space to form his administration…"

"There's something fishy about that story," said Ari. "Wonder if Laugherty saw that coming? And it's crazy! Who the hell *is* in charge down there now?"

"General Cornelius van Belt, it says," related Daryl. "Chair of the CG now. You know who he is?"

Ari nodded noncommittally. The others shook their heads.

"You know, the Army chief?" Ari laughed. "About two meters tall, old, white eyebrows like snow?"

"Oh God, really?" laughed Lara in disbelief. "I remember him from a parade in Blacksburg when I was a kid. He was already ancient then!"

"He was very imposing," said Jessica. "Commanding. I remember him well. He gave a speech on the Green, after the Fourth of July parade."

"Was that when there was that riot?" asked Daryl.

"No, no," said Ari. "It was quite a bit earlier. When you and your sister were teens. He came to speak, with a whole delegation of officers who were VMI and Tech alumni. Touring the state. Remember the Shamshir attack?" They all shook heads. "In China. Xinjiang." Ari labored to recall the details. "China blamed the US. Must have been '26, '27. Very deadly. Things got tense. And then China blockaded the Philippines and Okinawa, to try to force the US military out." He shook his head. "Very tense days."

"So, is he about—a hundred?" Jenny smirked.

This was met by one or two grunts of dismay.

"I know," said Jenny. "Sorry. I know it's not funny."

Blue lights suddenly flashed behind them. There were police vehicles approaching, climbing the hill. Everyone craned their necks to see. Ari squinted at the rear-view screen, trying to figure out what was going on. He slowed and eased over to let them pass. "I hope this isn't about Pittsfield," he said.

"Do you think!?" Jessica's face was blanched in the harsh, strobing blue flicker.

The police pulled to a stop behind and beside the truck.

"Shit!" said Ari shakily.

"Remain in your vehicle," a police loudspeaker commanded repeatedly. "Remain in your vehicle. Do not leave your vehicle. Keep all hands and heads visible. Do NOT leave your vehicle." They could already see police running swiftly from the vans and taking up positions. The red LED lights of several small sentry drones were suddenly visible dancing in the air ahead of and beside the truck's cab.

"Nobody move," cried Daryl. "Those are armed!"

They all sat stiffly, hardly daring to turn their heads, and waited.

"This is taking a long time!" whispered Lara after what seemed like many minutes had passed. Police were out moving around, shining lights at the truck and limber and carrying out a variety of scans. Then, with his pistol drawn, a policeman shone a light directly at Ari's face and instructed him to open the window. Ari complied.

"Please come with me," the policeman said. "Just you. Everybody else, stay where you are." He focused his attention on Ari. "Get down and follow me." Ari gently removed his seatbelt, swallowed dryly, and gingerly descended from the cab, conscious of the lights and weapons trained on him. He saw the police were from the Berkshire County Sheriff's Office. The policeman beckoned toward the other side of one of the vans. Ari followed, losing sight of the truck.

"Mister, uh, Daniels," said the officer, glancing at his HUD. "This vehicle was involved in a criminal incident in Pittsfield about four hours ago."

Ari swallowed again, trying to clear his throat, but was clearly not answering quickly enough, because the policeman angled his intensely bright flashlight right into Ari's eyes and barked, "Isn't that so?!"

"Yes, yes, we were attacked," stammered Ari. "We were jumped, and got out of there. That's all I know."

"All you know, sir? How about shots fired at unarmed men," the officer demanded. "How about a beating with a metal instrument?! What can you tell me about all this?" The police clearly knew something, although they did not have the story entirely straight. Ari realized that there must indeed have been a third person, who presumably ran away and somehow communicated his version of events to the police. Then his heart sank. The gun that had shot the bullet and the long wrench were both in the truck.

"We're just passing through. We're not here to make trouble. Don't you see?" Ari's tone was pleading. "We were attacked, and just got away as fast as we could. It was dark. Raining. We didn't see what happened next." He caught his breath. "We have young girls and little children with us. An elderly lady. *Of course* we're going to defend ourselves from an attack! There are bandits all over!"

"Attack is one thing, sir. But, whatever happened, you left the scene of the crime," said the Sheriff's Office officer angrily. "You did not report what happened. You just shot and took off. You're from away, I see." He surveyed the truck and its short trailer. "Now, you listen up, Mister Daniels from Virginia. We don't do things the way you folks do back home. If there's a crime and even if you injure or kill a man in self-defense, you don't just gawd damn go driving off into the night like nothing happened. Do you *hear* me!? You are not the law! Not in Berkshire County." He seethed. "We were called up to track you down from another crime scene other side of Adams. Several deaths. If you had reported this to the Pittsfield police when it happened, I wouldn't be standing here with my unit in the middle of the *gawd damn* woods, when we could be doing something useful somewhere else!"

Ari stared at him, nodding numbly. He was stunned, struggling with a sense of total unreality. Why exactly was he standing here on a dark mountain road somewhere in Massachusetts, being upbraided by this younger man in an accent he barely believed possible in real life? Upbraided. Odd word. He imagined braid on a uniform. Gold braid.

351

Scrambled eggs. Did this expression come from that? An officer with more braid yelling at the one with less? Because… No, but that had to be ridiculous…

"Are you listening to me, Mister Daniels!?" The police officer raised his voice another decibel with a note of irritation.

"Yessir!" gasped Ari with a start, his distraction vanishing. He had not heard a word. The policeman stared at him skeptically and raised an eyebrow.

"We're gonna take a complete report now," he said slowly. "This may take a while. I'll talk with you first, right here." He looked back over his shoulder. "Ronnie, get ready for statements." Two other police officers went toward the truck's cab. He turned back toward Ari. "We may need to take you back to Pittsfield," he said. "But, maybe not, if you cooperate."

"Good God," said Ari in contrite disbelief. "We are *so* sorry…"

"You and me," said the officer. He tapped the side of his AR glasses. "OK, what were you doing in Pittsfield, and when did you arrive?" Standing in the cold evening damp amidst the forest murk and the play of blue lights, they began a quick sequence of questions and answers. The same process seemed to be unfolding in the cab. Other police began to inspect the compartments in the truck and limber. A mountain stream rushed somewhere nearby in the darkness. Ari peered at the man as the distracting flashing continued. Maybe this was one of their techniques, meant to confuse and blind.

"Captain," said another police officer, coming around from behind the van. "There's a problem!"

"Come on," gestured the officer, now revealed as a captain. "Stay with me." He ushered Ari ahead of him. They followed the other policeman to the cargo compartment of the truck. Ari could see Mike slumped on the open tailgate. He was bent almost double, his face twisted in pain. "Mike!" he exclaimed. Mike was groaning, saying something Ari could not clearly hear.

"He wasn't like this a little while ago!" cried Honorée, who had been in the truck with her boys, all trying to nap deep among blankets. "We were asleep…"

"Gunshot wound?" asked the captain. A policeman stepped closer. They all peered at Mike's lower leg, which looked dark and wet in their lights. The captain reached toward it. "It's swollen up like a balloon!" He turned on his heel and confronted Ari. "Was this man shot?!"

"No, not that I know!" Ari was dumbfounded. "No, how could he have been shot?" He wondered if Daryl had accidentally shot Mike during the attack, but shook his head as he ruled that out.

"This man's gonna need medical attention quick," said the captain.

Claudia appeared, having climbed down from the wagon's cab just beyond the tailgate. "Oh, my God. Mike!" she cried hysterically. She lunged toward her inert son. "Why did they shoot him!"

"Nobody shot him, ma'am," the captain said, stepping toward her, realizing that the situation was deteriorating and required some tightening up. "Please stay where you are." Claudia whimpered, staring at Mike.

"She's his mother," explained Ari.

"Oh, dear God," said Honorée suddenly. "The animal bite!"

The others looked at her in incomprehension.

"He was bitten by a wild animal early this morning," she explained, her voice rising. "At the last camp. I, I don't know. Maybe a fox." Her hands went to the sides of her head. "We got an antibiotic there!"

"What, why didn't the rest of us know?!" exclaimed Grandma. "Good grief! He was fine when we left Pittsfield!"

"It was embarrassing," said Honorée in dismay. "He wasn't fine! He just didn't want…"

One of the Sheriff's Office police appeared with a medical kit, and quickly started cutting away the cloth of Mike's pants to gain access to the wound.

"He's very hot," said the man. "Fever."

Ari, Honorée, and Claudia stood watching in stunned disbelief. The policeman sprayed the wet area with an antiseptic foam and let it work for a second. Mike's calf was swollen to twice its normal size. Mike himself continued to groan incoherently, recoiling from the touch. The policeman tried to straighten Mike's leg, but could not. An ugly area of raw flesh and weeping fluid encircled several punctures that now gaped open like nail holes.

"This is very serious," said the captain. "Infections like this accelerate."

The policeman—apparently the medic of the team—glanced around at the travelers. "Is he allergic to antibiotics? Anything I should know about?"

"No, no," said Claudia, stricken, her hands to her mouth.

"OK. I'm giving him poly-ABX and glucocort," said the medic. "And pain meds." He dug through his kit. The captain turned to Ari. "We can finish the report later. I believe most of what you are saying. *Very* unfortunate. Don't *ever* do that again in Berkshire County. But right now you gotta get him to a hospital. Closest one is Baystate Franklin, in Greenfield. About thirty kilometers from here. Take you forty-five minutes, an hour. Drive fast but careful. No sense going back to Pittsfield."

"What's wrong with him?!" asked Ari, trying to process the rapidly shifting situation.

"I don't know. Some kinda massive infection. Seen a few of these recently. The ABX might do the trick, but you gotta get moving. We'll call ahead to the Franklin County Sheriff's and tell 'em you're on the way. We'll call the ER at the hospital." He ran his hand over his stubbly chin, shaking his head. "But they're awful busy with the migrants and the camps down there. All hell's breaking lose. You just get there as fast as you can."

"Let's get him up front," suggested Lara, who had appeared, unnoticed. "We need to watch him." She turned toward the captain. "I'm a nurse," she explained. Mike was weak and uncooperative, so a group of them lifted him awkwardly from the tailgate and staggered to the open door of the truck's cab, where they started hefting and pushed him into the back seat, Mike gasping and crying out the entire time. As they worked, somewhere in Mike's clothing a lapscreen started ringing, with the twangy chords of some old rockabot hit. It rang several times as they moved him from the tailgate to the cab.

"Somebody's calling Mike," muttered Honorée. "They'll have to wait."

"Oh. He's so hot!" exclaimed Jenny, aghast, when they had Mike leaning against the right-hand door. She knelt on the threshold below the edge of the seat.

"I'll get up there and pull from the other side," said Lara, running around the truck to the left rear door. Jenny climbed up the rest of the way. They both grimaced at the sight of his leg in the cab light's glow.

"I'm sorry, I'm sorry about all this," said Ari shakily to the captain and policemen, as they finished the lifting and the others quickly climbed back on board.

"You get going," said the captain. "He comes first. We know how to find ya. We'll be in touch. You're not finished with the Pittsfield matter." He gave Ari a firm, meaningful look. "Drive carefully. Just remember to turn right when you get to Route 2. It's well-paved from there." He hesitated. "But you might hit heavy traffic right outside of Greenfield."

Ari half-smiled, half-sobbed—riven by conflicting emotions. "Yes. Thank you." He jumped up into the driver's seat, started the truck, and they were off.

43—FLIGHT DELAY

Tuesday, November 6th (late at night)

"No, Jake. They can't spare a single one until tomorrow morning. With all the evacuations... They're using every helicopter they can get their hands on." Linda looked apologetically at Wilder and the others. After forty-eight hours in New York City, they were back at the Hotel Falk's bar for the third night in a row, and it was getting late.

"We should have rented that car yesterday, when we had the chance," groaned Lola.

"We never would have gotten through anyway," said Wilder. "It wasn't worth the chance. It's gridlock and checkpoints the whole way."

"Linda, are you *sure* that a helicopter will be able to come get us tomorrow morning?" asked Moriah. "I don't want that new hurricane to catch up with us."

Linda was on the verge of snapping at Moriah, but held back. "*I'm* not sure. All I'm telling you is what *they're* telling *me*. Ella Davis said there's a scheduled flight down here first thing tomorrow to pick up orders from an organ, blood, and tissue bank somewhere here, and they can take five of us back with them."

"They're running out of everything, I imagine," muttered Lola.

"But there are eight of us!" said Moriah.

"Doug has gone to stay with relatives here," said Linda. "And taken Selena."

"Maybe they eloped," whispered Lola archly to no one in particular.

"So, we're down to six," continued Linda, ignoring Lola.

"I can stay," said Mary. "My sister lives here and was away until this evening. I haven't seen her. I can take a train up later in the week."

"Great," said Wilder, his brows furrowed with concern. "I really appreciate it, Mary. That leaves five." He turned back to Mary Worthington. "I hope you don't get tangled up in the new hurricane."

Mary smiled back at him. "It's OK. It's a chance to play hookey an extra couple of days. Worse comes to worst, my sister can get us in a car away from here."

Wilder, with a nod of cautious relief, then turned to Moriah. "Moriah, I just saw that they're not expecting the hurricane to get here for three or four days, if it comes this way after all."

She nodded with a worried look.

"Where will they pick us up?" asked Steve.

"The West 30th Street Heliport," Linda answered. "Eight forty-five A.M."

"That's not too far from here, is it?" asked Moriah.

"Pretty close," said Linda, "but we'll probably have to do one of those flying wedges again with the NYPD." Several of them laughed.

"Who's up for a nightcap, before bed?" asked Lola. "I've decided to write a book about the Hotel Falk's lobby bar."

"Oh?" said Moriah. "What are you going to call it?"

"My Years at the Falk," sniffed Lola.

"Sounds falking boring," laughed Steve. "My three days here have felt like three years."

"Something like that," said Lola, who had already stood up and was turning to walk toward the bar. Moriah, Mary, and Linda joined her, while Wilder and Steve went back up to their rooms to work a bit more before turning in.

"Isn't that Rick Chen?" asked Linda in a whisper as they entered the bar's enclosure of trellises, screens, and potted plants that set it off from the lobby.

"Sure is," said Lola, following her eyes discretely toward a small group sitting at a table near a large window. "I used to work with his sister in Jersey."

"Didn't Jake say he had been arrested?" asked Moriah in surprise.

"Yes, he did," said Lola. "In Atlanta."

"What's he doing here?" wondered Lola. "Wasn't he arrested by the, um-".

"FBI?" Linda finished her sentence for her.

"No! It wasn't the FBI," she said quietly. "It was the OCI." Her tone became sarcastic. "The thought police."

"So how could he possibly be here only a few weeks later?" asked Moriah.

"Maybe he has special friends," said Lola.

"Maybe Lucia Morales arranged to have him released before she got arrested…" suggested Mary.

Lola was slowly nodding. "Mm. Yeah. Their family always had close family ties with China. I remember that with Li." She looked around. "His sister," she explained. "Not sure what that would have meant."

A table became available not far from where Chen sat, so they went over and sat down. Chen was speaking an Asian language—Mandarin?— and most of the people at his table were Asian. As they ordered drinks, Lola looked over at Chen a few times, hoping to make eye contact, but did not succeed. With the arrival of the women at the adjoining table, Chen and his companions lowered their voices slightly and moved more closely together.

As they waited for their drinks to arrive, the women chatted about the past day—the election, the tedium of waiting, things they had to do when they returned to Vermont. But Lola, ever attuned to the unfolding drama of news stories and political intrigue, grew increasingly curious about Chen's story and purpose. With the arrival of the drinks, Lola secretly turned on her T-pad, which lay on the table, and set the interpreter to Mandarin. Gibberish appeared in the English window. Lola scowled and angled the screen so her companions could see it.

"Tell the interpreter to ID the language," whispered Moriah.

Lola nodded, and quickly found this function. On her T-pad's screen, an icon orbited around the button she had pushed, searching for a match. It orbited and orbited, but finally chimed with the text "Match not found." Lola waved her finger for more information. The screen read, "The language in question may be a dialect of the Hui group of Sinitic languages. Probability 78%".

"Hm," said Lola. "Oh, well." She pursed her lips. "We tried."

"Cheers," said Moriah. She raised her glass of wine. "To home."

"To home, may we all get to ours without delay," laughed Linda.

"Hey, this looks interesting." Lola reacted to a news message that had just appeared on her screen. "'Laugherty leaves Crisis Group. Van Belt takes over as chair.' That was brief!"

"Pshaw," yawned Moriah. "These coups." She shrugged sarcastically. "Drama all the time."

Mary was shaking her head. "It's not funny, Moriah. Here we sit in a nice hotel in Manhattan, and the election today seemed, um, *normal*, at least in its process, and when we get home things will seem normal and stable, but are we just kidding ourselves? Are we just looking at the surface? I mean…" She clenched her fingers into fists and shook them. "… What on earth is going on? We were there in Philadelphia! We heard all that stuff. Now no one really knows who's running the United States of America from one moment to the next, but we're all walking around like everything's normal!"

"Speak for yourself," chuckled Lola softly. "Certainly not for all the refugees."

"I guess we truly are the chicken running around with its head cut off," mused Moriah. "The point not being the running around itself, but the fact that the body's just going on doing what it always did, unaware of the unavoidable consequences of having no head."

"Well said, professor!" smiled Lola.

"I couldn't have said that," laughed Linda.

"I never said you could!" grinned Lola wickedly, breaking into a giggle and then leaning over and hugging Linda in apology. "Sorry, hun!"

"It is really sort of chilling," said Moriah soberly.

Lola and Linda stopped smiling.

"Yes, it is," said Mary, standing up. "I've gotta go get some sleep. Early start."

44—KING FOR A DAY

Tuesday, November 6th (middle of the night)

Vulk's phone was ringing insistently. He awoke disoriented, still clothed in his formal attire, squinting in the hotel suite's bright lights. There was a poisonous taste in his sticky mouth. The 3V was on, streaming some news program. Gaudy tricolor balloons and streamers on the floor brought his awareness back. He could see Suzanna's feet on the bed through the open bedroom doorway. His eye lit on the 3V's screen. It was well past one in the morning.

The phone continued its urgent ringing. He grabbed it, trying to moisten his mouth, and answered.

"'Lo?"

"Prokop, it's Sharon."

"OK." Vulk struggled to think clearly and fully wake up. He had not intended to drink much during the Election Night celebrations, but now regretted the few drinks he had taken. "What's, uh, up?"

"Have you heard about..." She hesitated. He remained silent. "Well, guess not."

"Guess not what? Where are you?"

"Back at the office," she replied. "Martin's been kicked out."

"What?!" Vulk was now much more awake. "He just got elected!"

"No, silly, not from the Presidency. From the CG."

"What? Why? They can't just do that!"

"It's on the news already. Van Belt just gave a press conference. From DC, like, five minutes ago. One-fifteen AM and Van Belt is giving a press conference... Like a thief in the night."

Vulk was already standing shakily, pulling his shoes back on.

"Does Martin know?"

"I haven't called him," she said with a groan. "I thought you should tell him in person."

"For the love of Christ," said Vulk. "First, he's asleep. Second, he's probably gonna take my head off for delivering the news. Third, who the fuck is Cornelius van fucking Belt to tell Martin Laugherty that he is no longer welcome at CG meetings?" Vulk felt a fury swelling.

Sharon Denny hesitated. "Prokop, you need to calm down before you wake him up."

"Fuck that," said Vulk. "*You* can say that, but I am going to walk into a shit storm. I'll need all the adrenaline I can get." He was already stumbling toward the door, heading for the central section of the secure fifteenth floor, where the Laugherty suite was located. "Sharon, who told you?"

"I saw it on the news feed." She laughed ironically. "I went back to the office to get my stuff after the Election Night shindig and a screen was still on. Completely by accident."

"So this is public information?!" Vulk was incredulous. He stopped in the darkened foyer, feeling for the wall to steady himself. "Public?!"

"All over the place," said Sharon. "Everyone's starting to call here. My Dripf stream is moving so fast I can't read it. I guess no one sleeps anymore…"

"Did Van Belt say anything else important?"

"Not too much. Didn't announce a replacement. Didn't say that Martin was off the CG. Just off the troika and the executive committee."

"Why?" demanded Vulk.

"Conflict of interest," said Sharon. "Checks and balances."

"What the fuck," muttered Vulk. "So they just make a unilateral decision? Whatever happened to democracy?!" He rubbed his forehead. "Sharon, I'll call you back after I talk to him." He hung up.

Suzanna's sleepy voice emanated from the bedroom. "What's going on?"

Vulk turned back so he could see her. Suzanna was sitting up on her elbows, her face a small, pale patch amidst wine-red sheets and the billows of her black evening dress.

"Martin's got a CG problem," he replied distractedly and a bit harshly. "Gotta go tell him."

"Is it serious?" she asked, sitting fully upright. "Is he OK?"

"Is it serious?!" Vulk laughed sarcastically. "Are you kidding?" He swung toward the door and strode out into the hallway. "Is it serious," he muttered under his breath, leaving her stricken with concern. "Is he OK?!"

He almost ran down the corridor.

A Secret Service guard stood beside the door—a new one that Vulk did not recognize. He looked at Vulk in surprise.

"Need to talk to the President-elect," said Vulk with a tone of urgency. "Now."

"Sir?" The guard stood his ground, tense and puzzled. "The Speaker has gone to bed."

"I'm Vulk. Prokop Vulk." He directed his T-pad at his own eyes, and then flipped the screen toward the guard as the retinal scan signaled a successful identification. "Speaker's Chief of Staff. I have an extremely important message for Mister Laugherty."

"Yessir," said the guard. "I know who you are now." He knocked gently on the door. There was no sound from within. He knocked again, louder.

"Martin!" Vulk called out.

After a moment, there were sounds of doors and footsteps inside, and the door opened with a chain across the narrow opening. "Yes?" came Laugherty's hoarse, tired voice. "Joyce is sleeping."

"Martin," said Vulk, lowering his voice. He glanced at the guard, who had just been joined by two more from the nearby room that had been made a guard post. "Mr. Speaker," he said in a more formal tone.

"Prokop, what the hell are you doing?" asked Laugherty. "I was sound asleep."

"I just heard some disturbing news from Sharon," said Vulk. "May I come in?"

Laugherty closed the door, detached the chain, reopened it, and ushered him in, closing the door behind Vulk and bolting the lock. He was in a bathrobe, his bare legs skinny and pale, and his face puffy and bleary-eyed after a momentous twenty-four-hour day.

"So?"

"Sir, Sharon just told me that Van Belt just made an announcement that you're off the troika. You're not in charge anymore." Laugherty looked at him in shock. Vulk swallowed. "You're reportedly still in the

CG, but they apparently just had a meeting and decided that you, being the President-Elect now, should not also be governing with them."

Laugherty's face was a pancake of incredulity. "*They*? What gives *them* the right…?" He put his palm against the back of his head, looked down, and then looked back up, eyes drilling into Vulk's. "I am going to have Van Belt's fucking *head* for this! He—they—totally bypassed me on this. Why didn't they speak with me? And why the hell did they go *public* so fast!" Laugherty was turning his head slowly back and forth, neck down and extended like a boxer's, taking this news in. He was wide awake now. "So this is what starts happening when you let go of the Constitution and start inventing new governance to deal with a crisis. Every tin-pot general and his Minuteman neighbor start thinking that they're the goddamned Founding Fathers, and start re-inventing government randomly, late at night, whenever it suits them!"

Vulk had no comment.

"In case anyone's forgotten," said Laugherty, pulling his bathrobe tighter, "we talked about this when the CG first met. Transparency! Consultation! Precisely this kind of thing was not supposed to happen. Who the hell elected Van Belt!? I thought he was sounding awfully Authoritarian all through the meeting in the Burj, talking about states of emergency and the clear and present danger." He turned around on his bare heel. "I am so, so, SO mightily tired of the Front and their right-wing lunatic fringe constantly trying to beat me to the punch and show everybody how more conservative-than-thou they could be. But I'm still the President-Elect!"

"Van Belt a Homelander?" Vulk was surprised. He hadn't suspected that.

"Not openly," said Laugherty with disgust. "But look at him now!" He pressed both palms against his temples. "I gotta get dressed. So much for sleeping tonight. I need drugs. You talk to anyone else about this yet?"

"No, sir," said Vulk. "Just Sharon. She called me from the office." Vulk then remembered that Suzanna also knew something, but he hadn't related details.

"OK. I'll be right back. Get Rubino, Landers, and Bob and Sharon. I want a call with them in thirty minutes. Better get Jacobs, Zimmerman, Yoon and Laforte, too. But first, I wanna talk to Van Belt. And schedule a public statement for eight AM. You're gonna need Sharon's help for that, and I told her she could take tomorrow off, bless her, but tell her this trumps it, and she can blame me. And Van Belt, that fucker." He looked down at his watch, and sighed. "I am gonna need a nap at some point today…"

Vulk nodded.

Laugherty paused, looking back at Vulk. "You can help yourself to those drinks and food over there." He gestured toward a kitchenette counter with a plate of left-over party food covered in plastic wrap and an array of bottles and glasses. "Oh, and line up Rooney. And I wanna find out where Holt is."

"What about Guch?" asked Vulk. "And Douglas? You probably want your Leadership Council and some of the other 'garchs informed and on your side right away. You don't want Van Belt and his guys making deals with them before you get to them."

"You're right. Do it."

"Yessir," said Vulk.

Laugherty shook his head, recovering some of the energy of his Election Night triumph. "Who the hell elected Cornelius Van Belt, anyway?!"

Vulk looked at Laugherty, worried now about false moves and false confidence, worried about too much bravado. This was a very dangerous turn. The emotional gravitational forces were extreme.

"With all due respect, sir, no one did. But no one elected you, either. We have to be …"

He was going to finish with "careful," but Laugherty cut him off.

"The goddamn American People elected me, that's who!"

"Yes, to the Presidency, but not to the Crisis Group," replied Vulk cautiously, watching Laugherty.

"That doesn't matter now," said Laugherty derisively. "The People have spoken!"

"It does matter. To a lot of people," said Vulk. "It's part of the equation."

"Part of what frickin' equation?" laughed Laugherty angrily. "They just elected a President, and that's me, and I have the political capital to prove it, and I am not going to let Van Belt and a committee of self-appointed, unelected, supposed 'patriots' start dictating what happens next! We are *done* with despotism! I just won by a landslide! We live in a democracy!"

A landslide with eighteen percent voting, thought Vulk.

45—DARK STRETCH

Tuesday, November 6th (late night)

"They've got very good antibiotics these days," said Grandma. "I do know that those poly shots get constantly updated to stay a step ahead of the mutating bacteria and viruses."

Lara nodded encouragingly. "They do."

But Jenny did not look encouraged. Tears ran down her cheeks, glistening in the soft light of the cab. Mike was stretched out across the back seat, his head and back reclining against Jenny, and his feet against Lara's right thigh. Lara sat scrunched up against the left passenger door. They held him so he would not slip down off the seat from the truck's bumping and swaying. The floor area was full of bags and other travel items, so he would not have hurt himself, but at this point one thing the women could do was attempt to preserve Mike's dignity.

"God, he's hot," exclaimed Lara. "Poor Mike!" She put her hand on his uninjured thigh, feeling the heavy, greasy cloth. It was moist with sweat. She turned and opened the window partially. Cold night air blew across her and onto Mike. He did not react. Jenny wiped his forehead and temples with a towel.

Ari had not said much since the police stop. He sat hunched forward, peering at the road. The old blacktop was shattered, pitted, and frost-heaved, with weeds growing in the center line and washouts pulling the paved surface down into the ravines they skirted. It twisted and turned as they climbed out of one watershed and down into another, deep in narrow, forested valleys. Occasionally they passed small settlements, dim lights glowing up gravel drives, set back from the main road. Wild animals scattered from the road again and again, their eyes glowing like green and red LEDs: coyotes, foxes, raccoons? Once, to Grandma's gasp, they narrowly avoided hitting a person who was walking alone along the road in the darkness without a light or reflector.

They passed a post with a long, narrow sign that indicated the boundary between Berkshire and Franklin Counties.

"Look," said Ari, breaking a spell of silence. "Franklin County. Didn't that policemen mention Franklin County?"

"Mm hm," said Grandma. "Yes, he did. He did."

Ari accelerated slightly, as if in response. The truck fishtailed slightly in loose sand deposited across the road. "Dad!" said Lara in alarm. Ari slowed to a more cautious pace. Lights appeared ahead. Ari slowed even more. The lights approached. They seemed to be moving. Then they passed an old-fashioned wagon heading in the direction from which they had come, adorned with carriage lamps. The driver waved. The wagon was full of what looked like partygoers heading home.

After more silence and a dark tunnel of trees, they emerged with fields on either side. The lights of cross-traffic sparkled through a break of vegetation. A sign declared that the intersection with Route 2 lay just ahead, with options to turn left toward North Adams/Williamstown and right toward Greenfield.

"There it is," said Grand. Claudia gave a sigh of relief.

"It's still almost twenty kilometers," said Ari, eyes flicking between the road and the truck's screen. "But we can go faster." They bumped to a halt at a stop sign. Relatively heavy traffic—motor and non-motor—flowed in both directions. They waited for a chance to merge.

"Isn't this frustrating?" muttered Grandma. The wait continued. Then Ari saw his chance and they swung out into the four-lane roadway, passing horse traffic as they picked up speed.

The road's streetlamps were dark, but they could see fairly well by the headlights of many vehicles. It was much brighter than the dark stretch they had just traversed. Their hopes of getting to the hospital quickly began to rise. Then began a series of long descending straightaways. Greenfield drew closer. But congestion built, and then they were in slow-moving bumper-to-bumper traffic again. It began to seem like the roads they had traveled in Maryland and Pennsylvania.

"Looks like refugee traffic again," said Ari.

Grandma just shook her head and stared ahead down the crowded road.

"What's that odd sound?" said Ari. He listened to what appeared to be some sort of engine in the distance.

366

"Daddy, it's Mike!" Lara jerked upright and bent her ear toward Mike's face. "Jenny, do you hear that?!"

"Yes," said Jenny with a cry. From Mike's mouth was emanating what has sounded like a snore or distant motorcycle. It went on uninterrupted by breath for a long moment, rising and falling slightly. Then it suddenly stopped as Mike drew in a ragged breath. There was a pause. And then the sound resumed—a weird buzzing, keening exhalation.

"What's he doing?" sobbed Jenny. "Mike!" He did not react to her voice. She could see his eyes half-open in the faint light, his body tense against hers.

"What is that?" said Ari in a worried tone.

"His breathing," said Lara. "Mike, can you hear me?" She reached across his legs and lap, and stroked his cheek with the palm of her hand. "Mike?" His eyes remained half-open, unseeing. She switched on the salon lamp over her door. It cast light across Mike. His face, neck, and the backs of his hands had dark, purplish blotches. He uttered another long exhalation, and burped. A foul odor reached Lara's nostrils. She felt fear. "He doesn't look good at all," she said quietly. "I think it's a necrotizing fasciitis of some kind, some sort of sepsis, and rather than staying within the area where it first entered—the bite, you know - it seems to have gone deep into his body quickly…"

"Have you seen it before?" asked Ari.

"No, no," she replied. "Never. Well, not like this."

Ari rubbed his eyes with one hand. "I can't believe how quickly his health changed." Then he braked as the flow of the highway stopped. "Oh, damn. Is this the only route?" The traffic was jammed.

"Let me see if I can figure out another way," said Grandma, leaning toward the truck's screen. She studied the area they were passing through. "Not really any parallel roads… Hm… Oh, they look like such long detours, and you never know what we'll find down in one of these valleys." She pointed at the screen. "See, there are these long side-roads that seem to go up valleys and streams from this road, but they don't cross-connect for a very long time."

The traffic started up again.

"OK," said Ari as he pushed the truck forward. He looked at Grandma. "It is what it is, then. But we still might have to take a shortcut."

46—BATTLE IN THE MUD

Tuesday, November 6th (earlier that evening)

Molly Jeffries lived where she was raised: on a berry and vegetable farm in New Jersey's Pine Barrens, not far from Batsto. A sixth-generation Piney, Molly worked the farm as her ancestors had done, selling mostly blueberries and cranberries to the big markets in New York City and Philadelphia. The populous Jeffries clan made a good living, and were well-known and respected in the area. They were resourceful and self-sufficient in freshwater, food, energy, wood, and many other of life's necessities. When Rhiannon came, they were prepared. Their homestead sat on raised land within a rectangular levee, the compound elevated two meters above the surrounding coastal plain, with the levee cresting an additional two meters above that. The levee surrounded almost a hectare of dwellings, farm buildings, garages, and parked vehicles, and the two entrances could be sealed by water-tight sluice gates. It had taken years to build the levee fully. The Jeffries heads of household had always been well-informed about climate change and sea level rise, and learned long ago that the rural people in Burlington County, New Jersey (which lay only a few meters above sea level) had to take more than casual precautions against storm surges and unusually high tides in the Atlantic Ocean only ten or so kilometers to their southeast.

One precaution was the powerful electric pumps that Jacob Jeffries had installed twenty years before. Between the two of them, the pumps could drain the levee's interior at a rate of 4,000 liters per minute. They were powered by batteries charged by an array of solar panels on the roof of the main barn, and Jacob had the foresight to put the batteries and inverters on the barn's second floor, and at least put the pumps on a platform level with the top of the levee.

368

All of these precautions unfortunately came to naught on the night of October 27th. As its eye wobbled eastward, Hurricane Rhiannon reached the ocean a bit south of Atlantic City, and then stalled for almost eight hours before accelerating out over the Gulf Stream and northeast across the Atlantic. During its stall, it drove so much water inland that the levee was swamped, the pumps and their batteries were flooded, and—like thousands of their neighbors - the inhabitants of the Jeffries' homestead found themselves more or less adrift in the middle of a wild, dark, wave-tossed ocean, with no refuge but a few of the taller trees and the attics of buildings that could withstand Category 4 wind and surf. For hours, in the roaring blast, members of the family and their neighbors could only call out to one another through the salt spray and cling to whatever they could find. When the wind finally subsided and dawn came, one of Molly's children had disappeared without a trace, along with several of her relatives. The farm was in ruins. Homes had been destroyed, and food stores despoiled. Their silo had been blown over. The horses and cattle had been corralled beside the barn in the shelter of the levee, but despite the best efforts of everyone all night long, half the cattle had drowned—most trapped in the milking parlor between the rising water and the ceiling. A gate had broken open and they had sought relief there out of habit.

It was therefore with a mixture of shock, anger, desperation, and deep-seated pride in a life of resilience and self-reliance that the thirty-six surviving members of the Jeffries' clan decided to move together up to the refugee camps being established to the northwest on the outskirts of Philadelphia—to wait out the worst of the winter, regroup, and try to assemble enough resources to travel back down in the late winter before planting time, and get the farm working again. What choice did they have? There were more than a dozen children who needed food and medical care, and two more on the way. No buildings were left habitable. All of the equipment was damaged or lost, even if some was repairable. The decision was a bitter one, but the Jeffries needed to beat a strategic retreat, accept the charity of strangers, fight for whatever few insurance claims they could file, see whether there would be federal assistance, allow the land to dry out, and rebuild when they were in a position to.

After a two-day walk/ride up the Atlantic City Expressway, in carts and wagons with their herd in their wake, they were admitted into Camp Valleybrook. Their cattle were immediately commandeered because of their dairy and meat value, and because there was no grazing land for refugees' livestock. The New Jersey National Guard issued an IOU to Molly's husband Dan for the herd, telling him he would be able to redeem it for cash or camp scrip after ninety days. They were allowed to keep their eight horses in the camp paddock, but had to buy hay from private vendors who set up around the camp and charged exorbitant prices in euros, yuan, precious metals, Canadian dollars, milscrip—anything but U.S. dollars or camp scrip. The tents they were issued were cramped and smelled of mildew, and there were chronic shortages of everything from camp cots to toothpaste and shampoo, clothing of the right size, footwear, and planking to get things up out of the mud. The lines to get in and out of the camp were also long, with identity checks and x-ray searches on the way in and the way out. The camp guards were constantly on the lookout for drugs, alcohol, weapons, controlled metals, foreign currency, contraband food, and other forbidden cargo. Life in Camp Valleybrook was thus not easy. The Jeffries were wondering how they were going to stand another four months of it. But at least they had water, hot food, dry shelter, and emergency medical care. And each other.

On the evening of November 6th, Molly Jeffries went to the camp commissary with her November ration scrip to buy more food for the kids, especially nut-free bread and cereal for her youngest girl, who had a severe nut allergy, and gluten-free food for her surviving boy, who was gluten-intolerant. The line was long, and she stood for nearly a half-hour on the plankway beside the commissary that had been laid down because of the deep brown mud that seemed to be taking over the camp (which had, it seemed, been largely built in a marsh). It wasn't the sort of store or commissary where you could walk up to the shelves with a shopping cart and choose your own purchases; because everything was tightly rationed and guarded, you had to make your purchase at a counter, where an employee of an aid organization would go get the items you needed and place them in a box or crate.

The electric lights created a monochrome atmosphere of glare, deep shadows, and sharp contrasts.

"Polls close in forty-five minutes!" called a volunteer with an improvised megaphone, walking among the tents. "Voting closes in forty-five minutes!" She came near Molly. "You have to be a registered New

Jersey voter," the older woman explained to a passer-by's query. She took up her megaphone again. "Visit the voting tent by Gate B!"

"Useless waste of time," snarled a man in the line behind Molly.

"If we don't vote, then we've got no right to complain about who gets elected," answered an older man.

"Are you fuckin' juking me, paps?" The snarling man laughed roughly. "I'll complain when I want to. Anyway…" He turned toward the older man. "What's voting matter when who you vote for isn't allowed to stay in charge anyway. Look at Morales!"

Several people muttered in agreement. The older man looked at the muddy ground and shook his head.

"Vote one day, next day you got no frickin' idea who ya got," said the snarling man. "It's not up to the voters…"

Molly's turn came at the counter. A harried relief worker looked at her impatiently as Molly explained what she needed. Molly gave the worker her crate, and the worker went back into the warehouse to fill it. A few minutes later, he reappeared.

"Here's most of what you wanted, but not the nut-free or gluten-free."

"Are you serious?!" Molly's spirits sank. It had been like this often, in the week since they arrived.

"What, do I look like I'm lying?" the man replied with tired discourtesy.

"Why is it so hard to get these things?" asked Molly, adding, "If I were home, I would just make them myself."

"So, go home," said the worker dismissively.

Molly's irritation was rising, and she was not going to let him off the hook for this. "I would go home if I could, but—Hello!—we just had a major disaster." He looked at her blankly. "Do you think I like being treated this way by people like you?"

"You can get all that kind of food you want if you go up to the camps up north," said a woman behind her. "That's where they're sending it."

"Is that true?" demanded Molly, looking at the relief worker.

The man shrugged. "Maybe. I don't know."

"Why aren't they keeping some of it here?" demanded Molly, her irritation rising. "People need it here, too." The people in the line behind her had stopped talking and started listening in.

"I don't know," said the aid worker, backing down. "Maybe they want you to move north."

"Well, we are not moving north. And who is 'they'? I want to talk to somebody here in charge because it is *not* OK that things we need are being moved somewhere else like, like bait!"

"Just a second." The aid worker exchanged a look with the two armed and heavily armored guards at the entrance to the storage tent, and disappeared inside. Molly and the other people behind her regarded the guards in silent apprehension, surprised at the aid worker's prompt compliance. The guards stood impassively on either side of the door. Moments later, the aid worker returned. "She'll be right out," he said, and placed two frozen loaves of gluten-free, nut-free bread down on the table. "Here, I found these. That's twelve units."

Molly looked down at the loaves. "You 'found' them? Thank you, but why didn't you tell me about them to begin with, and then we wouldn't've hadda go through this in the first place?"

A man behind Molly who had already picked up his rations and was holding a partially filled crate drew closer to the counter and waved his free hand. "Hey, I wanted nut-free and you told me there wasn't any!" He pushed closer. "You go and get me the same thing you got for this nice lady and we'll be all right, OK, bud?"

The aid worked stared at him nervously, but did not react.

"Wait a minute," said a large, heavyset older woman behind Molly. "Yesterday you told me I couldn't get more than 2000 calories a person a day this week, and now you're giving way more to *some* people, and *fancy* food, too!" She shoved her way to the counter and put her empty crate on the table. "Go ahead, I'll take some of that, too, whatever it is."

The crowd was growing, and everyone seemed to have some kind of problem with getting enough food, the right kind of food, promises broken, unfair treatment, or something else they were upset about. At this moment, the aid worker's supervisor came walking briskly out through the plastic swing-door. She was a young woman wearing a tan baseball cap with a headlamp mounted on its visor and a wireless microphone extending down from her AR glasses, and like the guards she wore on her chest and arm the blue handshake logo of HelpServ, a for-profit disaster relief contractor based in Texas.

372

"What's the problem, folks?" she said brightly. She stepped in beside the aid worker, looked around at the many expectant faces, and homed in on Molly Jeffries. "Is this the lady?"

The aid worker nodded glumly. "Yes."

The young woman smiled blandly. "What can I do for you this evening?"

"You can give me the nut-free and gluten-free food when I ask for it, every day, if you have it," said Molly indignantly, "and not play games."

"Oh, I can assure you we're not playing games, Ms. -?"

"Jeffries."

"Ms. Jeffries. We're not playing any games here. We have a big camp to run, and a lot of needs to meet…"

The big older woman and several men stepped into the fray. "Well, you can start right here and now by better meeting *my* needs," said the woman. "You run along back in and get me the things you just gave this lady."

"Oh, see, I'm afraid I can't just do that, ma'am," said the female HelpServ supervisor, not bothering to get a name this time. "Everybody has a different rations profile, and if we started giving everyone what they simply came up and asked for…"

A man who had been watching this in silence pushed through to the counter and started yelling angrily at the camp staff. "How 'bout you start trusting us and working with us, not against us, and treat us like human beings and not like prison inmates! How would you like to be in our shoes?" He banged his food crate down onto the countertop, scattering the cards and pens that lay there. "I know all about you frickin' HelpServ parasites! You work for some oligarch who makes more money every time there's a disaster somewhere. Disaster capitalism." He turned around and started speaking loudly to the swelling crowd. "These oligarchs have been causing the bad weather and the storms and droughts using chemicals in the sky—you seen 'em?—and then sucking everyone dry who loses their homes because of that!"

"Sir, you are going to have to calm down or we'll need to close the commissary!" said the HelpServ woman urgently. "Why don't we go somewhere where we can discuss this?"

"I'll tell you where you can go, bitch!" yelled the man, completely out of control now. "You can go back to wherever the fuck you came from and put local people in charge of our food!" And then he threw his crate at the swing-door, managing to hit one of the guards with its edge. The guards, who had been increasingly tense and nervous during this exchange, now stepped forward menacingly. The man screamed incoherently at them, jumping up onto the counter. More out of curiosity than hostility, others crowded in around the counter and guards to see what was going on. The man was waving his fists at the guards from the counter, yelling. Afraid the man would jump down onto him, and spooked by the growing crowd, one of the guards raised his rifle and fired a burst of warning shots. The relief worker and his supervisor ran away through the swing-door, chased by several hurled crates and bottles of water.

There was an instant of pause, when both the guards and the perpetrators hesitated and sized one another up, and then the scene descended into chaos, with camp inhabitants vaulting over the counter and into the storage tent in search of supplies, others pelting the guards with anything handy, and many of the smaller, weaker, or older bystanders scurrying away from the violence. More guards appeared, savagely beating back the surging crowd with telescoping batons. Another guard fired into the air to quell the unrest. The crowd exploded into fury, with dozens of people rushing the storage tent while hundreds shouted their wrath and frustration at the guards.

From behind the crowd, a large piece of rebar was hurled through the air, hitting one of the guards in a gap between his helmet and breastplate. He went down onto his knees in pain. More debris flew through the air, and the guards took cover and started shooting teargas canisters in the direction they believed the missiles were coming from. Somebody in the crowd pulled out a pistol and started shooting at the guards, although the guards' chitrex body armor was more than enough to stop pistol bullets. Others nearby screamed at him to stop. People ran this way and that way in confusion, diving for cover.

A group of guards plunged into a knot of people across from the commissary and were seen dragging two young people—a teenage boy and a girl—out into the waiting area in front of the counters. They were struggling, and sustaining crack after crack from the baton-wielding guards. Others ran out to intervene, in dismay at the escalating violence. Neither the boy nor the girl seemed to be armed. Then, more determined gunfire with the deeper booms of heavier caliber weapons filled the area and people scattered, while the guards pulled back and started to return fire in earnest. In seconds, a gun battle was in full swing, although it was not clear who the guards were fighting. And pinned down in the crossfire was Molly Jeffries, winded by a teargas grenade that hit her in the belly. She lay in the mud, fighting to recover her breath, the contents of her crate strewn across the wet ground beside her.

47—END OF THE ROAD

Wednesday, November 7th
(early hours of the morning)

"Grandma, should we still be on this road?" The fear and apprehension in Jenny's voice were plain. "We have to hurry up!"

"Just a short while longer," said Grandma. "When we get to, um, Zerah Fiske Road, we take a hard left and go north again until we're back at Route 2. If Route 2 is still jammed, we can even take Old Greenfield Road, which appears to be a shortcut that goes right into Greenfield." She frowned, squinting at the truck's screen. "But the hospital is all the way over the other side of the town, so we have to figure out how to avoid getting bogged down in the center."

"Is there a stockade?" asked Ari. "Can you see main gates?"

"No… No complete stockade that I can see," she said. "But definitely security gates. Like…" She drew her finger along the screen, repositioning and expanding it. "Like where Route 2 goes under I-91. There's a big traffic circle. On the town side there's a gate. East side. Oh, we have to go through that anyway, even if we take Old Greenfield Road. And, by the way, it looks like there's an enormous camp near that circle…"

"Daddy," said Lara, interrupting. "It's urgent. I don't know how much longer he's going to hold out. I just don't know how he's doing." Mike was breathing more shallowly, and his fever remained high. He was still making his disturbing exhalation noise, with what seemed to be slackening frequency.

They drove at breakneck speed on the dirt road, over abrupt rises and down sudden dips, the truck shuddering as it skittered over short stretches of corduroy hardpan. There was little traffic, although someone else was far ahead of them—they caught glimpses of their tail lights—and someone was similarly following them at a rapid pace, its high beams on.

"There's Zerah Fiske Road!" exclaimed Grandma. "Left, left!"

Ari slowed down and halted at a stop sign. There was a steady flow of motor vehicles on the road—new and ancient vehicles of all kinds—traveling in both directions. "Isn't this strange?" Ari said. "Look at the traffic this time of night."

"We're not the only ones taking shortcuts, maybe," said Grandma.

The southbound traffic cleared momentarily, and a car heading north flashed its high beams for them to enter. Ari silently mouthed his thanks and pulled out into the traffic. "Thank God, a paved road again." The shaking subsided, allowing Lara and Jenny to loosen their grips on Mike and adjust their positions.

"We're very close now," said Grandma. "Only a few kilometers." And indeed, after scant minutes they drove over a ridge and could see Route 2 ahead and below, an unbroken line of headlights and tail lights that did not appear to be moving.

Ari groaned. "Florence, where did you say we should go if Route 2 is still jammed?"

"Old Greenfield Road. We should be passing it in a moment. We take a right."

"Should we risk it?" Ari asked.

"Please, anything that will get us to an ER the fastest!" begged Lara.

"It winds around and goes through some little valleys, but it looks like Greenfield is only about eight kilometers away now. I say we take it." And just as she spoke, the road sign appeared ahead. Ari slowed, and then around they skidded to the right, back on dirt, the limber chuttering and swaying, heading downhill among thin traffic toward the east.

"Doesn't it seem odd that we're still in such dense woods, just outside a decent-sized town?" Grandma muttered under her breath.

"Maybe this isn't the best place for food production around here," said Ari. "We still have the whole Connecticut River valley ahead of us, which I think is flat and has good soil."

"Isn't flat here!" said Grandma sourly. They swerved around a sharp bend and began climbing the side of a dark, wooded hill.

"Plus, maybe they haven't been burning up the woods for biomass here, like in Virginia," Ari muttered.

As they came around the hill and started descending again, vehicle lights appeared in the distance.

"What's that?" asked Lara in a worried tone.

"Orange flashing lights," said Ari. He slowed down. There were a number of vehicles ahead, and people in the road. There appeared to be a tiny village around a bridge. A man stood out in the middle of the road, waving a light to slow Ari down. Ari opened the window.

"What's going on?" Ari asked.

"Bridge come apart," said the man.

"What?" Ari narrowed his eyes against the bright flashing. "Is the bridge out?"

"Yup. What I said," said the man. "Just come off. Only built to take twenty tons, and all this migrant traffic's been too much."

Ari looked ahead, and managed to see that the short span seemed to be listing to one side. He realized that even his truck and limber might weigh at least ten tons with a bit more cargo.

"Looks like the bridge is OK but the foundation's giving out."

The man nodded, glancing between Ari and more traffic coming down the road.

"Is the only way to Greenfield either beyond this bridge or back up the way we came and around to Route 2?" Ari asked.

"Down here, yup, only that way…" He pointed toward the bridge. "Or back up the way you came from." He looked at the truck and rubbed his jaw. "Although with that you might get over the ford," he said, pronouncing 'might' like 'moit' and 'ford' like 'fow-ahd.'

"Ford?" Ari asked.

"Yes, down that road and over the brook. Comes up other side of the bridge. Water's low and your tires are high enough." He stepped back and started waving his light at another car coming down the road.

Ari turned back toward Grandma and the others.

"Should we try it?"

"Yes, yes," they all replied.

"We don't have much to lose at this point," said Grandma quietly so only Ari could hear her. He glanced at her as he put the truck in gear and waved at the man in the road, his eyes white and frightened in the strobing flashers.

"Lara, call back to the others and warn them what we're doing," said Ari. Lara was already picking up her T-pad.

They swung off the main road and onto a side road that sloped down extremely steeply into the little brook valley, past the hulk of an old water mill. The surface was bumpy with rocks and gravel. They all braced themselves against the forward tilt.

"Oh my God!' cried Jenny, hanging onto Mike so he would not roll off the seat.

"This is very, very steep," Ari confirmed, working the brakes and steering carefully.

"He's convulsing!" said Lara. "He's having a seizure." Mike's legs started twitching and jerking on the seat. Lara tried to hold him, but was thrown around by his movement. Mike's back arched and tensed, complicating Jenny's attempts to keep him on the seat.

"Ari!" said Grandma in alarm. "It feels like we're going to tip forward!"

"No, no," said Ari, his eyes on the screen. "It feels like that but it's less than a twenty-degree pitch." He searched around in the rear-view interior screen, trying to see what was happening with Mike.

"Grandma!" cried Jenny. "Look at Mike!" Grandma turned and looked back as the two young women fought to keep Mike in place. Mike was shaking so hard he seemed to be vibrating, and his jaw was tautly closed. A foam of blood and mucus swung from his nose.

"This isn't a good sign," said Lara, struggling to speak. "It means there's something neurological going on."

"Like what?" The truck leveled out as it reached the bank of the brook. Ari stopped, and turned around to see what was going on. He turned on the cab's interior lighting. The scene shocked him.

"Like maybe the infection—the pathogen and the sepsis—are affecting his brain. Circulating in his blood, getting up into his brain."

Under Mike, in his right thigh pocket, his lapscreen started ringing again. Ignoring it, Jenny looked at Lara in alarm. "What do we do?!" she sobbed. "What can we do for him?" Calls were coming to Lara from Daryl and Honorée about whether they should get out and come up to the cab, but she held them off.

"We keep going," said Ari with desperate determination. "Hold him." He eased the truck and its trailer off the bank and down a short sandy slope into the fast-running water. In the truck's headlights, it appeared to be about fifteen or twenty meters wide, with fewer boulders where other vehicles were clearly in the habit of crossing. There were washes of sand, deeper channels, and a few small logs and branches to negotiate. He inched forward. The truck bounced from side to side as it climbed and skittered off slippery rocks. Protests and shouts of dismay could be heard from the limber's passengers via Grandma's lapscreen.

"They must really be bouncing around in that light thing," said Ari, unable to do anything but keep rolling forward as evenly as possible.

"He's convulsing less," said Lara through gritted teeth.

"Yes," said Jenny. "Is that good?"

"I don't know," said Lara. "I don't have any monitors."

"You mean, like heart monitors," asked Jenny, her breath short.

"Yeah, and an EEG, EMG, that kind of thing."

"He really is calming down," said Jenny, trying to resist the temptation to feel relief.

"Mm hm." Lara reached over and felt his pulse. "Really weak." She felt his arms and legs. "The muscles are relaxing." She looked at his lifeless face, his eyes still half-open. "Mike, Mike!" she said. There was no reaction. "Jenny, honey. Is he breathing?" They had become accustomed to his noisy exhalations, but now they had stopped and he was quiet.

"I don't know!" said Jenny. "I can't hear anything." The truck lurched to one side. Jenny fought back to a sitting position, hanging onto Mike. She bent her ear close to the side of his face, almost colliding with his head. "Oh, something really smells bad." Holding her hand against her nose and mouth, she listened. "I can't tell!"

Lara took his pulse again. "Weak, weak." She searched Mike's chest for signs of movement, but the truck's jouncing made this impossible to discern. "Jenny, is there something cold and shiny you can put in front of his mouth so you can see the condensation?"

They both glanced all over. "Not my T-pad's screen," said Jenny. "It's too warm, from my pocket."

"Try this," said Grandma, pulling a folding knife from the dashboard and handing it back to Jenny. Jenny opened it quickly and held it unsteadily in front of Mike's face. No condensation appeared.

"I'm not getting a pulse!" said Lara suddenly. She pulled off her seatbelt and tried to get into a position where she could attempt CPR, but the cramped space of the cab's rear bench made it impossible. "Dad, Dad, stop the truck! I have to get him on a flat surface." The truck was only about halfway across the brook. In panic, Ari accidentally accelerated forward abruptly, throwing her back against the rear wall. The truck popped up over a small boulder and jammed a tire down into a hole.

"Ow!" she said, hitting her shoulder, her arm up to protect her head. "No, stop here!" Ari put the truck in park. Lara opened her door and jumped down into the cold, thigh-deep water, and holding the truck's side and front bumper for safety, scrambled around to Jenny's side. "Help me carry him over!" she screamed. Jenny was in the door's opening, pulling Mike's torso toward them. In moments, Daryl, Celia, and Honorée were all in the dark brook behind them, crowding around to receive Mike's body as one last heave by Jenny brought him sliding out the door. He fell head-first, back-down, and was submerged for a moment in the quick stream. They gasped at the water's chill as they grabbed him and staggered through the brook, sliding and stumbling over the loose rocks. They reached the bank, illuminated by the truck's headlights, and clawed their way up it, over an edge of sand, tree roots, and tufts of dead grass and weeds onto a narrow bench waist-high above the water's surface. Someone from the village came running down to assist, shining a light on Mike's face. Lara was down on him in seconds, pushing on his chest to initiate CPR, listening for breath, feeling for a pulse, pushing again, listening. The others stood around, aghast, faces pale in the glare, their adrenaline staving off any sense of the November night's chill.

Lara kept working on Mike, but nothing happened. Ari got down from the truck and waded across to them, hunched over, feeling for stable rocks with his hands in the dark water. "How is he?" he asked when he reached them. The shock on the others' faces gave a mute reply. Lara kept on fighting for long minutes, taking deep, gasping breaths, tears streaming down her face, and then stopped, on her knees, her forehead sunk down against the dewy grass, sobbing.

Jenny burst out with a wail and turned to Honorée, who held her, an expression of utter confusion and abandonment on her own face. Daryl and Celia stared at Mike in consternation. "How is he, how is he?!" shrieked Claudia from the middle of the brook. Grandma stood in the truck's doorframe, trying to see. Ari sat down on the cold ground, unable to speak. This had come upon them out of nowhere. What had they done wrong? How were you supposed to plan for situations like this? And it had been such a long, long day.

GLOSSARY & ABBREVIATIONS/ACRONYMS

3V: An advanced, 3-D, big-screen version of television, often placed in a living room or recreation room, for group viewing of movies, etc. It can obtain content from the VNET or tripleSD's.

AFK: Away From Keyboard, i.e., online but not at one's terminal.

Agricell: (Agricultural cellulose); a term for biomass energy crops like fast-growing willow and switch grass that are combusted in pellet or chip form.

Ailestrian: A person in individual flight (as in "pedestrian").

Andrometro: A flamboyant, theatrical style in which primarily men dress.

Aptitar: a universal identity object used in the VNET, Internet, and all other online systems that is associated with an individual at birth, linked to any and all nationalities and national personal registration numbers they possess, and used in for example financial accounts and transactions, taxation, and online subscriptions. Identity theft of aptitars is considered a felony and subject to capital punishment in many jurisdictions.

AR: (Augmented reality); a live, direct or indirect, view of a physical, real-world environment whose elements are *augmented* by computer-generated sensory input such as sound, video, graphics or GPS data. It is related to a more general concept called mediated reality, in which a view of reality is modified by a computer. As a result, the technology functions to enhance one's current perception of reality. By contrast, virtual reality replaces the real world with a simulated one.

Avacide: The voluntary termination of an avatar's identity and online account by the user of a virtual world; as in "sui-cide". Not to be confused with *avicide*, a poison that kills birds.

Avatar: A 3-D graphic image that a VNET user adopts to represent him/herself; could be anything, including him- or herself, a historical figure, another human form, an alien, an animal, etc.

Aztlán Movement: A Mexican nationalist, indigenous movement embracing pre-Columbian myth and culture with the political goal of creating an independent nation, Republica Aztlán del Norte, from the southwestern states of the United States.

Barriachi: Popular, high-tempo electronic music that fuses Mexican styles with techno.

Bat: A 3-D control device for a VNET computer, supplanting the mouse used for 2-D user interfaces.

BG: The Board of Growth, a secretive association of the world's hundred richest oligarchs. The Board of Growth originated as an informal lobby group within the World Economic Forum, but now functions as an independent body.

Biofleece: A synthetic insulating fiber made of polymers from plant oils.

CCC, also known as Triple-C: The Commonwealth of Christian Communities, an alliance of cities and towns run according to evangelical Christian values and principles, based in Fort Collins, Colorado, and with more than two thousand participating municipalities around the country.

Chinese Union, or CU:

Chitrex: A tough, slightly flexible non-petrochemical polymer material made from the polysaccharide chitin and complex bioengineered proteins, used for a wide variety of purposes, from automotive parts and aircraft bodies to body armor.

COE: US Army Corps of Engineers

Coalition for Renewal: A national political alliance of democrats, moderate republicans, progressives, and greens that emerged in the '30s and reached its apex in 2036 with the election of Morales on a platform of military disengagement from foreign wars, economic recovery, national reconciliation, and defossilization of the economy, which implied the dismantling of the Energy Trust and re-privatization of fossil fuels along with many other forms of energy. The Coalition for Renewal's principles were publicized through its "Renewed American Compact," issued in 2034.

Cogged, cogging: Tenses of the verb "to cog," in other words, to use cognitrol (see below). This could include using cognitrol to type and send a messge.

Cognitrol: A term for the control interface that uses a neural pick-up cap in a VRI headset to translate thought into executable commands in the VNET, including cursor controls, movement, and communication.

Conventionalism: The policy position supporting the idea that only fossil fuels (oil, gas, and coal) and nuclear energy can provide base-load electric power, district heating, and transportation energy, and that government funds should be primarily allocated to energy research and infrastructure for increasing capacity and efficiency in the fossil fuels sector, rather than to renewable energy sources.

Cybertropic drug: A drug used to enhance sensation and suspend one's disbelief in a virtual reality experience, using a mixture of subcortex stimulants, selective serotonin re-uptake inhibitors (SSRIs), and transopiates.

Cybriety: Moderation in the use of or abstinence from the VNET.

Cydub: Popular electronic dance music.

Cylph: N - An autonomous sex avatar that is operated by AI, not by a human user, and could either be a holomorph of a living person or an entirely fictitious graphic figure; V—*to cylf* means to holoscan a person in order to create an autonomous AI representation of that person for cybersex in online virtual environments. Unless one has the original person's permission, this is considered invasive and rude. However, it is quite common.

Dark Hill: An extremely radical anti-technology, nature-focused political and social movement with roots in New England, New York, and Eastern Canada. Often called a cult or animist religion, the semi-secretive Dark Hill is known for direct action and its profound effect on members' lifestyles and family life. Dark Hill has been accused of acts of terrorism against organizations representing modernity, the fossil fuel complex, Conventionalism, and the Federal government.

Diverse: [noun] A colloquial term for someone who neither wants to be associated with any majority nor with any distinct minority group, preferring instead to keep their identity ambiguous.

Downouter: Literally, "down-and-outer," a victim of poverty and joblessness

Downpowering: Reducing the use of energy through such things as shifting to smaller motors, increasing manual and draft animal labor, increasing the number of inhabitants of buildings, lowering thermostats, and replacing warm or hot industrial processes with cold processes.

DRR: The US Federal Department of Disaster Relief and Recovery, the successor to FEMA when dealing with disasters was elevated from a federal agency to the White House cabinet level.

Elevener: Nickname for a member of the Evangelical Church of the Plain Word of Jesus Christ Our Savior and Guide, also known as the Plain Word.

Eleventh Commandment: A principle of the Plain Word sect, usually stated as: "You shall love your neighbor as yourself, and accept men and women from every nation who fear God and do what is right."

Elimlets: Bracelets, anklets, and necklaces that ward off mosquitoes and other biting flies using complex ultrasound patterns.

Energy Trust (The): A corporation created by the US Federal Government which holds the monopoly for the production/importation, refining, and distribution of a variety of fuels and other substances based on oil, natural gas, and coal, including gasoline, diesel fuel, aviation fuel, and coal gas. The Energy Trust was created through an act of Congress in 2023, when large parts of the energy industry were nationalized in the name of national security and economic stabilization.

EROEI: Energy returned on energy invested; the ratio of the amount of usable energy acquired from a particular energy resource to the amount of energy expended to obtain that energy resource. When the EROEI of a resource is less than or equal to one, that energy source becomes an "energy sink", and can no longer be used as a primary source of energy.

Forest Reclamation and Stewardship Act (FRSA, "Forsa"): A bill before the US House of Representatives in 2040 that is intended to ease short-term fuel shortages for building heating by opening all publicly owned forests (federal, state, and local) to extensive cutting for fuel wood and wood-pellet production "until new energy regimes can be implemented," with highly streamlined permitting that the Energy Trust would control at the federal level. Most legal requirements relating to protection of endangered species, watershed protection, and other aspects of forest conservation would be waived when a FRSA permit is obtained. It would also make it a federal crime to attempt to slow or halt "expedient fuel wood recovery" or distribution of the resulting fuel wood, once permitted. The FRSA is essentially a federalization of biomass production and control.

Forest States Alliance (FSA): An alliance of mainly northern US states with higher than average forest cover that was created to protect forests and promote sustainable-yield forestry practices as a response to growing demand pressure from urban and less-forested areas that consume large quantities of biomass. The members are: Maine, New Hampshire, Vermont, Massachusetts, New York, Pennsylvania, Georgia, Michigan, Wisconsin, Minnesota, Idaho, Washington, Oregon, and Alaska. See also New Haven Compact.

Fort McMurray Declaration: A statement issued in June 2039 by a group of conservative members of the Legislative Assembly of Alberta, together with about four dozen US Congressmen and state legislators, demanding that Alberta secede from Canada, join the US as a state, and cut a favorable 50-year deal for retention in the provincial treasury of more oil revenues than it currently retains; all flow of oil to China and other markets would be curtailed; the US would protect Alberta from any "military retaliation or blackmail" (i.e., assertions of national sovereignty by the Canadian government); a pipeline would be constructed to transport oil to the US and another pipeline would be built to draw water year-round from the Great Slave Lake and pump it to the sand pits for use in oil production, potentially against the will of the Canadian government.

Fourth Crossing: A European political/social movement that believes it is Europe's destiny to send a new 21st-century wave of immigrants to North America. It bases its beliefs on three principles: (1) Equity, i.e., European population density is much higher than that in North America, with corresponding higher ecological pressure and difficulty in producing food;

(2) Justice, i.e., the notion that America's disproportionate greenhouse gas emissions for a century were the leading cause of the global warming that is (paradoxically) cooling Northern Europe; and (3) Destiny, i.e., the idea that Europeans have been crossing to North America since thousands of years before Christ (the Solutrean Hypothesis) and that this is part of "the divine order of things".

Frame, The: The perception (as in "frame of mind") of the virtual reality experienced through the VNET as equal in its actual reality to physical reality (RL).

Global Warming Pollution Reduction Act: Legislation introduced by Senator James Jeffords (I-VT) on July 20, 2006 before the US Senate. Jeffords was ranking member of the Senate Environment and Public Works Committee.

Go-suit: A comfortable jumpsuit made of biofleece, with both sportswear and business-casual versions.

Green Teens: The nickname for the period from 2012 through the end of the decade, when considerable consensus about energy and environmental policy existed across the political spectrum, and broad voter support fostered many steps toward greenhouse gas emissions reductions, investments in renewable and distributed energy generation, urban mass transit, and railroads. The legislative framework (tax credits and shifts, investment in R&D, permitting changes, etc.) was laid out in the New Energy Plan of 2015. This was a period marked by great optimism and enthusiasm, and in later decades was looked back upon with nostalgia and bitterness. Some social critics argue that the impetus of the Green Teens was doomed to run its course because the US continued its imperial involvement in other parts of the world, even as it tried to change the energy regime at home. Others have maintained that fossil fuel interests, buoyed by rising profits as oil prices climbed, fought and undermined the policies of the Green Teens. In any case, the public and policy atmosphere that marked the Green Teens came to an abrupt halt in 2021 with the Sanderborough tragedy.

HCE: Human cognition equivalent, a unit of artificial intelligence processing and sensemaking capacity equivalent to the capacity of one trained human analyst.

HF: Abbreviation of 'Homeland Front,' a precursor name for what became the Party for the Defense of the Homeland. This name was officially dropped when its members started running for public office and the party was registered as a political party, but it remained in common parlance. Carl Holt is its national chairman.

HFC: Hydrogen Fuel Cell, an electric propulsion system in vehicles that converts hydrogen and oxygen into water, generating electricity in the process.

Hive: A weapons system, formally named 'HV5', that consists of a dynamic network of hundreds or thousands of tiny dronecopters in a smart swarm that each target, track, identify, and if instructed kill individual soldiers on a battlefield. Each electric dronecopter is about ten centimeters in diameter and carries cameras, radar, avionics, and a five-shot 0.10 caliber rifle. They can travel at speeds of 100 km/h, and use intelligent algorithms to penetrate nets, fences, and other obstacles, and evade defensive measures. They are usually released from an aircraft or ground vehicle, and return to it when the mission has been completed. They can stay aloft for as long as 60 minutes.

Hokiesburg: Nickname for Blacksburg, Virginia.

Holomorph: A three-dimensional representation (avatar) of a person, with photographically accurate dimensions and textures of the real person (often the user behind the avatar). Holomorphs are created from a 360x360x360-degree digital scan ("holoscan") in a "holobooth," which is typically found at a V-tel.

Home Guard: The Southwestern Virginia Home Guard, a citizens' militia originally created by retired military officers to assist the Virginia Army National Guard and state police in providing security to communities and maintaining law and order if and when confronted with military-style threats. The Home Guard owes much of its origin in the Teens to Oath Keeper paramilitaries who were concerned that the US Federal Government might pursue policies that were unconstitutional and demanded armed citizen resistance. While this concern has remained an element of the Home Guard's culture, most of its efforts in recent years have been directed at guarding state and federal facilities and infrastructure, assisting the state police with travel control, assisting towns with stockades and other defenses, emergency response, humanitarian relief, and readiness training.

Homeland Brotherhood: A veterans' organization primarily active in the mid-South, existing ostensibly for social purposes, but increasingly used by racist, White supremacist, and fascist groups for recruiting and organizing.

Homeland Front (HF): See Party for the Defense of the Homeland.

Housemother: a southern expression for a woman who runs a rural working-class household where a family owns its own house and land, but is not wealthy enough to employ more than one or two servants or field workers.

HUD: Heads-up Display, a data display that a VNET user can open and close at will in their field of vision.

Humbum: The most common military nickname for a hurricane bunker.

Hunker: A common civilian nickname for a hurricane bunker.

Hurricane bunker: A large, heavily reinforced, flood-proof building complex that serves as a refuge from storms for several hundred or thousand people. Hurricane bunkers contain supplies of water, food, medicines, and other necessities, and also function as regional operations centers for DRR, the military, and state agencies.

Hypergrid: A set of standard VNET programming and communication protocols that allow users to move among different virtual worlds, essentially creating an unbounded metaverse.

I-ball: a wireless VNET-compatible video camera, powered by a photovoltaic cell.

IHC: Interstate Highways Command—the U.S. Army entity responsible for maintaining order on and controlling access to the interstate highways.

Inurb: Residential area embedded within a city.

Inworld: An expression for when one is in a virtual world (within the Metaverse) via an avatar.

Jambot: A VNET program that seeks out specific kinds of data and attempts to disable it or make it disappear from the VNET, using a variety of methods including transaction jamming and viruses.

KP: Kilopoint, also mistakenly expanded as "killerpoint"—a compact, lightweight Czech-made 4.5 mm electric machine gun that fires one thousand rounds per minute.

Landmark: A digital address in a virtual reality landscape allowing an avatar to return to it at will.

Living machine: An artificial wetland that treats sewage and purifies water using the natural ecological processes of a community of plants, bacteria, fish, insects, and other living organisms.

Metaverse: the universe of online virtual worlds, essentially equivalent to the VNET, although private virtual worlds exist that cannot be accessed via hypergrid links from the public VNET.

Milscrip: A currency used by the military and other federal security forces, existing only in debit-card form

Mindsurfer: A person who uses a mental-interface VRI headset and is able to control ("cognitrol") the human-machine interface mentally, including cursor controls, movement, text, and voice communication.

Neuronburg Rallies: The nickname for a series of Euronationalistic, extremist virtual political rallies taking place in the VNET.

New Energy Plan (NEP): Enacted by Congress in 2015 after a concerted bipartisan effort in partnership with the White House, the New Energy Plan charted a comprehensive course for US energy, transportation, housing, and related policy that was intended to move total US energy production to a portfolio by 2020 that was 50% conventional (including nuclear) and 50% renewable. This is considered the capstone legislation of the "Green Teens."

New Haven Compact: An agreement signed in New Haven, Connecticut in 2032 that created the Forest States Alliance. At the heart of the agreement was the principle that all wood biomass resources in a state were a public trust under the trusteeship of the government of that state, and that even federally owned lands and private property were subject to the terms of this trust, which included the principles of sustainable-yield forestry, net carbon gain, and habitat and water-resource preservation.

Oath Keepers: Oath Keepers is an American nonprofit organization that advocates that its members (current and former U.S. military and law enforcement) uphold the Constitution of the United States should they be ordered to violate it. The Oath Keepers' motto is "Not On Our Watch!", and their stated objective is to resist, non-violently, those actions taken by the U.S. Government that it believes oversteps Constitutional boundaries

Office of the Constitutional Inspector (OCI): A special police investigative and enforcement agency that deals with violations of suspensions of the U.S. Constitution's "Bill of Rights" (first ten amendments). The OCI is reports to the U.S. Attorney-General, who is equivalent to the Minister of Justice in most countries.

Offliner: A habitual, heavy VNET user who is not online; offliners can be seen drifting around buying food and taking care of other necessities between online sessions; they are thin and pale, with red eyes and often the habit of constantly glancing in all directions. They are usually drug-addicts.

Oil Sands Co-Management Initiative Act (OSCIA): A bill before the US Congress that would force Canada to sell most oil from Alberta to the US, exclude China and other foreign customers from purchasing this oil, and threaten Canada with annexation of Alberta if it did not cooperate. (This is a somewhat milder legislative manifestation of the Fort McMurray Declaration.)

Partisans: a blanket term used around the US for small, armed bands of radical environmentalists, socialists, and secessionists, often but not necessarily left-wing in their politics, who engage in opposition to the US Government, Energy Trust, industrial oligarchs, Homeland Front, and other conservative and right-wing causes through intelligence gathering, weapon and ammunition thefts, sabotage, and assassinations.

Party for the Defense of the Homeland (PDF): a conservative political party advocating a more robust defense against potential threats to US national security, and an aggressive position on US claims to a share of natural resources in Canada and Mexico, along with militant opposition to immigration. Also known as the "Homeland Front" (or HF), the name of the precursor movement that became the Party for the Defense of the

392

Homeland when its members started running for public office and the organization was registered as a political party. PDF membership is concentrated in the South, Midwest, and Rocky Mountain states. While formally a legal political party, the PDF is informally associated with innumerable grassroots militias, folkways clubs, and shadowy groups with racist, fundamentalist religious, and nativist-isolationist leanings.

PGM: Party of the Green Mountains, a state party in Vermont whose primary goal is secession from the United States, and which tends not to take positions in ordinary left-right policy debates.

Phase transition: When the phase of a substance, i.e., its material state (e.g., solid, liquid, gas), undergoes change to a different phase.

Plain Word: The Evangelical Church of the Plain Word of Jesus Christ Our Savior and Guide. Their "Eleventh Commandment" sets the Plain Word apart from other religious sects: "You shall love your neighbor as yourself, and accept men and women from every nation who fear God and do what is right." For this reason, the Plain Worders are nicknamed the "Eleveners". All the mainstream denominations and most evangelicals considered this heresy, a desecration of Moses' Decalogue.

Proxarchy: literally, the rule of the close; egalitarian government deliberately based on geographical nearness, similar economic means, and close social relations. The opposite of proxarchy has been variously called "siderearchy" and "abarchy," connoting distance in social relations, economic means, power, and social understanding, such as absentee ownership, great power distance, and extreme economic inequity.

RDD: Reality Dislocation Disorder, a psychological condition in which a person cannot remember whether memories, ideas, relationships, etc. originated in real life or in virtual reality experiences, interacting with bots or avatars. In more extreme cases, RDD may involve a disturbing, persistent lack of confidence that the reality one is conscious of is in fact bona fide reality. RDD is usually caused by heavy use of virtual reality combined with cybertropic drug abuse. RDD by itself does not involve hallucinations, although RDD may co-occur with other mental illnesses including paranoia and delusional and hallucinatory psychosis.

Rezz: To rez (or "rezz") in a virtual world means to make an object or avatar appear, or the process of appearing after for example teleporting or logging on.

RFID: Radio frequency identification, a technique that uses tiny electronic chips or tags containing memory devices, power sources, radio transponders, and antennas that can communicate a unique identity code to a radio receiver tuned to the appropriate frequency.

RL: Real life, i.e., physical reality experienced without the assistance of the VNET or AR.

Sanderborough: A small Western town that was entirely obliterated by an act of terrorism in 2021, with the deaths of nearly 35,000 people. The perpetrators, a radical splinter group of Al-Hijra who were in conflict with the Caliphate, carried out the attack to provoke further war with the United States.

Satcom/Satnet: the global wireless satellite-based data network that supports several communication systems, including the VNET, Internet, and a global positioning system. This serves as an alternative to the much cheaper terrestrial cellular networks. It is operated and maintained by an EU-Chinese consortium, and tends to be priced out of reach of most Americans.

SGW: "Since Global Warming," an abbreviation used when relating for example global average temperature or sea level to a hypothetical baseline prior to the point at which human-induced global warming became significant, often equated with 1900.

SHE-WEBS: Popular acronym for a list of what its proponents see as the key ingredients of a sustainable energy paradigm, made up of the first letters of: solar energy, hydro-power, eco-mimicry, wind, efficiency, biofuels, and simplicity.

SIF: Special Interior Forces, an elite federal military force for anti-terror operations and the maintenance of domestic civil order. SIF reports directly to the US President, not the Joint Chiefs of Staff or the civilian Secretary of Defense.

Skin: The surface appearance of an avatar, including hair, skin coloration, and hair.

Solarization: A concept according to which human society shifts to total reliance on solar energy alone in its many forms, including capture of direct radiation for heat and photovoltaic electricity, wind power, and biofuels.

Spawnport, spawn: A location in virtual reality where an avatar first arrives upon logging on.

Stim/sim: Stimulator/Simulator, a device consisting of a frame, seat, straps, cables, sensors, cognitrol harness, and electronics in which a person experiencing the VNET is supported, protected, and stimulated to feel motion and other effects matching what they are seeing and hearing through their headset. A stim/sim is usually used in combination with cybertropic drugs, to intensify the realism of the experience.

Sword and Shield: An elite and secretive militia associated with the Homeland Front, commanded by Carl Holt, the national chairman of the Party for the Defense of the Homeland. Sword and Shield was originally created in response to turbulence in the '30s when fears escalated among right-wing militias that a foreign take-over attempt of the United States federal government was imminent.

T-pad: A name for the ubiquitous wireless communication and computing devices that developed from cell phone, smartphone, satellite phone, laptop computer, tablet computer, e-book reader, and mobile digital media player technology. Other terms include "personal digital assistant" (or PDA).

Thermopolitics: Politics related to global warming.

TP: to teleport, or be transported from one place to another in a virtual world without the simulation of spatial movement.

Transmissionaries: Online religious evangelists from a number of Christian denominations who work virtually in the VNET to try to get people to give it up and adopt a simple, Christian, and drug-free/VNET-free way of life. One of their slogans is "There's No Salvation in Simulation." The Salvation Army is very active in transmissionary activity. They represent the "New Temperance" (or "Cybriety") movement that rejects drugs, alcohol, and promiscuity in the context of heavy virtual reality use.

TripleSD: A solid-state storage device for any kind of digital data. These come in many shapes, and because of their extremely high capacity (ranging from 256 terabytes to more than a petabyte) are sometimes used in place of online VNET data streaming.

Troding (to trode; troded): The practice of implanting several dozen electrode beacons the size of poppy seeds into selected parts of the body, especially joints, fingertips, and other extremities, so that a VNET scanner can map the movements of an avatar to the actual movements in real life of the avatar's human counterpart.

V, The: Nickname for the VNET.

V-bat: A virtual 3-D navigation and control device for a VNET computer, used inworld and held in an avatar's hand, supplanting interfaces devices such as keyboards, bats, verbal commands, and touch screens. In can be cognitrolled using the appropriate kind of VRI headset.

V-Icle: 3-D browser interface software for VNET.

V-mail: A message or messages sent via the VNET, sometime text-only, but usually video or other multimedia.

V-tel: A motel-like establishment where people stay in a tiny VNET cubical wearing a cognitrol cap and a full sensory suit, and spend periods of hours or days online in virtual reality; meals, washing & cleaning services etc. are provided; no windows or other distractions are present.

VDOT: Virginia Department of Transportation.

Viz-it: to virtually visit someone via the VNET.

VL: Virtual life.

Vlog: A personal 3-D, multimedia VNET format with which individuals post digital objects and receive comments, audio and video files, and other digital objects from visitors to the Vlog.

VNET (aka Vtopia): A convergence of broadcast & cable TV, Internet, entertainment arcades, movie multiplexes, and more, accessible online via internet-like "V-Icles" (3-D browser-type software). About 30% of Americans of all ages use VNET at least 12 hours a day. The VNET is also the virtual location of much commerce, education, and government activity.

VRI: Virtual Reality Interface.

Vtopia: A synonym for the VNET.

Wind barons: Industrialists (oligarchs) who own vast wind farms— mainly in the Midwest, Texas, and the Great Plains states - along with the electrical transmission capacity that serves them and a variety of related assets, like electrified railroads, natural gas pipelines, ethanol plants, fuel-crop farms, and water pumping and storage infrastructure. Sometimes compared to the railroad barons of the 1800's, they work in close concert with the Energy Trust.

ABOUT THE AUTHOR

Ralph Meima, MA/MBA, PhD, consults, writes, and pursues activism in renewable energy, sustainability, and community resilience. Born in the United States, he has lived in six countries and intermingled corporate, higher-education, and small business careers. He holds degrees in economics, engineering, international relations, and management. Ralph Meima lives in Vermont. *Fossil Nation* is his first novel.

Pbk fiction. Local author
(Ralph meima's son)

Made in the USA
Charleston, SC
13 January 2017